I0545632

Crazy for Cam
Bad Boys Book Two

Christine Young

Published by Rogue Phoenix Press, LLP
Copyright © 2020

ISBN: 978-1-62420-540-8

Credits

Cover Artist: Designs by Ms G
Edited by Christie L. Kraemer

Chapter One

1824 Glasgow Scotland

Lord Colin Angus Monroe MacEwen, Viscount of Rosehill, better known as Cam to his friends, stood on the balcony of his townhouse in Glasgow, Scotland, thinking over the last cowardly nine months of his life. He'd made promises to a lovely lass, Chelsea MacTavish. Promises he was unable or perhaps too terrified to keep might be a better word to describe his behavior.

The promise was to court her. Instead he stayed away, ran from her to be exact. Chelsea MacTavish was not for him. He was a womanizer and a cad and never expected to be anything else. Bad boys didn't change. Until he met Chels he had no intention of marrying until he was at least thirty-five and only because he wanted an heir. As his male friends claimed, he and his friends were the bad boys of Glasgow. Everyone knew they'd never reform.

Broc changed, he reminded himself. If one bad boy could do it, so could he. Blessed hell, but he wanted and yearned to have Chels in his arms, loving her for the rest of his life.

These last nine months had not been among his finer moments.

When Cam closed his eyes, when he tried to sleep, all he could see were Chelsea's lips and he didn't have to try very hard to recall the feel of them against his, their tongues dancing a beautiful duet. That night almost a year ago now had been a major mistake, one he was having a difficult time recovering from. When he saw her, in her quaint little hiding place staring at him, her sparkling, blue eyes huge which he read as desire, he couldn't resist her.

It was not well done of him, but he had to have her.

The bad boys were gambling and when he noticed her, she bolted from the room, dashing through the hallway to hide behind a door. The challenge she issued was explicit in the shimmer of her eyes. If he had any sense about him, he would have left her there, knowing she wasn't for him. Chelsea was a lady, and she deserved a gentleman who would treat her right. He could not leave though because he found himself inexorably drawn to her beguiling smile and passion-drenched eyes. A taste of her, he told himself, would be enough.

It wasn't enough. That one taste created an appetite he couldn't fill.

At the time, he believed that day had been the beginning of the rest of his life. She allowed him inside and he kissed her, not a chaste kiss, not one he might give a woman he was courting. No, this kiss was meant to seduce, raw and hungry, deliciously sensual. He found he wanted her in the most elemental and primal ways, and he craved to be her first lover.

Nothing else would do for him.

The wonderful thing was, he paused in thought to sip the brandy he poured for himself, well, she seemed to want him as much as he did her. She didn't resist or tell him no even though he suggested she do that very thing several times. The feel of her breast beneath his hand, the hardened nipple veiled by the fabric of her gown, haunted him day and night, awake and asleep. He should not have touched her so brazenly, but he'd been unable to resist her sweet siren's call.

The very next day he met her again and made more promises to her, agreements he now understood he could never fulfill, not unless he reformed. Her brother, Flynt, was right. He wasn't good enough for her. Hell, he never got rid of his mistress although that woman moved on when he stopped seeing her almost to the day he first kissed Chelsea. He'd been celibate for nine long months. Laughing at the irony, he downed the glass of brandy before throwing the crystal glass against the wall and watching it shatter into a million tiny pieces.

The violence didn't make him feel better.

The idea of properly courting a woman, not just any woman but Chelsea MacTavish, was not something he could wrap his mind around. When he was with her, all he could think about was stripping her naked and tasting every inch of her beautiful body. Bloody eyes, but he didn't even know what she looked like naked but he could fantasize. His imagination kept him in a state of constant arousal.

"What did that glass do to you?" Flynt MacTavish, Chelsea's older brother and proclaimed guardian of the MacTavish sisters clapped him on the shoulder. "Shouldn't you be getting back to the game so I can win more money from you."

The need to rid himself of the primal energy and sexual thoughts surrounding Chelsea pulsed through him. A ride and a cold swim in the river would do just fine. After all, it was almost dawn. Maybe he could reach his house near the ocean by the evening. Suitable company even for the other bad boys, he was not.

"You wouldn't like it if I told you," he said, smiling as he once more relived the few kisses he shared with Flynt's sister. "If you knew, you might string me up by my balls."

He roared with laughter. "That bad? Try me and it better not have anything to do with one of my sisters."

Cam was shaking his head, pacing the room now. "No. Like I told you. You wouldn't like my thoughts. Might even skewer me through." Cam laughed at the thought, knowing it was the truth.

"You want another glass of brandy?" Donal, another bad boy, stood by his side. "Don't know what's wrong, but it's got to have something to do with a woman."

"Like to drown in it." Cam knew a ride, a cold swim, nothing would stop the constant ache except possessing Chelsea, perhaps not even then would he find relief.

"That can be arranged," Leslie said, smirking as if he knew what was going through his head. "Let's get back to the game or call it quits so I can still find some bliss in my mistress' arms tonight."

"I'm not good company. Do whatever you like." Cam sat down on a chair, one leg slung over the arm, the other stretched out in front of him. The nearly full bottle of brandy sat on the table beside him. If he had it his way, he'd finish it tonight before crashing for a few hours.

"If it's not your mistress, who has you needing to see double and wake up with a pounding head?" Flynt asked, still laughing too hard for Cam's taste. "Must be a pretty special woman then. She denying you heavenly comforts or are you going to go the way of Broc and settle down, babies and all?"

Cam frowned at him, feeling the effects of too much alcohol and realizing the truth of Flynt's words. "Hardly going down that road." He didn't dare say more. If Flynt discovered his feelings for one of his little sisters, he'd keep Chelsea locked in her room until she turned thirty. Even her grams who seemed to take over the finding of suitable husbands for the MacTavish women wouldn't be able to persuade Flynt to hand over the key.

"Not until you're thirty," Leslie reminded them.

"Thirty-five, and she'll be out of the picture by then," Cam muttered, wishing he hadn't said the words but beginning to lose control of his thoughts and speech. Sullenly, he poured more brandy and hoped that in his drunken state he wouldn't reveal the woman of his dreams.

"Think it's time to leave this man to wallow in his misery. If you want the lady, do something about getting her. Shouldn't be too hard for a man of your specific talents," Flynt said, chuckling. "After all, what parent or guardian wouldn't welcome you into their fold? You've inherited money as well as a steady income. You're moderately good looking. Face it, you're a catch worthy of any young woman."

Any but a MacTavish lady. He was glad he had enough control not to say the words aloud. Or did he? The scowl on Flynt's face told him something else or was it a scowl. He downed the glass before closing his eyes and willing his friends from his townhouse. Truth be told he needed to wallow in his misery and wake up to a pounding head as well, just to remind him that he had to change his ways if he was going to court the woman of his dreams.

"You should see your mistress. A good douse of carnal sex might relieve the ache between your legs." Donal pulled his coat from the stand. "I'll see all of you next week at my place." Then he left.

"Good night," Leslie said, following in Donal's footsteps.

"Suppose I'll take my leave also. You're not in any condition to be good company. My suggestion," he paused, "find the chit and make love to her until you get her out of your system," Flynt said as he too exited Cam's home.

When the door closed behind Flynt MacTavish, Cam let out a loud roar of laughter. Find the chit and make love to her until you get her out of your system, he recalled the words. And wouldn't you just be the happiest guardian in the world when I threw your words in your face? Unknowingly, Flynt just gave him permission to ravish his sister.

Chelsea deserved more than that kind of behavior from a suitor. Yet that was exactly why he didn't court her. He knew he would do just that, make love to her until...

...but he didn't believe for a second he would ever get her out of his system.

The ticking of the clock was now the only sound he heard until the birds began to chirp nonstop. Sunlight filled the room and the pounding in his head was incessant. Squinting his eyes, he breathed in deeply, willing the alcohol-induced pain to vanish. Still, his head throbbed and his gut churned. A quick massage to the back of his neck as well as his temples did nothing to alleviate the horrendous problem.

Too many mornings he woke in this condition in a fervent yet unsuccessful attempt to rid Chelsea MacTavish from his thoughts. If he could go back to that night so many months ago, he would have never followed her into that empty room, never would have kissed her or felt her heart beat beneath his hand. Just the thought of the way her soft womanly curves felt against the hard planes of his body had him aroused and aching.

Rising, he ran his fingers through his hair until he was sure it was standing on end. His servant left a pot of hot coffee for him, anticipating his needs and when he wandered through his home, he found a still steaming bath had been left for him. Stripping, and with the cup of coffee in hand, he settled into the water, pretending he was ready to start his day.

Once more his imagination got the best of him though. He needed to do something about his condition. No other woman would do for him and he knew it. So, he would have to change the course of his actions but to what?

He had no idea how to court a lady properly. All he knew was how to bed them and give them pleasure. This was a predicament if bedding and pleasure weren't prerequisites for courting. He would have to make it a point to ask someone who might know. Problem was, he didn't really know or trust anyone like that.

Bloody hell, but he wasn't going to allow some other man to win over Chelsea's heart. He finished his coffee as well as his bath before heading off to the university. Some of his proper and stuffy colleagues might have some advice for him.

In the hallway and near his office, "Cam, you teaching today?"

"No, just have some paperwork then I'm heading home. Got business to attend to." The first matter on hand was to ride out to the MacTavish estate and discover if Chelsea was home and, in the process, get permission from Flynt to court her. Rumor was since Broc Wallace purged the waters, Flynt was a bit easier to deal with.

"Cam." Another colleague approached him. "What are you doing here today? You're not scheduled to lecture."

"Looking for advice and you're just the man I'd like to hear from." Cam opened the door to his office, waiting for his associate to join him.

"Advice from me?" Leod Donovan asked, pointing to his now puffed up chest. "Seems unusual. You've always appeared confidant. Never asked me anything before."

"Have a seat." Cam gestured to a chair while he removed his coat, thinking about what he should say or ask. He knew this man was courting someone, his gut clenching when he thought the woman might be Chelsea, but he also understood the man might have something more to offer than he could see on the surface.

The man cleared his throat, running a finger around his collar as if it was too tight. "What do you want?"

"Need to learn how you court a woman properly," Cam said, watching Leod's face turn a brilliant shade of red as his Adam's apple bobbed up and down. He poured two glasses of whiskey before holding one out to the man who ignored him. In one gulp he downed his, more curious now than he'd ever been.

"You're asking me that?" He coughed in a feeble attempt to clear his throat. "Don't know why you need help with something like courting. Heard you were a Casanova, one of the self-proclaimed bad boys in town. You shouldn't need help in that department."

For a moment, Cam was taken aback. He'd never thought of himself as a Casanova. He enjoyed women, true, but he never took advantage of a situation, at least not until he met Chelsea MacTavish and she had practically begged him to kiss her.

"Don't need to know why. My reasons are my own. Understand you're courting a young lady. Just have to know what's proper and what is not." Cam wasn't at all sure this conversation was going anywhere, and as the seconds passed, he was surer than ever this colleague would never be able to shed light on his question.

"Like what?" The man squirmed, fidgeting with his neck cloth. "What you're really asking me isn't apparent. I've heard stories about your prowess where it comes to women. I'm not like that. I don't bed every woman I call on, wouldn't want to in any case."

Cam waved his hand in the air. He also didn't bed everyone woman of his acquaintance. "Whiskey?" he queried again then immediately had a second thought on that matter.

"Don't drink."

"Mind if I do?" Cam understood how drinking might make this man uncomfortable. He would be shocked to learn Chelsea liked her brandy and wine. That was all he knew about her except the fact he craved her and she was sweet. Well, he also knew first-hand how she melted in his arms and the way her blue eyes shone with raw passion when he kissed her and how her beautiful blond hair shimmered in the sunlight.

"It's your office."

"I'll take that as a confirmation that you don't care." Cam poured a second glass of whiskey then sat on the edge of his desk, watching the man. Not liking the idea that people, his colleagues, talked about him behind his back, he asked? "What do you know about my, er, prowess with women?"

The man wiped his sweaty forehead with his forearm, "Just talk. You've had more than one mistress, I've heard. Women swoon when you walk by. No, perhaps that was an exaggeration. Not really sure in any case."

"True, all true." He tossed back the whiskey and grinned. "That's one of the reasons I'm asking for advice. While I'm an expert where it comes to mistresses and giving a woman her pleasure, I've no idea what a man can and can't do with a proper lady when they are courting. Do you give your women pleasure?"

"What?" Leod sputtered.

"Never mind, let's get back to courting part of this conversation."

"For instance..."

"Have you kissed this woman you've been seeing?" Cam asked, pretty sure what the answer would entail if he went into detail.

"Once," he confessed, the shade of his face had not changed since the first questions. His visage was still a brilliant crimson.

"And was this kiss chaste? A peck on the cheek or did you take her mouth into yours and taste her. Did you stick your tongue between her lips and deep inside her mouth?" Why the devil was he provoking this man when all he wanted was some answers to important questions?

Leod stood quickly, rocking the chair he'd been sitting on. "Sir."

"I take it there were no tongues involved." He rose, striding to the window. Looking over campus, he watched the people walking around and wondering just how many of those students would react to his question the same as his colleague. Perhaps he was a bad boy. He realized then he didn't like Leod at all.

"No, no, of course not. A gentleman wouldn't do such a thing. A peck on the cheek is all that is proper, if you must know. Nothing more, no body parts involved." He was breathing hard and sweating profusely, clearly agitated by his questions.

Cam couldn't help himself. He sighed heavily, understanding all too well he would never be able to keep his hands to himself let alone his tongue where Chelsea was concerned. The thing was, he didn't believe she would ever tell him no. "Haven't you ever wondered what it would feel like to taste the woman you want to marry before the nuptials? What do you think?"

The man was shaking his head back and forth while he righted his chair and sat down. "No, no I haven't. Don't know what you mean by tasting. Doesn't seem at all proper to me."

For a moment Cam thought the man might swoon. "You should really try it sometime. I can find you a lady of the night who is clean, a woman who could teach you how to make love to a woman so she has her pleasure not just you. You don't want to be selfish, do you?"

"I don't know what you mean," he said, droplets of sweat running down his face and into his shirt, his armpits soaked through.

"Would you like a woman to teach you?" Cam persisted, wishing all men would discover the secrets before they wed. Women deserved better than fumbling fingers and grunts that led nowhere.

He could still remember the woman his father brought him to at the tender age of fourteen. The lady was a widow. Her husband left his fortune to his son from another woman, failing to provide for his wife. At the time the lady needed funds just to live. He also remembered just how beautiful she was. If he ever had a son, he would make sure he treated his boy to that very valuable education.

"I can't imagine doing such a thing."

Cam turned his attention back to his associate, discovering a bit of disdain for this pious self-satisfied man. "Have you held her hand? Traced tiny intoxicating circles on her wrists and heard the first tiny sounds of desire a woman makes when she likes what you are doing?" Cam was beside himself. This was turning out to be detrimental to his case.

The man was sputtering now, "I've held her hand but not the other. Why would I want to do that?"

"You should try it, and you could suck her fingers into your mouth. I guarantee you'll enjoy the tiny sounds of pleasure your actions will cause. You do want to pleasure your woman."

"Professor MacEwen, I daresay the things you are proposing are outrageous, very improper. Doing those things would ruin my reputation. Why, people would talk about me the way they do you."

Cam grinned again, wondering for a moment how people talked about him but then realizing he didn't really care. "Of course they are improper. That's why I needed to know how to approach this woman properly. You see..." He was about to tell this stuffy and oh too prim man that he'd done all he'd said with the very woman his colleague might be courting. No, he hadn't sucked her fingers into his mouth but he would. Not for a moment did Cam believe Chelsea would ever give her heart to a man who only kissed her chastely on the cheek. At least that's what he presumed had been done.

"I don't see anything at all," he objected. "The young lady I'm seeing would never allow me to do such things and neither would her brother, Mr. MacTavish. I would most likely go to hell if I only tried."

Cam let out a huge sigh, realizing suddenly he might have been giving the man ideas. The last thing he wanted was for this man to taste any part of Chelsea. "Yes, yes, I suppose you're right. It was a crazy notion of mine, and you haven't touched her breast either, felt her nipple tighten beneath your hand. That is all good and proper. I'll try to remember your advice."

Cam couldn't stop the outrageous statements. Truth be told he had no interest in making his coworker uncomfortable, but jealousy swept through him the moment the man told him he'd kissed her and held her hand. He was pretty sure this person would never follow through with his suggestions, thank god.

Months had passed since he touched Chelsea, and his body pulsed with need night and day just to see her let alone run his hands along her waist to her breasts kiss her deeply. Bloody hell, but he was going insane just thinking, talking about sex with Chelsea's face prominent in his head.

Imagining himself sitting next to Chelsea while doing nothing more than holding her hand made him sweat. Where she was concerned, control like that didn't exist for him, and he realized he was doomed before he even began to try the proper way to court her.

The man stood, starting for the door. "This is all none of your business and very inappropriate." He left, slamming the door behind him.

Cam plopped down on the chair behind his desk, closing his eyes, head back and wondering what the devil he was going to do about courting Chelsea. The man was right, of course. Flynt wouldn't let him anywhere near his sister. Flynt knew all too well his reputation around women. They'd honed that very reputation together.

But what would her grams, Catherine, do? Probably feed him ginger cookies. He groaned. In any case, she was the official guardian now having assumed the position after Flynt made so many mistakes with Bliss, the oldest sister. Of course Catherine would never approve of him either. If she knew the things he and Chelsea had already done, she would ban him from the home.

All I need do is behave myself when the older woman is close and if I'm lucky enough to find privacy, well then, I don't have to behave. He smiled, realizing right then his next stop would be the MacTavish

10

townhouse. He'd prolonged this moment far too long. Chelsea was in town for the next few days. He remembered that he heard that tidbit from Flynt just last night.

Playing by the rules had never been a strong suit of his. Now, if his end game were to be achieved, he would have to do just that at least around the chaperones.

Play by the rules... A new concept for him, one he meant to cultivate where it was advantageous.

A different colleague poked his head into his office, laughing. "Heard you've been asking questions about proper courting."

"You heard right..." Cam was no longer in the mood, his answer sounding gruff.

"Got a drink for me? I can tell you many a tale if that's what you'd like," he told him.

"I think I've heard enough about proper and prim. Not something that appeals to me."

The man let his head fall back, roaring with laughter. "She's really got you by the balls, doesn't she?"

Cam thought about that for a second. "True." His eyebrows rose a notch, studying his friend. "I want her and the only way I can have her is to seduce her or court her."

"I know which I'd prefer," the man said. "But do you want her for more than a week or two or is this for a lifetime?"

Cam felt his nerves begin to snap while his fingers tightened around his glass. "Don't know yet." He hadn't thought that far ahead. What did he want? Now, he needed her this very moment.

"You should make up your mind before it's too late for either scenario. If you seduce her and toss her away, you'll ruin her life as well as her prospects for a decent marriage. If you seduce her and mean to keep her as your wife, your life will change in too many ways to count."

"I'm not a cad," he growled, yet at the same time marriage had never been in his thoughts. His plan was to marry when he turned thirty-five and not a moment before. He wanted an heir too. He was only twenty-four, eons stretched in front of him before he would need to make a commitment.

"If you go through with your plans, you will be just that, a cad, unless of course, this lady is mistress material. Hardly believe that though. You'd already have her set up in your old mistress' home if that were true."

Cam drummed his fingers on his desk, thinking and wondering if his set-in stone plans could change. Chelsea would never wait for him eleven years. She would be wed and bedded before he could blink.

He thought nine months had been a long time to stay away from her. Hell, eleven years was a lifetime. What to do?

"Think about what I said." His colleague left.

Silence, cold and hard, echoed in Cam's ears. Everything he planned and saved for would vanish in a blink if he let go of his dreams. Yet, he craved Chelsea, his body did anyway. Wasn't there more to a relationship than just sex or lust? He didn't have an answer for that. Sex, for him, had always been the driving force where women were concerned.

Bad boys, he mused thoughtfully. They all had been christened as such, by themselves of course. Now the community did the same.

Bad boy, what's she gonna do when I come for her?

Cam was determined to do just that. He was coming for her and he craved her in every way a man craved a woman. She would have to tell him no if they ever found privacy or he would teach her everything he knew about lovemaking.

So far she'd never told him no. Chelsea was older now though. And he'd also ignored her for a significant amount of time.

Anything could happen.

~ * ~

"There's a young man waiting for you downstairs," Catherine told her granddaughter as she stepped inside Chelsea's bedroom, a large grin on her face. "He seems a bit impatient to see you. While he was polite enough, there was an edge to his voice."

"And he wants to sit in the parlor and talk?" Chelsea asked, incredulous. "I've had enough of that for a lifetime. I don't even want any of these men Flynt has found to court me for a friend, let alone a partner for life." No, she craved more and the only man who could fill that had lost interest in her despite his promises.

"You should at least give this man a chance," Grams said.

"Why?" she asked stubbornly.

"Most who have courted you don't know how to ride a horse, and I for one am heartily glad I don't have to chaperone you and your suitors in a carriage. Sitting in the parlor and engaging in polite conversation is just fine with me." Catherine laughed, still smiling fondly at her granddaughter. "I would have your word you won't let this beau touch you below the waist though or do anything but kiss. Kisses are just fine."

How was this man different from the others? For a few seconds she stared out the window, wishing no one was downstairs and she could go for an unchaperoned ride all by herself. She knew just where she would go if given the chance. No, she wouldn't. It would only make her recall Cam and his kisses, the way he played her body. Not chaste, dry kisses her suitors had given her on the cheek, but deep soul shattering, heat raising delicious kisses only Cam could give her. She wanted to taste him again and feel his tongue dance with hers.

Then, with a heavy sigh and a reluctance to exist in the next few hours, "Why would I have to give my word now? Most of the men who visit me don't touch my hand let alone somewhere below my waist. I'm really not up to this, Grams. Tell him to go away."

"Stop moping around. You've got the rest of your life in front of you. If you want him to go away, you'll have to tell the man yourself. I don't want to hear what you have to say if he leaves without your seeing him," Catherine said with another chuckle while she smoothed her skirts and donned an exasperating look.

"You're far too secretive for my taste. Just spit it out. Tell me who this man is, and I'll make the decision. I'll tell him to go away if that's what I want." Chelsea was plucking at her skirt, nervous energy seeming to sweep through her. The air around her seemed charged with raw energy.

"Tell who to go away," Daryl and Lacie, two of her sisters joined them, plopping down on the bed together. "Tell us. Who exactly do you want to go away?"

"Whoever it is in the parlor," Chelsea began with a huff and a very negative attitude. "I don't know who it is, and I really don't care anymore.

I'm never going to marry anyone anyway. Grams seems to think I'd like to see this man. Don't know why." Considering suitors just to make Flynt and Grams happy had her exhausted and wishing she could run away to some island and never have to talk to or see another man.

"Would you like us to see who it is for you?" Lacie asked, cocking her head to the side as if she was studying her. Then she grinned, her signature Lacie smile that told Chelsea her sister had something devilish in mind. "I know I'd want to know who was waiting for me in the parlor, especially if Grams thinks you might want to see him."

"Who would you like to see, Chelsea?" Daryl asked, prompting her curiosity as Daryl well knew there was only one man she would consider, and he was on her bad side now. Cam broke promises to her. "You can narrow down the possibilities if you look at the situation that way."

The only man she'd like to see right now was Cam just so she could tell him what she thought of the abandonment as well as the broken promise. She wanted to rail at him and hit him until she felt better inside. Anger at his rejection of her simmered deep inside, had for the last nine months, growing more as each day passed. At her sides her fists clenched and unclenched, frustrated that there was nothing she could do about this situation. Obviously, she couldn't just show up at his townhouse. If she were a man, she could call him out.

Irritated, she crossed her arms in front of her then clenching her teeth, she gritted out just for spite, "I don't want to see anyone. They can all go...they can go..."

"Jump in a lake. Perhaps that would be a good remedy for what is probably ailing your man. Of course it would have to be an icy cold one," Grams offered with a wink as if she knew something no one else knew. "I'll tell him you're under the weather and he can come by tomorrow. That should suffice for today, but you'll need another excuse tomorrow and the next day and probably the one after that."

"Why would you get rid of him today just to invite him back tomorrow?" Chelsea asked, now furious with her grandmother. "It's obvious to most people that your words make no sense. If I didn't know better, I'd wager you're playing matchmaker and that has to stop."

"No." Lacie blocked the way, holding her hands out to stop her grams from leaving the room. "Let me see who it is then you can decide. Is that alright? We shouldn't make this permanent, at least not yet. It might be Cam."

"I don't want to see him either."

"Of course you do," Lacie said. "Quit acting like a fool and denying yourself something you desperately want, the one person who has you moping around the house. Grams is not the only one who is tired of your moods."

Chelsea wasn't sure how to react to her well-meaning sisters and the groping suitors who came to see if she would be a suitable wife for them. This had to be another one just like the others. The man downstairs wasn't Cam. She wasn't anyone's suitable wife. "I suppose you can go see. Nothing you discover will make me want to go somewhere with whoever it is or sit in the parlor and talk nonsense about the weather or who is performing at the theater. And I won't pretend for anyone that I don't like brandy and wine."

"Good, then it's settled. You'll have much needed information to make up your mind with." She turned to Daryl, grinning as if she couldn't wait to see who sat in their parlor. "You coming with me?"

"Keep me away? Not on your life. I bet it's Cam," Daryl said, just as the pair exited the room. "And what do you suppose she'll do if it is him?"

"Maybe he's finally come to his senses. We'll be back in a few minutes with the valued information. Don't go anywhere," Lacie said when she turned to look at her over her shoulder.

"Where would I go?" Chelsea sighed softly with a little emphasizing lift of her shoulders. Almost nine months ago she'd seen a future with Cam, now... There was nothing now and if it was Cam in the parlor, what the bloody eyes did he want? To play with her emotions before he left her again? She wasn't going to allow that to happen. He'd have to get down on his knees and grovel on the floor before she'd consent to anything he might have planned.

"You could sneak down the servant's staircase. If you got to your horse before anyone knew what you were doing, well...you could be miles away before the man knew you'd left the house just to get away from him,"

Lacie said, returning to the room to further irritate her.

"If it's Cam waiting for you down there when he found out, I bet he'd go after you and just like on that night you'd let him catch you," Daryl said, also returning, pointing a knowing finger at her. "You'd do it again, let him catch you, kiss you, fondle parts of you, intimate parts."

"I did not do that." Chelsea protested to no avail, understanding just how astute her sisters were. "Would not," she protested, but her voice was weak and she knew the lie.

"You told us you did and you also told us he kissed you. Is that why you don't like any of the other suitors? They can't kiss like Cam?" Lacie asked, now tapping her toe impatiently and seeming a bit reluctant to accomplish her mission.

Bliss walked into the room. "What's Cam doing downstairs? He finally come to his senses? Did he decide he wanted to court you properly?"

"You ruined our fun," Lacie said, hands on her hips, a pout on her pretty face. "We were teasing Chelsea about her anonymous suitor, and now she knows Cam is waiting to see her."

"I don't understand." Bliss sat down next to Catherine. "What are you talking about?"

"Chelsea's debating whether or not she wants to go downstairs and talk to him. Of course until this moment, she didn't know it was Cam waiting for her," Daryl said. "Now that she knows, she should be racing down the steps eager to tell him what she thinks."

"Really, Chelsea." Grams leaned over and placed her hand on hers. "You absolutely should see what he wants. You might be pleased. I'm certain I don't want to watch you mope around the house for another second let alone another nine months. Go see the man and stop wallowing in self-pity. This might well be the dawn of a new life for you."

"How can I just forgive that man after what he did?" Chelsea felt betrayed and abused by him. He made promises to her he didn't keep. "I can't trust him now, never will."

Grams chuckled softly, "He's a man. You will have to learn that where their women as well as their hearts are concerned, they don't seem to know what they want. I'm sure he meant what he said at the time, as I'm also sure he will move heaven and earth for you to grant your forgiveness."

"They want sex," Bliss said softly, smiling as if she understood the opposite sex better than most. "Nothing else matters to them until other things jump in and blind side them. Deny him what he wants the most and see what happens."

"Look how that worked out for you." Chelsea couldn't help the sarcasm. "You barely had your babies before Broc wed you."

"That's just it. I didn't deny him anything, and it took forever to work out, forever for him to come to the recollection he loved me and wanted me in his life," Bliss said. "Perhaps if I'd told him no..."

"Flynt still wouldn't have let him court you," Lacie said and that was the crux of Bliss' problem. "You forged the way for the rest of us, even though nothing is perfect yet."

"That wasn't how it all started though. Even before...well I allowed Broc to do things I shouldn't have," Bliss said.

"And he won't let Cam court me anymore than he would have let Broc court you. Perhaps I should visit him at his townhouse and get pregnant."

"No!" They all chorused.

Then Catherine cleared her throat, "Lest you forget, I'm in charge of those chaperone duties now, not Flynt. Getting yourself with child is not the solution. It might be a means to an end but never the answer."

"Flynt doesn't understand the fact you are now our guardian. He's still searching out men who he deems worthy husband material and presenting them to me."

"Where are the twins?" Grams asked in a not very subtle attempt to change the subject.

"Broc needed to see Flynt for some reason I didn't quite understand. He has the babies, and I'm sure he will bring the twins to me as soon as either one starts crying or needs a diaper change. Right now he just wants to show off his heirs. So, I'm going to enjoy a few minutes with my sisters."

"You're sure it's Cam you saw?" Chelsea asked, her heart in her throat while she tried to figure out what she would say to the hideous man. If she should chastise him for leaving her alone for so long without a word as to why, or if she should count her blessing and try to find some time alone with him.

"Yes," Bliss said, "I'm sure I know who he is and that I saw Cam. If you want him, you have to decide how to proceed. Walking down those stairs to the parlor could be the first step toward a new tomorrow. Staying here, well, it certainly won't put you one step further in your quest to wed him."

"What does that mean? How to proceed?" She breathed in long and deep, her emotions in a jumble of incoherent thoughts that made no sense. "Walking down a set of stairs won't change the fact he broke his promise and my heart. Won't change the fact he abandoned me for whatever reason."

"Can I assume you've allowed him liberties you've granted to no one else?" Bliss asked, prying into Chelsea's private life. "Of course you don't have to answer anyone but yourself."

Chelsea gazed at Catherine then back to Bliss, unwilling to say the truth with Grams present even while she understood her sisters knew most of what happened between herself and Cam. She licked her lips before sucking the bottom one between her teeth.

"I did let him kiss me, a couple of times and I—they made me..." she paused, staring at Bliss as if waiting for an answer.

"As if you can't think," Grams answered for her. "As if you don't have any bones in your body. Dear, we've all been there. And some of us, including me, have given liberties to their men they shouldn't have. You have nothing to be ashamed of or feel guilty about. If you didn't care for Cam MacEwen, you wouldn't have let him kiss you or touch you either."

"When you're in love it's terribly hard to deny them anything. Especially when they caress you in certain ways," Bliss said with a starry eyed look. Then shrugging, "I still can't deny Broc when he looks at me in a certain way."

"I never thought you lacked courage," Daryl said directly to Chelsea. "You've always been the boldest and the most fearless; a bricky lass is what everyone calls you. Don't change now. Act before it's too late and you have regrets."

"You all really think I should go see what he wants?" Chelsea felt her knees begin to wobble. "Not sure I can actually walk down those steps. I'll most likely fall flat on my face."

"He'll be there to pick you up," Daryl laughed, "and that will give him another chance to kiss you."

"Put on that beautiful blue day dress with the Belgium lace you purchased the last time we went shopping. We can all help you and lace the corset tight so you have the tiniest waist. He won't be able to resist you," Grams spoke fondly to her. "Bliss can help you with your hair and Lacie, you go down and keep Cam company until Chelsea looks more than presentable."

"I'd like that. I used to talk to Broc, too, but I never knew it was you, Bliss, who he fell in love with. He was always so elusive and secretive. At least this time I know the woman of his choice, and I can give him the proper incentive to treat you right." With that set, the youngest of the MacTavish clan vanished from the room so quickly it seemed she wasn't even there.

"What if he doesn't wait for me? We've all been talking for quite some time. He might have left already." Chelsea felt a wave of insecurity pass through her as her sisters and grandmother dressed and coifed her. Cam was a busy man, although she didn't know what he did to make money. It had always seemed he was on the go doing this or that.

"Some powder on your cheeks, a bit of tint to the eyelids and lips; after that we'll blacken your lashes and you'll be even more gorgeous than you are already."

"It's time," Bliss said, holding out her arms before twirling her around. "I'll walk down the steps with you. Steady you if you think you're going to fall. You can do this. Cam is a lucky man if he can catch you. Mark my words, don't make courtship too easy for him. It's best if they have to work a little bit."

"You don't have to hold me," Chelsea whispered, discovering the corset was cinched in so far she could barely take a breath. "Really, I want to think I'm a grown woman even though at the moment I'm realizing I'm not acting that way."

"I'm sure Broc is ready to hand over the twins. He's lasted longer than I expected." Bliss patted Chelsea on the hand. "As soon as you say the word, we can confront this man you want."

Chelsea nodded. "Ready as I'll ever be."

In the parlor, Chelsea's feet seemed to freeze to the floor. Not only did Cam sit in the room, but also the sultan as well as someone who'd been here once before. When she first saw Cam, she had the horrific urge to run into his arms then anger began to build inside. He abandoned her and as Bliss told her, he should have to work for her affections.

If he crooked his little finger, she'd undoubtedly give in to him and whatever it was he was asking for.

She fanned her hot face with her hand, yet she couldn't seem to cool herself or the uncontrollable fury rising to the surface. Her gaze remained on Cam, but it was Arie, the sultan, who had followed Hope, Broc's sister, to Scotland who seemed to understand her predicament.

Arie suddenly stood beside her, his hand on her shoulder as he bent close, "Are you all right? I will sweep you away from all this. Just say the word, my petite. We will run away together, you and I."

"No." She was shaking her head and trying to swallow, knees trembling. "That's Cam." She tried not to look at him again. "What does he want with me now?"

"I know who he is. If you recall you've told me a lot about what transpired between the two of you," he whispered close to her ear, laughing. "May I escort you into the room where you can confront the beast? Be sure to make him beg before you forgive him as I know you will."

Her shaking head turned to nodding while she remained thoughtless, very nearly spineless and without any notion of what was happening or how she would make him beg. Arie seemed to have this meeting under control. He brought her to a chair to sit in while he poured everyone a glass of wine and graciously handed the drinks out.

When she looked at Cam, he appeared so arrogant and cocky her fury grew. She would throttle him if they were left alone, beat his chest with her bare fists, toss her wine in his face. The silence echoed in the room as her discomfort grew.

"Well, it seems Chelsea has several suitors to choose from. This is such a fine day." Catherine entered the parlor with her hands clasped in front of her. "The conversation does seem a bit boring, nonexistent to be exact. Perhaps," and she turned to Chelsea with a look of encouragement on her face, "you would like to take a stroll in the gardens with one of these men."

Cam stood as if she would pick him, but the way her sensibilities were tumbling all over themselves she dared not. Turning to Arie, she began, her heart pounding out of synch, "I think perhaps..."

He was quick to reject her preliminary choice, seeming to understand after seeing Cam she needed more time, "You should take this other man." Then looking at the third man in the room, "What is your name?"

"Leod," Chelsea said but she didn't want to go for a walk with him in the gardens or anywhere else. "He's been here before. I thought I made it perfectly clear to him. I did—"

Arie cut her off, seeming to have some other agenda in mind. "I would like to speak with Lord MacEwen privately. The viscount needs to understand a few things before he's left alone with you. So, I'll come find you as soon as I've had a word with him."

"I don't know why you'd want a word with me. I've nothing to say to you." Cam rose, extending a hand to Chelsea and ignoring Arie. "I've come to see the lady and don't want to speak with anyone else."

"Go on," Arie said with a smile and a push of his hands in the air. "Have faith in me and in what I plan to do here, petite. Go with Leod. One of us will be with you shortly."

"I do have faith but..." She didn't trust Cam one tiny bit, but she was coming to trust Arie even given his role here and what they all expected of him. He had come to reclaim Hope, who had run away from his father's harem. The story was long and involved but despite his father's intentions, Arie wasn't attracted to Hope and Flynt was. Now Arie was just having fun, enjoying the Scottish atmosphere and the women in Glasgow as well. Chelsea didn't think Arie ever had plans for Hope.

"Wait in the gazebo. Whoever survives this encounter will find you." Arie laughed a full rich belly laugh.

"Come, Chelsea," Leod said, holding out his arm. "I want to clear the air. We've much to talk about."

Chelsea didn't accept his arm but she did follow him. "Don't talk to me as if I'm your lap dog. As far as I'm concerned, we've nothing in common, and therefore there is nothing further for us to speak of to each other. I'm only accompanying you because Arie asked."

Leod looked back to the room then to Chelsea. "Of course I don't think of you as my lap dog, you're a woman. I'd prefer it if you accepted my arm." His voice cracked when he said preferred.

"Don't need any man's arm to walk," she muttered softly. "Been doing it alone since before I was one." In truth she didn't want to touch the loathsome man.

"What?" he demanded, touching her chin and making her look at him.

"Nothing." She jerked away from his hold then inhaled, praying Arie would not be much longer and that he would also find a way to send Cam home. Despite feeling eager yet apprehensive to see Cam earlier, she no longer felt that way. Her anger was just too close to the surface and unpredictable as well.

Chelsea had no idea what Arie had been thinking sending her to the garden with Leod. He knew she didn't want anything to do with this person who she despised and had express instructions along with her grams to turn him away if he ever came to the house again.

So, why had her wishes been so blatantly ignored?

Arie obviously didn't know how to follow instructions or keep a promise and neither did Grams. "Men," she muttered, hoping Leod didn't hear her. They do exactly what they want, when they want.

Outside, the scent of roses filled the air as did the site of all the lovely summer flowers beginning to bloom. The blue sky and sunshine should have brightened her day but it didn't. Chelsea tried desperately to keep her mind focused on herself and what she needed to say to both men. When Leod placed her hand in his, she cringed, jerking away, but he held it tight.

"Let me go," she grit out. "I don't want you to touch me."

"Never." His voice was gruff, determined and different from the way he usually spoke to her.

She told herself this was only for a few minutes more but when they walked into the gazebo and he placed an arm around her pulling her to him, she panicked. Her hands on his chest, she tried to push him away, but he was too strong. His lips slanted over hers while he forced his tongue inside her mouth.

Chelsea didn't know where the strength came from, but she shoved him hard, screaming, "No!"

Turning, she ran into Cam's arms, her body quivering and so grateful he was there for her. He held her close, her head on his chest while his hands ran the length of her trembling back. "I suggest you leave, Leod, and never return here," Cam growled low in his throat. "Chelsea is mine."

"You were the one who told me I should do that." Leod tried to shift some of this problem on to Cam.

"Only to a willing woman. If you recall, I offered to find one for you. Chelsea seems far from agreeable."

"I didn't know we were courting the same woman," Leod said, seeming to be taken aback by Cam's appearance and the way he held Chelsea in his arms.

"We're not." Cam spoke calmly. "I'm the only man courting Chelsea. Best you don't come around here again," Cam reminded him.

This time Chelsea pushed away from Cam, staring into his eyes. "You told him to do that? Stick his tongue in my mouth?" She inhaled, coughing when she couldn't get enough air.

"Yes and no." Yet he didn't release her but turned her and helped her to find a place to sit inside the gazebo.

"Yes and no, what the bloody eyes is that supposed to mean?" She couldn't believe Cam would tell another man, anyone to do that to her. "You are a cad of the worst sort."

"If you'll have me, I'm your cad."

"If..."

Sitting down beside her, he placed her hand in his, slowly tracing tiny circles on the underside of her wrist then running his fingertip up then down her arm. She shivered at the gentle strokes. "It's a long story. Are you willing to listen?"

"Does it begin nine months ago?" She wanted a complete explanation. "You're a cad," she told him again, turning her head away, unwilling to fall victim to his compelling eyes as well as the wide charming grin that stole her heart every time he flashed it at her.

"Yes and no about the time period, not my being a cad. Where you're concerned, I guess I deserve the title, but I intend to rectify that." When she looked at him again, he placed a fingertip on her lips, stopping her comment. "Let's start with my discretions and what happened this morning in my office."

She meant to remain cautious. Cam could rip her heart out and tear it into tiny shreds if she let him. Arie had told her as much, caution, and don't give him everything he asks for, her sister's advice.

"I'm listening." She moistened her lips, almost as if she anticipated a kiss.

"This morning I asked Leod for some advice, and I ended up giving him some of my own which, when I realized what I was telling him, he might apply to you since in the process I discovered he was courting you. At that point I wasn't sure what to do, so I offered a willing woman to him, one who could teach him how to treat a lady."

"You asked Leod for advice? I've a hard time believing that." The confession nearly made her laugh and quite literally stole her anger for the moment. She would have to remain stronger.

He traced the line of her neck, sending goose bumps down her arms. "It's the God's honest truth, but I do find I won't be able to use any of his advice. His way of courting just won't work for me. I wanted to do this properly, and I'm still going to try but—"

"Why is that?" she interrupted, needing to run her finger along the smile forming on his lips. She realized instantly he would suck her finger into his mouth and she would allow him to do anything. If this was her version of not giving into this man, it wasn't going to work.

"You're just too beautiful and hard to resist," Cam murmured, his mouth so close to her ear she felt his breath as he spoke. She thought he might touch the tip with his tongue.

"Cam...why really." Her voice shook as her body seemed to be melting with desire for this man who treated her despicably.

"Because I'm going to kiss you like I did so long ago, not a chaste kiss but one where I'll hear those tiny sounds in the back of your throat. The ones that make all of me smile."

"Arrogant." She did touch him then, traced his lips with her finger, wishing she dared give into everything he asked for. Perhaps that ploy would result in all her dreams coming true.

"Self-confidant." He pulled her finger into his mouth, sucking, biting gently, licking, teasing. "I truly don't like the word arrogant."

"You didn't do that before. Suck my finger into your mouth. What's a girl supposed to do when she's angry and wants you to beg forgiveness?" She closed her eyes, trying to inhale a deep breath of air and finding the task impossible. "Dear lord, my corset is too tight."

He laughed, a deep belly laugh. "If you like, I can fix that." His mouth descended on hers before she could answer. Her lips encased in his, his hands on both sides of her head holding her still, he slipped his tongue deep inside, played and dueled with her, nipping at her bottom lip.

She recalled all the vivid sensations as he bit and laved her mouth with his teeth and tongue. Over and over again, he kissed her and kissed her until her body cried out for him, for something more. She did want him to touch her breasts, cup them in his hands like he did before, run his thumb across her clothed nipple, perhaps even take the tip into his mouth as he did her fingers.

When they parted for a moment and he gazed into her eyes, "I really can't breathe. Cam, I think I might faint."

"I promised Arie I wouldn't do anything to compromise you," he whispered, even as his nimble fingers unfastened the buttons on the back of her dress. Before she understood what he was doing, he untied her corset then laced it back, much looser. "You should turn now. Not too sure if I can fasten the buttons without seeing the tiny things. Let it be known, though, this is the last thing I want to do at the moment."

"Thank you." She inhaled long and deep. "My sisters..."

"They did this to you? Truly I cannot understand anything about women's clothing, least of all corsets."

"They wanted me to look my best for you and well...a tiny waist..." She was amazed by the myriad of expressions crossing his face.

"Good god, woman, you're so tiny without the corset I can wrap my hands around your waist. Why would you want to be smaller?"

She shrugged her shoulders, unable to think of an answer to his question but needing a diversion. "I'm still angry with you, Cam. Doesn't matter that you kissed me and I liked it and want more. You have a lot of months to make up for, and I don't intend to be an easy conquest. I'm not going to give my heart to you again and have you toss it away as if it's worthless."

"I'm just glad you still like my kisses." His smile captured her heart again.

"I wanted to hit you and hit you until all the anger vanished, but I let you kiss me instead."

"Ach lass, is the anger gone now?"

"Not yet." She touched his lips again, needing more of him. "You should kiss me again and maybe I'll forgive you."

He roared with laughter. "So, if I kiss you again, you won't be quite so angry and you won't take your fury out on my humble man's body. Hmm...should I just keep kissing you until there is no more fury to vanquish? Kissing. That's my choice."

"Or until Grams finds us. Don't do anything that will have her banishing you from the house. I don't think I could live through another desertion. Grams told me kissing was fine. Just kissing. Nothing below the waist."

"And what would that be, my sweet one? What could I possibly want below your waist?" He laughed and she somehow thought he knew more than he was allowing her to know.

"I'm hardly sweet and you know that," Chelsea protested, hitting him on the shoulder with her fisted hand.

"Not at all. Now, what would get me banished from the house?"

Arie handed Leod a glass of whiskey that he wished was laced with arsenic. "Drink this." The sniveling little man tried to take liberties the lady didn't want to give. Chelsea valiantly fought her own battle and won. He'd been a few steps behind Cam when he watched her shove Leod away.

"Don't drink." Leod told him. "Don't like the stuff."

"Very well. Let it be known from this day forward you're not welcome to court the lady MacTavish. She doesn't want your attentions nor does she like you. You need to set your sights on someone else, someone more appropriate for your expectations." Arie cared more than he wanted to admit that Chelsea touched his heart. If she wasn't so averse to becoming his fourth wife, he would spirit her away and make sweet love to her, make her forget Cam. Lord MacEwen didn't deserve her.

"Why should I pay any attention to what you, a foreigner has to say?" Leod sneered, seeming to have no idea the power the sultan possessed. "I've no intention of finding a different woman."

"Slavery is something my people enjoy. They've found it easy to abduct women and men to work for them, serve them in any way they please, physical labor as well as sexual slaves. There is little the various governments can do to stop them once a person disappears behind harem walls." Arie spoke slowly and pointedly, watching the play of expressions on Leod's face.

"You wouldn't dare. I'm a free man. You have no right to enslave me." His voice wavered on the last words.

"Only as long as I want you to remain free. Do something I don't like..." The sultan spoke nonchalantly, staring at Leod, looking for any sign of weakness of which there were many.

While he was surprised his subtle threat didn't seem to register with this man, he was pleased too. His unwillingness to believe would make the task so much easier if it ever came to his enslavement.

Arie could think of no greater pleasure than watching this man labor throughout the day for the rest of his life. Or, he paused in thought, he could sell him to another man as a paramour. The thought got better with each passing second, and he almost hoped Leod would defy him and in doing so test the truth of his words.

Leod didn't have the courage for defiance. Arie was sure Leod would crumble to his will.

"What's that supposed to mean?" Leod asked. "I am free. I won't work for any man unless it's of my choosing."

"You should look around you and see everything as it really is. My people don't live by the same societal rules as you do. I've money, power, friends and the means to abduct you to my country. If I do so, you'll never leave, never see Scotland again, and you will be under another man's thumb for the rest of your life, and you will have to please that man if you value your life." Arie knew just the man to sell Leod to.

Leod grumbled for a moment then chose not to speak.

"I was sent here for another purpose but found it didn't appeal to me. You, on the other hand..." He let the sentence hang, wondering what spin Leod would put on this.

Leod downed his whiskey, sputtering and coughing as it seemed he felt the effects of the alcohol as it slithered down his throat. Then after setting the glass down hard, "Are you threatening me?"

"Of course not." Arie loved the way this was beginning to play out. "Me? I would never threaten something so dastardly or a loyal Scotsman. This is just a version of what could happen in the future if you don't play by my rules."

Leod held his glass out silently, asking for more whiskey. "I should be able to do anything I want."

Arie smiled while he filled Leod's glass. Thoughts of getting this man so drunk he couldn't think and putting him on ship bound for some place far away flitted through his head. He couldn't though, but what he could do was serve him a lesson he wouldn't soon forget and perhaps put fear into his heart.

"You can do anything but court Miss MacTavish," Arie persisted as a plan slowly took shape in his head. "Where you are concerned, I've only one consideration, and that is for you to leave this lady alone."

"I want her," he said, his eyes closing. "Don't want to give her up. One way or the other she will be my wife."

Once more Arie filled Leod's glass.

"Sadly, for you my friend, there is no choice in this matter," Arie said before he nodded at one of his retainers. From the earlier conversation, the man in Arie's employ must have guessed his intent and left to return a few glasses of whiskey later.

"Where is she?" Leod stood, unable to keep his balance sat down. "Need to say goodbye."

"Let my men help you to your carriage, or did you ride a horse?"

Leod held up his glass, "Like this stuff better than I ever thought possible."

Arie obliged as he smiled and watched his men escort him from the house. His man stopped, waiting for further directions.

"Take him into town, strip him of all his clothes save his small clothes and leave him in the town square. No, perhaps you should leave him naked. If that doesn't bring the point home, nothing will."

"Or we can resort to stronger measures."

"Only if he doesn't learn the lesson we are teaching him." Arie sat back, grinning and thoroughly enjoying the scenario he set in motion.

Chapter Two

Cam sat at his desk in the Glasgow townhouse, thinking of Chelsea and their next meeting. Two days ago he apologized for treating her so badly and promised again he'd court her. Trouble was courting her properly was a lot harder than it seemed at first. There were rules. He wasn't much for rules.

Damn rules.

At the moment, he was opening an invitation to attend a play at the theatre in Glasgow to be followed by a quick appearance at a ball being given in honor of the university, proceeds to go to his department, the department of astronomy. Hoping she'd accept, he planned to send it immediately.

He'd never appreciated the theatre or balls, but he'd spent the last day and a half searching for some proper way to see Chelsea. It seemed the best way to accomplish such a feat was just that, a ball or a play, yet she was still supposed to have a chaperone and that just wasn't something he could tolerate. Finishing the letter then ringing the bell beside his desk, he waited for his servant to appear.

Instead of his servant, his mother surprised him.

"Cam..." She walked into the room her arms open wide. "Do you have a hug and a kiss for your mother?"

"Carmine, what brings you back to Glasgow and where is my father? Did he find somewhere dangerous to do his research? Thought the two of you agreed that now you were older you would make sure the sites were well-secured." He stepped from behind the desk to give his mother what she asked for. "Don't want to lose my mother and father."

"Well..." She poured a glass of whiskey before sitting down in the chair across from his desk. She smiled at him while frowning at the same time. It seemed she was thinking about how to proceed. It was very

Carmine like, cautious and thoughtful. She wouldn't want to say anything more than necessary. She especially didn't want to give away her intentions

Cam sat on the edge of his desk, smiling. "It's good to see you. It's been a while, mother. Catch me up on any news."

"I got tired of traveling. Needed to come home for a while. Your father just wants to look for old dusty bones." She brushed off her skirts to emphasize her statement.

"That does sound like father. Where's he off to this time?" Cam appreciated the theatrics at least for a short time. He hoped she would find some way to occupy herself as he was hardly in the position to entertain her, his plans now revolving around Chels.

"Egypt somewhere. Heard about some tomb raiders and wanted to make sure everything was preserved. As you well know he can't stand thievery." She sipped then waving her hand in the air, "Enough about me. What have you been up too these days? Am I going to have a grandchild anytime soon?"

Cam coughed on the whiskey going down his throat. A grandchild? "Not wed yet and I'm not going to have a child before the nuptials are said and everything is permanent." He wasn't going down the same path as his friend Broc Wallace who very nearly had the child a few minutes before the wedding.

Carmine pointed a finger at him, shaking it while she spoke, "You need to think about finding a special lady you can spend the rest of your life with. Don't want you to become a lonely old man with too many regrets to count," She paused, "and of course siring a few babies for me to spoil would be nice."

"Don't want to put the cart before the horse so to speak." Cam told her, wishing he dared tell her about Chelsea but that would cause way too many problems, difficulties he didn't want to have to deal with or explain until Chelsea committed to him. Besides if he told her today, all of Glasgow would know tomorrow. His mother might be cautious at times, but she was also a gossip.

"Excuse me." His manservant poked his head in the door, asking, "You called for me?"

"Could you have this delivered to the address on the envelope? I'd appreciate it if you have the messenger wait for the answer."

"Ah." His mother rose, walking toward him as if she wanted to get a closer view of the address, "Could this be an invitation to a young woman. What is it, Cam? You can tell me."

"Of course I could but if I did confide my dearest secrets, the rest of Glasgow would know within the hour. I'm not complaining mind you. It's just that I know when to keep a secret. This moment is one of those times," Cam spoke softly, appreciating his mother as well as her need for chatter with her cronies. She'd spent so much time away from home, supporting his father in all his scientific endeavors. When she was around her friends, she talked incessantly about anything that popped into her head.

"Sorry to disappoint you. It seems I'm lonely and getting on in age. My husband's travels exhaust me while he just keeps going as if nothing phases him." She sighed softly, a slight droop to her shoulders. "I've found I need something more in life."

"How long are you staying?" Cam poured her another drink. Then, "You obviously can stay as long as you like. I don't use the townhouse that often."

"At least a year. I want to stay for the summer and traveling in the winter is not to my liking. By then your father might decide he'd like to stay home for an extended period of time, especially if there is a pending grandchild. I'm really not looking forward to traveling again." She rose then and with a heavy sigh, "I suppose I can take one of the guest rooms. Is the one overlooking the park acceptable?"

"Whatever you like, mother. If you decide you need more privacy, I've another townhouse you're welcome to occupy." He didn't think his mother would appreciate being placed somewhere his mistress had lived, but he needed to offer and he needed his privacy as well. He wasn't used to having anyone underfoot, least of all a mother.

She was nodding and the expression on her face told him she knew more than she was going to say, "At the moment I crave company. Old bones don't talk and while I know you're a busy man with a life of your own, you'll prove to be more company than your father ever was. Even if I only see you once a week there will be more conversation."

He mulled that over in his head and before she left the room, "Why did you marry father?" he asked, suddenly craving some answers. "Not that it's any of my business."

She stopped at the door, walking back inside a wistful look on her face. "I loved him, do love him. Sometimes love isn't enough and it seems I followed his dream forever and never mine."

"I never thought about a woman having dreams," he said slowly, wondering at the idea. "What were yours?"

She sat down again, slowly rearranging her skirts. "Not what you might think. Nothing too major or surprising, I too enjoyed academia. I always wanted to study medicine and the human body. So," she paused closing her eyes, "at first the bones intrigued me. Now, looking back on all that has happened..." She shrugged her frail shoulders. "Now I just wish I'd had more than one child as well as grandbabies. I've spent an entire life doing what my husband wanted." She stood up again. Then waving her hand in the air, "No more talk of unrequited dreams."

"Let me know what you need," he said, slanting her a smile he knew she'd understand.

"Of course I will, don't even know what those could be. But if I'd had another child, say a girl, I might have a grandchild by now." It seemed she would not stray from that notion anytime soon.

He sighed, thinking more than once about telling hear about his plans with Chelsea. "You'll find out soon enough."

"What?" She suddenly looked more alert than before a tiny smile hiding the few age lines on her face. "Find out about what?"

"I'm courting a lady. Her name is Chelsea but...." He held up his hands at the brilliant smile appearing on her weathered face and what he knew she must be thinking. "We are not even close to marriage or having children. I've just begun to court her, and truth be told I'm having a devilishly difficult time trying to figure out how to be proper."

"For you, one of the bad boys," she began, laughing.

He cut her off with a wave of his hand. "How did you hear that name?"

She chuckled, seemingly pleased and began again, "For one of the bad boys to give up his mistress without plans for another means he's more than serious about the lady he's courting."

"How did you hear?" He wasn't going to leave the question unanswered.

"Rumors abound no matter where you live. Chelsea MacTavish, I presume. A lovely girl who I'm sure is even lovelier as a woman. I approve, not that you need approval from your mother."

"If she accepts my invitation tonight, I'll be gone tomorrow evening. You might even enjoy the ball we'll be attending after the theatre."

"A ball, I'll think about it."

"But you won't attend."

"Probably not. I've a few friends I'd like to see then I'd like to go to the country estate."

"Thought you wanted company."

"Perhaps, I just don't know what it is I want." She sighed again then inhaled deeply. "Without your father, I don't know if I'm coming or going. Sometimes I want to surround myself with people and other times I just want to be alone with my thoughts." Once again she turned to leave. "I'll take the room looking over the park. Enjoy your evening with the MacTavish lass and the ones to come."

His mother was home. He hadn't seen her or his father in at least six years. The day after he turned eighteen, they left for parts unknown, and he supposed to follow his father's dream. During his childhood they'd come and gone, gone more than they lived here in Glasgow. Truth be told, he barely knew either one of them. When he thought on it, he didn't know how to be a husband or a father.

The majority of his time had been spent at his friend's homes. First his nanny then his tutors provided little company for him. When he was fourteen, his father returned and introduced him to the widow who taught him all he knew about sex and women.

Well, the message had been sent. Now all he had to do was wait and wonder what dreams Chelsea had. Would she deny herself those dreams for him, and did he have the right to expect something like that? He realized once again he didn't really know who she was other than a beautiful woman he couldn't get enough of sexually. There had to be more to a relationship and marriage than just lust. Perhaps all a man really needed to be happy was good sex.

He didn't believe that for a moment.

Talking with her could quite possibly be necessary. He wondered, what was her favorite color or her greatest fear? Could she paint as well as her sister Bliss or perhaps better? Did she like to swim or could she swim? Would she enjoy looking at the night sky with him? Suddenly, the list of things to ask her grew in his head. Before the conversation with his mother, all he'd thought about was kissing her, discovering every part of her that lay beneath the fabric of her gowns.

The knock on the door startled him from his musing. "Come in."

"Cam, is it alright with you if I visit? Thought I could bring you the answer to the invitation in person if you're not too busy." It seemed she saw the clutter on his desk, all the papers he'd not been able to concentrate on because he was thinking about her.

"Chels." He sat up so quickly he knocked over the chair he'd been sitting on. "Of course you can visit. Come in." He set the chair to rights then walked toward her. All thoughts of discovering more about Chelsea and her dreams vanished as he pulled her into his arms.

"I'd like to go." She had just enough time to answer him before he took her mouth in his for a long sweetly passionate kiss, ripe with desire. When he finished and drew away, she was breathing hard.

"I'm sorry," he inhaled deeply.

"Whatever for? I like your kisses." She sat down, a beautiful and innocent smile on her face.

"That wasn't very proper of me." How the hell was he going to court Chelsea MacTavish in the proper way?

"Where you're concerned, I don't care a fig about proper. You can kiss me anytime you want for as long as you want. I want you to be yourself." She paused for a breath of air. "Can I stay a little while if I promise my corset isn't too tight and you won't have to fix it?" She laughed then a strange expression graced her face.

"Loved unlacing it. Could do the same thing even if it's not too tight." He smiled at her laughter, wishing he dared ravish her then remembered his mother was in one of the rooms upstairs. He no longer had the privacy he craved.

"Probably not a good idea. We need to know more about each other before you unlace my corset again." She looked away for a moment, hiding her expression from him. When she looked back, her eyes were wide and sparkling with raw passion and her lips shimmered with moisture, beckoning to him.

"Would you like to go for a walk in the garden?" He remembered the walk two days ago, once more thinking only of discovering more of her. The MacEwen townhouse also had a gazebo.

"That might be nice. I really don't know why I came here." She smushed her lips together as if thinking.

"Perhaps you wanted to see me as much as I do you. I've a better idea," he tossed out without really thinking but wanting to show her something about him she couldn't possibly know.

"I'm open to any suggestions," she said, shrugging her delicate shoulders, "Unless it's to see your bedroom. I'll have to decline something like that. Don't want Flynt to do something we both might regret." After the words blurted from her, she blushed a beautiful shade of red. "Please tell me I didn't say that."

His brows rose then he belted out a deep laugh. "Showing you my bedroom was on my mind, and someday I'm sure we'll take a look at it. No, I'd like to show you the observatory where I work. You won't be able to see any stars or planets today because..." he paused... "let's eat dinner first then go to the observatory when it's dark. I can show you so many things." Yes, he could show her stars and planets, but he'd have to hold back on what he truly wanted to teach her.

"You have access there?" She appeared astonished. "I thought only a few distinguished scientists were allowed access."

He held her by the waist, close to his body. "I'm both, distinguished and a scientist. I'm an astronomer at the university. Don't really do a lot there but I am one of those," he paused, "Distinguished professors."

She tilted her head looking at him a bit sideways. "Then why..."

"I lecture occasionally so they give me access for research and information for said lectures." He traced her eyebrows then down the side of her face with a fingertip. At the moment, he'd like to research Chelsea, all of her. He was sure that type of research wasn't considered proper.

"Really?"

"Don't look so surprised. Don't know if my tender ego can withstand such intense scrutiny or disbelief."

"Show me after dinner then. What does that entail and what does one do in an observatory?"

Kiss, he mused. Although he'd never done that but he'd also never been in an observatory with Chelsea. "Did anyone know you were coming here? Should we send a note to Catherine?" he asked, not wanting a search party interrupting any of his plans.

"Told Grams I was riding home and would be back late morning. Told her I needed some privacy so I could think. Arie knows I'm here though," she told him, suddenly studying her hands.

"Do you tell that man everything?" Jealousy swept through him at the notion the sultan might know more about her than he did. "What does he know about you I don't?"

"He doesn't kiss me and he's never..."

"Touched your breast or unlaced your corset?" he asked, hoping the answer would be no.

"Don't want to talk about Arie." She turned then, walking away from him, her back stiff. "It's a waste of time, yours and mine. Arie is a friend, a good one but he will never be anything else."

It seemed he would have to leave his inquiries about the sultan to another time, but he didn't like the close relationship she had with the man even though he was pretty sure she'd never shared any type of intimacies with him. "Where would you like to go to eat?"

"Someplace private, intimate where there aren't a lot of people," she told him, smiling again. "I want you all to myself."

"Me too. You, all to myself. Don't want anyone around to ruin the evening. Need to discover more about you." He extended an arm, pleased when she placed her hand on his forearm. "I know a place close by. We can walk and enjoy the beautiful afternoon."

He grabbed her cloak from the coat stand as they exited and walked in silence for a few minutes. "Now that we're alone I don't know what to say," she said, staring up at him.

"Don't always have to say anything. It occurred to me today that I know very little about you." He patted the hand holding on to his arm then let his, rest on top.

"What do you want to know?"

Everything Arie knows. "What's your favorite color?" The question was unimportant in the scope of things. He understood that but for some reason he needed to know.

"Guess." She challenged him the sparkle in her eyes growing brighter.

Grinning he looked her over from head to toe, "If I have to guess," he paused touching his chin with a fingertip, "I'm going to say blue since you've worn blue the last two times I've seen you."

"Observant. I think I like that although I can't return the favor. I've no idea what your favorite color is and unless I got lucky, I would probably name all the colors in the rainbow before I guessed the right color."

"Believe blue has just become my favorite color." He was beginning to feel as if his mind left him and was replaced with a bowl of jelly.

"Why? Because it's mine?" She challenged him with a small and very girlish giggle.

"No, because it's the color of your eyes. They're the shade of a summer sky and they darken with simmering passion when I kiss you." His eyebrows rose as once again his thoughts strayed from his original purpose to thoughts of seduction. He wasn't just thinking of kissing but other less appropriate things.

"Oh, I'm not sure what to say to that."

"Don't fash yourself lass, say what's in your heart. Perhaps we can try another question, something my mother posed before you stopped by."

"Your mother is in town?" She blinked a few times before saying, "That's a rare event, isn't it?"

"You surprised me so I forgot to tell you. She's in town or the estate now for at least a year and before you ask, Father is continuing his voyage and research in Egypt, at least that's what Carmine thought he might be doing."

"What kind of question would you pose? You know my siblings and... What did your mother ask or what question did she provoke?" she asked, suddenly looking curious.

"Do you have dreams, Chels? Is there something you want so much in your life you can barely breathe thinking about it?" He held his breath waiting for the answer.

He watched as her eyes widened and the color deepened, just as they did when he kissed her. Knowing he'd touched upon something substantial, he waited patiently for her answer.

She moistened her lips, shaking her head as she tried to speak for a moment then stopped. "I shouldn't say."

"Why ever not? Don't you trust me?" He touched her chin; tilted it upward so he had a breathtaking view of her entire face.

"Because... Can you not ask me that? Please?"

His gut rolled and for a moment anger simmered. He didn't like the fact she wouldn't answer such a simple question. He'd never be sure why he pursued this further. "Does Arie know?"

Frown lines formed on her face and he understood he'd hit a sore spot with her, something she wanted to keep from him. Silence encompassed them for longer than Cam could endure then, "Yes, Arie knows but..."

Jealousy swamped him, nearly sent him to his knees. "Tell me. No, I'm sorry. If you don't want to confide in me, I won't insist. I'm not going to do that to you. I promised myself. No pressure." He let go of her, turning his back to her for a moment. Inhaling several long deep breaths, he turned again, forcing a smile.

She looked down for a second then up, "Thank you. Ask me anything else. I promise I'll answer everything."

Then a notion took hold and he decided to run with it. "If you don't want to answer a question I pose then I get to kiss you," he told her, trying to put the jealousy aside and live in the present. After all it wasn't Arie walking beside her, talking to her. It wasn't Arie kissing her.

"Are you giving me an out?"

"I am and now I intend to collect on the last question."

"In the middle of the walkway?"

"What better place to show the entire world that I'm courting the most beautiful lady in the world?" His mouth met hers again and he thought this could be a delightful evening. He teased and tempted, lightly brushed his lips across hers but decided not to deepen the kiss, wanting her to look forward to more tonight, much more.

The private time in the observatory could be his chance to discover her more intimately. So much for proper, he pulled away, "Shall we?" He offered his arm again, enjoying the feel of her fingers encircling him.

Inside the restaurant they found a small table in a back corner. He wanted to be away from the few people who entered the restaurant, needing Chelsea all to himself.

"I've never been here before," she said as she looked around, "In truth I've been to very few places in Glasgow. Never spent much time in town. Always preferred the country."

"Do you have any idea what you'd like to eat?" He handed her a menu, touching her hand in the process, flirting and setting the mood for later this evening.

"No, what's good? What do you order when you come here?" She moistened her lips watching him and her hand shook when she held onto the menu.

"Wine or Guinness?" he asked as the waiter stood beside the table.

"What do you like?" she asked him, staring at him, at his lips. "I'll have whatever you choose."

"Both. I enjoy both." He wasn't about to have her make her decision on his preferences.

Her arms stiffened and she took in a breath of air. "Well," she paused, "today is about being bold and trying new things. It's an adventure, my adventure. That's why I wanted to deliver the answer to your invitation in person. So, I'll have the Guinness. I've never before..."

"Good, then one for the lady and one for me." He directed the waiter. Then to Chelsea, "What would you like to eat? Anything on the menu you've never eaten before?" He liked the adventure idea and trying new things as well.

"It's pretty common fare but I've never tried oysters. Are they good?" She looked at him, her eyes shining with trust.

He shrugged a laugh trying not to bubble up and ruin the moment. "I like them but are you sure? People say they are a potent aphrodisiac."

Time seemed to freeze for a moment then she tilted her head

sideways. "I'm not sure what that is supposed to mean. What's an aphrodisiac?"

It seemed he forgot he was talking with an innocent young lady. Indeed, he wasn't too sure what to tell her, having expected her to get the gist of his comment. "An aphrodisiac, hmm...it's a food that is supposed to get you in the mood," he told her drumming his fingers on the table and wishing for a diversion.

"In the mood for what?"

Hell, why not tell her everything she wanted to know. She asked the question after he let the potent information escape. "For love, for my kisses and sex."

"I don't need anything to get in the mood," she blurted, turning a beautiful shade of pink.

"I like that. Would you like to try oysters since you've never had them?" he asked, feeling totally at ease now, loving the facts about herself she told him.

"Yes, please." She leaned forward. "What comes after kisses? You've touched my breast but..."

"Well aren't the two of you a sight. I wanted to talk with you, Cam, but you've kept yourself hidden," Leslie pulled a chair from another table before sitting down then he signaled the waiter who was delivering the beers.

"You're courting Chelsea. Does Flynt know?"

~ * ~

"Must be the lovely lady Chelsea MacTavish who is occupying all of your time. We haven't seen you in a while. I'll take a Guinness too." Donal pulled up a second chair also joining the pair.

Chelsea wasn't sure what to do at this point. Truly she didn't want to share Cam tonight with these two, and she certainly didn't want either of them reporting back to Flynt that they saw her in the restaurant with Cam. Flynt would believe she was with Catherine and Catherine would take her at her word that she rode to the country estate. After tonight her grandmother would never trust her.

Cam appeared speechless, politeness seeming to be prevalent at this point but the look on his face was not pleasant. Frown lines deepened on his forehead as it seemed he noticed the second friend stride up beside them and grab another chair.

"What are the two of you having?" Leslie asked as he sat down a devilish grin on his handsome face.

It didn't seem Cam wanted to answer. So, she paused, looking to him for something she wasn't quite sure of. They didn't order yet but she decided she'd make a choice then perhaps they would leave.

"Oysters, I believe," Chelsea said looking to Cam for approval and was surprised by the shocked expression she saw, "Not that it's any of your business. It's supposed to put me in the mood but I already am... in the mood."

"You are not staying," Cam said pointedly with a cough meant to clear his throat. "The two of you are just passing by, stopping to say hello. You didn't see us here and we didn't see you if you get my drift."

Chelsea sipped slowly, savoring the taste and deciding she liked the beer. She watched the subtle nuances between the men and wondered what they meant.

Donal leaned forward laughing. "He's privy to things I'll bet you've never heard of. "Don't let my friend here take advantage of you. Oysters could be..."

"You are nefarious, Cam. Feeding this young innocent oysters without telling her their effects." Leslie said, joining in the laughter.

"I know the affects and I approved," she blurted.

Cam graced her with a startled look and it seemed the two men were choosing to ignore both of them.

"Guess it's a good ploy. I'll have to remember it when I decide to court a lady properly but until then, I believe I'll choose ladies who already understand the effects of certain foods."

Donal slapped his friend on his back, the jest at Cam's and her's expense seeming to go on far too long. "That's never going to happen as well you know. Court? Marriage? Children? What's the fun in that? I'll keep my mistress and freedom, thank you."

"It's time for the two of you to leave," Cam gritted out clearly unhappy at the turn of events.

"Well that's not polite, dear friend. Where have your manners vanished to? We're simply making conversation," Leslie asked seemingly unable to stop his laughter as two more beers were placed on the table in front of the men.

"We did wish for a bit of privacy," Chelsea said, trying for the sweetness she always claimed she didn't possess. "While another time we might enjoy your company..."

"Now is not that time," Cam pointed out, seeming to agree wholeheartedly with her.

"Seems like perfect timing to me," Donal said, leaning back and stretching his legs out, obviously making himself comfortable. "Think we're keeping you from a big mistake, one that might have consequences. The two of you need chaperones and who better than the two of us. Friends who won't judge." Donal pointed to Leslie then back to himself.

"Not making a mistake." Cam smiled politely, seeming to change tactics. "Don't need any one watching us. No chaperones tonight."

"It's a dinner, nothing more," Chelsea said, exasperated with the good natured teasing but wishing she could figure out how to get rid of these two men.

"You must have some plan for afterward," Leslie pointed out with a wink and a wicked grin. Then lifting his eyebrows, "A play? A stroll in the park? Or perhaps a trip to the observatory."

"Kissing. Cuddling and maybe something more inappropriate," Donal added to Leslie's list.

"What?" She couldn't help the surprise in her voice or realizing she'd just given something away that would have been better off if left private. She looked to Cam whose frown lines deepened.

The waiter stood at the table again, seeming to expect an order from the two men.

"They're leaving," Cam said.

"Think I'll have the salmon." Donal said.

"Sounds good to me," Leslie agreed. "Don't have need of oysters tonight."

"They won't be eating at this table." Cam looked over the room.

"There's one in the front that will do just fine for these two jokers. Won't it?" His gaze riveted on the oldest of the pair, Donal.

"Suppose so since it doesn't seem we're wanted here," Leslie frowned. "Always thought you'd have room for us. Didn't think I'd be put aside so easily all because of a not so proper courtship."

Unmoving and less than eager to depart the table, Donal sipped the beer. "Did you hear about the man they found naked in the city center the other day? Quite the spectacle."

Chelsea was shaking her head and when she looked at Cam, it seemed his mood brightened.

"Ah, I see at least one of you heard," Leslie said, sitting back down at the table his hands clasped over his stomach. "Rumor has it someone made a threat to Leod, I think that was his name, and Leod didn't understand that the man meant it. So, I guess Leod had to be taught a lesson."

Chelsea couldn't help the tiny gasp of surprise, "Leod?" Arie must have been responsible for this. The sultan told her he would take care of the odious man who dared touch her when she told him no.

"You know this naked man. Do you also know who is responsible for sharing his naked white body with all of the city?" Donal asked, laughing all the while. "Heard one of the bystanders gave him a tiny handkerchief to put in front of his private parts while he tried to make his way through the growing throngs of people to his apartment. He wasn't even given shoes."

"Too bad he lived so close to the city center. Have you seen him at the university?" Leslie posed the question as if he already knew the answer.

"Haven't seen the man and I haven't heard anything about the incident. Haven't been at the university either. Been busy," Cam said, slowly sipping his beer and glancing at Chelsea. Then back to his friends, "The two of you are leaving now."

"Only if we can accompany you to the observatory," Donal chimed in. "Don't want you to take advantage of the lady."

"No," Cam said.

"You have to have a chaperone and what's better than two chaperones?" Leslie said, restating the earlier point. "Beside I always wanted to look through one of those..." He waved his hand in the air and looked to Donal. "What are they called?"

"I don't have any idea what you're talking about," Leslie said as both men looked at Cam.

"Telescope," he said, leaning back in his chair, his anger or frustration seemingly vanished. "No one is chaperoning us."

"What about Chelsea's reputation?" Leslie pointed out.

"Unless the two of you mention anything about seeing us or our destination, no one will be the wiser. We won't need to be concerned," Cam said, smiling. "There will be no blight on her reputation."

Chelsea wasn't too sure why she wasn't part of this conversation even though she didn't have a thing to say. Then she blurted. "I don't need or want two chaperones. I'm a grown woman. Cam and I wanted to get to know each other a little better." When she heard Cam's groan, she stared at him, her head tilted a bit sideways in confusion.

"Get to know each other better?" Donal asked, nodding his head and grinning. "I'm sure that's what Flynt is afraid of, the two of you knowing each other better. It must be what keeps him up nights. Would have been the same with Bliss if he'd known."

"Never a good thing. This getting to know someone better," Leslie agreed. "A young innocent female."

"I'm sure if I give the word, the sultan will find a way to humiliate the two of you as I believe he did with Leod. Arie and I are good friends. While I don't understand half of what the three of you are bantering about, I know what I want. I want to spend the evening with Cam. Alone. Private. No one watching over us." She was delighted by the play of expression over the men's faces when she reminded them of the sultan as well as what was done to Leod.

"I suppose neither of you are adverse to being found naked in city center. 'Fraid you two would have a lot farther to walk, but at least you might be a bit more pleasant for the women of Glasgow to look upon. Probably wouldn't give you even a skimpy handkerchief to hide your private parts because they'll be too busy ogling." Now it seemed Cam goaded his friends.

"Have an enjoyable evening. I've heard more than enough to put an end to the teasing." Leslie stood, bidding them goodbye before strolling to the front table Guinness in hand.

"Don't do anything I wouldn't do," Donal said with a wink. "If I was courting a lady that is," he added as an after thought.

"Finally," Cam said leaning back in his chair before motioning the waiter for another beer.

"I think they were harmless," Chelsea said, sipping on the beer and grimacing slightly. Next time she'd order wine. "Actually, they are handsome and fun to talk to." At the look crossing Cam's face, she quickly added, "Lacie is sweet on Leslie, but he doesn't even know she exists and Daryl seems to like Donal. And if it will help wipe the frown from your face they aren't anywhere near as handsome or gallant as you."

He seemed to brighten at her words and she'd give just about anything to know what he was thinking. "How old is she?" Cam asked.

"Lacie turned sixteen last January. I know, at least at the moment she is way too young for him. But it doesn't stop her from dreaming about him."

The oysters were set on the table.

"These are cooked," Cam pointed to a plate, "and these are not. What's your pleasure?"

"One of each," she told him hesitantly, wondering why she agreed to trying these creatures. The beer should have been enough of a challenge for one night but she'd wanted to impress him.

"Good girl." He placed a few of each on her plate then dished up his own. "Take a swallow of beer before you try the uncooked. Just let them slide down your throat."

She rubbed her arms then tried for a deep breath of air. "I've never been one to try new things." The need to renege on this seemed to rise to the forefront of her mind the more she looked at the animal sitting on the shell. Was it an animal? Then she looked at Cam who seemed to be sending her a reassuring smile.

"You will survive," he chuckled softly.

"I know but..."

"Like this," Cam sipped his beer before he began, "Take your fork and sort of move the oyster around the shell. You want to make sure it's detached. Then pick up the shell, and slurp down the oyster like this. "There."

"You don't chew it? Just swallow it whole?" She certainly didn't know what to think about that.

"Once or twice but you don't have to because it will just slide down your throat." She was sure he laughed at her shocked expression.

"If you don't chew it, you won't taste it. Perhaps that's for the best." She felt her insides churn.

"True, but if you don't taste the wee sea creature, then you won't know if you like it. I thought today was about boldness and trying something new." He leaned forward briefly taking her hands in his.

For a moment she stared at the plate and with a huge breath she sipped her beer once then twice, then she did as he told her, slurping the oyster from its half shell. She did chew once then let it slide down her throat. Two gulps of Guinness later, she opened her eyes.

"I did it." A smile on her face as if she'd just accomplished the impossible.

"Did you like them, oysters?" he asked, seeming to stifle the laughter but was unable to stop the huge grin on his face.

"Slimy. Do you think the cooked ones are that way too?"

"But did you like it?" he asked again, touching her hand with his.

"I don't want to lie."

"Of course not, I won't be offended if you don't like raw oyster. Don't ever feel as if you have to lie to me or protect my feelings in any way." His smile turned serious. "I mean it, Chels. Always tell me what you're thinking."

"The taste might grow on me. It was unusual but the texture was abhorrent." Lord but it was horrible, so she did lie to him in a way. But the taste might be acquired. "I'll try one more."

"Together?" he asked, holding up a shell while seeming to wait for her to do the same.

She nodded, emboldened by him then together they sipped the beer and downed the oyster. She blinked a few times thinking it might taste a tiny bit better the second time around but it didn't.

When he looked to her for an answer, she shook her head. "Don't suppose I want to try another one of these, but I'll try two of the cooked. I like the Guinness though and I can fill up on bread although my stomach is telling me it has had enough food." She picked up a slice of bread, chewing on it while she searched for the courage to try a cooked one, believing she wouldn't like it any better than the raw ones.

"I'm sorry this is not to your liking," he told her, "Perhaps the rest of the evening will be better than the food. I'll make it up to you."

"I'm not. Life has to hold surprises and challenges. If I don't try new things, can I say I've really lived?" She wondered at her spontaneous words. Never before had she challenged herself in any way. Cam helped her see something different in life.

"You're right. I need to challenge myself, too, and the way to do that is sitting right in front of me confirming what I vowed to myself when I decided to court you properly."

"How is that a challenge? You're completely at ease with women. Just like my brother." She didn't like thinking about all the women who came before her and who might follow.

"But not debutantes, you're my first one. Shall we eat two more of the cooked variety?"

Together they ate two with no better results. Cam finished the oysters and she finished the bread. Another Guinness and she felt a bit lightheaded and a lot sleepy.

"Are you ready to go?" he asked as he stood, holding out his hand. "To the observatory."

The sun had set when they left the restaurant and the street lamps lit the way to their destination. Cool night air served to waken her and when she stepped inside the room she was in awe at the site of the huge telescope. The instrument stole her breath.

"You can really see the stars when you look through this?" she asked, her voice soft, amazed at the very idea. "And planets too?"

"Let me set it on a planet, Mars perhaps. Then you can see a better version of it than when you just use your eyes." Cam went to work and a few minutes later he finished.

She watched as he seemed to know what he was doing unsure of exactly what was happening, but when he finally stepped back with a smile on his face, she said, "I can't believe I'm going to..."

"Look into my world," he told her and directed her to the eyepiece.

She stared at the object for several long seconds, turning into at least a minute. When she looked up, "I'm amazed and intrigued. What kinds of things are whirling around in your mind? I had no idea you knew about things like this or that you were even connected to the university. I just knew you as my brother's friend and a bad boy."

He grinned when she mentioned bad boy. Then, "The moon is beautiful tonight. I'll set the telescope so you can look at it. Have you ever wanted to walk on the moon?" he asked as he made the necessary adjustments.

"Can't say that I've ever had that thought," she told him as she gazed through the telescope at an object that until now she'd always taken for granted then realizing there were depths to Cam beyond anything she could ever imagine, she knew she loved him.

"Someday people will walk on the moon; they might even live there." He wrapped an arm around her pulling her close. "Can you even imagine anything like that?"

She felt his sincerity as well as the warmth emanating from him. His hands were around her waist and her back pressed against his chest. Closing her eyes, she tried to find a way into his thoughts, his world. How could this contact with him be wrong in anyone's eyes?

"You amaze me," she whispered. "I want to find a way into your thoughts as well as your brilliance. I never thought about anything that wasn't right in front of me until now. Never looked beyond the fact stars were pretty and the moon was nice to look at, romantic."

"My thoughts about you, Chels." His chin rested on top of her head. "Do you have any idea how much I want to make love to you right now. Everything about you draws me to you. I can't even think of anything but discovering more about you when I'm with you, despite how hard I try to think of other things. I intended asking you questions tonight so I could learn more."

"But I wouldn't answer the second question."

"No, you wouldn't and that fact put a sudden damper on my intentions."

"Then Leslie and Donal turned up, embarrassing me."

"Indeed, the two of them could put a damper on anything romantic."

She didn't turn in his arms even though that's what she wanted. Instead she enjoyed the gentle press of his hand on her belly. He drew her close as he wrapped his arms fully around her, encompassing her within his embrace.

"I want you to make love to me," she spoke softly, needing to experience more with him even though she wasn't too sure what those experiences would entail. "What seems like a long time ago, you told me you'd give me lessons in love. Could we start tonight?"

"I did, didn't I and I will, just not right now. Now I have to do this right even though there are no chaperones." His voice was tight, strained. "I want to court you properly, do things in a suitable order."

It seemed to Chelsea he held himself back. She turned in his arms, determined to do everything possible to help him change his mind about her lessons about making love to her. "Please," she whispered while she trailed a fingertip up his neck to his ear.

"You need to stop doing that," he grit out, clearly distraught by her actions. When she placed a tender kiss on his neck. "Chels..." His voice was deep and raw, deliciously throaty. His hands against her shook as they tightened.

She hesitated for a moment, concerned she did something terribly wrong. Then, "What if I don't want to stop? What if..." Her voice seemed to purr and grow husky.

His groan gave her reason to smile, pleased she could do that to him. Briefly he touched her lips with his, brushed them across hers once then twice before he rested his forehead against hers. "I can't do this right now. I made promises to myself. I would do this right and not take advantage of you. Anything I would do right now would be reaping the benefits of your innocence."

She stood on tiptoes and even then when she tried to kiss him, she could not reach. He was doing nothing to help. "You don't want to kiss me? A real kiss?" she asked, her feelings unraveling. "I don't understand what has changed so much."

"Ach, Lass, it's not like I don't want to kiss you. I told you I want to make love to you more than breathe. I promised myself though. Promised I would be proper and take care of your tender sensibilities. You are a lady born and deserve to be treated with respect." He repeated his vows as if in doing so it would help him.

She pushed away from him laughing, "Since when have I had tender sensibilities? Bloody hell, I'm not even sure what it means, but I've never expected or wanted you to be proper, Cam MacEwen. I like you just the way you come."

He groaned again, his fists clenching as even now he held them to his sides as if that was his only recourse. Then he laughed. "I do like it when you swear, my sweet one."

"If I keep swearing, will you make love to me or at least teach me one more of those lessons you promised? I'd be happy with the next installment as you said a long time ago." She smiled at him, wrapping her hands around his neck and trying to think of some other ploy to entice him. She just had few ideas about how to seduce a man.

Now he was shaking his head, laughing even more. "No matter what you do, I'm not going to give into your seduction. I—"

"Promised yourself," she cut in, frustration as well as anger building. She turned away, sitting on one of the seats, arms crossed in front of her in a determined pout. "I don't understand what I've done wrong." She pushed back the moisture clogging her throat, determined not to cry in front of him.

He sat down beside her, drawing her onto his lap. "You've done nothing wrong, Chels. It's me and something I have to do right. Where you're concerned, I've done too many things wrong."

"Then why won't you even kiss me? I can almost understand the other part," she paused, "the part about making love to me. Almost. Broc didn't care if he was proper. He made love to Bliss before..." She hesitated simply because she didn't want to say the marriage word. He failed to mention it in the last few days. Maybe he didn't have any intention of marrying her.

That could be a problem... What then?

His heavy sigh sent a wave of guilt through her then he spoke, "Not kissing you goes against everything I want right now. If I were to kiss you, really kiss you I might not be able to stop myself. One kiss would lead to another then one more and I'd be tempted to do other things." With a callused fingertip he traced the line of her bodice.

Shivering beneath his touch she persisted, "I don't want you to stop, never stop wanting me. Please kiss me."

It seemed he meant to oblige then he stood, striding to the door to the observatory and casting his gaze outside. "It's getting late or should I say dawn will come soon. I don't know where the time has gone. I should get you home."

Tears in her eyes, she walked to him, and placing her hand on his back, "I'm sorry I've made this so hard for you." Understanding him was difficult for her. Understanding a man, she decided, was impossible. It seemed they were perverse, one minute touting one thing and the next minute something completely different.

"No apologies necessary. Perhaps I shouldn't have promised something that would be so difficult to keep. Even in protecting your reputation I'm damaging it by bringing you here and keeping you until the sun rises. People will think," he began slowly.

"That you made love to me." She inhaled deeply then let it out slowly. "What are we going to do now?"

"You're supposed to be at your country estate but instead you're here, with me," he spoke softly as if in distress. "Leslie and Donal know the truth."

"I'm here with you. Catherine will wonder if I show up before noon."

"Or before the sun rises," he added, wrapping an arm around her before pulling her close once more. "I'm sorry. It seems that once more I put my needs in front of yours. I wanted to show you the telescope."

She didn't have the strength to push away, "Did you hear me refuse?"

"No, but that still doesn't give me the answer to our problem. I can't take you home without causing more difficulties for you."

"My problem," she corrected him. "It seems you can go home without anyone questioning your appearance there." Men, they could come and go as they pleased without any repercussions to their statuses in society.

"When you're with me it's my job to protect you." His voice turned gruff as he ran a hand through his hair. "You'll have to come with me. I've an idea."

"You're going to make love to me." She grinned at him thinking that perhaps he might be listening. "After all, my reputation will be in shreds if anyone sees us together right now. So why not make everything valid?" She blinked a few times, wondering why she still persisted when he made it clear he would not give in to base desires.

"Come, we'll take the less traveled streets. My mistress' house is close by. We can go there and you can sleep. You must be tired."

She bristled at his suggestion and pulled away from him. "I'm not sleeping at your mistress' home."

"Why not? I've no mistress and haven't had one for almost a year now." He sounded indignant. "It's just a house that I own. Why not use it?"

She turned to him, angry and frustrated as this evening had turned sour when it had once held so much promise. "Because," she blurted, unable to figure out how to explain the reason if he couldn't figure it out for himself.

"Because?" he prompted softly, playing with a tendril of hair that had escaped her chignon.

Her body shaking, "You slept with her there. I won't sleep in the same bed as the two of you..." She couldn't say anymore. Walking down the path that led to the observatory, all she wanted was to put distance between them.

~ * ~

When Chelsea didn't show up at the country house as planned, Arie borrowed a horse and raced into town. He was worried about her. To his knowledge she never did anything spontaneous, and if she told someone she would be somewhere that's where she should turn up.

He arrived in the city soon enough to watch the lovely couple walk from Cam's home then down the street to a nearby restaurant. Chelsea appeared to be enjoying herself but then why wouldn't she?

He knew firsthand how much Chelsea loved the man. She didn't know it was love yet but again he recognized love when he saw it. One of his wives actually loved him, the other two tolerated him at best. He could have fallen in love with Chelsea but her heart was already held tightly in someone else's hands. Trouble was Cam MacEwen didn't know what he held, either that or didn't care. Someone needed to knock some sense into that stubborn pigheaded man.

"What do you want us to do?" His best friend, Victor, a man who spent most of his life enjoying the good times as well as lamenting the bad stood by him. "Enjoyed the last mission you sent us on. Interesting to watch Leod try to escape the crowd of people watching him."

"No lessons for Cam unless he hurts her in anyway including breaking her heart. I've an idea and hope it might work," Arie said. "Problem is she loves him and he has yet to discover what true love is. We'll wait and see what happens."

"So, do nothing?" Victor asked.

"Follow them discreetly." Arie folded his hands in front of him, hoping this sweet lady would find love with her chosen man. He would do anything to help her, even deposit Cam in the city center naked if necessary. Chelsea would have his head if he tried such a thing. Perhaps he could think of something else to help her.

"All night?" the man asked.

"Until she is safely in the MacTavish townhouse and he goes home. Then I want to know where they went, how long they were there, everything." Arie now invested himself in this relationship more than he'd ever done before. In truth he never cared about any other woman this deeply.

Too bad her heart was somewhere else.

Chapter Three

Cam ran his hands through his hair, frustrated beyond belief. He didn't know what to do or how to ease Chelsea's feelings about sleeping in his second townhouse. Bloody hell but he saw tears in her eyes and he knew he was a cad for putting them there. Any other woman he would have swept off her feet and made love to her when she asked. Hell, any other time with Chelsea he would have done the same.

He watched as she strode down the path, her back stiff as a board, her anger at him simmering. What to do? Presenting the most logical choice he could come up with to her, she thought his suggestion abhorrent.

Where was she going?

Kicking his body into action, he raced after her. "Chels." He set a hand on her shoulder in an attempt to stop her.

She shook it off, "Leave me alone, Cam. Right now you're the last person I need or want to talk to."

He wanted to give into gut instinct as well as his pulsing rod, sweep her off her feet and in the privacy of the observatory make love to her. Instead, "Please, stop and listen to reason." He tried to step in front of her.

"Staying in your mistress' house, sleeping on your mistress' bed is not tenable." She continued walking. "It's not reasonable to think I would ever do such a thing."

"Of course it is. It's the only solution we have. Do you want to ride to your country home right now then turn around and make the trip back to the city or would you like to sleep? I know you're tired." He tried for reason and understood she was not feeling sensible or reasonable at the moment.

"How would you know any of that? Did you ask or did you just come up with this manly opinion? Will you always presume to know how I feel or what I want?" She continued walking, her breath seeming to catch in her throat as she picked up the pace.

He wanted to ask her if he could unlace her corset so she could breathe more easily but didn't dare. She would either let him and in that case, he'd be doomed or she would take offense at his suggestion.

At the moment he was damned and left with no feasible alternatives.

He tried to backpedal and explain his words. "I'm tired and would love a few hours of sleep before I have to confront the world, so I assumed you must also be tired. If you don't want me near you, I won't sleep in the house with you." He wasn't at all sure how any of this would work, but at first the solution seemed to stare him in the face. It had been so practical and easy.

Now he wasn't so sure.

"Is there more than one bedroom?" she asked.

"There are three. You can have your pick." It seemed she was thinking over his suggestion and perhaps realizing it might be the only possible way to accomplish this innocent deception without entirely ruining her reputation. Of course he would have to rely on the silence of Leslie and Donal, but they had no idea Chelsea told her grandmother she was riding to their country home yesterday afternoon.

"So, I wouldn't have to sleep on her bed." She told him with an emphasis on her.

"Even if you stayed in the master chamber you wouldn't sleep on the bed we once shared. I always replace the furniture when I take a new mistress." He spoke from the heart believing he understood her reasons better than she gave him credit.

"I'm not going to be your new mistress." She nearly shouted the words, her hands once again fisted at her sides while her body shook with her anger.

Cam was sure if there were other people nearby they would have certainly heard the words and there would be no reason for a deception of any kind. "Of course not, if everything goes as planned, I'll never have another mistress in my entire life." Despite his efforts he found he was also speaking much louder than he intended.

"Then what are you implying by suggesting I sleep there?" Her hands were still fisted at her sides as she spoke. "I would have you tell me exactly what you're thinking."

"Nothing." He was shaking his head, unsatisfied by the events of the evening and irritated this was happening. "Nothing, absolutely nothing. Just wanted you to have a place to rest before encountering the world. I was trying to think of your needs and what would be best for you."

"Nothing?"

"Absolutely nothing." He recognized the fact she was thinking now, not reacting to whatever he said. "Can you think of some other way to save a reputation that isn't even close to becoming tarnished? I'd be happy to entertain another solution if you have one."

"No." She hung her head, looking at the ground. "No, I'm sorry. It's just that this has been such an emotional evening for me. I don't understand who exactly you've turned into but you're not Cam, at least not my Cam. What have you done with him and when am I going to get him back?"

Turned into a man who cares about you more than he cares about himself. Cam couldn't ever remember a time where another person except perhaps his mother came first in his life. "Chels, I want you to be happy and tonight you were for a short time. Seems I've ruined the special evening, but I promise I'll make it up to you in the future."

"Tomorrow night?" she asked.

"Tomorrow?" He was trying to move from one conversation to this new one and was a bit confused.

"The play and the ball."

She looked at him as if he'd lost his mind. He scrambled to remember how this evening began. "The play and the ball." He ran the words over in his mind. "You delivered the answer to my invitation in person."

"Do you still want to take me?" Her smile was tentative as if she doubted herself. "Will you be my Cam and not some strange person I don't recognize?"

He'd done that to her, made her second guess his intentions and all because he needed to court her properly. Perhaps proper was much ado about nothing and he should act more himself before he singlehandedly drove her away. "Yes, more than anything I'd like to take you with me, although I do believe it will be a dull affair, a bit boring."

She sighed deeply then bringing her hand to her mouth she made a gallant attempt to stifle the impending yawn. "I do need to sleep and while I don't want to admit the fact, your ex-mistress' house is probably the perfect place to spend the early morning hours. I do believe I just forgave you."

"Good, I'm glad you see the wisdom of the choice and I've fully noticed the use of the word ex where it concerns my mistress. Would you like me to find a cab to take us there?" He made more progress than he expected in the last few minutes, thrilled she was coming to see things his way. Yet he couldn't promise she'd get her Cam back this night. It seemed neither realized that this was indeed a new day. He still wanted to court her the right way and attendance at these two affairs would provide no privacy for anything other than a chaste kiss or two.

"Not if it will take less time to walk." Once again, she started down the path, but this time the pace wasn't quite so fast or her back as stiff.

He caught up with her, offering her his arm again. "We should be there in a few minutes."

At the house he brought out a key and opened the door. The furniture was covered with sheets, waiting for the new arrival. At this point the only possible new arrival would be his mother, Carmine, if he could convince her to move here instead of continued residency at his townhouse. He wasn't ready just yet to have a roommate.

"Did you decide where you want to sleep?" he asked, looking up the stairs and wishing they could share the bed.

"I want to sleep with you." Then she held up her hands as if to stop his next words. "Just sleep and share the bed. You told me enough times tonight that you wouldn't sleep with me, make love."

Cam wanted to give in to her request, needed to hold her through the rest of the night. He was glad, too, that she seemed to understand what he'd been telling her all along was not that he didn't want to make love to her but that the dictates of proper courting would not allow him to do so until they were married. He was trying his damndest to follow those rules. "I do want to hold you," he whispered the words, forcing other thoughts to the back of his head.

He watched her start up the staircase. This time when he raced after her, he swept her into his arms before carrying her into the bedroom. He almost set her on the bed, intending to come down on top of her, kiss her, touch her, explore every inch of her. Something he'd dreamed about almost every night since that first kiss too many months ago to count. Then he caught his breath, common sense and prudence rushing to the forefront of his mind.

When he stopped himself, he set her down. "Do you need help with the dress, the corset? You won't get any rest at all if you keep everything on." His voice shook with raw emotion as he needed to clear his throat just to finish the offer.

"I should sleep in my dress," she said, watching him as if hoping he would tell her no.

He found that despite her earlier challenges she became suddenly shy. "That wouldn't be relaxing. I guess I didn't think this out very far. I should go in the other room so you can be comfortable."

"What are you going to sleep in?" she asked, her eyes wide with some emotion Cam couldn't read.

"Tonight, it seems my clothes." He wanted to tell her he always slept naked, never wore a stitch of clothing and in the future that was the way they would both spend the night hours.

"That won't be very comfortable for you either," she said.

"Or for you." Hell, sleeping with all his clothes on was hardly appealing, but he suggested this scenario and now he needed to see his creation to its proper conclusion. "You could take your dress and corset off and sleep in your underclothes." Lord, he knew women wore more layers than necessary.

"And you could..."

"I'll sleep in my clothes." He decided then he would stay with her just until she fell asleep. That way the temptation wouldn't goad him the remainder of the night. He was fooling himself if he truly thought she would no longer tantalize him.

When she turned her back to him in seeming agreement, his nimble fingers quickly divested her of her dress and corset. "Thank you." She smiled at him, holding the fabric of her dress to cover her breasts. Once again, she seemed to hesitate, more unsure of herself than he'd ever seen her.

He pulled the bed covers back before she slipped into bed, watching him while he pulled off his boots. He climbed onto the bed and on top of the covers. "Bloody hell," he swore, slipping underneath and pulling her to him, needing her now and in the most elemental ways.

"You don't have to swear," she whispered as he felt her breath across his chest. "I won't seduce you. I promise."

He let out a roar of laughter. "Do you even know what that would entail?" In his state of arousal, seduction could be achieved in a matter of seconds. If she had any understanding of what was happening here, he would possess her, take her virginity without a second thought.

"No, but someday I hope that will be one of my lessons." She looked up when he swore again then she placed her head on his chest, exploring him with her fingers.

"I promise you it will." He groaned, his voice turning rough with unrequited hunger, "Perhaps you know more than you think."

He knew the moment she fell asleep. Her body molded to his, and her roaming fingers stilled, thank the heavens above. He closed his eyes, telling himself it would only be for a few seconds and he would rise.

When he woke, one hand rested on his chest and the other had found its way beneath his shirt. She was now running her fingers along the waistband of his pants. He stopped her and sat up slightly, fully aroused and trying to ignore the location of her hand. "Did you sleep well?"

"I did," she said. "And you?"

Her blue eyes were wide, while tendrils of her hair that had come lose during the night fell around her shoulders. My God, but she was beautiful. Disheveled as she was, she appeared a wanton angel. The slight swell of her breasts could be seen beneath her shift as well as the dusty rose color of her nipples. He knew he wanted to wake up to this sight for the rest of his life.

"Never better," he told her even though it had taken him hours to fall asleep. He'd not planned on sleeping this long and now he had to figure out a way to get her home with no one recognizing her. "Are you hungry?"

"Starving," she told him as her stomach rumbled.

He hopped from the bed, tucking in his shirt. "I'm going to the bakery nearby. You do whatever you need to do and I'll be back before you know it with some pastries."

She nodded at him while he pulled on his boots, leaving the room with a lingering look at her and wishing when he returned, he could truly have her, all of her. Ideas formed in his head as he understood the growing difficulty he was having keeping his hands to himself. Proper was just not going to work much longer.

Perhaps the vow to himself needed to be changed. Possibly, if he could find a private place with no interruptions, they could explore their relationship further. When he stepped outside, a warm summer sun filled the sky above and a cool breeze swept from the river. With a light heart and filled with hope for the future, he whistled as he set off down the street.

Stepping inside the bakery, the bell clanged when he entered, setting off a cheery sound that aligned with his feelings. Scents of freshly baked bread and sweet delicacies filled the air. His stomach growled as he tried to remember the last time he ate. Recalling the oysters, he chuckled softly.

"It's a beautiful day, sir. What can I do for you?" The proprietor stood behind the counter, a broad grin on his aged face. "Everything's fresh baked this morning."

"Four croissants, no, *pain au chocolate*, and do you have coffee?" Cam wanted nothing more than to soak in the ambiance of the wonderful day while he found a way to improve his relationship with Chelsea.

"Chocolate croissants, *tres bien*, and I can give you a large container of coffee that should stay hot for a while." The man busied himself filling the order. Whistling a bawdy tune as he worked, he set the ordered items into a bag.

"Thank you, have a nice day," Cam said before he left with their breakfast. He wondered what she was thinking now and if she understood how much he cared for her. All his actions had been for her.

And yet...

She wanted her Cam back. Fortunately, he wanted him back too. This celibacy thing was not to his liking despite the fact it was supposed to be the right way to go about courting a young debutant. Chelsea and their relationship didn't fit that mold. Especially when she announced to him more than once she didn't want to be considered a debutant.

When he stepped inside, Arie sat on the steps leading upstairs, a broad grin on his rugged face.

Cam's gut tightened, anger bristling beneath what he hoped was a carefully constructed façade. "What are you doing here?" He'd had few feelings for the foreigner Chelsea befriended until these last few days. Now he disliked him with an intensity he wasn't sure he understood. Just knew the man was too important to Chelsea and he didn't like it. In her heart it seemed he assumed a brotherly yet not so brotherly place in her life

"Waiting for you. What took you so long?" Arie rose, extending his hand in friendship and greeting. "Seems you took advantage of the wee lass last night. Not a good choice, no, not at all a good way to proceed. No, no, no, no, you should treat Chels better."

He bristled more at Arie's use of his pet name for her. "Why are you here?" he insisted again, gritting out the words. Cam was tempted to ignore the haughty man but decided where the sultan was concerned, rash behavior never boded well for anyone. Arie tended toward the unexpected and where Arie was concerned the ends always justified the means.

"I've made Lady MacTavish my concern, since it seems Flynt has abandoned her for his new love, Hope, and Catherine is far too lenient. Where your behavior leans to impropriety, she seems to ignore it. Chels spent the evening as well as this morning in your company. I want to know your intentions."

"Isn't that for the head of her family? I believe that's Catherine not Flynt or you." he repeated, understanding Arie might not see this his way. As far as he was concerned, Arie was insinuating himself into something that was not his business but if he wasn't careful, he could end up naked in the city square.

"As I said earlier, had you been listening, Catherine gives her too much latitude and Flynt is all tied up in knots over Hope." His words were gruff and to the point. "It's up to me to make sure you're not hurting her and you're what she wants. Of course you also must have her best interests at heart, which I don't think you do. You have yours, just as any man."

"Hope is the lady you came all this way for." Cam searched for another topic of conversation besides his relationship with Chelsea. "Why don't you concentrate on her instead of Chelsea? Shouldn't you be vying for her hand instead of allowing Flynt to run rough shod over you?"

"You spent so much time at the observatory you weren't able to get her home at a reasonable hour so you brought her to your mistress' home. Not well done of you, Colin." Arie went on, every once in a while gazing up the stairs while he ignored Cam's pointed remarks.

"Ex-mistress," he gritted out, disliking this supercilious man more with each ticking of the clock as well of the use of his first name. Only his father and his mother called him Colin, however they usually included his other two names and sometimes his last name as well.

"Ah, yes, ex-mistress. What are your intentions? I've offered her my hand in marriage. Can you say the same?"

"She told you no." Breath suddenly rushed from his lungs. Bloody hell, Arie asked her to marry him? Cam looked around Arie, hoping to see Chelsea dressed and coming down the steps. Only her appearance would ease his fears. "She doesn't want to become another one of your wives."

"Chelsea won't be down for a while. I brought a few servants with me and she's bathing." Arie's smug pronouncement slapped Cam in the face.

"You did what?" Anger for this man as well as loathing simmered inside Cam even hotter than it had a few minutes prior. Arie's words stung.

"See to her needs? You shouldn't have any objections. You should have thought of that before you left her to fend for herself."

"I will see to Chelsea's needs not some sultan from thousands of miles away who will be returning to his country soon. At least one can hope he's returning." Cam wasn't at all sure why he let Arie goad him, but that was exactly what was happening right now. Every smug smile as well as every pointed word brought him closer to throttling the man

"Perhaps you should understand a woman's necessities better. It seems to me you're quite lacking in those fundamental skills." Arie provoked him further, his grin growing broader as if he understood exactly what he did.

Petulantly and almost childlike, Cam held up the bag of food as if the gesture would prove to Arie he could take care of Chelsea. "I brought her breakfast, coffee and croissants."

"Coffee and a few pastries." Arie directed his attention to the kitchen, "That's no way to feed your woman. Why she'll wilt away to nothing if that's all she gets for breakfast. My cook is seeing to a proper meal for the beautiful young woman. He's in the kitchen as we speak. I'm sure there will be enough for you also if she wants you to join her."

This was untenable. "Get out!" Cam lost his patience as well as his temper, his emotions seething. All the frustrations he'd felt for the last several days reached a boiling point he had limited control over.

"I don't see how that is possible," Arie said, still smiling seeming to have this scenario under his command. "Can you smell the bacon sizzling in the frying pan and..."

"Arie, I knew it had to be you who made sure I had a bath." Chelsea ran down the steps and into Arie's arms not his. "That was so sweet and considerate of you." She never looked at him.

Cam cleared his throat in an attempt to get Chelsea's attention, but she paid no heed, having eyes only for the sultan. Arie was whirling her around in circles while she giggled. "Put her down," he gritted out, his jaw tense, his fists following suit.

"Do as he says, Arie," Chelsea said. "I see you're back from the bakery. Can you smell the bacon? It's heavenly. Nothing in the world is better than chocolate and bacon." She inhaled a deep breath smiling at both men. "We should eat then you can take me home with my virtue intact just as you wanted."

Chelsea had no idea what her innocent affection for the sultan did to him. Gulping a long deep breath in hopes of tamping down the rising jealousy, he said, "I'd prefer it if Arie left right now," he grumbled, staring fiercely at the man who got under his skin like no other.

"That's not very nice," Chelsea said, tugging on Cam's arm. "You should apologize. Arie has always been sweet and thoughtful to me."

Arie glanced his way, the pompous grin still present. "Yes, do as the lady says, apologize. That would be ever so nice."

"Not going to happen." Offering his arm to Chelsea. "Shall we proceed to the kitchen?" When she accepted the proffered arm, he felt a small measure of relief and she did say she liked chocolate.

"Not without Arie," she protested, glancing from one man to the other. "I don't understand you, Cam MacEwen."

"Very well, if you insist." He had to agree with her. It seemed there was no other course of action.

"That's quite alright and thank you for your generous invitation. I've eaten this morning. My men and I will leave the two of you alone."

Cam tried to smile through his emotions. Arie knew how much his actions irritated him. There was no reason to continue this charade. He would have to ignore the man in the future and let his words vanish into the air rather than getting under his skin. If he could help it, the man would have no control over his thoughts where it concerned Chelsea or anything else.

"Good to hear," Cam said. "Didn't relish your company anyway."

Arie hugged Chelsea one more time then quickly departed, the door clanging shut behind him.

"You don't like Arie very much." Chelsea made the point while she held his arm. "Why is that?"

"We should eat then I'll get you home." He ignored her question having no intention of explaining his opinions about the sultan to anyone, especially not Chelsea. Pure jealousy was not something he was used to experiencing. Before he said anything more about his feelings to her, he needed to figure out why Arie was able to prickle him.

"Cam." She tugged on his arm. "What is wrong with you?"

He pulled her into his arms, his lips meeting hers, softly at first then deepening the kiss, he bit gently on her lower lip. Hoping she'd forget the question, his tongue slid across her lips, pushing inside. The little sound she made in the back of her throat pleased him immensely. He'd wanted to do this for so long now, he could barely breathe.

"Now, if you two don't get on with breakfast this little ploy you created to save her name will be to no avail." Arie spoke from the back door.

Slowly Cam pulled away from her, his mouth so close to hers, he felt the soft whisper of her breath against his cheek while he glared at the odious and intrusive man standing in front of them.

"About time you left," Cam said, keeping his eyes riveted on Chelsea. "We can't get on with breakfast until you leave."

Instead Arie stepped farther inside and pulled up a chair, looking to his cook. "We do have enough for three." When the cook nodded, "Then dish up the plates. The two of you can either eat or do whatever it is you were doing. I for one can use another good meal since it is getting close to noon."

Cam pushed down the thoughts filling his head, determined to best the sultan at his games despite Arie's decided advantage. He pulled out a chair for Chelsea, one as far away from Arie as he could place her. Unfortunately, across the table from the man, she looked right at his grinning face.

"Eat up," he told Chelsea after she sat down. "We've got to get you home. Despite Arie's insinuations I do have your interest at heart. Gossip with your name in it is not tenable to me." He set a croissant on her plate, ignoring Arie even though he had enough for all of them.

It didn't seem Chelsea wanted anything Cam said to go without further discussion. "Cam, Arie means a lot to me."

Chewing thoughtfully on a piece of bacon and ignoring Chelsea's comment as well, "Thought you said you ate already."

"Our discussion here made me hungry, besides the two of you need company. Wouldn't want you to do something you'd come to regret."

"And we appreciate your unfailing concern. Don't we, Cam?" She turned her gaze toward him.

She wanted him to like this man. It was simply something he couldn't do.

"I'll give you credit for one thing. You do care for my lady." Cam spoke slowly and with an emphasis on *my lady*.

"So appreciative of the fact you noticed. Where Chelsea or any of her family are concerned, you can always count on me to do the right thing." Arie reached for the bakery sac and pulled out a chocolate croissant.

Gritting his teeth and vowing to stop the reply he was about to blurt, Cam smiled and politely nodded. He tried to let the conversation between Chels and Arie run unnoticed.

"Well just who is this?" Carmine stepped into the kitchen. "And what are the two of you doing in the ex mistress' house?"

~ * ~

Cam rose quickly, pushing his chair away from the table. "Who is this?" Chelsea asked, staring at him with wide innocent eyes. "Certainly you wouldn't think to bring a new mistress into the house while I'm in it?" The woman seemed a bit old but she knew nothing about mistresses or whom Cam might want. His desire for her seemed to waver daily so there was nothing she could be sure about.

"Never," he told her, chuckling softly. "This is my mother and I'm truly curious just as you are as to what she's doing here at this hour of the morning."

"Colin, it seems you need to explain yourself, not me. If this beautiful young lady isn't a mistress then who is she?" Carmine asked, her voice holding a wealth of disdain so much so Chelsea felt goose bumps rise on her arms.

"No concern of yours," he blurted unthinkingly before seeming to think better of his hasty reply. "Rest assured she is not my mistress or anyone's. Are you here to look around?" It seemed to Chelsea he meant to change the subject before any more damage was done.

Chelsea felt the color drain from her face just before heat flooded her cheeks during the conversation. Needing to explain, "I'm a friend and this is Arie, another friend of your son's." She remembered Cam telling her about his mother, but she never expected to see her this morning.

"Then why on earth would the three of you be eating breakfast here?" she stared accusingly at her.

Chelsea stood then, feeling the need to leave as soon as possible. "I've got somewhere I need to be. Things to do, you understand." She turned to Arie, "Can you see me home?" Then to Cam, hoping he wouldn't change his mind because of this, "The play tonight?"

Chelsea didn't wait to hear Cam's acknowledgement to her question or to see if he meant to nod. Instead, eager to leave, she headed out the door, her legs shaking. Once she reached the door she stopped, her hand on her throat, trying desperately to breathe.

Before she was able to step from the house, she heard Cam's mother say, "Don't you dare follow that woman."

She closed her eyes, wondering if Arie hadn't followed her how she would get home. From this place she wasn't even sure what streets would get her there. "Chelsea."

She spun, shocked by the sound of Cam's voice behind her and relieved to feel his hand on her back. "I'll see you home. Not the sultan. Don't want him anywhere near you."

"I...I thought you would do what your mother asked."

"She's my mother but she doesn't command me. I'm not a child. Haven't taken orders from her ever, mostly because she was never around. Not going to start now."

While she tried to think of something to say, he hailed a cab. Once inside, he drew her close, his arms around her. For several minutes they rode in silence while she tried to absorb his warmth into herself.

"Are we still going tonight?" She tried not to sound insecure but so much had changed in the last few minutes. Arie arrived and his presence seemed to make Cam angry and she didn't understand why.

"Seven o'clock. Why did you ask Arie to take you home?" he asked, an edge to his voice reaffirming her notion that Cam disliked Arie.

"I thought you would have to speak with your mother. Tell her why we were in the townhouse." She turned in his arms, looking for a kiss.

"My mother can wait and our reasons as to being in the house are private. Her surprise visit, while it's nice, she isn't going to take over my life. Be ready to meet me at seven and we'll have fun." Frown lines creased his handsome face as he drummed his fingers on his thigh.

An urge to touch the lines on his face crossed her mind. "Why are you making faces at me?"

He laughed then shrugged his broad shoulders, giving her a quick hug. "Heard the play was very bad and the ball is for the professors. Don't know if you'll have any fun either place."

"We could play hooky and go somewhere else," she told him, feeling her emotions lift a tiny bit.

"Well," he paused, "you can do that, but I'm expected at the ball. It's part of my work at the university meant to raise funds, an obligation I can't refuse. What would you like to do and I'll make sure we do it? If not tonight another one." He caressed her cheek with the back of his hand.

"Look, we're here."

She didn't want to leave him. Last night as well as this morning had been confusing and frustrating. Not knowing how to answer his question, "I'll be ready at seven."

He pulled her closer, kissing her quick before letting her go. She realized this was the type of chaste kiss she had best get used to because she certainly never knew which Cam would show up.

"You look disappointed." He touched the tip of her nose with a finger. "Whatever for?"

Chelsea forced a smile. "No, never disappointed." She waited for him to help her from the vehicle. His hands on her waist he lifted her, holding her for a moment longer than proper. Sighing softly, "Will you come inside the house?"

"Tonight, not now. I take it Catherine will want to give us some directions. Does she know what we've planned?"

"No, I suppose I should tell her. You realize of course that I haven't been home since you proposed the outing." Chelsea sighed heavily, unable to look forward to any encounter with Catherine or Flynt. She was exhausted from the night before even though she did sleep for a few hours.

"Catherine rather than Flynt. Is he in town?" Cam asked, touching her cheek with the back of his hand as if he didn't want to leave her.

"He wasn't yesterday when I met you. He's never been predictable though. Just like any man, he comes and goes as he pleases." She was pretty sure if Flynt knew her plans, he would either play chaperone or forbid her to attend with Cam. If he did, she would sneak out a downstairs window. She'd done that often enough as a young girl. It would be more difficult in her ball gown but if necessary, she would find a way.

"Don't let him coerce you or change your mind. I need to see you tonight. We..." he paused, seeming thoughtful then with a quick nod he disappeared back into the carriage.

Chelsea watched the buggy trundle down the street until it vanished from sight. Stiffening her back while praying for the best-case scenario, she walked up the porch and into the house, hoping she would find Catherine sitting in the parlor knitting or reading, not Flynt.

Her hopes or prayers, might be more apropos, were not answered.

Flynt and Hope were chatting in the parlor. She stopped midstride, deciding to head up the stairs and in the process avoid a conflict she didn't feel up to. Flynt would ask questions she was ill prepared to answer.

"Chelsea, where have you been?" Flynt rose, striding toward her as if he meant to stop her, his voice accusatory.

"I was at home," she said softly her voice whisper thin and strained. "Really, Flynt where I am at any moment of the day is no longer your business."

"Hiding in the third floor or did you just never come out of your room?" He placed a hand on her shoulder, stopping her from departing from the room and his questions.

"You're not my guardian." She shrugged the hand off but he wasn't going to be dissuaded so easily. Two steps and he stood in front of her.

"Where were you?" he persisted, scowling.

"I told you. At home."

"Grandmother isn't here so it's my job to make sure you're courted properly. Were you with Cam? If so..." It seemed he stopped just short of calling her a liar.

His pointedly direct question surprised her. "He was a perfect gentleman," she blurted before she gave herself time to think.

"Where were you?" he asked again. "It will go bad for you if you lie to me."

"Go bad for me? What the bloody hell does that mean?" Her temper rose several notches. "You have no power over what I do."

"What it means is that I'll confine you to the house."

"Really, Flynt, don't you think that's a bit archaic. Your sister is a woman grown." Hope walked up behind Flynt, resting a hand on his shoulder. "Besides you should hold her to the same standards as you do yourself. Trust her and Cam."

"At the observatory," she told him, unwilling to let him intimidate. "Now if you must know, I'm going up stairs, that is if I can get by you, and get ready for a play and a ball with Cam."

"Not without a chaperone," he ordered, paying no heed to Hope's comment that she was a grown woman. "Since Grams isn't here the chaperone will be me. Hope and I will go with the two of you."

"I don't suppose there is any way to get out of that." She looked to Hope as if she might be able to provide an answer. When she shrugged before making a small grimace, Chelsea understood there was no way around her brother's autocratic demands.

"What did you do after the observatory?"

It was time to ignore him. If she didn't, he would never stop questioning her and she wouldn't be able to take a short nap before getting ready for tonight. "Nothing," she mumbled, stepping around him and up the steps. At least that was the truth. Cam did nothing despite her best efforts.

In her room she collapsed on her bed, arms spread wide, eyes closed. She needed a nap. Taking a quick look at her clock near her bed, she curled up with a pillow and a quilt.

A few hours later she woke to the scent of food wafting through the room. Her ladies' maid, Jana, arranged the table with dishes and silverware. Chelsea sat up, pushing her hair from her eyes.

"It's nearly four, seems if you sleep much longer, you'll miss your dinner as well as the pleasant evening you and Cam have planned. Hope told me about it and that I should help get you ready. Also said she was sorry she couldn't figure a way to keep Flynt from making your life miserable."

"What else did Hope tell you?" She sounded just as suspicious as she felt. While she wanted to trust Hope, she didn't know her very well and she was close to her brother who she didn't trust at all, not one little iota.

"That Flynt was taking Hope and you to a play then a ball. I've ordered a bath for you and set out a few dresses for you to pick from. Then she went on to say the hasty outing was spurred by your announcement that Cam was taking you. Suppose there's no way out of Flynt playing chaperone tonight. Just curious who is going to chaperone Hope and Flynt."

With outrage at her brother's brashness, "How dare he put himself into my life and leave Cam out of the scenario."

"What was that?" her maid asked.

"Did he say anything about Cam being part of his plans or was that all Hope?" she asked, sure she knew the answer.

"No, milady. Not a word about your beau from Flynt. Hope told me we need to work together so you can outsmart Flynt."

"Cam is going to come here for me. I'm not going anywhere with Flynt and Hope no matter what my brother is thinking." She fisted her hands determined to get her way in this but horribly afraid Flynt would find some means to force her to leave with him.

"Yes, he most likely will but all you need to do is sit down and wait until Cam arrives. Flynt's not going to pick you up and carry you to a carriage, now is he," Jana said with all practicality.

She thought the knock on her door meant the bath water which she didn't need had arrived but when she called out, Flynt stuck his nose in the door then warned, "Don't even think of defying me."

Her heart skipped a beat but once again she blurted unthinkingly, "Already thought of just that," she told him petulantly. "Now get out and let me take my bath and eat. I need to relax for a few minutes then dress. Blessed hell, but the hot water sounded devine."

He let out a roar of laughter, backing from the room. "You're my little sister and you will not win this game you play. I will always hold the upper hand."

Sure she could do that very thing and remembering Jana was in love with the stable boy, "Would you get a message to Cam. Send your beau. I'll pay as soon as I get my allowance. Do you think he'd do that?"

"I'm sure he would love the chance to earn extra coin. Not sure he would want to defy your brother, his employer, but if Flynt doesn't know, of course helping me out would be a priority."

"He might guess," Chelsea said, hoping he wouldn't speculate. If he did, he might report to Flynt.

"Do you want to take the chance?" Jana asked.

"Yes. Then go right now," she told her as she scribbled on a piece of paper she pulled from a desk in her room. Quickly she explained how she would meet Cam in the back of the house at six thirty. If he could please get the message to Cam MacEwen, she would appreciate it ever so much.

The bath water arrived while Jana was dashing from the room, note in hand, to the stables. Chelsea slipped into the hot water, enjoying the heat and finding a way to relax, her nerves stretched thin by the confrontation earlier today with her brother. Until now, she'd been looking forward to the evening even though Cam had told her the play was horrible and the ball would be boring.

Nothing was boring when she was with Cam. Well, it depended on which Cam showed up. She corrected herself, uncaring which man appeared as she was in love with the man not the seducer of debutantes or the man who tried to court properly. The real Cam was a man somewhere in between.

By the time she finished washing her hair, Jana returned. She poured the rinse water over her head before handing her a bath sheet.

"There you go. Let's get your hair dry and you dressed so you can meet your man outside. I'll distract Flynt so he won't be the wiser or accidentally find his way into the kitchen while you go out the back door."

Chelsea decided on a blue and green stripped gossamer dress, the corsage cut straight and rather high, the upper part full and ornamented with narrow blue and green satin rouleaux. A trimming of bouffants, separated by turban folds, rose from the waist and formed a stomacher the front extending over the shoulder and meeting behind. Two rows of very full bouffants, fastened to the dress by blue and green color satin turban folds, ornamented the bottom of the skirt.

She held the dress up, shaking out the nonexistent wrinkles in the skirt before Jana helped her with her underthings then the dress. Smiling at herself in her mirror then turning sideways and back, she was satisfied she looked her best.

Whirling to Jana, "Do you think Flynt will be horribly angry when he discovers my ruse? I've never defied him this way. I know Bliss did. She lied to him by omission all the time. He'll probably blame this on Cam and he's the innocent one this time."

"Your brother is being autocratic and stubborn, but he does have your best interest at heart. It's just that he doesn't know what that is."

"They are both bad boys and Flynt just doesn't believe Cam could want anything from me but sex." She wished she knew exactly what that entailed and if Flynt was right in his assumptions.

"If your brother truly believes that's all Cam wants then he doesn't think too highly of you, does he? Think about all the implications. What man wouldn't want more from you than just your body in his bed?"

"He doesn't treat Hope that way, does he?" Chelsea asked, thinking about Jana's words and how they applied to her. Cam tried so hard to show her he was different from what most in Glasgow believed him to be.

"No, your brother does not understand anything about a man who truly cares for a lady," Jana told her emphatically. "He has no right to treat you so poorly or Cam for that matter. Now step back and let me look at you."

Chelsea stepped backward then twirled around, seeking Jana's approval. "How do I look?"

Jana clapped her hands together. "You're stunning. Cam will swoon when he sees you."

"What I hope is that he turns into the bad boy he's supposed to be." She laughed then thought about his kisses and the way they liquefied her to her very soul. She wanted some of that tonight.

"And, you mean what by that statement?" Jana seemed to be more than curious.

"I don't want him to court me properly or keep his hands to himself and his kisses chaste. I want more. He's kissed me a few times as if he wants to devour me, and I liked the way it made me feel."

"No." Jana was backing up and shaking her head. "Chelsea, don't think things like that. Remember Bliss. You don't want him to compromise you. Promise me you won't do something foolish at least not unless he asks you for your hand in marriage."

"Foolish? I do want to be foolish with Cam or anything else he asks me for. I'm crazy about him." She placed her hands beneath her chin, the longing in the pit of her stomach amplifying. "When he touches me, I can't breathe and..."

"You get so hot you can't think." Jana finished for her. "And that's just the way these bad boys want you to feel so they can have their wicked way with you. You must learn to tell that man of yours no or you're going to be with child. Promise me, Chelsea."

Chelsea couldn't believe what her maid was telling her. "It's not that way with Cam."

"Of course it is and you're just too naïve to understand what is happening here. You should have had a mother who could tell you about the ways of men not a brother who wants to keep you hidden away until no one wants you. If you ask me, Catherine is shirking her job. She needs to sit down with you and explain everything that happens between a man and a woman to the minutest detail." Jana stood back, her hands on her hips and expression stern.

"If I'm so naïve and you're so smart, you should tell me and stop expecting someone else to do the job," Chelsea challenged, wishing people would stop alluding to things she didn't know about. What she did know was how Cam made her feel and she did have to acknowledge that she couldn't say no to him, didn't want to any case.

Jana turned away for a moment and when she glanced her way again, "It's not my place, Chelsea, and I'm sure I don't know a lot more than you do. As I said before, your grandmother should have spoken to you about the ways of men. With your mother gone, it's her job."

"She's been busy." Chelsea tried to defend her grams.

"With the twins, I understand. They also keep Bliss too busy to help with you. You have very real needs though. You're with a man of the world and you're an innocent as well as completely naïve. It's not right someone doesn't have your best interest at heart."

"Arie does," she said softly, thinking about the way Cam reacted to the sultan.

"Pshaw, the sultan has his best interest at heart not yours. He loves you and would enjoy watching this relationship you have with Cam fail. Can't you see what he's trying to do? As soon as possible, and if Cam fails to ask for your hand, Arie's going to try."

"No, I suppose I don't. He already has and the last thing I want though is to be his fourth wife. Besides, I don't love him and I'm definitely not crazy for him as I am with Cam." She thought Arie was giving her good advice and he always was there to help her where Cam was concerned. Yet Cam seemed to dislike the sultan intensely, and she certainly couldn't be sure she understood why.

"Well anyway, we've run out of time here. Go on down the hall to the servant stairs. I'll find Flynt and..." she paused thinking.

"What exactly will you tell my big brother?"

"Not really sure what I can say to keep him from the back door if he wants to go that way. I'll try though. Good luck."

"Hope I don't need it and I pray Cam is outside waiting for me. Not quite sure what I'll do if he's not."

"No worries. Your handsome beau won't let you down."

Handsome beau, yes, but if he didn't receive the message no one would be in the backyard and all her plans would dissolve. With a long indrawn breath of air, she nodded. "I'll keep my fingers crossed all the way. Good Lord, how tight did you lace my corset? I can barely breathe." Later of course, Cam could loosen it just as he did the other night and he might not be able to resist her. She grinned at that thought.

Jana poked her head out the door. "It's clear. I'll go first and check the kitchen before you leave the staircase."

"If this goes well, I'm beholdin' to you."

"Let's go then."

Down the hall then the stairs, Jana stopped to check the kitchen. "Is anyone out there?"

"No. You can go."

Chelsea stepped through the back door and into the fading light of the day. Looking around she didn't see Cam at first, just dancing shadows of the trees cast by the disappearing sunlight.

Her heart in her throat, she turned in a complete circle before she heard booted footsteps behind her.

"Chelsea."

"Cam, you got the message." Good lord, he was handsome. Dressed in his kilt and other Scottish finery, he presented a magnificent figure. He stole her breath.

"I did." He drew her into his arms for a quick hug and a soft brush of his lips across hers. "You didn't think Flynt would let you go with me?"

"He said as much or that he would be my chaperone. He planned on leaving for the theater without you." She placed a hand on his cheek. "When I'm with you, I don't want a chaperone."

"Not even Arie?" he asked, a disdainful tone to his voice.

"Arie's not a chaperone of any kind. He's a trusted friend." But Chelsea had second thoughts about that fact after what Jana said. "Why do you dislike the sultan?"

Cam wrapped an arm around her pulling her close. "Because you've shared things with him, you haven't with me. Besides, I can see through his ploy. He wants you for himself and he's just waiting for the right chance. If you give it to him, he'll take it."

She bristled at his comment, but Jana told her the same only a few seconds earlier. She would have to rethink her relationship with Arie. "He was there for me those nine months you were ignoring me. If you don't like the fact I confided in him and he made me feel better when I was hurting, that's just too bad. You're going to have to deal with that and the fact Arie is my friend, but he'll never be anything more."

"Point taken and I feel bad about the way I disregarded you. Simply put, I was a coward who has now seen the error of his ways. Want to make it up to you now though if you'll let me," he told her, one eyebrow rising a fraction. "This morning I was jealous and wanted him out of my house as well as your life. Still do."

"Don't be jealous of the few things I've shared with him. He's never kissed me and if he does, I'm sure I'll tell him what I think of it."

"And what would that be?" He continued the questions.

"I don't want kisses from anyone but you."

"Is that true?" He chuckled softly, seeming pleased with her answer. "Think I like the way that sounds."

"You should." She tried to sound confident even though she was anything but self-assured.

Cam helped her into the carriage. Stepping in beside her, he seemed to study her as they drove. The silence was comforting and she didn't feel the need to fill it with chatter even though she understood there was a lot that needed to be said between them.

She closed her eyes, thinking of all the questions about their relationship that needed answering. "What is it that everyone is afraid of where you're concerned? And why do they say I'm too innocent to understand?"

"Don't fash yourself," he cleared his throat, "everyone is warning you away from this bad boy, most likely for good reason. They are all afraid I will take advantage of you as Broc did with Bliss. They think all I want from you is your delicious body. While some of that is true it is not everything."

"I'm not listening to the warnings. Besides, Broc didn't know who Bliss really was. He would have done everything differently had he known from the very start."

He laughed softly. "Perhaps you should listen to your words but I promise you..." He ran his fingers through his hair, leaving it disheveled but endearing.

"Promise me?" She opened her eyes staring at him and trying to see inside his soul.

He took her hands in his, "I promise I won't get you with child or take advantage of your innocence in any way. I'm not going to compromise you. I'm doing this as a proper gentleman should."

"What if I want a child?" she asked, trying to discover more than he seemed willing to tell her.

"Of course you do, but not before." He paused and she watched the twitch at his temple. "Not before..."

"Don't keep anything from me. Before what?" She needed to have all the information possible and seemed everyone stopped short of telling her exactly what she needed to know leaving more unanswered questions.

"One of these day's soon I'll show you exactly what I'm talking about, what others are talking about. You need patience."

"Everyone who knows me, knows I'm anything but patient," she told him indignantly, turning from him even as it seemed he wanted to kiss her.

~ * ~

"You could have her if you really wanted her," Arie's servant and best friend told him while they shared food and drink in one of the more posh restaurants in Glasgow.

"Perhaps." Arie focused on a woman a few tables away, instantly mesmerized. Her red hair caught the glow of the setting sun, appearing as if fire touched it. The myriad of colors dancing in the strands tantalized him, drew him as never before.

"You could have that lady also." Victor sipped his drink. "All you need do is ask and she'll be with you on the next ship back to your homeland."

"Yes, I could act like my father did and take what I want. I could kidnap Chelsea and hold her against her will, but I won't. She doesn't want me or to be a fourth wife. If I did that to her, she would never be happy." Arie mused thoughtfully, comprehending the truth of his man's words, but what about this woman? She did intrigue him.

Victor waved a hand in the air, clearly disagreeing. "What does it matter if she's happy? She's just a woman, meant for a man's pleasure. Your happiness is paramount here and I've watched you the last year. You've been sad, depressed, moping around."

"I will find someone to love, someone who returns that love so much she won't care if she's my fourth or my tenth wife. She will want me for who I am." His wives didn't love him, tolerated him because they had no choice. Here in the western world he realized how much he was missing. Well, one loved him; at least she said as much.

"What will you do about Chelsea then? She is carving out your heart one tiny piece at a time." Victor rested back on the chair. "I will get that red head for you. You can have her tonight."

"As tempting as that sounds, no. I'm going to spy on Chelsea and Cam tonight. If I can find a way to stop her brother from humiliating her, I will do just that." He pulled out his pocket watch assessing the time. "They should be at the play by now and in their private accommodations. If I take a balcony seat across from them, I can watch with the aid of my binoculars."

"Would you like company? I do love spying."

Arie laughed, enjoying his good friend. They'd been through so much together. "You are well suited for the job I employ you to do. We both understand the truth of those words. As to the redhead, on second thought, I'll consider your offer. Perhaps you can get her for me later tonight."

"Glad to hear that, at least for the near future a new lady would take your mind from Chelsea MacTavish. Perhaps this lady will make you happy."

"While I'm at the play and the ball, follow her. Find out who she is and where she lives. If my compromising her won't stir up a hornet's nest in the aristocracy here in Glasgow, bring her to me."

"Tonight?" he asked eagerly, a broad grin on his face.

"Tonight, if possible. I believe I've been too long without a willing woman." He paused. "She must be willing. Tell her everything or nothing. I don't care."

"How willing?"

"Never mind." He waved a hand in the air again. "I'll find a way to convince her she is willing and eager to become one with me."

Chapter Four

Cam wasn't at all surprised when Flynt entered the box seat in the Theatre Royal in Queen Street sitting down with a smirk on his face. He heaved a sigh, looking to Chelsea for an expression he could read. From here on out the conversation would be stilted or nonexistent. He'd been looking forward to time to discover more about this woman who intrigued him more with each second, the woman who seemed to have an iron hold on his heart.

"You're not welcome here." Cam's voice was a whisper but he was sure Flynt didn't miss the underlying anger.

"My sister needs a chaperone." He sat down opposite Chelsea, his gaze moving between them. "Wouldn't want anything to happen that can't be easily explained."

"You've no right to follow me around," Chelsea said, her fists clenching. "I'm a grown woman and can make decisions without your help. This is a public place. Cam isn't going to do anything to compromise me here."

"That's all right." Cam directed his words to Chelsea, a casual softness to his voice. "At least if your brother is here, we know he isn't having any fun either. Perhaps we can take this time to make his life miserable."

"No, I suppose it can't be too much fun, relegated to babysitting your little sister." Chelsea seemed to agree with him, laughing as she spoke the words while looking at Hope. "What does Hope think about all of this?"

Cam casually picked up her hand, daring Flynt to say something. He brought the back to his lips for a gentle kiss. Smiling at Flynt's grimace he was so tempted to carry this a bit farther but chose not to at the moment.

"I'll enjoy the play despite your school boy antics," Flynt said.

Cam squeezed her hand trying to reassure and hoping she would understand this wasn't what he wanted. "Let's just pretend he's not here," he said, pointing to the stage. "Look, they're starting now. Do you think it will be as bad as the critics say?"

He wrapped an arm around Chelsea and pulled her close despite the fact Flynt cleared his throat in an attempt to voice his disapproval. He set his attention on the actors and relished the way she felt sitting next to him. If Flynt weren't here, he would steal a chaste kiss. Then he recalled his last words to Chelsea, deciding to take action.

His finger on her chin, he gently tilted her face so he could brush his lips across hers, sweep his tongue lightly along her bottom lip before withdrawing. The rough sound spewing from across the tiny room gave his heart a lift, understanding Flynt would do nothing to garner unfavorable attention. He shifted his focus in Flynt's direction before briefly kissing her again.

When he ended the caress, he slanted a harsh gaze in Flynt's direction. Hoping Flynt would take the hint and leave, he was disappointed yet delighted when Chelsea placed her hand in his. She had never been the aggressor when it came to sensual things. He ran his hand up her arm then back watching a tiny hint of color paint her cheeks, enjoying the view immensely.

However good his intentions were to ignore Flynt, the task was harder than he thought it would be. His nerves as well as his patience seemed to be stretched to their breaking point. He was relieved when the play finally ended and they would go to the ball.

As they left the theatre, Chelsea was laughing and holding on to his arm for support. "Was it as bad for you as me?"

"Are we speaking of Flynt or the play?" he asked, grinning broadly and pleased with himself.

"The play of course," Chelsea said, leaning into him, her breast pushing against his chest.

He couldn't help but chuckle along with her. "I haven't seen many plays but this one was the absolute worst. The singing, raucous but the acting was in the gutter."

"You should demand your money back," she laughed.

"No, perhaps it will go to a good cause," he said, looking into her eyes and hoping she still wanted a kiss.

He looked to Flynt whose mind seemed to be somewhere else before he brushed a quick kiss across her lips. "Soon there will be more. I promise."

"I'll take you at your word on the kiss but what good cause could you possibly be speaking of?" he asked.

"Money to hire better actors." He touched the tip of her nose. "And singers. Ones who can actually sing and act."

"Perhaps the ball will be more fun," she said, skipping toward the carriage. "We could lose Flynt in the crowd or mayhap he'll find something to interest him. Hope just isn't doing a good job at diverting his attention." She shrugged her delicate shoulders as if that might truly be a possibility. He knew Flynt and Flynt would never forget his purpose here.

"It can't be any worse than the play." Leaning close, "Perhaps I can find a dark corner where I can kiss you the way you want to be kissed, a bad boy kiss for my Chelsea."

"Do you think I would allow such a thing?" She gazed at him, her eyes shimmering with what he hoped was desire.

Squeezing her hand, he hailed a carriage.

"Always." Cam helped her into the carriage, grimacing when Flynt followed without a word.

"Don't you have someplace to be? I'm sure Hope would like to see a little more of you tonight or you could carouse with your friends. Do bad boy things, you know," Chelsea pointedly spoke to her brother. "I've certainly seen enough of you for one night. Your departure couldn't come a minute too soon."

"Need to make sure you get home in one piece, unscathed and reputation intact." Flynt smiled, leaning back and crossing his legs. "Hope understands."

Chelsea turned to Cam, "I remember when mother and father would host balls. We, my sisters and I," she moistened her lips, "would sneak up to the third floor and watch. We could always find a place on the balcony where no one would see us."

"Which is why you all knew how to hide that night when I first kissed you." He paused, rubbing his chin, studying the grin on her beautiful and intriguing face. "You wanted me to find you," he hesitated seeming to think. "And kiss you."

She looked away for a moment as if she tried to hide the emotions playing across her charming face. He knew the answer to his statement and felt pleased. Tracing gentle circles on her wrists, he delighted in the shivers he felt against his chest. Entwining his fingers with hers, he brought their hands to his lips, kissing hers.

Across from them Flynt cleared his throat again, interrupting their conversation, suddenly not so relaxed. "When was that? The first kiss. No one told me about it."

"About ten months ago when you hosted the gambling night at the country home. I believe it must have been August or September." Cam tried not to smirk, knowing he was successfully goading Flynt. Little did Flynt know that he'd practically ravished his sister that night. Might have if she'd been older.

"I was terrified you would find me and frightened that you wouldn't." Chelsea admitted. "I didn't know what you would do but I did want to find out. You've always fascinated me, and I did want you to be my first real kiss."

And her last, "You wanted me to kiss you then." Cam realized as he spoke, the truth of his statement. All his guesses were right. That night she wanted him to catch her, led him to the abandoned room.

Chelsea looked to Flynt then with a quirky little smile, "I had no idea you would kiss me and... I just wanted you to know I existed. I always thought you looked through me."

He chuckled softly, resting his head against the seat. "You accomplished your mission, my sweet treasure. Before that night I didn't notice you or at least when I did, I looked on you as Flynt's little sister. Any relationship with you was obviously off limits."

"And after you kissed me?" she queried.

"I saw you as a woman, a very attractive woman and one I craved to know better. I think you managed to make me very aware of you." He didn't want to give away too much, especially in front of Flynt. Revealing his feelings was not a task he was ready to do, especially tonight. It was just too soon to lay his heart out there. He had plans that had yet to be put into motion and he wasn't about to risk anything.

"Really?" Her eyes were wide with disbelief. "Then why..."

"It's all true. As to why I didn't pursue you when you turned eighteen, I can't say for sure." Telling her he was terrified didn't sit well with him, yet in time he would explain everything.

Flynt shifted in his seat, seeming uncomfortable or in disagreement. "Don't believe anything the cad says. He only wants one thing from you."

"Do you think so little of me and our relationship? Do you think so little of your sister?" Cam directed his anger at Flynt. "If all I wanted was to toss a woman's skirts, I wouldn't go after one of my best friend's sisters. Chelsea is more than a great horizontal," he tossed out before thinking better of what he said. Then, clearing his throat, "Not that I would know."

Flynt's face had turned red with what Cam could only assume was rage, the man's fists clenching and unclenching as if he meant to hit him. "That's why I'm boring myself with the job of chaperone. Chelsea is not going to be anyone's horizontal."

"And why is that?" Chelsea asked, seeming to have missed the reference to sex. "Because Cam likes me for me? We don't need someone watching over us all the time."

"I beg to differ," Flynt spoke slowly. "What I've garnered from this entire conversation is that you need someone next to you every second you're with this man."

"Between the theatre and the ball," Cam spoke slowly, "Most of the time we are in the company of others. We don't need you tagging along."

"You and I both know there are ways to remedy that problem. I'm only here to make sure I stop anything more that might transpire than a chaste kiss. My sister will be a virgin when she is wed."

"Stop arguing about me, both of you." Chelsea's hand was on her chest as she struggled for air. "I can speak for myself and my actions are private, between Cam and myself. You have nothing to do with them, Flynt."

"I'm sorry. Seems I forgot myself." Cam scowled, wishing he could start over and wishing even more he could have spent the evening alone with Chelsea. He had so much to talk over with her. Much of which could not be done with her brother sitting across from her.

"Seems we've arrived," Flynt said as the coach drew to a stop and the door was opened.

The walk to the house then upstairs to the ballroom seemed to take an eternity. Cam kept Chelsea's hand firmly settled in his while Flynt strode behind them.

Lilting highland tunes echoing around the ballroom seemed to put a smile on Chelsea's face as her toe tapped in time to the notes. After they were introduced, he whirled her into his arms for a fast paced Scottish Reel. Cam let thoughts of Flynt and his overbearing ways slip from his mind as he twirled her around the dance floor.

After a few minutes, he stopped then bending toward her. "Can I get you something to drink or eat?"

"I'm sure we can go together. It looks as if there are tables on the balcony where we can eat."

"Hopefully without our chaperone," Cam said, looking around the room for Flynt and content to see him dancing. "Perhaps he'll forget about us."

"We can only hope," Chelsea murmured softly.

A few minutes later with food in hand they found a table that was semi secluded. "What are you thinking, lass?"

"This would have been more fun if a certain brother wasn't following us," she said. "I was hoping that when I escaped without him he would give up and find someone else to plague."

He tossed her a grin, which he hoped she'd find charming. "Other than that. A penny for your thoughts?"

"I was surprised, but then perhaps not, when they announced the honors you won with your research when they introduced you. If you didn't have that bad boy persona, you would be exactly what Flynt is hoping to find for me, a man who would spend all his days and nights with his nose in a book."

Cam couldn't help himself, he let his head fall back, roaring with laughter. "Intellect is hardly enough to turn me into one of those men who were sitting in your parlor waiting for his permission to court you. Although I do enjoy a good book, poetry also."

"I don't understand."

"Do I look like any of them?" He challenged her for an answer that would give him reason to preen. To keep his body the way he liked it, he boxed. Did other things too. He never intended to sport a sagging belly created from overindulgence. She would find no comparison between his physique and her other suitors.

"You're handsome as sin," she told him, seeming to look over his body. "They were not."

He leaned close, his breath whispering against her ear. "You haven't seen me naked yet."

A blush rushed to her cheeks. Her lips pursed together when she gazed at him. "I think I'd like that," she whispered, moistening her lips. "I want to see you with nothing on."

"What would you like tonight?" He pursued, needing to push this to the admission he was seeking. Holding her hand, her pulse throbbed quickly beneath his fingertips.

"To see you naked." Her gaze shifted downward as if attempting to avoid looking at him.

He touched her beneath the chin, lifting. "I'm glad of that. But not tonight and don't ever be afraid or embarrassed to tell me the truth or even what is rolling around in that quick discerning mind of yours. I want to see you without a stitch of clothing on also."

"No, not tonight." She was shaking her head but he wasn't sure at all what she might be thinking.

Time to change the direction of their conversations. He rose, extending a hand. "Another dance and perhaps we can escape without our chaperone in tow. I'd like to have a few minutes of privacy with you before I take you home."

She accepted the hand as he drew her into his arms, stepping in time with the music. He whirled her around the room, enjoying the way she felt in his arms. The pipes now changing to a slow tune, he didn't want to let her go.

Arie suddenly stood by him tapping him on the shoulder. "If the lady wishes." He directed his statement to Chelsea. "May I have this dance?"

"She doesn't." Low in his throat, Cam growled.

"Cam." Chelsea tapped him on the shoulder with her closed fan. "Of course I'll dance with Arie. Don't be rude."

Slowly stepping back, he allowed the sultan to take her into his arms, despite his gut protesting the invasion of what he considered his. With narrowed eyes, he watched them twirl around the dance floor. The need to step in and whisk her away was ever present.

"Someone take what you mistakenly think of as yours?" Flynt stood beside him. "Get over it, old man. Chelsea won't ever be yours. I simply won't allow that to happen. She'll have someone who will want only her."

"If you have your way. Have you forgotten so soon? I make my own rules." He would take this one step further, and he would find a way to be alone with Chelsea despite her brother's efforts to the contrary. Proper courting be damned.

"As do I." Flynt's gaze remained on the dancers. "Wouldn't you love to know what they're talking about?"

"Arie is a friend to Chelsea, nothing more." Cam repeated the words Chelsea tossed at him earlier. He supposed it didn't matter how Arie felt about Chelsea when she didn't return those same sentiments. She would never consent to becoming his fourth wife.

"So you say." Flynt bated him. For the last nine months, he's been her confidant.

"You're just gloating because you've Hope living in your house with you. How is that going for you?" Cam needed to change the subject from his personal life to something that would cause Flynt problems. "Have you bedded her with no regard to the fact she's Broc's sister? If you have restraint, then you must ken I do too."

"Hope is not your business neither is our relationship," he shot back and it seemed to Cam he did hit a nerve.

"Perhaps we, the bad boys, should ban together to protect Hope from you. Too bad her father isn't here to protect her. I'm sure he'd have some way to torture you." Cam laughed, thinking of all the things he'd heard about the man who sired Broc and Hope as well.

"Grandmother is there to chaperone, if you're thinking there is no one at home to keep Hope safe from me. Besides I've no designs on the young woman. She is nice enough and pretty enough, but I'm not ready to settle down. I still have my mistress who sees to my needs."

"We both know one doesn't have to marry a woman in order to find pleasure with her." Cam's thoughts swirled to Chelsea, but the sentiment didn't mean he didn't long for her to be in his bed.

Arie brought Chelsea back with a smile then handing her over to him. "She is all yours." He grinned as he held her hand out for Cam to accept. "The two of you have a nice chat?"

"Not really," Cam said as he pulled Chelsea into his arms, dancing away from two men who irritated him more than he'd ever thought possible.

"Are you angry?" Chelsea was looking at him, and all he wanted was to kiss her, show her the pleasures they could share. He would have to have patience understanding all his plans would come to fruition soon, despite Flynt and his overbearing ways.

"Should I be?" He bent close to her ear, touching it lightly with his breath then his tongue. He felt the tiny shiver sweep through her. "Good, right now it's just you and me. We should take advantage of this rare opportunity."

"We certainly don't get many. But Cam, while I was dancing with Arie, you looked as if you wanted to murder someone and I hope it wasn't me."

"Just your brother and Arie."

"My brother yes, but Arie has only my best interest at heart. He told me he met a girl." They danced into a corner only to find Flynt leaning against a pillar, arms crossed over his chest.

"A girl, you say." He headed back to the dance floor. "Is she someone who would be willing to become a wife number four is it?"

"Well, he didn't tell me much. His man is looking for her and he didn't really meet her yet. He just saw her and knew he wanted her and would have her."

"So he can kidnap her and take her back to his harem?" Cam felt the sarcasm rumble in his chest.

"Would that be so bad? If she was willing?" Chelsea asked. "Can we sit? I know Flynt will hover, but I'm having trouble inhaling."

"Corset too tight?" he chuckled wishing he could loosen the

contraption for her.

"Possibly, I'm just not used to dancing so much. I'm winded."

"We can get something to drink and you can tell me about this lady Arie has met." With drinks in hand they walked to the tables. "Here comes Flynt just as expected. Doesn't he have anything better to do?"

"Perhaps we should put an end to the night." Chelsea touched his hand. "I think it's time for you to take me home."

Cam's fists tightened at her words, his gaze shifting from Flynt to Chels. "Don't let him ruin our evening."

"He already has," she spoke softly. "No matter how much I try to ignore him, he's there, hovering around us."

"I'll get you home but I promise we can have time together soon. I'll make arrangements in the next few days and let you know." He had a home on the coast overlooking the Firth of Clyde. All he had to do was make sure Flynt was distracted for a morning and they could escape his parental stare.

"I don't know how you can promise something so impossible." She wrapped her hand around his arm as they walked to the coatroom, Flynt behind them. "But I'll be ever so grateful if your assurance comes to fruition. I don't care what happens."

"You going home so soon? Imagine that," Flynt asked, his grin an irritant Cam wanted to erase.

"We wouldn't want to ruin your evening. Why don't you stay?" Cam shot out, hoping Flynt would take him up on the offer while knowing he wouldn't.

"This fete is not much fun. A bit stuffy for my taste," Flynt said, stepping quickly to the door. "Shall we?"

~ * ~

"Tell me all about the play and the ball," Daryl sat in Chelsea's bedroom braiding her hair, three days after. "And Cam of course. Is he a gentleman or a bad boy?"

Chelsea shrugged as she stared at herself in the mirror, wondering if Cam liked the way she looked. "Flynt happened along to ruin everything.

He's such a bore. I hope he finds something or someone to distract him when you have a beau. Believe he is worse now with me than he ever was with Bliss."

"If you recall, he didn't know about Bliss."

She let out a long breath of air, admitting the truth and wishing Cam had decided to keep their relationship secret. "True."

"I can't believe he's acting so domineering. Seems he should have learned from what he did to Bliss that he's going to force you into Cam's arms as well as his bed. He doesn't realize how stubborn all his sisters are." Lacie plopped down on the bed, a cream puff Daryl made in one hand. Then with her mouth full, "These are really good. What else can you make?"

"You should know. You've eaten everything that has come out of the oven. How can you put so much food in your stomach and stay so slim?" Daryl asked. "It seems you never gain a pound."

"You should sell them," Chelsea said as she artfully arranged the tendrils of hair framing her face. Lord, but she hoped she would see Cam today. She was going for a walk with Arie as soon as she could get ready, and Arie promised her they would run into Cam. She turned to Daryl. "Maybe Bliss could help you with a bakery shop. The funds you know. She really has more money than she knows what to do with, and she won't even have to ask Broc to help financially in any way."

"I wouldn't know the first things about setting up a place of business. Besides, baking is just a hobby," Daryl said as if she might truly be thinking about that very thing. "I don't believe I'd like to make things every day if it was work. And I don't relish waking up at the crack of dawn."

"But you would be independent. Isn't that what we all want, to have our own money?" Lacie said, licking her fingers before looking at the tray to see if there were more delicious goodies. "I could help. You know how good I am with numbers. I could be your accountant or business manager if you like. I would keep all your books in order so you wouldn't have to worry about anything save baking the most delicious delicacies."

"Have you heard anything from Cam? It's been three days since the ball. One would think he'd be ringing the door bell," Daryl said.

"He's sent messages. Poetry," Chelsea said, smiling then with a small sigh, "He told me he likes to read books as well as poetry. The poems are really quite romantic. I must have read them a thousand times."

"So, now he's trying to prove the fact," Lacie said, seeming a bit skeptical. "He doesn't strike me as being the romantic type or even a man who..." She paused, capturing the last crème puff from the tray. "Literary."

"Can we see the message?" Daryl stacked the plates and cups on the tray she'd brought into the room for a quick brunch.

"Of course." Chelsea cleared her throat as she began to read. "But only the poem, nothing more. That's private."

Moer stilis,

"It means sweet treasure. This is from day one," Chelsea began a smile on her face. "It's a Lord Byron poem."

She walks in beauty, like the night
Of cloudless climes and starry skies;
And all that's best of dark and bright
Meet in her aspect and her eyes;
Thus mellowed to that tender light
Which heaven to gaudy day denies.

"It's not finished. He went on to say he would send more of the poem the next day. He's tempting me with promises and expectations, and I absolutely adore him for it."

"And did he send something yesterday? Lacie leaned forward as if trying to read the rest of the note.

Before she could see more, Chelsea folded the paper with a smile on her face. Tucking it neatly in the bodice of her dress, "The rest is for my eyes only. And yes, he did send more the following day. The second verse, and no, I've not received anything today. I'm hoping to see him instead. As I said earlier, Arie assured me he would make sure we meet. Don't have any idea how he's going to go about something like that, but I do trust Arie in matters of the heart."

"Agreed. I don't see how Arie can make promises like that." Daryl sat on the end of the bed, her tray still in her hands. "There are too many things that could go wrong. He shouldn't have promised."

"His schedule at the university." Chelsea paused inhaling slowly and feeling as if all her dreams were about to come true. "Arie says he was able to get a look at it and he knows where Cam will be this morning at eleven. That's why I have to hurry. Arie is probably downstairs right now waiting for me."

Lacie put a finishing touch on her hair with a beautiful sapphire butterfly hairpin. Then stepping back to look at her. "You are so gorgeous. He will not be able to stop looking at you. And your dress, well, it brings out the color of your sky blue eyes."

"I do feel beautiful. Cam has promised we'll have privacy soon, and he doesn't care how Flynt feels about it or Grams for that matter." Chelsea stood, smoothing her skirts and glancing one more time in the mirror.

"Would you like us to walk downstairs with you, run interference in case Arie wasn't able to distract Flynt."

"Yes." She breathed in deeply, striving to vanquish her shaking arms and legs. "I don't know if I'll be able to walk down those steps. Every part of me feels wobbly. If Flynt sees me all dressed up, he'll guess that I'm going to see Cam and do his best to put a stop to anything Cam has planned."

Downstairs, Arie waited in the parlor, sipping some of Flynt's expensive French brandy. When she entered, he rose, a smile plastered on his face before bowing.

"You're lovely. Cam is sure to appreciate what is about to happen and take action. No more proper for you and your handsome beau. I hope you will get everything you wish for." Arie turned politely, offering his arm.

"I pray that is so, yet my nerves are on edge and I don't understand why every part of me is quivering." She looked up the long curving stairs to see her sisters still at the top and waving.

"Because something momentous is about to happen today. Shall we?" With her hand wrapped around his arm, they moved toward the door. "I've my coach to take us to the University Park. There, we will stroll toward the building housing his office. His meeting will be over by the time we reach our final destination, and we should come across him quite unexpectedly on the sidewalk."

"Then what?" She wasn't at all sure she liked surprises like this. He would be shocked to see her with Arie, and she was sure that dark shuttered look would cross his face while his brows would draw together. What he would do was something she couldn't predict and she realized neither could Arie.

She replayed the second verse of the poem Cam sent her in her mind where he changed the word raven to blond.

One shade the more, one ray the less,
Had half impaired the nameless grace
Which waves in every blond tress,
Or softly lightens o'er her face;
Where thoughts serenely sweet express,
How pure, how dear their dwelling-place

Outside, Arie helped her into the ornate carriage he always traveled in and tried to reassure. "You will like this. I promise." Then it seemed he paused for the longest time. "Eventually."

"It's just, Cam really doesn't like you at all, and I believe you know that for a fact. Is this thing you have planned today meant to infuriate him or help us find some private time together?" She couldn't help the inquiry, yet there was something about Arie's behavior today that seemed different to her, almost diabolical. He was hiding something from her, definitely keeping a secret.

"Fury at what I've planned might well be his first reaction, but it most certainly won't be his last." Arie chuckled before suddenly sobering. "I know men well, just as I know women. Chelsea, promise me you will think and not just react to what he's going to do. I don't want you to have any regrets about today. This will most likely be a turning point in your life."

"Whatever does that mean?" She didn't understand anything he was trying to tell her, turning points and regrets?

"Ah, it seems we've arrived. Take a deep breath now and try to remember everything I've told you. Play along with me and remember everything I'm doing is to help you with Cam."

"You're not going to tell me your plans, are you?" Indignant, she wanted to shake him until he explained things.

"My darling, if I tell you too much it will take the spontaneity out of the situation. And we must have spontaneity, or this strategy of mine simply will not work. Now..." He stepped from the carriage before offering her his hand. "We will see what is about to transpire. I promise I'll run interference with Flynt if that action becomes necessary."

She slanted him a weary look but could think of nothing to say. Together they strolled through the park, watching the birds and the squirrels play in the late morning sunlight. The day was warm and the sky was dotted with only a few clouds. She really wished she knew what Arie planned. The man could be quite devious.

"Have you seen your redheaded lady?" she asked, hoping to keep her mind from the scenario playing out in front of her. "The one in the restaurant."

"Do you seek a diversion?" he asked her, chuckling softly before patting her hand. "No, I've not seen her, but I did purchase her from the whorehouse she was sold to. She is now mine even though I've no idea what her name is nor have I had a chance to speak with her. I plan on doing that soon. Perhaps today I'll go see her and find out what will transpire between us."

"You bought her?" Chelsea felt anger rise from the pit of her stomach. "How could you? People don't buy other people."

"I could because I'm a man and it is my right. She is, after all selling herself. Simply put, I was the highest bidder. As you surely must recall, my father kidnapped Broc's mother. There was no compensation in that arrangement."

"Don't take advantage of her, Arie." Chelsea understood all too well her command would go unheeded. Like every other man Arie would do as he pleased.

"My darling, the lady is a whore, a beautiful and very tempting one, but a whore none the less. I could not take advantage of her. She probably knows more about lovemaking than I do."

Chelsea let the gist of Arie's words rattle around in her head for a few minutes before she spoke. "You could hurt her and what if she's not willing. I've heard of women who did not want to be prostitutes but were forced into that position by the men in their lives."

"Most likely the absence of a man in this woman's situation has caused her to sell herself. My idea is to remedy that condition. I will be the man in her life, and I won't hurt her. I promise you. I've never taken a woman against her will and no way in hell will I start now."

Once again Chelsea felt baffled. "I'm not even going to try to figure out what you mean by that comment. The absence of a man..." She let go of his arm, striding in front of him until he caught her arm turning her.

"Act as if you mean it. Now." Arie's lips found hers as he drew her to his body. His fingers closed around her waist, bringing her closer to him while one hand drifted lower pressing her derrière against his lower body.

She squirmed but his fingers tightened while she gasped for air. He deepened the kiss, running his tongue along her mouth. Suddenly, she found herself yanked away. A chasm of air separated them and while she stumbled backward, she watched Cam land a hard punch to Arie's face.

Pointing a warning finger in Arie's direction. "You stay away from Chels." Turning, "You're coming with me." Cam swept her from her feet and into his arms, striding down the walkway. He didn't say anything but his jaw was tense and his eyes hard, dark, foreboding; nothing good.

"Cam, put me down. I can walk." She was breathless even though she wasn't the one nearly running. "Please."

"Not fast enough," he muttered some more words she didn't understand beneath his breath.

"I didn't know what he was going to do."

"Doesn't matter."

Just as suddenly as she was swept off her feet, she found herself inside a small vehicle, sitting close to Cam. "Whatever is wrong with you?" She pushed stray pieces of hair from her eyes.

"You need to ask?" he shot out as he urged the horse drawing the carriage to a faster pace.

"No, I don't suppose I do." Her words were soft and she wasn't sure he heard, yet for some reason she knew he wanted her to explain herself. "Men." She didn't understand anything about them, and she wasn't about to explain something she didn't understand.

"Care explaining why you were kissing Arie?" He turned to look at her, his features still menacing.

"No." She sat back, her arms crossed over her chest seething. "Do you care to explain all of your mistresses to me? Besides, I just told you a few minutes ago I didn't know he was going to kiss me."

"In the past, not this morning, not five minutes ago. I've had no mistress since I first kissed you. Been celibate the entire time. Which is most likely my problem now." They stopped moving. Almost as quickly Cam jumped from the vehicle and swept her into his arms again.

Practically running he two-steeped the porch stairs until he reached the door. He set her down until the door swung open and once more she found herself in his arms as he continued to the second floor and what must be his chambers.

"What are you doing? What are you going to do?" She pushed on his shoulders, remembering Arie's words of warning, think don't react. This could be a life-changing event, Arie had told her.

The silence emanating from him frightened her. Yet, when his lips met hers, touched hers, she forgot the fear if it ever really existed. He set her on the bed, fumbling with the buttons on the back of her dress, his movements seeming frantic.

"Bloody hell." His lips, teeth and tongue explored her neck then her ear. He bit gently then turned her over so she was on her stomach. As he unfastened the buttons as well as her corset, he touched her flesh, trailed kisses along her spine. Explored and tasted every inch as fire rushed through her.

She shivered as her body heated passionately and once more she tried to recall Arie's words of warning, but it seemed they vanished from her brain. She couldn't think or move. "Cam..." A tiny mew caught in her throat.

He turned her over, spreading her legs before settling between them. His eyes darkened with desire and passion, not anger. Before this she never knew there was a difference. His exploration with his lips continued across her collarbone as he drew the corsage of her dress lower, exposing the rounded globes of her breasts to his hungry gaze.

This was what she wanted but...

"She walks in beauty, like the night..." he quoted before his mouth molded on hers, his teeth tugging on her lower lip drawing the tender flesh inside his mouth. He kissed her again and again. She sighed, her breath floating into his mouth as he pulled her tongue inside.

Her body responded to the delicious enchantment he wove around her and through her, heating as she arched her hips trying to get closer to him. His lips and teeth found a tender spot on her neck, biting and licking, sucking on the skin until she thought she could stand no more. Her fingers wound into his hair, her nails scoring his neck as she tried to pull him closer.

This must be heaven and she never wanted it to end. He pulled away for a second, gazing down upon her, appearing pleased with himself. Then he gently kissed the same spot on her neck he'd been caressing before.

"That spot will tell Arie you are mine. Don't ever let him kiss you again." Slowly, he drew her dress lower, the tips of her breasts now completely exposed to him.

"Arie surprised me. I didn't know he was going to kiss..."

His lips and teeth settled on one hardened tip while his fingers touched and squeezed the other. "Cam..." His name on the air seemed to give him delight.

When he looked at her again, he was grinning. "He should not have kissed you, and I hope he has a black eye to remind himself of that fact. Perhaps a broken nose."

And she realized then Arie had foreseen the anger or jealousy and planned this. She would have to thank him. "What are you going to do now?"

"Colin Angus Monroe!" His name spoken by his mother seemed to stop him.

Chelsea heard the low growl of displeasure. Then, "Mother."

"Stop this instant."

"Please leave. While you've brought common sense to the forefront of my mind. Chels is in a bit of a compromising position. I won't have her embarrassed." He made a feeble attempt to cover her.

"Have you forgotten I'm a woman?" her mother bit out indignantly.

"I'm not concerned about your sensibilities, mother." He slowly pulled the fabric of her dress higher. "You need to leave, now."

In his arms, Chelsea felt the shaking of her body and she couldn't stop herself. The harder she tried to stop the tremors, the more intense her shaking became. Heat from his kisses as well as the embarrassment of discovery swept through her. Mortified, she wanted to slip from the room and never see anyone ever again as she suddenly realized she was very nearly naked beneath his big hard body.

"Everything will be alright." He whispered close to her lips, touching them gently as she heard the door close. "I promise there will be no repercussions from this. I've got a plan. It's just that Arie shocked me, and I'm going to have to implement this strategy now instead of tomorrow because of mother."

"I don't see how." She closed her eyes and he kissed each one. "I've no idea what you're talking about, plans and strategies."

"I promise you, I'll fix this before today is over." He drew her to a sitting position, rearranging all the clothing he'd sent askew. "Turn around."

He was so tender, gentle. The anger had vanished minutes ago and now the passion turned to protectiveness. "What are we going to do now? What is this plan?"

"First, I'm going to finish dressing you. Do I make a good lady's maid?" He placed a gentle but not so chaste kiss on the back of her neck. "Not so good with hair though." He picked up a long tendril running it through his fingers. "Soft, silken, possessing the heat of the sun, I want to wrap it around me."

"I can manage my hair, but I don't want to see your mother when we leave. I never told you that I like your first name, Colin." The last thing she needed was to see the disapproving gaze of the woman who raised Cam. If she were judged she'd come up lacking, but she didn't regret this moment. She had the old Cam back and Arie had done that for her.

Thank you, Arie.

"You won't have to see mother and no one calls me that except mother. I will personally escort her from my home. She's supposed to be living in the other townhouse. Don't know what she was doing here today." He finished with the buttons. "There, you look almost as good as new."

"Almost?"

"Well, I like the way you look better now." He smiled at her as if that tiny gesture would give her confidence as he gently touched the spot on her neck.

"And how is that?" She had the decided impression she should not have pushed for an answer when she watched his handsome smile change to an all male and very possessive grin.

He touched her lips with one fingertip. "Your lips are kiss swollen and the tiny mark on your neck tells the world you're mine even though it will embarrass you. Should probably wear a scarf for a few days until it goes away." He touched her lips again, this time with his thumb, "You don't need the lip tint. Now you have color on places that shouldn't have the tint."

He rose then, striding to a pitcher and washbasin. Pouring water into the bowl, he collected a cloth before walking back to her.

"Let me rid you of your wayward face paint."

Truly, she didn't know what to say. She watched the damp cloth as it touched her face, gently caressing. Heat rose within once more. His simple movements mesmerized her.

He moved back, "I love that sweet dusting of freckles."

"So..." She moistened her lips, unable to speak or move.

Then he began, "And on that cheek, and o'er that brow,

So soft, so calm, yet eloquent,

The smiles that win, the tints that glow,

But tell of days in goodness spent,

A mind at peace with all below,

A heart whose love is innocent!

Then, "We're going to head out the back door. While I didn't plan on any of this, at least not for today it's for the best." He waved his hand in the air, "This...or my mother, I'm not unhappy about anything that just happened. Do you have any regrets?"

"That you kissed me?" His kisses were what she wanted, nearly begged for. The rest she wasn't so sure about except for the way she felt. "No, nothing to regret."

"Nay, lass, that I took liberties I didn't have the right to take." He paused, touching a fingertip to her lips once more. "I lost control and I ken why but it doesn't absolve me from what I did."

She wound her hair into a tight but messy chignon. "Dinna fash yourself. I've no misgivings. Indeed, I would not protest if you..." She didn't know how to describe what happened.

"If I took all your clothing off?" His chuckle rumbled up from his belly.

"I'd rather you took your clothes off."

Now he roared with laughter. "I'll give you the chance to take my clothes off soon if you like."

"That's not exactly what I said." For a moment she looked away. "I don't think I could do that?"

"What can't you do, lass?" he spoke softly, touching her heart.

"Take your clothes off." Her voice wavered.

He brought her hands to his lips, "Someday you will. I promise. Someday in the not too distant future."

Shaking, she closed her eyes for a second. "This is so unreal for me. I'm at a loss for words and thoughts as well. Would it be proper for me?" She touched him. "To take your clothes off?"

"Only if you want to..."

"We should probably leave before your mother comes looking for you." She tried to get off the bed.

"Let her look. She won't find us. Let's head down the back stairs. I've something I want to show you." He stood then, extending his hand to help her from the bed.

"Something besides the observatory?" He sparked her interest.

"Yes, my sweet treasure," he tapped her on the nose, "but I'm not going to tell you yet. Are you ready to start out on another adventure?"

"With you, yes." Her heart was racing and she had no idea what he was asking of her but she trusted him with all her heart.

After a quick look out the door and down the hall, he motioned for her to come to him. Stifling laughter, she followed him until breathless they raced across the back lawn to the stables. A large carriage drawn by four horses waited for them.

"Here we are." He seemed proud of himself.

"Where are we going?" She stopped, realizing this was something bigger than she expected.

Suddenly he got down on one knee. "Will you marry me, lass?"

~ * ~

Arie stood in the whorehouse where the little redhead lived. From the madam he learned several important facts about her. Before Arie's man purchased her for him, a man calling himself her father had sold her to the brothel. Her name was Alison and a short time ago she lived on a small farm just outside Glasgow.

Arie smiled, so far pleased with his purchase and the promise it would bring. She would do well with him. He didn't know the circumstances surrounding the sale and he wasn't sure he wanted any knowledge. He preferred to keep her past where it belonged and as far as he was concerned, the reasons for the sale were in the past.

He held the only key to her rooms in his hands. Victor made sure the girl, Alison, was in the best suite in the house and he'd purchased an array of clothing for her including sheer lingerie he meant to enjoy as soon as possible. She would stay here until he found more suitable accommodations in the city. His man was out looking for something as he stood in front of her rooms, waiting to meet her.

Inhaling a long breath of air, he unlocked the door, unsure of how he would find the girl. The madam had also told him she'd been drugged and forced against her will. When he pushed open the door, it was to find Alison on the sofa, her head buried in her arms sobbing.

His breath caught. Dealing with crying women was not something he needed and disliked intensely. Yet his heart went out to her, understanding she no longer determined her future. He vowed he'd protect her and treat her as gently as humanly possible, but soon she would understand that she was his and pleasing him would be best for her future.

"Alison." He stepped into the room. "You need to stop the tears now. They will do you no good. You must come to terms with this situation you find yourself in now. You are mine. I bought you and your destiny is in my hands."

She turned, her eyes swollen and red. Her words ripping through him, "Did you come to rape me?"

Taken aback by the brutal accusation, he stopped midstride. "I don't rape women."

"Then you won't touch me." She rose, wiping the tears from her eyes then with her hands fisted at her sides. "I won't let you and will never be willing no matter how you try to charm me."

"Never is a very long time." Arie knew he could persuade her to his ways. For a man well practiced in the art of seduction, it was child's play.

"I mean what I say."

Arie cleared his throat, searching for the right words. "While I won't force you, I will touch you, touch you very intimately. I've spent a great deal of money to have you—exclusively. You won't want for anything."

"Before I found myself in this room, I had everything I wanted." She strode toward him and for a moment Arie thought she would confront him further.

He reassured himself understanding this was not going to be easy, his gut had told him as much when he saw her at the restaurant. "I will give you the world if you allow it."

She stood her ground, her eyes blazing with passion. "I don't want or need the world, only my freedom."

Stepping closer, he prayed she would not flinch away from him but would hold her ground with the courage he was witnessing. Gently he stroked her cheek, wiping away an errant tear with his thumb. "Your freedom is nonnegotiable. In the world I come from, women are bought and sold every hour of every, day but I can assure you I've never mistreated a woman in my possession."

She gulped a breath of air, her eyes sparking with anger and what seemed to Arie desperation. "I will claw your eyes out if you touch me."

His hand settled on her shoulder, one thumb tracing circles on her flesh. "Really. Should I be afraid right now?"

Whirling, she moved to the window, staring at the grounds below her, shoulders shaking. She didn't answer nor did she turn to confront him again.

Arie followed her. At the window he placed a hand on Alison's back. "We can make an agreement, you and I and proceed slowly. Will you give me a chance to win your heart?"

A sob wracked her body. "No, I cannot." Once again tears flowed from her eyes and down her cheeks.

"So be it." Anger swept through him but he suddenly had second thoughts. Truly he needed to continue with her best interest at heart. If he did, they might both reap the benefits, but he would have to rely on patience. Something he had little of at the moment.

Chapter Five

Cam pulled Chelsea into his arms for a quick kiss. Love struck and gazing into her eyes, "We are wed. Are you happy, lass?"

With her eyes wide, she touched his face, a smile on hers. "What do we do now?"

I make love to you for the next week. "A honeymoon before we announce to the world our new status would be in order. I've plans and I know the exact right place to consummate our vows. We are already halfway there." His eyes darkened with desire as he absorbed into his soul all that happened today. "I want you, and to me, it seems I've waited a lifetime. No more proper."

"I've no clothes. Shouldn't we go back to town?" Chelsea ran her hands across his chest seemingly unsure of herself.

"No clothes? I believe I love that idea. What do you need clothes for?"

"Cam." She hit his shoulder with a tiny fist before tracing his jawline with a fingertip.

His body shuddered at the intimate caress while his mind traveled to the sight of her on his bed this morning, her hair disheveled around her face. "Lacie and Daryl packed a valise for you and I took the liberty of purchasing a few things I thought you might like to have. We've no need to return to Glasgow."

"You've taken care of everything."

"I have." The smile in his heart grew as he realized she was beginning to trust him.

"Then where?" They walked from the small church where they were wed and to the waiting carriage.

She turned into his arms. "A surprise. Can you wait an hour for us to arrive?" Cam wrapped an arm around her waist, drawing her closer, enjoying her soft and willing compliance to his affections.

She pushed away from him, laughing. "You know I can't wait. I've no patience. Tell me now or I won't kiss you in the carriage and I know you want to do that, kiss me."

One eyebrow rose, "You threaten me?" He knew he could steal a kiss despite what she just told him and meant to prove it to her before they stepped inside the vehicle.

"Making a promise," she corrected him.

"A promise you will be unable to keep."

Placing a finger beneath her chin, he lifted her face. The sparkle in his eyes drew him into the web she unknowingly wove around him. He watched as she moistened her lips in anticipation of the kiss she told him she would refuse. In the few months they'd known each other, they had shared few kisses and he meant to make this one a promise for this evening as well as their future.

Slowly, he brushed her lips with his, his mouth settling gently on hers. He smiled at the tiny sounds of passion she was making in the back of her throat. Teasing with his mouth and teeth, he pulled her lips inside his. She leaned into him, her body begging for more. His hands, he ran up and down her back before they settled on her derriere, molding her close to his arousal.

Needing to stop before he tossed her skirts, he ended the kiss, grinning at her. "See you want this as much if not more than me. You can't refuse me. Try to deny the fact and I'll prove you unable to sustain the promise."

"We are not inside the carriage." Her laughter delighted him as she skipped away from him.

He knew she couldn't possibly want this more. She didn't even know the end game. He caught up with her and setting his hands on her waist, he helped her inside then followed, sitting close to her. Tapping on the roof, he signaled they were ready to start.

"Champagne?" He rummaged in a basket on the opposite side. "We should only have the finest."

"To celebrate our nuptials, I'd love some. Are we really married?" She pursed her lips together, watching him intently. "I can't believe it.

Everything happened so fast I didn't even have time to breathe let alone think. Arie told me I should think first and not act or react to things you did."

"Please breathe," he laughed, wishing Arie wasn't still on her mind. Nodding, he popped the cork, holding the bottle away for a few seconds while the liquid bubbled out. When it stopped, he held the bottle to her and with a lift of his shoulders, "No glasses and yes we are really married. Drink and enjoy, anticipate the night to come."

For a moment her lashes fluttered downward then when their gazes held, she reached for the bottle. Downing a few swallows, she gave it back to him. "The alcohol won't sway me to your kisses. Tell me the surprise or I'll withhold my favors."

He drank before pushing the cork on the bottle and setting it in the basket. The slow wicked grin forming should tell her he wasn't going to heed her threat. "I don't have to kiss your lips to give us both gratification or to ravish your beautiful body."

"A kiss is a kiss." Her prim voice gave him cause to laugh. "Don't you dare try to sway me with a different definition."

"Only a kiss if the act is on the mouth. Anywhere else would be a caress and you didn't tell me nay to touching and caressing." Cam pulled her onto his lap, his hands settling on her tiny waist then traveling higher to rest beneath her breasts. He didn't want to stop his exploration nor did he intend to cease.

"Cam..." His name on her lips was a soft moan of pleasure, delighting him as well as encouraging his efforts.

His questing hands found the hem of her skirt and petticoats, drawing them higher. He explored and searched, tracing gentle circles on her ankles then higher, enjoying himself as her body responded sweetly to his attentions. Her flesh was soft, silken.

"Do you like this or do you want me to stop? Tell me now. Your threat...you know." He watched as she opened her eyes, sighing softly as he found naked flesh above her stockings. He pressed kisses along the bodice of her gown, testing her resolve.

"I don't suppose you're kissing me, but Cam," she paused, seeming to think, "I do want to know where you're taking me. I don't like surprises and as you'll learn as you get to know me, I'm not patient, not patient at all."

"You want to know more about where we are going than you want me to do this, and this?" With his teeth he slowly pulled her gown downward until he saw the deep curve of her breasts and anticipated the view of her turgid pink nipples that he needed to take into his mouth.

"Yes, no." It seemed she didn't know what she wanted.

He chuckled softly as she let her head fall back against the seat giving him sweet access to more alluring places. "What was your answer?" Then his lips explored, touched and tempted, promising sweet pleasure she'd never experienced before. Still he wanted to wait until they were on his bed and he could truly give her every consideration, but there were things he could do now, in this moment to give her pleasure and help initiate her to his lovemaking.

Slowly, he unfastened her dress, drawing the bodice beneath her breasts. He pulled back, watching as they were revealed then inhaled a swift deep breath. Then he bent close, touching each tender bud, enjoying the movement of her hips as he pulled one into his mouth, bit gently before laving with his tongue.

"Please." The soft sigh following his actions, delighted him even while her passion seemed to spill into him.

His hands shook with the power he held over her as well as the need to make this evening, their wedding night, one she would never forget. He craved to hear the words from her. "Please what?"

"Please." She heaved a deep breath of air, the movement of her breasts tantalizing him. "Keep doing what you're doing."

"So now you want me to kiss you?" He teased her, wanted an affirmative answer.

"Yes..."

His hands once more found their way beneath her dress. While he was staring at her, enjoying the soft flush of color on her cheeks as well as the sheen of moisture on her face and bared flesh, "So now you want me to kiss you." He persisted in search of another affirmative.

She squirmed on his lap. "I didn't say that exactly."

"Precisely, how is a man to know what his wife wants if she doesn't tell him?" Liking the word wife as it pertained to Chelsea. His hand rested on the bare flesh of her belly. Tenderness assailed him, thinking that after tonight there would be the possibility of a child growing in her womb. He didn't want to consummate his marriage inside the carriage, yet she enticed him like no other, his control wavering more every second.

"If you don't want this then..." He set her away from him. "Tiny temptress, you enchant me, deliciously set the blood boiling inside me," he whispered as he pulled the bottle of champagne from its resting spot. "More? If we're not going to kiss, we should drink. I need to keep my bad boy image intact." He drank long and deep, realizing he needed the liquid courage as he was more determined than ever to keep from making love to her for their first time inside this vehicle. If he continued to tease, he would succumb to his baser needs and primal instincts.

"I've done nothing. You." She pointed a shaking finger at him. "You do things to me. I can't think straight and well you ken that fact. You do it on purpose, but I wouldn't have it any other way." She tilted the bottle he offered, taking two gulps before handing it back to him.

Needing some distance from her and her beautiful body, he watched disappointed as she pulled the corsage of her dress to cover her breasts. "I wonder if your sisters packed us food."

The rise of her breasts as she inhaled long and deep several times had him questioning his withdrawal in favor of a bedroom. Uncovering her once more seemed to take over all his senses. He gritted his teeth while he clenched his fingers in an effort to stop himself from finishing this before they reached their destination.

"I'm sure Daryl put food in the basket for us, some pastries, too, I hope. She loves to bake and when I left this morning there were blueberry muffins in the oven." She reached for the champagne again.

His stomach rumbled hungrily as he searched for the muffins. Instead he found two ham sandwiches. "You hungry? You should eat. Keep up your strength for tonight."

"Can't say that food is what my body is telling me it needs. Seems as if butterflies are flittering around inside."

"Butterflies, hmmm... What is your body telling you?" he asked between bites, studying her intently and hoping for a certain answer. "I bet it's telling you it craves my mouth on yours and my hands beneath your dress discovering sensitive and oh so tender spots, soft places."

She leaned forward, ignoring his questions. "Think I'll have that sandwich now and quit grinning at me as if you know something I don't." Her words sounded indignant. "Even though you do."

"Believe I know quite a few things that you don't, but if you're trying to get me to reveal our destination, you can't."

Her lips pursed while her brows drew together. "I wasn't thinking of our destination. I've resigned myself to patience as well as your obstinate silence about it." With a soft sigh she sat back, closing her eyes, her hands folded in her lap.

"Then you're speaking about where my hands have explored this last hour." Closing his eyes, he sat back, contemplating the evening ahead. "We should be there soon." He peered out the window, searching the landscape for something familiar. As the carriage traveled the last mile to his home near the beach, he watched waves crash against the giant wall of rocks. Spray flew high each time the ocean water hit the solid land barrier.

"And then I'll know where we are going?" She wrapped up the food she'd only taken a few bites from before setting the sandwich in the basket. "Can I look?" She ginned.

"If you want to ruin the surprise. You've not so patiently waited all this time..." He let the sentence hang, hoping she would decide not to look.

"Wouldn't it still be a surprise if I'm just seeing it now?"

"No," he told her thoughtfully. "Don't believe it would be. I want you to get the full effect. If you peek now, it won't be the same."

"Have it your way." She sat back, eyes closed with her arms crossed delightfully beneath her breasts, pushing them up and nearly freeing them from her loosened bodice, which he neglected to refasten.

"Next time I will let you have your way." He wanted to laugh at the look of annoyance she shot him.

"I don't believe you." She sat up, staring at the curtain shade on the window and even reaching out before she drew her hand back.

"Good girl."

"A few more minutes and we'll be there. As I promised before, the sight will be worth the wait. I guarantee you." He leaned forward, touching her leg beneath her dress and wishing for that bed he was waiting for. "This will be a wonderful honeymoon. I hope I've thought of everything."

"I'm sure you have," she told him.

The carriage slowed. Cam pulled out a cloth, slowly running it through his fingers. "I'm going to blindfold you. It will heighten the affect if you don't see anything until the proper time."

"Really, do you think that's necessary?"

"I know it is since you've not so patiently waited. Now turn around." He paused, watching the myriad of expressions crossing her face. "Please."

She let out a long breath of air then turning, "If you insist and I like the softer touch, when you say please."

"I do insist." He placed the cloth on her eyes before tying it in back. "You won't regret this."

"What if I fall?" She sounded petulant.

"I won't let you." His breath whispered against her neck and delighted in the little shiver it elicited.

He opened the door, jumping down and reaching inside to hold her by the waist. Drawing her from the carriage, he let her length slide evocatively down his chest. For a few seconds he held her close, her head tucked beneath his chin. He closed his eyes, realizing this moment would be one of many. Chelsea was his now. He'd let no man take her away from him.

The sky was dark, clouds covering it, disappointing him. He had hoped the night would be clear with the stars bright. Perhaps another night he would be able to point out constellations while holding her in his arms.

"Wrap your arm around my waist and I'll make sure you arrive unscathed. You won't fall on my watch."

He pulled her close while she did as he asked. "Cam, really, isn't this going too far? A blindfold?"

"When we get there, you'll appreciate the wait as well as the blindfold. I promise." It seemed he promised her something every few minutes just so he could get his way. He closed his eyes for a moment, praying. This was after all the beginning of their new lives together, a life where he meant to share everything with her, good and bad.

When they had children, he would stay at home, bring them up. He would never leave them to be raised by a nanny as he was. His children would be a part of his life, and they would learn his values as well as Chelsea's.

"Cam." She stumbled. He pulled her closer.

"I was distracted for a moment. We have stairs to go up. I won't let you fall." *Ever.* It was his job to protect her now, keep her safe from all the problems of the world and make sure she was happy.

"How much farther?" She sounded winded and a bit unsure of herself.

"Two more steps." He guided her to the railing surrounding the rooftop balcony. "Hold still. I'm going to take the blindfold off." He held the cloth, anticipation gnawing at his gut. He wanted the view to steal her breath. She was silent for too many minutes to suit him.

"It's beautiful." She turned to him, her eyes wide then back to the scene in front of her.

"I'm glad you like what you see. This home is very special to me." His hand settled on her waist, his fingers tightening.

"It's spectacular, Cam. Is this where you stargaze?" In his arms she turned, looking at him, her tongue gliding across her lips as if she was asking him for a kiss.

"Yes. I'd hoped the sky would be clear this evening. It's amazing how bright the stars are when you get away from the city lights." He kissed her then, a long slow kiss one that seemed to go on forever but when it was finally time to end it, he almost didn't.

"The house is yours?"

"I'll show the rest to you in a minute. Are you cold? The wind seems to have picked up. We really should get inside."

In the house, he lit the lanterns even though the sun had not yet dropped below the horizon then showed her around the home. The first floor then the second but in the kitchen a feast for two was set on the table.

"My cook arrived earlier as I planned and prayed you would accept my marriage proposal. You didn't eat much earlier. Would you like to wait for dinner or eat now?" Quite frankly he was a man long starved, but his hunger was for Chelsea not food.

He'd waited so long, months he deprived himself of her charms because of her brother and weeks where he was trying so desperately to be something he wasn't and never would be, proper.

That first kiss in the servant quarters of her family home seemed a lifetime ago. Now, with nothing to get in their way he would make love to Chelsea, his wife, from now into eternity. He inhaled a long deep breath of air, suddenly feeling a bit nervous and insecure. He'd never made love to a wife or a virgin only a mistress.

"Suppose we should eat, although I don't feel like eating any more now than I did a little while ago. My stomach is in knots."

"I understand. Try to relax." He found a tray, placing a few of the prepared dishes on it then found a bottle of wine and two glasses. "Let's go outside and eat. We can watch the waves and the spray as the water hits the rocks."

A blaze of light flashed across the sky followed by a roar of thunder then another. At that moment the heavens opened, hail pummeling the ground as well as the rooftop. The thunderous sounds were deafening.

"A storm." Showing no fear, she strode to the front of the house then out the door to the enclosed porch.

"You're not afraid." He followed, setting the tray on a table in front of the porch swing. For a few minutes they stood together, his arms enfolding her and watched. She leaned against him, her back pressed against his chest, his hands beneath her breasts.

Lightning slashed across the sky while the following thunder boomed. He felt the mist from the waves as the storm and the high tide pushed the spray higher and harder.

Reveling in the energy created by the tempest, he held the woman he was falling for in his arms, thrilled she was not terrified while he found himself amazed at her courage. He prayed the energy and emotion between them would fill their evening with the same raw and mercuric sensations.

"No, not afraid, never afraid. I love storms and the energy."

A bolt of lightning flashed from cloud to cloud across the sky. She settled into his arms, watching the tempest in front of them. "This might be better than star gazing."

"You would admit that?" she questioned him. "I'm surprised."

"Only once in a very long while. This is spectacular yet perhaps it's because I'm holding you in my arms." He rested his chin against the top of her head. "Should we sit? I brought a quilt from the house. We can wrap it around us." All he wanted was to hold her, enjoy the tender closeness he was feeling now. This was so different than the sexual drive he always felt before. He needed her in so many different ways.

"I'd like that."

He shook out the blanket before wrapping it around her shoulders. They sat on the swing. She curled her legs onto the seat, leaning into him. He held her hand, their fingers intertwined.

"I used to watch the storms in the valley from our third-floor balcony. Viewing it with you by my side is much nicer than seeing the thunderstorm alone."

Chelsea didn't answer with words but she nodded, seeming to agree with him. Warm silence ensued as the storm's fury increased.

She pushed flyaway hair from her eyes and with a long sigh, "We, my sisters and I, when a storm hit at night, we would all run into Flynt's bedroom and jump on the bed. Even after we got older, we would do the same thing, simply because it annoyed him. Although he would never admit to the fact, he liked to have us there also."

"And Flynt didn't shoo you girls to your bedrooms?"

"No, we all missed mother and father so much, and the storm gave us a chance for closeness we weren't able to get any other way. We never really understood how much we needed each other." With one hand she turned, touching his chest then gazing upward. "Now I have you."

He brushed a gentle kiss on her forehead, unwilling to change the tenor of the moment between them. "What was it like having so many siblings? I was always wishful but of course mother and father were always too busy and it was probably for the best they never had more children. They were not good parents."

"I'm sorry. The house was always hectic. My sisters and I were all so close in age, and Flynt was so much older. We loved to play tricks on him, take his things and hide them."

"Can't imagine him having very much patience with that," Cam laughed, trying to imagine the scenes and wishing somehow he could have been part of something like that.

Chels was still staring at him a strange expression on her beautiful face. "Are you going to make love to me tonight?"

Struck by her question, he hesitated a few seconds. "Yes." Then he laughed. "Are you impatient, little one?"

Drawing her lips together and shaking her head, "Nervous. The waiting makes me anxious. I'm thinking I would just like to get it over with."

"Ach, lass, get it over with...never. Soon, *moer stilis*, I was enjoying this time with you in my arms while we reminisced about our childhoods."

She fiddled with the buttons on his shirt, undoing them while she seemed to let him have his way for the moment. Yet when her fingers caressed him, touched his nipple, his indrawn breath of air was quick and harsh. The sound gave her reason to look into his eyes and question.

"Was that bad?" Her smile was hesitant but her eyes sparkled as the lantern he hung behind them illuminated her face.

Letting his head fall back and roaring with laugher, "It was very naughty."

"Then we must be well suited for each other if you're a bad boy and I'm a naughty girl." She spread her fingers, stroking his chest.

The easy moment between them vanished as if it had never happened. The tempest and the thundering of the waves seemed to enter into him spiraling with raw energy and rising to an inferno of sexual need he couldn't control. He had to orchestrate this first time with her, but the raw hunger coursing through him might put that in jeopardy.

"Slow down," he whispered, placing his hand over hers. "Slow down or this won't turn out the way I planned for you. This is about you, about your first time, our first time." His voice was husky and his fingers quivered with expectation. He pushed the blanket from them and drawing her into his arms, carried her through the house and up the stairs to his chambers.

~ * ~

Perhaps she started something too soon, had messed this up. His face was so dark and his jaw so taut, he frightened her. Yet all his actions were gentle and sweet. He set her on the bed then he was kissing her and the feelings cascading through her were exquisite. So was the taste of Cam, his heat, the textures of face stubble and lips, tongue and teeth.

He melded her mouth with his and she returned the passion just as they had done before. A ring on her finger didn't make a change in the inferno he sparked within her with just a kiss or the magic he created with his hands. Everything he'd done before she imagined he would do again.

"You need to get out of this dress..." He turned her over just as he'd done earlier in the morning, unfastening and unlacing all her clothes.

"I want to see you naked too," she murmured into the pillow before he gently tugged her to a sitting position then pulled her dress over her head. Everything except her chemise fell away.

Quickly he shrugged from his shirt. Sitting he pulled off his boots and the remainder of his clothing. Then he stood in front of her.

She knew her eyes were wide with wonder. Her gaze roamed the length of him then again. "Cam..." She breathed in then slowly let the air rush out in a soft rush of air. She stared at him. His eyes were a vivid fire against the heightened color of his skin. Each time his head moved, light shimmered over his face casting ever-changing shadows. His lips were dark and moist from the pressure of their shared kiss. "What now?"

He grinned shamelessly, his voice deep and husky with desire. "You match me, take everything off so I can see all of you."

"I've never been naked in front of you." She didn't want to be embarrassed or refuse him but she truly didn't know if she had the courage or if he would find her pleasing.

"There's a first time for everything. Do you want me to help?" He sat on the bed, his gaze riveted on her, on her mouth then her breasts and lower before he looked into her eyes again.

"I won't have anything on."

"What you wear now does little to cover you. I can see all of you, every beautiful part." Lightly he traced the contour of her breast then the other.

She pulled the chemise over her head and watched the shine in his eyes darken. "I want to kiss every part of you and keep kissing you until the honey flows and you're as soft as I am hard and we..."

With a sharp breath he reigned in his words, moistening his lips. Chelsea waited, watching him with her eyes wide. She felt both passion and wariness yet passion outweighed the other emotion.

"Ach, lass, you put the sun and moon to shame as well as all the stars."

She was watching his mouth rather than his eyes even while heat rushed through her from the impact of his words.

"I..." She had no words to respond.

"Isn't that the idea?" he said huskily. "Watch me. Watch us kissing. I need to kiss you everywhere, every luscious part of you."

"You told me it wasn't kissing if the kiss wasn't on the mouth."

"I lied to get my way with you."

His lips were silky against her ear, her neck, the pulse beating hard just beneath her skin. When his tongue probed the hollow at the base of her throat, her breath broke. He sucked on her skin, bit her tenderly, and shared the ripple of response that coursed through her.

She had never known this before, yet she wanted, craved what came next. His naked flesh against hers sent raw mercuric sensation rippling through her. Her nipples were firm rosy crowns seeming to beg for his attention.

He bent lower. His lips parted over one taut nipple.

In response she touched his, needed to give as much as she received from him. "Cam..." throaty little sounds she couldn't control seemed to delight him.

"Kissing, mean to kiss you everywhere," he said, his voice deep with raw emotion and a vibrating hunger that sent the flames of their shared passion higher.

"I need to kiss you too."

"In time. Watch."

The sight of him nibbling gently on her breast made an odd, breathless feeling twist through her. The stark contrast of dark masculine stubble and fragile pale flesh somehow heightened the intensity of the caress. Her hips seemed to move of their own volition, upward begging him for some type of fulfillment.

Slowly, deliberately, he licked the rosy taut bud, her body quivering with passion and desire. Lifting his head, he gazed at her.

Sensations flashed through her as the lightening slicing through the night. Fascinated, held in a delightful net of pleasure, she watched as he now gave attention to each nipple.

Before she knew what was happening, the tip of her breast vanished into his mouth. As he had once seduced her lips, now he seduced her breast, stroking it with tongue and teeth.

Instinctively her back arched, rubbing her nipple even more firmly over his tongue. He responded by increasing the sucking pressure until she whimpered and held him to her breast.

When Cam finally lifted his head, her body was flush with color and a sheen of moisture covered her. This was so much more intimate than anything they shared before and she knew she should be self-conscious to see herself so clearly and to know that he was seeing her in the same way, but her heated cheeks came from rising passion as well as the joy he seemed to share with her and embarrassment no longer played a part in what they did.

She loved watching him caress her.

Delicately, repeatedly, he sipped at the tight pink crown, kissing her then kissing her again. When his teeth closed tenderly around the nipple, she shivered and unexpectedly cried out.

He lifted his head, concern in his expression.

"Did I hurt you?" he asked.

She was shaking her head, unable to respond. In any case, words eluded her. There was nothing she could think of to say.

"Your eyes are wide and dark, a dark, vivid blue," he whispered. "I've never seen them such a deep color."

Chelsea couldn't help herself, she looked at her breast, where his mouth had been.

"What did you do?" she asked, wonder in her sensations. "I've never looked like that, even on the coldest morning."

"This?" He touched her nipple with the tip of his tongue.

"Yes."

"It's your body's way of telling me it likes being kissed. It's kissing me in return."

"Just kissing," she repeated his words wondering what would happen next and if he would kiss her again and exactly where he would kiss her.

He made a rumbling sound in the back of his throat, which she thought was pleasure.

"Of course," he said deeply. "I would love to touch you more places while I'm kissing you. I want to discover every soft, tender spot you possess, caress you everywhere and I hope to do the same every night for the rest of our lives."

"Cam please, you're tormenting me on purpose." She let out a ragged little breath.

"Would you have it any other way? We've the entire night and I want you to feel my mouth and my hands everywhere before the sun rises then I pray you will beg for more."

He bent and smoothed his face against her, from her collarbone down over each breast and back again, kissing and stroking every bit of the way. Bracing himself on his elbows, he dipped his face between her breasts, stroking her. He shuddered, gazing at her before he redoubled his caresses, tenderly devouring her.

For Chelsea this was what she'd waited for since that night he first kissed her. The storm outside had settled and only a soft rain drummed on the roof but the tempest inside her raged with uncontrolled raw energy. The silk of his lips brought her breasts to aching peaks that were soothed by his tongue and caressed by his fingertips and palms. Her breasts were flushed and taut, fully alive for the first time. It seemed they too begged him for his attention.

She made a hoarse sound and jerked when his mouth closed over a nipple again, realizing she would never get enough of this or deny him anything.

"I've never made love quite this way with a woman an innocent woman like yourself," Cam whispered, lifting his head. "You'll have to tell me if I do something you don't like."

At first, she didn't really hear the words, for she was too caught up in the pleasure that rippled and shimmered through her to understand what he told her. Then she really heard his words.

"Never done this?" she managed finally. "I thought..." she could barely speak, licking her lips she tried to form the words. "I thought..."

"Not like this."

"I don't understand. You've had mistresses."

"That's exactly what I'm talking about. They were all women who were paid to have sex with me. I paid them. They were experienced and well versed in the ways of making love. Before now all I wanted was..."

His voice died as he softly kissed the inner curve of her breast, then raked his teeth with exquisite care over each nipple. The jerk of her response and her fingers clenching suddenly in his hair sent a groan of pleasure through him.

"Hell," he said huskily. "I can't even remember how it was before. I just know the sex has never been like this."

"Should I be pleased?" She worried over his statement then, "Is it a good thing that you can't remember?"

Ignoring her questions, he lowered his head and delicately consumed her breast, lingering over the hard pink tips.

"It's time to move on. There is more of you I want to pet and pleasure, places I've neglected," he said. "Would you like that, for me to kiss you in different places?"

Her only answer was a dazed sound and her fingers silently urging his head back to her hungry breasts.

"You know I will. I've waited for you, longed for you but I don't know anything, don't know what you expect of me. I want to please you too. Tell me what I should do?"

"Nothing, I want except for you to enjoy each moment."

"That's not too hard."

"So, you'll like the next part even more than what I've done so far," he told her. "Before this night is over, I'm going to touch all of you, kiss every amazing part of you."

"When can I touch you?"

"Patience. I'm wanting to give everything I can to you before you make it so difficult for me to hold back that I cannot. Have you ever felt something so good it almost hurts?" he whispered.

"You mean like the sound of the first bird in the spring? Or the sight of the first crocuses bursting from the frozen ground? Things like that?"

His fingers tightened at her words. "Pain and pleasure combined. I'd never guessed anyone else felt like that after winter's long cold silence. Yes, like a silver needle stitching through your soul. That's not real hurt, is it? It's sweet painful pleasure, agony that turns into bliss."

"No. It's beautiful, like you so strong and sure of yourself. I never really understood all that drew you to me or me to you. At first, I just the thought it was the way that first kiss made me feel. But now I know there is more, so much more."

"Even before that first kiss you were drawn to me. I saw it in your eyes every time you looked at me. I was drawn to you too but you were always too young. Now, it seems you've grown up right before my eyes and you are mine."

"No longer too young," she murmured. "Yes, I am truly yours."

Cam kissed Chelsea very gently.

"I'd give my soul to make our lives together last forever," he whispered, gazing at her. "I want to make everything perfect for you, for us and I want you to remember this night from now through eternity."

With a hoarse sound, he put his forehead against her heart. She ran her fingers through his hair, realizing this amazing man would be part of the rest of her life. Slowly very slowly his mouth slid down to her navel. He probed the sensitive hollow with his tongue before moving lower still.

She gasped in surprise at the sensations radiating through her and the clenching of her belly and lower with each enchanting movement of his lips and teeth. His hands circled her breasts and plucked the aching peaks while his tongue worked its magic lower, more intimately. Her back arched as she cried out unable to stop herself.

Above her she felt an answering wave of passion sweep through him, shaking him. He repeated the caresses again and again, tenderly and at times recklessly.

Then he began smoothing his forehead and stubbled cheeks over the top of her thighs. His silky mouth and sensuously hard, hands followed. The sweetly conflicting textures were intensified by the tender raking of his teeth.

Gently, he seduced her legs as completely as he had seduced the rest of her body. She forgot that she was vulnerable to him and only savored what he so willingly gave. She forgot everything but the pleasure gathering deep inside her with each kiss he gave her, each caress, each husky word telling her how much he cherished her body.

The fear of the unknown as well as the stiffness of her legs melted away before his tender assault. Distantly she realized he was kissing and stroking the inside of her knees, her thighs, her...

"Cam." Her voice wavered.

He made a hungry questioning, oddly soothing sound in the back of his throat. "This might hurt."

She closed her eyes, tensing then feeling a tiny moment of pain then only the pleasure he spoke of. "You're inside me."

"Ach, lass. You're pure honey, velvet soft, perfect in every way. Your heat...it warms my soul."

He moved his hand again slowly, caressing and exploring places so sensitive she needed to cry out with the pleasure.

Silken heat flowed once more.

"So much fire, the flames would melt any iceberg," he whispered, moving slowly inside her.

She tried to speak. She couldn't. A flash of intense pleasure was bursting through her, arching her back, drawing him farther inside.

Shock and surprise overwhelmed her. She no longer questioned his hands and where they explored intimately between her legs. Instead she gave herself to his caresses with a trust she'd never given to anyone else in her life.

A ragged throaty sound rumbled from her lungs.

"I didn't hurt you too much did I?"

Her sultry response seemed to encourage him. He shifted. Then he repeated the caress slowly, deeply, again and again.

In that instant she truly realized where he was and that she was completely exposed. This was what she'd wanted for so long but never quite realized what this was or what it meant. When she started to speak, her words became a husky cry of pleasure as his hands moved again. Still, he was deep inside her, his thumb rubbing over a most sensitive spot.

Intense, shocking pleasure burst inside her, drenching her with heat.

He shifted again, moving over her in a gentle, overwhelming wave. He was everywhere, hot and powerful, tender and caressing, surrounding and the pleasure seemed to go on forever yet she somehow knew this wasn't everything, understood instinctively there was more.

"Tell me if I hurt you," he said huskily, his voice ragged with emotion, seemingly just as affected by this lovemaking as she was.

She barely heard the words. She knew only a sense of heat and sensations that went on and on, delicious, frightening, endless, sensuous beyond belief. "I need more," she whispered. "There must be more."

Cam made a throttled sound as she placed her hands on his chest, caressing his tiny nipples.

"Chels?" he asked hoarsely. "Am I hurting you?"

"No, it's just that I feel so strange and hot." She shivered rhythmically. "What you're doing doesn't hurt," she said. "Not exactly."

He grinned, rolling over and taking her with him. "I'm glad to hear that."

She made a surprised sound when she found herself on top of his hips, straddling him. "What are you doing?"

"You're so sweet and tight. I feel as if I'm encased in velvet," he said, his voice thick. "This way you can decide how much of me you want then I won't need to ask if I'm hurting you."

"I'm not sure I understand." She ran her fingers along his chest, bending close to touch a nipple with her tongue, her breasts brushing across his chest. She sat up again, looking at him.

The corner of his mouth lifted in the smile she adored. He was holding her up. "Look down and you'll have your answer," he told her.

Chels did. Her eyes widened when she saw that their bodies were joined in the most elemental way possible. When he entered inside her, she didn't think about it at all or even comprehend exactly what was happening or what they were doing.

"We're..." Her voice dried up. "I think I knew but..."

"We sure are. "Well," he amended, "we're halfway there. The rest is up to you. Do you want all of me?"

"How?" She didn't have any idea what he meant or what he was encouraging her to do.

"If you want more of me, settle down on me a little, then lift up a little, then come back down."

Hesitantly she moved her hips her hands pressed on his belly.

"How does it feel?" Cam asked through gritted teeth.

"Amazing, wonderful, nothing I've ever felt before. Different than when I was on my back."

She moved again and again.

He made a hoarse sound in the back of his throat. "This way you have all of the control."

Chelsea froze. "Does it hurt?"

"Like a warm summer breeze caressing my face. I don't want it to ever end."

She hesitated then smiled, understanding.

"This seems like heaven to me," she murmured. "You like it too?"

"I'm not sure," he told her, his eyes darkening further. "Why don't you try it a few more times so I'll know for sure."

Slowly she slid up and then down, then up again.

His hand moved. Fingertips searched through her intimately until he found that sensitive spot that seemed to intensify everything they did together. He circled it, retreated, circled, retreated, spreading the liquid heat of her response between them.

Eyes closed, shivering, whimpering with each breath, Chels tried to get closer to his maddening, wildly arousing fingertips. Her hips rocked less tentatively over the aroused male flesh between her legs. He was a hard, full presence that wasn't hurting her at all, not any longer.

Eyes smoldering, watching her, Cam teased her until her pleasure drenched both of them. Then he retreated.

Something both wild and beautiful spread up from their hot, joined bodies. Chelsea's eyes widened. She shuddered and rocked hungrily, craving more of Cam, needing to feel every bit of him as deep into her as she could get him. His hands were on her hips and he seemed to be helping her move.

Suddenly his body tensed. With repeated, throttled shouts he spent himself inside her. When the sounds and throbbing pulses went on and on, she became still, afraid she had somehow done something wrong. Anxiously, she looked down at his face.

It was drawn as though in pain. Sweat glistened on his forehead. "What happened?"

"Don't move please. Stay where you are. I don't want you to leave me. In a second, I'll make sure you have your pleasure. This just was not well done of me yet I tried. A woman should have her pleasure first."

"I..." She lifted herself away from him.

With a hoarse sound he slid his hands across her thighs and buried himself inside her once more. Then he rolled his hips against her. Hard.

Sweetly painful pleasure burst through her. She couldn't move her hips in response, but she discovered she could move secretly, measuring and caressing him even while he pulsed deeply inside her.

The shivering sweetness doubled. She clenched her body around him again and again, gasping at the expanding pleasure. Talons of fire seemed to slide into her, pulsing, releasing, pulsing again throbbing uncontrollably.

She groaned, moving against him, trying to get even closer, desperate for something she couldn't name. Yet she knew there was something more, something so close she could almost feel it but not quite. She wept with the need of the unknown.

Cam put his hands on her hips again, jerked forward and drove into her.

A wild heat pounded through her, beating and throbbing, the fire inside her escalating. Then she realized what she knew hovered just beyond her reach. Each broken breath she inhaled was a cry of ecstasy that was also his name, spasms of pleasure ripped through her over and over again.

He seemed to understand everything about her, seemed to know what her body craved even while she didn't. When she fell against him spent, he pulled her close settling her head on his chest.

A crash outside stopped her heart for a moment.

~ * ~

Fletcher Donovan paced the first-floor townhouse of his nephew

Leod. Running his hands through his hair, he tried to figure out why the man they called Sultan purchased his daughter for more than he received from the bordello. Something was wrong here and he meant to get to the bottom of it and get what he deserved.

He cursed the fact that if he'd known the sultan liked redheads, he would have approached him first. He would have never had to deal with the madam and her disapproving stares.

"What's got you all in a dither?" Leod tossed back a whiskey, a newfound vice before setting the glass hard on the end table.

"Sold the girl, thought I got top dollar for her but was wrong. Could've gotten double the price if I'd gone to the right buyer."

"What girl?"

"My bastard daughter," Fletcher grit out. "She was never worth her upkeep, never did an honest day's work."

"Why'd you sell her?" Leod strode to the liquor cabinet then poured himself another drink. "Not that it's any of my business."

Fletcher shrugged his shoulders. "Needed the money. Thought it was about time she helped out a little."

Leod rocked on his heels, staring out the window before turning. "And her mother didn't object? I've a hard time believing that."

"Gave her a small pittance." Fletcher laughed. "Her mother was a pretty little thing. Caught her one day walking home with a heavy bundle. Don't even remember what was in it, not that it mattered. I gave her a ride and she gave me pleasure not even complaining too much about it. From then on, we shared a bed and her home."

Leod sniggered. "That's what I'd like to do with a certain little lady, but she won't even look at me. Prefers a cad, a bad boy, over me."

"In this world you need to take what you want." He tossed back a drink. "Can't wait around for anyone to hand you something you crave on a silver platter. No, just can't wait for something like that when it's never going to happen." His words gave him an idea that he wasn't about to wait around to put in use.

"I can't even get close to her. This sultan you were just talking about keeps men guarding her. They only let MacEwen inside the perimeter they've formed around her."

"You don't say." Fletcher stroked his beard. "He's interested in two ladies or just one and protective of the other?"

"Can't say. Don't really know anything about your daughter. Don't believe he's set his sights on Chelsea either."

"If he's guarding two ladies, his resources will be cut in half and we'll both fare better." Fletcher decided to pay the brothel a visit. The next day would be soon enough. He had a few plans to put into action. "What are you going to do about your lady?"

"Not too sure. Think I should just take her? Don't know how to go about doing something like that, but maybe if we put our heads together, we'll figure it out."

"We need to find her alone and to do that you're going to have to discover what she does every minute of every day then you can plot the attack. What are you going to do with her once you have her?" Fletcher smirked. He knew what he'd do but he doubted if Leod had the wherewithal to figure out all the things a lady was good for.

"That's exactly what I plan. I'm going to take everything from her she refused to give me."

"Plan this out well, my friend. Do you have somewhere you can keep her where no one will look?" He wouldn't mind sharing the farm home with Leod and the pretty little lady that captured his nephew's heart. Well, Fletcher didn't think it was really Leod's heart; more like she had him by the balls and Leod didn't know what to do.

Leod drummed his fingers on the arm of the chair, scowling. "Nowhere. Nowhere at all."

Fletcher's smile began slowly then grew. "I've got the perfect spot."

"You sure about that."

"I am. Alison's mother has been bothering me for more money, and I've become quite tired of her. She's a bit over the hill now, but I could sell her to one of the lower-class whorehouses. Then we'll have her home, which I paid for, all to yourself and the lady you covet. I'll start the process on the morrow when I pay a visit to Alison."

Chapter Six

"Stay there!" Cam pointed to where she sat trembling, eyes wide, covers pulled to her chin.

Naked, he strode to the window as the sky was lit with a bolt of lightning. While he peered out the window, thunder boomed, seeming to surround the house in noise. The storm had died an hour ago, but it now seemed to take on another life.

The crash they heard was a tree. Splinters of it scattered the ground while a small fire simmered inside what was left of the tree's trunk, the rain keeping the flames from growing.

"What is it?" Reaching for her chemise, she rose from the bed before she slipped the garment over her head.

"Nothing really, just more of the thunderstorm we were admiring earlier." He was amazed at what the powerful tempest had done.

She stood by his side, one hand resting on his back, her body pressed close to his. "I thought the storm had passed by."

Once again, the impeding weather proved them both wrong. Flashes of light followed by more thunder penetrated the tiny room where they stood. "Probably not a good idea to stand so close to the window."

Cam walked to the fireplace, tossing in a couple pieces of wood in hopes the coals wood ignite the tinder. A spark caught on a dry piece then another and with a bit of tending, flames took hold, leaping merrily in the grate.

Chelsea sat down on a fur rug near the fireplace, moving her legs across the fur as if she enjoyed the sensual glide of the softness. At the sight, his body hardened, needing her again. He had not expected this so soon and naked, he could do nothing to hide his condition. He supposed and hoped the rest of their lives together would be just like this.

With a sigh and gazing at his beautiful wife, he picked up the tray of food the servants must have left for them before their arrival. In any case when he set her on the bed earlier in the evening neither had been hungry. He'd only had one thing on his mind.

Placing the platter on the hearth, he retrieved the glasses then poured wine for both. This was all so new to her he was hesitant to question her yet the need to understand her emotions inexplicably drove him.

"How do you feel?" He handed her the glass, studying her, knowing she could even now carry his child. Thinking about a baby, their baby, gave his heart a small leap of joy.

"Exhausted, happy, wanting you to make love to me again." She touched his chin, smiling then her hand wandered lower to his chest, her gaze following the direction of her hand before it seemed she noticed his arousal.

He picked up her hand, kissing the back then the palm, "I want the same thing, but we're going to wait and we're going to eat first."

"Because you're hungry." She twirled her glass of wine before looking over the rim at him, her eyes sparkling with desire. He wondered if she had any idea how she looked when he pleasured her. "I am." She picked up a strawberry, taking a bite before feeding the remainder to him, her fingers lingering softly and enticingly on his lips.

"We should eat but I'm not going to sit here naked if you're wearing clothes." He laughed when she looked at herself, smoothing the fabric so it inadvertently molded to her body.

"I'm practically naked." A soft blush of color rose to her face while her eyes narrowed as if she concentrated on something. Then lifting her shoulders in a miniature shrug, "Doesn't much matter does it?"

"Sheer fabric veiling your soft curves doesn't count as naked to me even if the sight is beguilingly enchanting." His shoulders moved upward, shrugging, knowing his grin was shameless. "Naked is naked and you're not."

"But you can see all of me," she blurted, gazing at herself again a hint of pink on her cheeks.

"Not the same." He handed her another strawberry, trying not to laugh while thinking of something else to talk about.

"Seems the same to me."

"If it's the same then take your chemise off." He challenged her, hoping she would comply to his wishes all the while understanding she thought of the clothing as protection. "You don't need security from me." Yet perhaps she did.

She was shaking her head, watching him and he knew she was desperately trying to do as he wished.

"I would not feel comfortable." Her lips quivered as she reached a soft spot in his heart.

He chose to leave this conversation behind while moving on to learning more about her. "You know I want children, more than one or two," he told her as he drank deeply of the wine.

"Because you're an only child."

"True, in part." He was attempting to put his feelings into words, and he was pretty sure he'd want a lot of children even if he had siblings, unsure how to broach the subject with Chels, "I love children."

"How so?" She smiled at him over the rim before partaking of the wine.

"They are so innocent and sincere, unlike most adults. Children have a way of making me smile with their sweetness. I would love to have a lot of children," he paused, "as many as you like."

"They have more energy than heavenly possible," she added, laughing. "Do you think you can keep up with more than one child? I would make you watch them whenever you're around."

"I heard the word them. Does that mean you want more than one?"

"Could you match their energy?" It seemed she avoided his question. "And change their diapers, kiss their tiny hurts when they fall down?"

"Can you?" he challenged, pulling her close to him for a grand hug. He wanted to hold her for a while, creating a different type of intimacy than sex, yet this closeness was something he craved. The personal confidence, a woman he could tell his wildest dreams to as well as his darkest secrets. Someone who he trusted with his life.

"Perhaps we will get to see," she told him, placing her head against his chest, touching his arm with a hand while tracing his forearm with a delicate fingertip. "I would just hope we do not have twins as Bliss and

Broc did. Two babies at the same time is difficult."

"Perhaps we will and it would not be so bad because I promise you I will help." He agreed with her, grinning. "Now, what would you like to do for the hours before dawn. Would you like to sleep?"

"Don't believe I can do that, sleep." She walked to the window, enticing him while the candlelight as well as the occasional light from the storm silhouetted her tiny waist then accentuated her hips. His body tightened with need just watching the delicate sway of her body as she walked.

"Why?" He enjoyed watching her, every aspect of Chelsea. He was crazy for Chelsea and he wondered if she felt the same. *Crazy for Cam...* He realized he wanted her to feel that way about him, didn't want her thinking about anyone but him. He needed to bind her so thoroughly to him she would never want anyone else never the sultan.

She turned, the fabric of her chemise moving with the sway of her breasts. "Too excited and on edge. The lightning seems to send sparks along my arms." She rubbed them, appearing to need something. "I can't stop thinking about—you and me—together in that bed. The way we looked when you were inside me. Don't know if I'll ever be able to sleep there."

He stopped the laughter at her words from bubbling up in his throat. "I certainly hope you'll be able to sleep in our bed. If not, you'll be exhausted night and day. Can't have my wife too tired to play."

"When the storm passes, can we go for a walk? I want to feel the spray of the waves against my face, smell the sea."

He relaxed back, leaning on an elbow. "We would have to dress. Don't believe I'd let you go outside even in this remote area in just your chemise."

"See, I'm right," she told him, a sparkle in her eyes, making them darken with desire. "Even you think I'm not dressed." She crossed her arms beneath her breasts, pushing them upward.

"We have to eat more than a few strawberries. If you lie down and sleep, we'll explore the area around the house and if the waves die down, I can take you to the beach." Ah, he'd like that, making love to his wife on the beach with the surf crashing in front of them.

"Don't want to sleep," she whispered softly, her voice fading. "Need to be with you, want to feel you inside me again."

While he adored the sentiment, he knew better. She needed rest as well as food in her stomach. "Come here." He motioned to her to sit by him. "When you finish eating, I'm going to take you to the bed," he paused, "For sleep, nothing more."

"You too?"

"Holding you in my arms while we sleep is everything I've dreamt of." He didn't know how to tell her holding her while not having sex with her was going to be the hardest damn thing he'd ever done.

Closing her eyes, she nodded her head in seeming agreement. "If you insist. I suppose I can try." When she opened her eyes, she looked at him with trust and desire.

The way she gazed at him was everything he'd ever wanted. Strangely though, until he met Chelsea he didn't understand the emotion he now knew he could not live without.

After they finished eating, he carried her to the bed. He didn't ask her to remove the flimsy garment she donned earlier but pulled her into his arms. She set her head against his chest, his arm around her. He knew the moment she fell asleep; her breathing eased and she seemed to give herself completely to him.

In the hours before dawn he must have dozed. When he opened his eyes, it was because of the crowing of a rooster. In his arms she stirred, her hand running the length of his chest then lower to stop inches from his sex.

"You are bold this morning and a wee bit naughty, *moer stilis*." He kissed the tip of her nose before placing a finger beneath her chin then turning her so his lips could brush across hers.

"Do you like bold and naughty?" She touched his lips with the tip of her tongue then grew braver, wrapping her fingers around him.

He felt her shudder at the contact.

"Making love to you will have to wait, my sweet treasure. I want to explore the beach with you this morning." He held her hand, bringing it to his lips so he could kiss her fingers.

"The storm has passed through?"

He pointed to the window. "Look outside," he told her, waiting for her to turn her attention to the window. As she pushed away, her silken hair slid across his body. Closing his eyes, he gritted down, trying for control. If she knew the power she held over him, she could sway him to whatever she wanted.

Sunlight shone brightly through the window and one could see the brilliant blue of the sky which was dotted with a few white clouds. This would be a good day. He smiled thinking about the plans he had made.

"What are we going to do?"

"Hmm..." He laid back, his hands behind his head smiling. "I'm going to show you around. After we eat that is. You've slept and now we will eat so we can do whatever we want."

She straddled him, her legs sleek and silken against him, her core resting on his arousal. A groan rumbled up through his chest even while he was pleased she enjoyed sex with him. He'd wanted to wait until the beach and the waves. It seemed to him she had different ideas.

"Are we just kissing?" she asked, a beautiful smirk on her face.

"No."

Above him, she gazed down, her eyes darkened with passion. This wasn't supposed to happen. Yet, he rolled her over, settling between her legs, stroking her intimately, exploring everywhere. Open to him, she gave herself over to his control.

"I look at you and I want you," she whispered, her face flushed with passion. "Is that alright?"

"You're incorrigible and your wanting me is everything I've ever craved." He couldn't help but chuckle as he thrust inside her, pleased with all she said and did. If she remained this way, the rest of their lives would be filled with bliss. Bloody hell, but he was crazy about his wife. In his wildest dreams he had never believed anything like this could happen.

Beneath him she cried out, "Cam..." as intense waves of pleasure passed through her into him. He thrust inside harder until he touched her womb.

He shouted when he filled her and when he was spent, he rested his elbows on either side of her head. Moving damp strands of hair from her face, he grinned at her. "You're so beautiful. It seems I'm doomed by the mere fact I can't say no to you."

"Not as beautiful as you." Her hands rested on his shoulders, her breasts pushing against his chest.

His laughter echoed around the room, "Men are not beautiful." He kissed her softly, then, "Time to get up. Would you like a bath before or after we eat?"

"Before."

Cam rolled off the bed, sauntering to the bell cord and ringing it. "You should cover up," he told her as he pulled on his doeskins.

He was at the door almost the same time as the knock. "Sir."

"We need hot water to bathe. As quickly as possible."

"We anticipated your needs. The water is boiling on the stove as we speak. I'll have it here in a few minutes. I'll tell cook to start breakfast," the man said.

"Good, we'll be down when we're finished bathing."

The buckets of water arrived; the bath filled with steaming water.

When he turned to Chelsea, she was sitting with the sheets pulled in front of her, looking well loved by him, her lips slightly swollen and her hair disheveled around her head.

"You first."

Fifteen minutes later they were sitting in the dining room, eating. A feast had been prepared for them per his instructions. He watched her pick at her food and wondered if she usually ate this sparingly.

"Eat. It might be hours before our next meal. I'm going to take you down to the beach. Would you like to fish?"

She broke off a piece of bacon. "Don't know. Never fished before. Do they smell?"

"Yes."

"If we don't fish, can we make love on the beach?"

"I do believe I've created a very naughty girl." He pushed his food around on his plate, feeling his body pulse with need. How did she do this with a look in her eyes or a few inappropriate words?

"We can do whatever you'd like. Make love, catch fish, it's our honeymoon and I want you to be happy. You pick what we do and I'll be satisfied." He watched her, mesmerized by the changing expressions on her face

"We only get one," she told him, smiling while she ate, her gaze shifting upward for a second.

What was in her mind, he craved to know but he wasn't going to ask. He would wait and see what transpired during the day. Truly, if she wanted to spend all day in bed, he wouldn't complain even though he did have an agenda. Perhaps it would wait until tomorrow.

"Cam..." She pushed hair away from her face.

"What?" He wanted to smile at the way she pursed her lips together then touched them with the tip of a finger.

"Are you afraid of anything?" For a moment she looked down but in less than a second, she met his gaze.

"Are you?" he asked, hoping she wouldn't notice he turned the question back to her.

"Cam." Her eyes narrowed.

"I'm afraid of your brother or I used to be. Now that we're married, I've no reason for terror where Flynt is concerned." He laughed thinking about the way that sounded. Before he wanted to court her, he couldn't say as much. Flynt was not the type of guy to put terror into anyone's mind.

"Be serious, please. What's your greatest fear?"

"If I give you an answer, will you return the favor?" He wasn't too sure about a greatest fear now that they were wed; he was terrified of losing her before that... He'd never thought about things like that before. Life was made to be lived at its fullest, and he didn't have time for apprehension.

"I believe so..." She strode to the window. "Let's go for a walk. Take me to the beach."

For a few moments, he didn't answer. Then, "As I said before, we can do anything you like. So, you either don't want me to tell you my greatest fear or you don't want to confide in me."

She whirled, shaking, "Perhaps both. I'm not too sure. Sometimes not knowing is safer than discovering the truth."

Meeting her by the window, he drew her into his arms. "I'm terrified of losing you. Now that we're wed, I don't think I can live without you." His whispers floated against tender flesh beneath her ear. In his embrace she shivered as if feeling the intensity of his voice as well as the heat from his words.

"We should leave soon. There could be another storm. There are clouds on the horizon" She pushed away from him.

"Not thunder clouds yet, though," he told her, studying the horizon. But she was right, they could grow into storm clouds.

Poignantly, he felt the loss, wondering what ideas entered her mind that had her pulling away from him so dramatically. He followed her through the house to the front door where he wrapped a shawl around her shoulders before grabbing a jacket for himself. As an afterthought, he picked up the blanket from the front porch so they would have somewhere to sit and perhaps make love.

Taking her hand in his, "The path is this way."

They strolled along the edge of the cliff then downward as the hill began to slant toward the ocean. Silence seemed normal, but he still had her last question rattling around in his head. He decided not to bring it up again, at least not right away.

When they reached the beach, they sat on a large piece of driftwood. She leaned into him, her head on his chest.

"Did you mean that—that you were afraid of losing me? That's your greatest fear." She pushed far enough away so she could see into his eyes. "You're not going to lose me."

He was nodding his head, smiling like a besotted fool. "Every word, my sweet treasure." But was she going to confide in him? Truly he didn't know if he cared enough to pursue the answer.

"I don't want to lose you either." She turned away from him, hiding her expression. Slipping her shoes off, she pulled her skirts to her knees and ran into the surf, giggling.

While the ocean water washed across her feet, she turned. "Join me or are you afraid of the cold water?" She ran away from the incoming surf then followed it as if daring the water to come back.

He couldn't help but smile at her obvious joy, unable to remember the last time he played in the surf. Content to watch, he sat with his hands folded in front of him.

"Are you coming?" With a huge grin she kicked water in the air, showering herself with droplets. "It's so cold."

He shrugged out of his jacket then his shoes before rolling up his pants. Still he knew if an unexpected wave hit, they'd both be drenched. Water already seeped through part of the fabric of her dress, where the layers touched the ocean. She would be cold soon, colder than she should be.

With a sigh and knowing that in a matter of minutes they would be thoroughly soaked, he ran toward her then swopped her into his arms, twirling her around and around. Slowing, his lips found hers for a soft brief kiss. He drew away, "We could make love on the beach. That's why I brought the blanket."

"And someone would find us." She laughed. "You would want to risk such a thing?"

"My beach is private. No one would dare intrude on our intimate moments." This was a pretty isolated part of the Scottish coastline. He would be shocked if anyone stumbled upon them. The danger excited him, even though she had a point. An interruption would not be pleasant.

With his tongue, he stroked the sensitive spot on her neck where her pulse beat rapidly. Her body trembled as she pushed closer to him as if giving her consent to his outrageous proposition. "Are you sure," she whispered softly, giving him more access to her neck. "I don't want anyone but you to see me without clothes on."

"Positive." He carried her to a spot well away from the tide and the possibilities that the ocean would interrupt them, which seemed more threatening than another person. "Is that a yes?"

"We'll get all sandy." Her fingers wound into this hair, pulling him closer, moistening her lips in anticipation of his kiss.

"That's why I brought the blanket," he told her continuing his ardent exploration of her neck while pushing her sleeves lower. His lips found hers, his hands settling on either side of her face. He kissed her again and again, lips, teeth, tongue continued over and over. "You taste so damn good, sweet, delicious, intoxicating."

"You knew at the house that..." She drew away, smiling at him. "I still don't think..."

"Hush, little one. Let me pleasure you. Out here in the open, trust me." He spread the blanket before bringing her to the ground with him.

"We're going to get naked?" Her voice wavered. "I just don't think... know if..."

"I'm sure we can figure this out without shedding all of our clothing if that's what you want."

"That might be the best idea," she agreed with him.

He rolled so she lay on top of him, his hand settling on her rear. "I don't think I'll ever get enough of you."

"Best you get out from under my sister now before I kill you."

~ * ~

Chelsea tried to push away but Cam held her close, his hand roaming up then down her back in a soothing motion. There was nothing sensual about his touch, still it was somehow reassuring in the face of adversity. "Stay calm," he whispered. "Let me handle this. As you well know, your brother has no authority over you."

She couldn't stop the shaking, which seemed to consume her body. This wasn't supposed to happen. They were supposed to have a honeymoon, a week to themselves. "Please."

Then he sat up, bringing her with him, holding her protectively close to him. "My wife."

It seemed Flynt didn't hear or chose to ignore Cam's words. His shoulders stiff and seeming to bristle with fury, Flynt stepped forward. "Chelsea, you're coming with me." He was reaching for her even as she pushed herself closer to Cam.

She was shaking her head in an attempt to tell her obstinate brother no, her heart in her throat while she tried to speak but no words seemed to clear her throat. Looking to Cam for support, she found he was smiling, a huge grin plastered on his face, yet the smile didn't appear in his eyes. She realized then that Cam was enjoying lauding his position over her brother.

"Chelsea is staying with her husband," he paused for a moment, seeming confident he would get his way, "Where she belongs, I might add, with her husband." His voice assumed a furious growl, the smile disappearing as quickly as it appeared.

"Liar," Flynt spoke softly. "You vowed to never marry at least not until you turned thirty-five. You're nowhere near that ripe old age." He turned his attention toward her again, "Chelsea, come with me," he repeated with more force this time. The two men bristled with raw energy each, vying for the prize.

Chelsea didn't like the feeling.

"Changed my mind about marrying. Knew I didn't want to live without Chelsea." He turned, blocking Flynt's view of her while adjusting Chelsea's clothing as well as tenderly pushing wayward strands of hair behind her ears. Then he whispered, "You've nothing to fear. Your brother will come to understand our position probably later than sooner, but he will understand then he will leave. I will make sure of it."

He rose then, pulling her to stand beside him, his arm wrapped protectively around her waist.

"When?" Flynt growled. "You had no time for a wedding."

"That's where you're wrong, old man." Cam seemed to want to goad him, perhaps even shame his friend, but Chelsea poked him in the ribs as if warning him against this new thought.

"We were married yesterday afternoon in a small church between Glasgow and my beach house. You should turn around and go home, Flynt. You're not wanted here. You should try to make your relationship with Broc's sister something more than tarnishing her reputation. What is it between you and Hope?"

"'Fraid I need some proof of your marriage." Flynt rocked on his heels, staring at her, his gazing boring into her. "I'm not going to stand by and see my little sister compromised without putting up a fight in her behalf."

Chelsea was sure her brother saw her flushed cheeks and the slight dishevelment of her hair. He knew what they were doing, about to do and he judged her, making untrue assumptions.

"Even if we aren't married, you've no rights where I'm concerned. You've had numerous affairs and probably as many mistresses. Why is it fine for you, a man, to have sex out of wedlock and not a woman," she paused for air, "not that this out of wedlock?" She held tightly to Cam's hand, never wanting to let it go.

The look on her brother's face almost made her regret the question as did Cam's hand tightening on her waist. "You probably should stay out of this argument, little one. This is best left to the men."

"Why, and let the men fight it out?" She wanted to stomp a foot at the arrogance but wisely kept her temper. "I'm just as much a part of this relationships as you are, and I've every right to speak my mind. Flynt, you need to leave. I would not be here if I was not Cam's lawful wife." Well, that was a small lie but it was worth the untruth to see the look on her brother's face.

"No, because a man does not get pregnant," Flynt's voice was barely controlled. It seemed to Chelsea her brother's temper was rising quickly. "A woman is vulnerable and needs a man's protection. Have you forgotten Bliss and her mistakes so soon?"

She felt the wrath of his words and understood what he was trying to tell her even though she whole-heartedly disagreed. Perhaps she was with child even as they spoke. Her heart skipped a beat, thinking about the possibilities. "I don't need or want your protection, Flynt MacTavish. I'm hoping I do carry Cam's child as does he. An heir for the new year would be nice, don't you think?"

"You've plenty of time to turn your horse around and return home," Cam said, placing a chaste kiss on Chelsea's forehead as if he wanted to antagonize her brother further. "You're not welcome here right now, particularly in your frame of mind."

"Show me the wedding certificate and I will do just that, turn around and leave the two of you alone to do what honeymooners do." It seemed Flynt challenged him, still disbelieving Cam. Yet in the alternative there was hope they would be left alone before the night ended. They did have the documents Flynt requested.

"When we return to the house, I'd be happy to do just that. As it is, Chels and I were enjoying the day. I'd rather not have my time with my new wife interrupted by something so inane as proving to you something I know to be true. Feel free to return by yourself. I'm sure you can scavenge something to eat while you wait. Make yourself at home." Cam finished with a smile before gesturing toward the beach house. He had the upper hand right now, and it didn't seem he would do Flynt's bidding any time soon.

Flynt stepped forward. The look in his eyes didn't bode well, but once again Cam blocked her from Flynt's view. "Don't even think of touching my wife or forcing her to go with you. She will not. Chelsea is mine for all eternity. Go away, Flynt. Seems you have things to answer to Broc for, regarding Hope. Look after your business and stop sticking your nose in everyone else's."

Furious with both men for ignoring the fact that she was also here in the present, she stepped forward, pushing herself around Cam, finding suddenly she didn't really know what to say. Then, with one finger she jabbed at Flynt's chest. "I'm married. You need to trust in that fact. Trust your sister. Trust your friend. We would never lie to you. Do as Cam asked, go away and leave us alone."

"Not in this, I can't," Flynt said, striding to the edge of the surf then back. "I want proof before I leave the two of you by yourselves." He paused then, "Why did you do this in secret?"

"Because of you, Flynt." Chelsea didn't believe for one second she needed to explain anything to her brother. "Because you are autocratic and won't see what is right in front of your face."

"Because we both thought you would have denied us," Cam said. "And, honestly, I couldn't wait the days necessary for a wedding. If it will make you feel better, I will host a celebration of our marriage when we return."

"A reception would be nice," Chelsea agreed, smiling and hoping her brother and husband would come to some type of agreement before this ended in fisticuffs.

"In town or at the summer home?" he asked her, as if he tried to ignore Flynt's presence.

"Doesn't matter." She turned to her brother. "I wanted Cam with all my heart, have for a very long time," Chelsea said, softly. "Please, do what Cam asked and go back to the house. We will follow in time. There is much to be said between all of us, but when you're satisfied, I hope you will return to the city and forget that you came here to drag me back by my hair if necessary."

Flynt ran his hands through his hair, leaving it disheveled and standing on end, clearly wishing he could have his way in this. "Against my better judgment, I'll do as you ask." Facing them, he slowly backed away then she saw his posterior as he quickly made his way up the hill. A few minutes later she heard the hoof beats as he left, whether to return to the house or go home, she couldn't know.

When the sounds of his retreat vanished, she sighed, relaxing into Cam's arms. "I didn't expect Flynt to come here. Didn't think he would leave either. Do you think we convinced him we're married?"

"Neither did I and I doubt if we've convinced Flynt of anything. I'd like to know which of your sisters betrayed our confidence," Cam said, his arms encircling her, securing her close.

"Does it really matter? Flynt would do anything in his means to get his way. Even though Grams is our chaperone, we all know the position is in name only. Flynt doesn't like to relinquish control over anything let alone something he feels so strongly about, and grams would never gainsay him."

"If you had to guess?" Cam asked seemingly out of curiosity. "Knowledge won't make me judge your sister."

She looked skyward then back to Cam, "Probably Daryl. Lacie is too strong willed. She'd like nothing better than to stare Flynt in the face and defy him if she thought she was right."

"Should we make love or walk to the house for another confrontation?" Cam eyed the blanket he laid out not too long ago.

"The mood has vanished," she spoke softly, wishing Flynt had never shown up and ruined this glorious day. "Perhaps we should walk for a little while and allow Flynt's mood to cool somewhat. On the other hand, if we want him to leave, it might be best to confront him before it gets too dark for him to return to the city."

"Wouldn't want company overnight. I've plans and they don't include your brother." Cam ran his hands through his hair, clearly frustrated. "By the time we get to the house, it most likely will be too late for him to ride back to Glasgow."

Cam retrieved the blanket before joining her. For a while they walked along the path leading from the house. She didn't want to return, didn't want to see her brother again. Depressed and out of sorts, she leaned her head against Cam, closing her eyes as if that small gesture would make everything go away.

"I didn't think anything would happen to ruin this day. It started on such a bright note after the storm. I felt as if the air was clear and nothing could ever go wrong for us." She inhaled a long deep breath, moisture clogging her throat.

"I promise you, we'll get the ambiance back. Tonight, we can stargaze if there is no cloud cover. I'll show you some constellations and you won't believe how brilliant the stars are out here away from the brightness of the city." He pulled her closer, seeming to sense the depression that had come upon her with the arrival of her brother.

"I'd like to look at stars with you, see into the universe. I don't understand how you hid your profession from everyone. Does Flynt know what you do, or any of the bad boys?"

"Never tried to hide anything and it's not so much a profession as a calling. I didn't make my fortune from astronomy. Most of what I do at the university is volunteer lectures. Flynt knows as do the others."

She wondered what he did do to make money but decided it didn't really matter to her. If he were dirt poor, she would still love him with all her heart, and she would defy Flynt to be with him. The realization gave her reason to smile, thinking if that were true, Flynt would probably drag her away. That ploy would never work because she'd always run back to Cam. She was his after all and he was hers.

She was crazy for him.

"What wicked thought is putting a silly smile on your face?" Cam asked, turning her and before she could answer, his lips brushed across hers, distracting her.

He deepened the kiss, sending waves of wonderful, enchanting pleasure pulsing though her, raw and delectable energy. If he kept this up, she'd let him do anything right here on top of the cliffs where any passerby, including her brother, would be able to watch.

He drew away, running his thumb along her bottom lip, his eyes darkening with desire. "Well?"

For a moment she looked down, "I..." She smiled at him again but stopped herself from telling him she loved him. The feeling was too rare and too new for her to blurt out.

"I?" he queried, brushing his lips lightly across hers again, teasing her with teeth and tongue.

"If you were dirt poor, I would still marry you. If Flynt tried to drag me home, I'd run right back to you. Wealth makes no matter to me." She held her breath, wondering what his answer to this new information would be.

"You unman me, yet I would have always prayed my wife would feel that way. Does that mean you love me?" He pushed for something she didn't want to give just yet.

"Do you love me?" Challenging him, she had second thoughts when his brows drew together while the lines in forehead deepened. As a young child she learned it was never a prudent idea to challenge her brother. Flynt and Cam were so much the same in too many ways to count.

He cleared his throat as if to answer, gently tracing her jawline with a calloused fingertip. Something else she wondered about. What did he do to put callouses on his hands?

"I believe in romance and the love espoused in poetry. Don't think I've ever been loved or in love. Understand, neither of my parents could possibly have loved me because it wouldn't have been so easy for them to leave me for such extended periods of time. I don't really know if two people can love each other or if that type of love even exists."

Impossible to keep the disappointment from her expression, she turned away until she could school her features. Then, "I suppose you're right. I don't know what love feels like either. Until now, I always thought my parents loved their children, but even if they did, I was too young when they died to know what love feels like, what it looks like. How do two people react to each other when they are in love? Perhaps what we feel for each other is just lust."

"I wouldn't want to lie to you and say the words if they weren't true. What I do know is that I don't think I can live without you by my side. You've found a way to become part of me, and I do believe you have stolen a piece of my heart. When I'm with you, I feel a magic that can't be explained." His words wavered, ripping through her soul.

"Do you think we'll ever understand what love feels like?" she asked as he wrapped his arms around her, securing her against him.

"Anything is possible. We should get back to the house. I've a feeling we've made Flynt wait long enough."

No words were said between them on the walk back. She was sure now Flynt would most likely stay the night just to be obdurate. He wouldn't like being proved wrong, and his stubborn nature would most assuredly kick in as soon as he witnessed the documents.

"I suppose our night of stargazing will have to be put off," she said as they approached the front porch and Flynt was sitting on the porch swing, a glass of beer in hand, waiting for them.

"Took your sweet time getting here," he said as they stepped onto the porch. "You two do that on purpose?"

Cam poured wine into the two empty glasses sitting on the tray before handing one to her. He helped her with her shawl, placing it on the coat stand inside before returning to the porch. "Here's to our marriage." He held up the glass, waiting for confirmation.

Flynt's scowl was plastered firmly on his face, but he held his glass up in what seemed to be a reluctant salute to the newlyweds.

"Where's the proof?" Flynt asked, setting his glass on the table.

Slowly Cam sipped the wine before turning into the house. A few minutes later he returned with a document then handed the papers to Flynt. Cam stepped back, arms crossed over his chest and with more patience than Chelsea ever remembered seeing. He waited as Flynt perused the marriage certificate, seeming to read every word.

Begrudgingly, he handed the paper to Cam. "Take care of my sister or you'll have me to answer to. Make her happy and I'll let you live to breathe another day."

"I intend to." Cam rocked back on his heels, his hands now behind his back. "Suppose you're staying the night."

"No reason to ride home in the dark. See you brought your cook. What's for dinner?" Flynt lifted his glass to his lips.

"Fish, I suppose. Chels and I will be taking our meal on the third-floor balcony. We're stargazing tonight since it's a clear warm night. Don't want company, but you're welcome to any of the bedrooms on the first floor."

Chelsea was pleased as well as amazed at Cam's generosity. She was sure his pleasantness was taking everything within him. Then he turned offering her his arm. "Shall we go upstairs to the top of the house?" He grinned at her, one eyebrow rising in question.

"I'd love to stargaze with you." She accepted his arm, walking outside in order to access the steps to the top of the house.

"May I?" He took the glass from her hand so she could pick up her skirts.

"What? No blindfold tonight?" she asked, wanting to laugh at the memory as well as her impatience from their wedding night.

"Eyes wide open now that you're experienced and no longer a virgin. I plan on learning everything about you, and how I can pleasure you in so many different ways, I'll have you begging me for more. What you enjoy and what you do not but tonight is different."

"How so?" She loved him when he wanted to share his knowledge with her. Adored the look on his face when he taught her new things about life and love.

"Well, you'll just have to use some of that patience you're not so famous for and wait." He chuckled softly as he paused for her to ascend the last few steps.

Her breath caught in her throat at the sight in front of her. She looked at him then turned back to the scene. "We're going to sleep here too? I just thought..."

"Is that alright with you?"

"Do you do this often?" The huge bed sat in the middle of the deck, a sturdy cover over the bed would protect them from the elements in case of rain. Large pillows had been set at the head of the bed while a thick quilt covered it.

"When the weather is nice as it is tonight, I sleep up here. I can't wait to share this with you. It's like sleeping outdoors in the woods but with all the amenities of home. Did you and your sisters ever do that?"

"No, doubt if something like that would have been allowed and while we pushed some rules, we weren't that bold."

"For a moment I forgot rules are different for boys and girls," Cam said thoughtfully.

"We have dinner I see." She felt the need to change the subject to something that wouldn't start an argument. Rules shouldn't be different, but she was forced to agree that they were.

"As well as more wine. If I ring the bell by the bedside..."

"Your cook or servant will appear out of nowhere." She wondered where the man would be waiting. Somewhere close because they'd have to be able to hear the bell."

"Not out of nowhere. We've more than enough food for the evening. I've ordered another bottle of wine to appear in one hour." He brought her to the railing overlooking the ocean where she stood that first night. "Look at the stars. It's not even dark yet and they glimmer so brightly. This will truly be an amazing evening."

Suddenly the sound of carriages and horses reverberated through the air.

"What? What is that?"

Together they turned their attention to the side of the house. A small carriage with the MacTavish shield on it appeared then two men on horseback behind the vehicle.

"My sisters? What could they possible be doing here and at this hour?" Chelsea questioned, appalled at the thought that once again their privacy was being invaded. Their honeymoon would be denied them. "We don't have to be polite and go see them. We both ken why they are here."

"And with the other bad boys..."

"Do you think Flynt organized this?" she asked, her hand above her heart. "I don't want to see them. I choose to stay here and let Flynt run interference. The only conversations I want tonight are with you," she paused. "Do you truly believe Flynt would do that?"

"I've no idea what he will do now that he has proof that our marriage is legal. What we do know, however, is that he won't send anyone home." Cam spoke through gritted teeth, "but I agree with you. We're not going downstairs. This is our magic time and I don't want to share you with anyone. If necessary, explanations can be made tomorrow and not a moment before."

"And I don't want to share you either." Chelsea said, watching as the carriage and horses were delivered to the stables and the four people strode purposefully to the house.

"Do you think they'll trust Flynt's words or will they seek us out?"

he asked, holding her close, his hand tightening on her waist. "I'm not going to worry about any of this. Let's eat and by the time we finish, the stars will be brilliant." He lifted his broad shoulders in a manly shrug, a quirky smile on his face. "By then we'll know if anyone is going to invade our privacy."

"If anyone comes to see us, we'll shoo them away." She laughed while they ate. Holding her glass near her lips, she watched him watching her. His smile brought warmth to her heart. Recalling everything he did with her last night sent another surge of heat through her.

"Do you want me as much as I want you?" he queried softly while he stroked the sensitive flesh beneath her ear. "The blush on your beautiful face makes me wonder what you're thinking about."

"More." She couldn't help herself, the one word shivered with passion. Then, "I need you more."

"That's impossible." He leaned back on an elbow, his straight white teeth showing.

At the way he looked at her, her breath caught in her throat. "No, Cam, perhaps we should look at those stars before we do something else or we get interrupted." She rose, striding to the railing.

Earlier the sun had vanished beneath the ocean. The sky was dark except for the brilliant lights dotting the sky. A cool breeze wafted off the ocean.

Cam held her close with one hand then waving the other at the night stars. "This is one of my passions. Not just stargazing but learning about the universe. I want to learn everything I can about those beautiful and amazing lights we are looking at now as well as what lies beyond them. Have you ever wondered if there is life out there?"

She leaned into him, relishing the warmth of his hard body in opposition to hers. "I don't know what to say. I used to think the stars were pretty sparkles in the sky, but you've changed the way I see them. And no, I've never thought beyond what's on earth. Thinking about the universe and other life forms seems so abstract to me."

He squeezed her waist then, setting his glass on the railing he pointed to the north. "The brightest star there," he paused, "is the north star, also called Polaris. Sailors use it during the night to navigate. If not for the stars, ships captains would not know what direction they are traveling when it is dark."

"I think I see it," she said, squinting and hoping she really did see the star he was pointing at.

"Very good, once you find Polaris you can find other grouping of stars, constellations that revolve around it. They all seem to spiral out from the center."

"Really." She was in awe of Cam and his knowledge, understanding what he shared tonight was just a tiny bit of what he knew.

"Just a few tonight, look downward from Polaris and you should be able to see four stars that look like a cup with three more that make a handle."

"I see it." She clapped her hands together, excited by the prospect of becoming part of Cam's world.

"That constellation has other names too: Ursa Major, Big Bear and Big Dipper." When they looked at each other, he kissed her softly, brushing his lips across hers. "I'm not boring you, am I?"

"Of course not." She moistened her lips, wishing for another kiss or one that would touch her soul.

"We could always do something else."

"Do you want to do something else?" She was surprised and disappointed as well at his words.

"Later, we'll do other things later."

He continued then, showing her the constellations surrounding Polaris. He showed her Cassiopeia the queen also circling around Polaris. There were others too; the Pleiades and Taurus the bull.

"You can tell time by the position of Ursa Major."

She felt as If she absorbed so much information, "But only if it's dark outside."

"What am I going to do during the day?" Chelsea wasn't sure if he would have an answer for that, but at this point nothing would surprise her.

"The sun, you can use the sun to tell time during the day or at least approximate time. Not as good as looking at a watch but it still works."

"Really." She turned her attention back to the sky. "A shooting star." She pointed, thrilled to see one.

"Did you make a wish?" he asked, his voice soft.

"Absolutely."

She stood in front of him now, his arms wrapped around her. "What you saw is not really a star falling from the sky."

"What is it then?" Her curiosity grew.

"A large rock falling through the sky and burning up in the heat of earth's atmosphere as it enters." He turned her so he could look into her eyes, laughing at her shocked expression. "Enough." He handed her their glasses then swept her into his arms carrying her to the bed. After he set her on the bed, he placed the crystals on the bedside table.

"We're going to make love now." He straddled her, kissing her, his hands on her face holding her still. "Would you like that?"

"Yes," she breathed out in a long slow whisper, the anticipation intense.

~ * ~

"Flynt told us the marriage is legal and binding," Donal said. "You need to leave this crazy notion you concocted alone."

"It doesn't matter what Flynt told us; I want to talk to Chelsea. She's my sister. I need to find out first-hand what she really thinks and feels." Daryl was beside herself with worry, walking back and forth in the parlor. Lacie helped Cam plan everything and she knew exactly how impetuous her little sister could be. This could have been something gone terribly awry, something Chelsea couldn't get out of without help.

"You really want to go up there and interrupt them?" Donal questioned. "Not a good idea, if you ask me. They could be doing something very intimate and private. Something you shouldn't witness."

"Not asking you. If you don't want to come with me, you certainly don't have to." She was angry now, her purpose clear to her but this self-appointed guardian she picked up accidentally wanted to stand in her way. He wasn't going to even if he believed it to be in her best interest.

She picked up her skirts striding out the front door. His footsteps pounded behind her.

With a hand on her arm, Donal stopped her. "Ach lass, you might not want to intrude. Seems to be a bit of a private sanctuary up there, romantic and all, the stars and the moon shining brightly, meant for sweet romance and love making."

"What would you know about romance?" she asked, suddenly aware he must know a lot more than she did. "You keep a mistress. That's hardly romantic." She challenged him, still not too sure of herself or what he was talking about.

Not answering the question, he stoically walked beside her until they reached the bottom of the steps where he stopped her again. She turned with an impatient shrug, questioning him without words.

"What are you going to do when you get up there and find them in the throes of one of the most basic but intimate acts in nature, something that shouldn't have human witnesses?" he asked, his voice stern and intimidating.

She gasped, thinking he was saying strange things to her. Starting up the steps again, he followed once more. Half way...

"Cam..." Her sister's voice rang out, settling around her, veiling her thoughts.

Daryl picked up her skirts, intent on racing up the steps. "You can't go there. You'll regret it if you do. They will regret it and your sister won't forgive you for the longest time." Donal's warning seemed to give her pause.

Then, "No. She's in trouble. I ken it. That was a scream."

"That was a cry of passion and those other sounds you're hearing," he paused, looking upward, "those are sounds a woman makes when she's being sweetly pleasured."

"I don't have any idea what you're talking about," she said indignantly, her hands on her hips. Yet he made her question her intentions, unsure now what she should do. If Chelsea needed her, she meant to be there for her.

"Not now but you will in a few minutes." Donal braced his hands on either side of her head. "I'm going to kiss you now and give you some idea where those tiny little breathy sounds are coming from and what they might mean."

She moistened her lips, staring at him, thinking he had gone a wee bit crazy, but she did want him to kiss her, remembered the last kiss and the way it made her feel inside. Then his lips brushed hers, gently at first, soft, moist then wet and so very hot she felt as if she burned. She inhaled quickly as his tongue danced across her lips before insinuating itself into her mouth. His taste was exquisite a bit of brandy and something indefinable, something very male. "Donal," she whispered into his mouth just as their tongues met and danced together.

"Yes, lass, do you like this or should I stop?"

"Don't stop, whatever you do, don't stop" she sighed softly, wishing these sweet sensations would never cease. "I don't think I can stay upright."

He laughed then lightly bit her lip before sucking the soft flesh into his mouth only to lave and nibble. Holding her against the wall, he pushed his leg between hers, helping her stand.

"Sweet, so delicious, raw and primal." His hand slipped to her waist then up her ribcage, resting just beneath her breast.

She felt his hand curve around her breast then brush across her fabric covered nipple. Feelings of heat and pleasure ripped through her, danced through her body. When his lips closed over her bared nipple, she'd never noticed his fingers unfastening her bodice. A tiny mew flitted from her as her hips seemed to move against him and with him as well.

"Donal," she gasped as small throaty sounds from her lips seemed to make him smile. Her head fell against the side of the house giving him accesses to her neck then lower until his teeth tugged on her nipple again, dancing attendance.

"Ach, lass, what you do to me. I've never felt anything like this or tasted anyone so sweet as yourself. Tell me to stop, Daryl. Don't believe I can end this unless I hear the words."

She couldn't answer, in any case didn't want to tell him no. More than ever, she needed him to do more and more. "I don't even care that you're looking at me," she whispered. "I want to look at you. I want to see you without any clothing on."

"Do you believe me now, lass?" he asked. "Have you heard the sounds coming from your lips? It's all good up the stairs."

Daryl didn't have any idea what he was talking about. Her mind had gone blank. Now all she could do was feel and react to the wondrous, amazing things he was doing. The glide of his hand along her leg sent more heat to parts of her she'd never really thought of before.

"Don't know what you're asking me."

"This is some of what your sister and her husband are doing. Would you like someone to intrude on us?"

"You're, you're touching me..."

"Intimately, that I am, lass. Do you love this as much as I do?"

"I'm so hot, and wet and... Donal do something." Her hips were moving against him and she needed something she couldn't define. In any case she was beyond rational thought.

"That's your body telling both of us you're ready for me to be inside you, but I'm not going to come inside you tonight. No, another time," he said softly, his whispers against her ear.

Then a wave of sweetly painful pleasure consumed her body, followed by more spasms, uncontrollable delicious waves of delight, agony and bliss all wrapped into one feeling. The sensations went on and on. "Donal, please..." She fell against him, her body so spent she couldn't move, and she was thankful he was holding her.

Then it seemed he was soothing her, whispering nonsense to her and running his hands up and down her sides. Slowly her body was calming, no longer pulsing with a craving she didn't understand.

"Daryl, are you alright?" He held her head, in one large hand.

She pressed her cheek against the warmth of his hand. "What did we just do?"

"Nothing to worry about," he told her, his voice hardening. "Nothing at all."

"Didn't seem like nothing to me." Her smile wavered as he brushed a soft kiss across her lips.

"How old are you, lass?"

She bristled at his words, beginning to understand things. "Nearly eighteen."

"You should shoot me now."

Chapter Seven

"What the devil are we doing here?" Cam asked as he searched the faces of his friends. If given the choice, he'd rather be home with his Chelsea, not here in Flynt's third floor.

"Appears we're playing cards and drinking." Donal lifted a dark brow along with his glass. "What did you think we were doing?"

Cam searched his mind for a wry comeback but couldn't think of anything funny to say.

Flynt chuckled, "You're missing your wife and it's only been a few hours since you left her. She's got you tied up in knots. After a year you'll be happy to get some free time away from home with the bad boys."

"Don't see why they need a girls' night out," Broc tossed in his cards. "Can't stop thinking about Bliss and the twins. If he's anything like me, it will take one hell of a lot more time than one year to untie the knots I feel when she's not with me."

"Left them with Grams again, did you?" Flynt asked, seeming amused once more. "Must be hard to have both a wife and two children. Never bargained for that, two babies in one shot. Keep you on your toes, do they?"

"Best thing that ever happened to me." Broc picked up the new cards that were dealt, narrowing his eyes as he looked over the top at the other men.

"How long are we supposed to wait for the girls to come here? That was the plan wasn't it?" Cam thumbed through his cards. For some reason his gut churned with worry. This wasn't something he approved of but Chelsea insisted, leaving him with a quick kiss to his forehead then she told him, don't worry too much. Everything will be just fine. You'll see. What could possibly go wrong?

"Bliss told me they would send word when they were finished

eating," Broc said. "Thought we were to meet them at the restaurant."

"They changed their minds, "Donal said. "Daryl told me they were going to walk home when they finished."

"Just doesn't sit right. Arie told me he would put a man to watch them in the restaurant but he's been distracted of late," Cam thought about his words. Now he depended on the man he'd been jealous of for so long. What if Arie forgot and something happened to Chelsea?

There had been rumors at the university that Leod was acting strange and saying even stranger things. Leod lusted after Chelsea, and he didn't know how far the man would go to have her. To top that off, Leod hated him. Cam knew revenge could always be sweet. Every instinct Cam possessed cried out that he was not where he needed to be. Even the hairs on the back of his neck stood on end.

"I can't do this." He slammed his cards on the table. Standing, he strode the length of the room, remembering the night he first kissed Chelsea. He stepped quickly out of the room and down the hallway to the servant quarters where she chose to hide from him.

Thoughts of that night made him smile. After all, that evening changed his life for the better as well as forever. After pushing the door open and stepping inside, he inhaled deep and long. Now something threatened his happiness, their happiness. His fists tightening, he felt the sensation bone deep.

Something was threatening Chelsea and he wasn't beside her to help.

He leaned against the wall, closing his eyes while reminiscing about the promise he made to Chels. *I won't interrupt your dinner for any reason or feeling of doom I might have.*

She made him repeat the words several times after she told him how she had survived all by herself for almost nineteen years, no one protecting her or following her around. She could survive one night out with her sisters. True, Flynt had protected her somewhat, but he really hadn't paid much attention to any of his sisters. The girls ran the countryside, exploring and going pretty much anywhere they pleased, doing as they wanted.

From Chelsea's words she'd told him how she rode over the MacTavish estate by herself as well as with her sisters. One thing for sure, she was confident of her abilities, but what she never considered was how tiny she was and exactly how ill prepared for an encounter with a man, the wrong man, she was. She'd bested him several times, but only because he allowed it. Now, he wished he'd never given her that kind of confidence.

"Hey, you going to mope around here the rest of the night or play cards?" Broc knocked on the door. "What are you doing down here anyway?"

"Don't want to lose any more money. Tempted to ride to the restaurant and wait outside. Don't trust Arie. His head's not on straight right now." That was true. Arie wouldn't hurt anyone, least of all Chelsea, but for the last few weeks the sultan had been enamored of this little red head he bought at an exclusive brothel down by the river.

"Perhaps we should all do that. Broc's in a dither and for some reason I don't understand Donal isn't any better than the two of you," Flynt said. "Didn't know until now that Donal is a bit enamored of Daryl. Guess there's one more of my sisters that's going to get involved with a bad boy."

"You're not concerned about Hope?" Cam was having a difficult time believing Flynt was the only one besides Leslie who didn't appear apprehensive.

Flynt's heavy sigh followed by his words, "I'm more than anxious about Hope. She's barely been outside these four walls since she arrived almost a year ago. Before that she lived in a harem. What does she know about men and nefarious things transpiring in the outside world? I promised her, however, I would not do anything stupid that might embarrass her."

"Then we should..."

With a wave of his hand Flynt cut him off. "No, we have to trust them. We all know they are level headed and capable women."

"Isn't that the total opposite of the way you thought for the last year and a half or perhaps more?" Where Chels had been involved, Cam had spent so much time avoiding Flynt and trying to find a way around his autocratic ways, he found himself in disbelief now.

With a masculine shrug and wry smile, "I was wrong. Thought I was doing what was right for my sisters. Instead I messed things up." He shot a look at Donal who was just making his way into the parlor. "Doesn't mean I won't make your life difficult if you hurt Daryl in any way, but I intend to behave differently from now on. Hope has played a major part in my rehabilitation."

Taken aback by the admission, Cam wasn't sure how to reply. Finally, "I don't believe we are wrong in our suspicions this time. Something is happening to Chelsea tonight. I feel it in my gut and know it just as clearly as I inhale each breath of air. She needs me and they need us because somehow all the girls are involved."

"You can't know that," Flynt spoke slowly, seemingly unconcerned despite the frown lines on his face. "Come back to the room, drink, play cards if you want or mope around the room but we can't forego our promises. If we do, we'll regret the moment that happens."

"Believe we'll have to atone this decision if we decide to forego our promises. I'll try to keep my mind off Chels." He didn't want to admit it to his friends but there was no way he could stop thinking of his wife and what might be happening to her as he played cards, pretending to remain pleased with her demands.

They had only been married one month, but he was sure she carried his child. Her body had changed in subtle ways. Now he was protecting a wife as well as a baby. He wasn't about to take chances with their lives but here he was, doing that very thing, playing cards and drinking.

Feeling as if either one was in danger left him short of breath. At this moment he was holed up in his brother-in-law's house frittering away his time as if he didn't have any responsibilities.

"Cam? You coming?" Flynt poked his head back inside the door.

"You're enjoying this aren't you?"

"No," he paused, "well, a little," Flynt chuckled.

Brooding in the servant quarters even if this room wasn't in the same house wouldn't help Chels if she needed him anymore than playing cards with the bad boys would help her. There were only two bad boys left, Donal and Leslie, and he had a feeling Donal wasn't going to be one for much longer. Something happened between Daryl and Donal at the beach house, he was sure.

He didn't know what but the way they looked at each other was remarkably different.

Cam followed Flynt back to the card room. He poured himself a brandy before sitting on a chair absorbed in his thoughts.

Broc sat beside him. "I don't like Bliss away from me but what do you think is happening to Chelsea. It's a restaurant and dinner. What could possibly go wrong?"

"Don't know. Probably nothing." He sipped his drink, thinking of everything that could go wrong if someone planned well. Gossip at the university led him to believe Leod sought some sort of revenge. He would have thought the vengeance would be directed at him, not Chels, but what better way to hurt him than to do something to his wife?

"I'm willing to listen."

"Been some talk around my office. Before I courted Chels, there were others. Leod, one of my colleagues, showed a bit of interest in her. I wasn't worried about him at the time."

"So why now?"

"Fletcher Donovan, his uncle."

"I've heard of him, none of it good," Broc said, thoughtfully tapping his glass with a finger.

"Same here," Cam said.

"Think there's more to be said on the subject."

"No proof, just hearsay, but talk has it that Fletcher sold his daughter to a certain exclusive brothel. He had gambling debts that the proceeds covered," Cam paused thoughtfully. "I believe the woman he sold is the same woman Arie purchased from the brothel for himself."

"Really." Flynt joined the conversation seeming to forget about the on-going card game.

"That's why he's been distant the last few weeks. Seems the woman isn't willing and Arie has the good sense not to force the issue but not the good sense to let her go." Cam strode around the room, the feelings of unease growing. He set his glass down, thinking once more he should go after Chelsea. He gulped a lungful of air before deciding to stay put for a little while longer. Seconds ticking by seemed like hours to Cam as he fidgeted with his drink.

"So, why doesn't Arie release her?" Broc asked.

Cam shrugged, looking at the clock, which just chimed eight times. With each chime, he shuddered, his nerves frayed. "Where would she go?

Chelsea told me a lot of this. Mind you, she still sees Arie and as much as I dislike the fact, they confide in each other."

"You've nothing to be jealous of," Flynt said with a chuckle. "Seems when my little sisters fall in love they fall hard and fast. Chelsea doesn't have eyes for anyone but you. Back to my question, why doesn't Arie let her leave?"

"Seems she doesn't have any place to go except back to her mother's home and from everything I've heard, that woman has as much to do with the sale as her uncle." Cam was disgusted with the thought anyone could sell or purchase a woman, let alone kidnap his niece and barter her to a whorehouse for the best price.

On the other hand, he didn't see how Chels condoned what Arie did. Thinking of this in a different light, Arie would probably treat the woman with more respect than she would have received in the brothel. Perhaps he needed to overlook the details or the kidnapping and concentrate on his life and what was happening to his wife.

"So, that's why Arie's been distracted," Donal said, sitting down beside them. "He should be here to explain himself."

"Don't understand why any of us has to explain ourselves or our actions to each other. It's his life and he was brought up with different cultural values. What's strange is that Fletcher felt no qualms at selling his niece," Leslie said, joining the conversation then with a shrug and a smirk, "The men treat women differently in the Ottoman Empire."

"I don't think she is really his niece," Donal said.

Cam spun on a heel. "I'm going to find Chels and bring her home. They said they would come here when they finished with dinner. Plenty of time has passed for them to eat and walk the half-mile home. Anyone who wants to join me is welcome. Someone should stay here though in case they arrive before we find them." He strode from the room and to the stables, not waiting for anyone to follow.

When he saddled his horse, to his surprise both Leslie and Donal were beside him. It seemed Flynt and Broc chose to stay put.

"Got a vested interest, in Daryl," Donal said, his voice raw. "She reacts to things before she thinks. If you're worried then I suppose we should all be anxious. Going after her seems prudent."

Cam searched Leslie's face for some of the same. "Lacie's too young for me right now, but I'm hoping she's still around in another year or so. She caught my interest a long time ago, and I hope she feels the same way I do."

"Let's go then."

The hooves of their horses pummeled the cobblestone streets. Breezes off the river cooled the night air to a pleasant temperature. He saw no one as they rode through the city to the tiny restaurant he first took Chelsea to over a month ago. That night seemed a very long time in the past.

They pulled up in front of the small eatery, tethering the horses in front. Cam strode through the door, fists clenched at his sides, searching the room for the girls.

"Can I help you, sir?"

"Earlier there was a group of women. I don't see them now. Can you tell me when they left?" Once again, Cam's gut churned with apprehension. Only one logical path existed between this place and Flynt's townhouse. They did not pass the girls.

"Perhaps thirty minutes ago. I'm not sure."

"Did they walk or take a carriage?" Leslie asked as he too looked over the eating area.

"I heard them speaking of walking, but they might have changed their minds because one of them said the husbands wouldn't be pleased with the fact they might walk home in the dark." The waiter turned, setting the table in front of him.

"They couldn't have walked." Cam breathed in a deep sigh of relief as well as pleasure that they made a safe decision and not an impetuous one. "We didn't see them." Perhaps his worry had no basis.

"True, if they walked, we would have seen them," Donal agreed with Cam.

"Thank God, this ride was unnecessary. I'm sure we'll find them safe at the house and laughing at us for all our manly concerns," Leslie said.

"I hope that's true." Cam still had the gut feeling of danger and he knew well enough that just because they took a carriage instead of walking, didn't mean they arrived safely at their destination.

"We've no proof anything happened. Let's retrace our path and proceed from there," Donall said, seeming as worried as Cam.

Cam wanted to see inside Chelsea's head. It seemed he felt her terror, saw the sheen of anxiety in her beautiful eyes. What the hell happened to her? Yet he could do nothing more than return to Flynt's home.

The return ride was somber. Cam searched the sidewalks for possible clues to Chelsea's whereabouts. Beyond any possible doubt and without confirmation of the fact he knew Leod kidnapped her. With Fletcher's aide he might well sell Chelsea to a whorehouse. What better revenge?

A light cloth on the ground caught his attention. Stopping his horse, he dismounted. "Chels' shawl," he murmured, his heart stopping. With renewed purpose, he continued his search. He found nothing further and had no idea in which direction she could have been taken.

"You should come back to the house." Leslie sat his horse in front of him. "We need a plan and we need to get Arie."

"Arie?"

"If Fletcher is involved, Leod might well approach the same brothel his uncle used to sell his niece."

"Then you no longer doubt she's been taken." Cam had no misgivings, but he did need the support of the others.

"I don't. The question remains is whether or not all of them were taken," Leslie said, his words sounding urgent now that the scenario might involve Lacie.

"You're right. Every instinct in my body cries out to race forward and find her, but I've no idea where she is." He wondered if he was repeating himself or the words were echoes in his mind.

Too many minutes later, Cam and Leslie along with Donal stood in the parlor of the MacTavish townhouse. Apparently, Arie had arrived before them. He sipped brandy with the other bad boys. Bliss was there, her husband standing behind her, his hands resting protectively on her shoulders. Hope sat in front of Flynt as well.

"We should try the brothel where I bought Alison," Arie began, standing while he set his glass on a side table. "We should hurry."

"Where are Lacie and Daryl?" Leslie asked, his voice cracking with seeming apprehension.

"They tried to follow the carriage," Bliss swallowed hard, wiping tears from her cheeks. "They should have either found Chelsea or returned. They promised not to go too far or take any chances trying to rescue her."

"How long ago?" Cam asked.

"Seems like hours," Bliss said, setting her hands on her lap, fingers enfolded together.

"How long?" Cam persisted. The need to know everything circumvented all rational thought.

"Maybe an hour."

"Do you have an idea the direction they took?" Donal asked, pacing the room, his gaze riveted on the door as if that would make the girls appear.

Bliss was shaking her head and sobbing. "I've no idea. My sisters should be back by now." She turned to Arie. "We'll stay here and wait for Lacie and Daryl. Please go do what you do best, what sultans do, you know. If you have to, please buy her back."

Flynt ordered his man to saddle a horse for the rest of them and bring them around to the front.

"You should take a carriage," Arie said. "If we find the girls, we don't know what their condition will be. I'll talk to Victor and have him send my men to visit all the major brothels in town. He's waiting outside the door. He knows how to be discreet."

Flynt nodded to his man who stepped out the door to do his bidding.

"Flynt, drive the carriage and tie your horse to the back," Cam directed. "Arie, you lead the way." A few weeks ago, Cam would never have guessed he would have to rely on the sultan for his help. Now, he thanked God for Arie's unique abilities and his friendship with Chelsea. If not for that he didn't know what would happen.

The ride to the brothel seemed to Cam to take hours, but when they strode up the steps united in what they meant to accomplish, he felt a tiny measure of hope. His ragged breath and snapping nerves didn't help him control his anger though.

The madam appeared, a smile gracing her features hand held out in polite greeting. "What can I do for you gentleman?" Then it seemed the sultan caught her attention. Her voice dripping sugar, she spoke, "Arie, you've returned. I pray everything goes well with your purchase of a few weeks ago. What can I do for you tonight?"

"All is fine. I'm looking to make another purchase, perhaps three if the price is right."

Cam wanted to race through the house, throwing open doors to discover Chels' room. Arie seemed to understand the emotions driving him and placed a hand on his shoulder to stop him.

"There are guards. You would be stopped and either issued outside or restrained in a room if you did what is in your head. Trust my judgment in these matters and all will turn out the way you want."

"Are you looking for a particular type of woman?" she asked. "Another redhead perhaps?"

"No, the women who arrived tonight. Probably only a few minutes ago." Arie's voice took on a hard edge.

"Ah, she is not for sale that one. There have been promises made and invitations sent. It was all done earlier this afternoon in lieu of her arrival." The madam looked over her shoulder as if protecting herself.

"Only one? We were looking for three possibly," Cam spoke quickly, his body tensing with apprehension and fear, sweat dripping down the sides of his face while he clenched his fist.

"Just one girl?" Arie asked speculation now in his tone. "You only have one woman and she is not for sale. I can make you an offer you won't be able to resist or refuse. Why isn't she for sale? I thought we had a special understanding."

"We only have one lady and at the moment, she is not for sale. I purchased her from a certain gentleman I've done business with before and would like to make my money as well as some profit back before I let her go, even to you. Your last purchase cost me a great deal of money, and I'm not willing to forego my own profits."

Cam felt an urgent need to learn the name of the woman even though he was certain he knew. While he wanted to hear his wife's name on the madam's lips, he knew Chelsea would be the name he heard.

"If I doubled the purchase price?" Arie queried. "Would you be more interested? This woman is not suitable for the profession here nor could she ever be suitable for a man's special needs."

Cam understood Arie would somehow get his money back. Arie wasn't the type of man to take anything for granted or lose money in the purchase of a woman. Arie had his ways and if the madam refused to sell, she would find her brothel would no longer make a profit. Then there were worse things he could do to this woman who rebuffed him.

"Not even a doubling would sway me this time." She took Arie by the arm, strolling to a more private section of the main room their heads bent close together.

Cam tried to hear the spoken words but he could only catch a few, understanding enough to know there were extenuating circumstances. Nothing Fletcher could do to the madam would come close to the forces Arie could bring down upon her if coerced.

None of this made sense.

Arm and arm the pair returned after a while, a grim expression on Arie's face and a smile on the madam's.

"We need to leave now," he told the men before he gallantly kissed the top of the madam's hand.

"No!" Cam thought he would explode at Arie's words then he gritted out. "I'm not leaving until I have my wife."

"Patience, this situation is under control. I'll explain everything outside." Arie left the room, looking over his shoulder just once to see if they followed.

"What the hell do you think you're doing?" Cam asked, furious with the outcome of the confrontation inside the brothel. He didn't care if Arie thought this was under control. He believed he'd have Chelsea in his arms as soon as she returned from dinner. "You were supposed to broker a deal with that lady."

"Getting your woman back unscathed is what I'm about. You are going to have to trust me in this. At the moment Chelsea is subdued. She is unconscious and could not come with us even if the madam would allow it. We will have to figure out another way to procure her. Tomorrow morning will be the best time to negotiate."

"Chels' is a slip of a girl. I'll carry her." Cam started inside but once again found himself restrained by Arie.

"Nothing untoward will happen to Chelsea tonight. She understands the forces I can call into play against her if anything happens to your wife as well as my personal feelings for Chelsea. I promise you, Chelsea will be back in your home soon."

"Where is Daryl," Donal asked.

"And Lacie?" Leslie added.

"She didn't know. Neither Daryl or Lacie were brought in with Chelsea," Arie turned to the man. "They must have escaped and are most likely trying to find their way home. We can spread out and trace their path. The madam told me Daryl and Lacie managed to elude their captors a few blocks back when Leod tried..." Arie waved his hand in the air. "They both got away because Chelsea made it possible, no other reason. Lacie was behind Daryl and escaped also."

"They've had one hell of an evening. Girls' night out, never again. I'm going to search for Daryl as well as Lacie. The rest of you can figure out what you want to do," Donal said, his anger seeming to rise with each spoken word as he left.

"I'm going with Donal." Leslie said.

"When the two of you find the girls, bring them home. Cam, come with me. We'll wait and plan our next step.

"I'm not waiting for anything. I'm getting her now."

~ * ~

Earlier in the evening the sisters chatted happily as they dressed for their first girls' night out. They planned on walking the short distance to the restaurant and if it was dark when they left, they would take a carriage. Chelsea smiled, looking around the room at her sisters and realizing just how blessed she was.

"What's Cam like as a husband?" Bliss asked as she tinted her lips, smiling into the mirror. "Are the two of you happy? I know it's none of my business, and you don't have to answer if you don't want to."

"He's so sweet. He wouldn't want me to say that about him though. Before we were wed, I would have never, ever called him sweet; determined, autocratic, confident but never sweet. Cam does whatever I want before I know I want it. Seems as if he can read my mind." Chelsea had always known Cam would be a good husband, a provider but everything else, the pleasure, the raw mercuric passion filled energy that passed between them, she had never expected.

"That's the way Broc is to me too. The twins already have him wrapped around their tiny little fingers," Bliss said, gazing into the mirror while readjusting several strands of hair. "I dread what could happen when they get older. They are already incorrigible."

"And... It sounds as if you have Broc wrapped around your little finger," Lacie laughed, seemingly delighted about that fact. "I wish I was old enough..." Lacie plopped down on the bed and as if attempting to divert her last statement, "Do you have anything here for us to eat?" She turned her attention to Daryl who always provided them with something delicious straight from the oven.

"Old enough for what?" The girls chorused.

"For Leslie to kiss me and other things I've heard the two of you talking about. He's so much older than me, I'm sure he isn't going to wait around for me to grow up."

The huge sigh following gave Chelsea a feeling of deja vous. She remembered all the time she spent wishing she reached that magical age.

"You've got plenty of time for that," Bliss told her. "You don't have to be in a hurry for kisses and to grow up. There is so much more to a successful relationship than kisses and what follows."

"Donal kissed me then said he should shoot himself. I never quite figured out what he meant by that," Daryl said with a long drawn out sigh that seemed to permeate the room. "What do you all think he meant?"

"Did you like the kiss?" Lacie asked as if she wanted to learn as much as she could.

"Heavenly," Daryl whispered softly. "But he did more than kiss and I think it was because he wanted to teach something to me. At least he said something like that. Don't know if I learned anything because I still don't understand what he was talking about."

"So, you didn't learn anything," Chelsea laughed, realizing all men must be the same when it came to sex and the women they wanted. Donal kissed her and when he learned she wasn't yet that magical mystical age of eighteen, he realized he must have done something wrong.

"I suppose I did learn something. He stopped me from intruding on you and Cam when you were on the rooftop during your honeymoon. I thought Cam was hurting you so I was going to race to your rescue." Daryl looked away for a moment, her cheeks painted in a blush of color. "His actions helped me realize that wasn't the case."

Chelsea felt heat rise to her face. "I'm heartily glad he managed to stop you before you reached the deck. That's when he kissed you?"

"Yes, and he touched me places I don't think he was supposed to. It's only a few months until my birthday," Daryl spoke with a whisper thin voice. "Was it so bad what he did? What we did? Why does a few months make such a huge difference in what I can and can't do?"

"That depends," Bliss said with a smile. "If you didn't tell him no, then you must have liked the sensations he introduced you to. I'm certainly not one to judge given the liberties I allowed Broc before we were married. It's important though..." she paused thoughtfully. "How he made you feel and if you liked it."

"That you don't let him take advantage of you or get you pregnant," Hope said pointedly. "Before I escaped the harem, I was sure I'd be with child before I turned eighteen. What I didn't know was that Arie wasn't interested in me. He thought of me as his little sister, not a potential wife. I also learned, after he caught up to me, that along with my mother he actually helped me leave the harem and find you. The accident did not help though, and it did take him a few months to locate me and make sure I stayed safe."

"If Arie didn't want you what would have happened to you?" Daryl further distracted them from her story.

"I would have been sold to another sultan." Hope moistened her lips, pushing her hands down her thighs. "Despite what you all think, I haven't let Flynt touch me sexually. The other women in the harem along with my mother schooled me as well as to what would be expected of me when I was sold. If I was to wed a man, I had to be a virgin or I would become a slave, not a wife."

"Well, I truly believe you should school Lacie and me in the ways to say no," Daryl said. "I had no idea what Donal was doing to me until he finished, but it was the most exquisite pleasure and I wanted more of it, still do."

"He took your virginity? I'll shoot him myself," Hope said indignantly. "He had no right to do such a thing."

"I don't think so. Wouldn't he have to..." It seemed Daryl wasn't quite sure how to continue.

"He would have to put his sex inside you. There would have been some pain if he did," Hope continued, a strange expression on her face. "Well?"

"There was no pain, only the most sweetly painful pleasure. He did, I think put his finger..."

A collective sigh of relief swept through Bliss, Chelsea and Hope.

"You're still a virgin then. Your man showed a few tiny signs of control, but he was right. The act was not well done of him," Hope pointed out. "He is older and should have had more restraint with you. Just as women need control, so do men."

"A man is supposed to wait until you are wed to him," Lacie told her sisters with a matter of fact voice, her nose sticking into the air.

"But few do that, wait," Bliss told them.

"None of your husbands waited?" Daryl asked, looking around the room at her sisters, seeming to need confirmation of what, Chelsea didn't know.

Bliss laughed, "Well, it was obvious to all Broc didn't wait. Just moments after we were married, I gave birth to twins. His twins."

"Cam waited, but I wish he hadn't. I hated the way he tried to act all proper and the perfect gentleman. There were times I wondered where exactly my Cam disappeared. He did introduce me to the most exquisite kisses and a wee bit more then he took it all away," Chelsea told them with a heavy sigh. "I told him I wanted my Cam back and a few days later we were married and he made love to me."

"It's not right that men can live by a different standard than women," Lacie spoke up, a tinge of anger in her voice. "Why should they be able to have mistresses and not be condemned as sluts or whores? Instead, they are looked up to for their manly prowess with women then they strut around as if they were peacocks."

"I agree," Chelsea said, speaking softly, remembering all the confusion she had when it came to Cam and the way he treated her one moment and how different the next. If things had been equal between them, none of that would have happened. "Women should have just as much freedom to explore relationships as men."

"As do we all," Bliss said. "Perhaps in the future life for women will be different. The biggest problem, however, is that women get pregnant and men want to know if the child is theirs. That's why they are so possessive of the women they believe will become their wife."

"An unfortunate fact at best," Chelsea said, wondering when she would carry Cam's child or if perhaps she already did. "Or maybe it's fortunate. I'd like to have children."

"You're not with child? I'm surprised. You've been together for a month now and..."

"You think I might be pregnant?" Chelsea asked, resting her hands on her stomach, feeling eager to learn the truth.

"I would guess you are," Hope said a smile on her face.

"Well, to our earlier conversation, one can only hope for things to change in the future. It seems we are stuck with these manly dictates. We should push for equality in all things, at least within our own households. Now, are we ready? I'm famished and I'm looking forward to a night with my sisters." Bliss rose, smoothing her dress and smiling at everyone.

The restaurant was just as Chelsea remembered, small, intimate and inviting. Recalling the oysters made her blush. She had the distinct feeling they affected only her. Cam had been so detached that night. Still, the observatory had been magnificent, breathtaking actually. Perhaps in the future they could have another night in the small room gazing at the universe.

They chose to share and thankfully for Chelsea oysters wasn't one of the preferred dishes. When all the food was ordered and set on the table, there was more than they could eat.

"Do you really think I might be pregnant?" Chelsea looked to Hope for an answer, unwilling to let that conversation die.

Hope took Chelsea's hands in her, "Have you had your monthly?"

"No." Chels tried to remember everything Grams taught her and there was nothing in the conversations about pregnancy and monthlies going hand in hand. At the time, though, she had to admit she'd only been about twelve or thirteen, so she really didn't pay much attention and obviously wasn't concerned about getting pregnant.

"When was your last one? Do you keep track? It's something you should learn to do." Hope went on, seeming to look to the other women to see if they wanted to continue this conversation.

Chelsea was shaking her head and looking to the ceiling for answers. "Maybe a month and a half ago. I am late. Does that mean..."

"Yes, dear. It means you are probably one month along. You will start showing in a couple months' time. I would guess your man has noticed the very subtle changes in your body and guesses the truth even before you. He's probably just waiting for you to tell him."

"You have to talk to Daryl and me about all this." Lacie scooped potatoes onto her plate. "I want to know everything. When and if Leslie ever sees me as a woman, I need to know what he's doing and what will happen. I don't want to be pregnant before I want to be pregnant, if any of that makes sense."

"Then I will make the time for the both of you. I feel old beyond my years," Hope sighed, thoughtfully.

"You should learn how to ride a horse. In return for your advice, Daryl and I will teach you how to ride then you can go riding with Flynt. He must care an awful lot about you. He seems to hover around you even though he tries not to let anyone notice."

"I'd like that," Hope said, seeming a little bashful at all the attention. "And, I don't know why you think he cares so much about me. I haven't noticed him hovering or doting. Now he's constantly talking about finding a suitable woman because he has decided he needs an heir."

"What happens next?" Chelsea asked, interrupting Hope. "And when will I know for sure if I really am pregnant."

"Wish our mother could have lived long enough to teach us about life and love," Lacie said. "Flynt certainly isn't cut out for sex talks, although I'd wager he knows as much as Hope about these things as does Cam and Broc."

"Leslie and Donal too," Daryl chimed in. "They keep it all to themselves then suddenly we're faced with things we've no idea how to react to. Maybe he should shoot himself although I wouldn't want him to really get hurt."

"They might know a lot of things, but I can tell you how to keep from getting pregnant and still enjoy the men in your lives. The women of the harem, while they were never allowed to say no, many didn't want to spend most of their lives swollen with child."

"There are ways to prevent pregnancy?" Lacie asked seeming to be avidly curious, "I'm not entirely sure how to get pregnant. I can make guesses but it all seems like a haze in my mind."

"Now is probably not the right time for the lessons to begin," Hope's voice was gentle as she reached out to touch Lacie's hand, "But Chelsea wanted to know what would happen next. I suppose she deserves an answer."

"Yes. I really do need to know." Chelsea pursed her lips, trying to think of all the questions she wanted to ask.

The chatter as well as the food and drink seemed to continue nonstop until the last bite of food and the last drop of wine was consumed.

"I'm so full. Truly, we need to walk back to the house," Bliss leaned back in her chair with a tiny groan. "I don't know why I ate so much."

"Because everything was amazingly good," Lacie said. "And this is a rare holiday of sorts."

"You know how angry they will be if we don't take a carriage," Daryl said as if she was already planning to keep Donal happy with her and on his good side.

"I don't really care what they think. It's still light outside," Chelsea announced as she pushed away from the table. "What could possibly go wrong? I'm going to walk. The rest of you can do whatever you want."

"I'll walk," Bliss said with a heavy sigh as if thinking how much Broc would dislike the choice as well as the pursuing to lecture her on keeping herself save. "I do need the exercise just so the food will settle and I won't feel huge tomorrow."

"Me too." The rest chimed in.

"Then it's settled." Chelsea rose, setting her napkin on the table. She motioned for the waiter.

With the bill paid, the girls set off, leaving the restaurant behind and making their way down the street. Chelsea recognized Victor, Arie's main man following discreetly behind. She smiled, laughing at herself as well as her sisters. They had never been alone. If Victor was present, there were other men. Arie wouldn't leave them unprotected and neither would Cam or Broc and Flynt for that matter. She realized she didn't care if they had guards. The city could be a dangerous place, and she needed to have a small taste of independence knowing at the same time that if anything happened someone would come to her aide.

With the knowledge of the protective guard surrounding them, she let her mind run in whichever direction it seemed to wander. Positive she was pregnant, she smiled, relishing the opportunity to tell Cam even though, as Hope said, he probably already knew the truth. Appreciation and excitement swept through her even though the thought of spending an unknown number of weeks being nauseous was not appealing.

The summer day was warm and a cooling breeze swept from the river and the sun hung just above the horizon. Chelsea enjoyed summer nights and while she thought about the evening to come with Cam, she realized she wanted to go back to the beach house and stargaze.

If business didn't interfere, Cam would say yes. Whenever he could, he always said yes to her.

"When are you going to tell Cam about the baby?" Hope asked, walking beside her.

"Tell Cam?" Chelsea was shocked out of her inner and intimate thoughts.

"That you're expecting," Lacie prompted, laughing. "Have you forgotten so soon?"

"No, I haven't forgotten. That's all I've been thinking about. Tonight, or perhaps I'll wait. If I can convince him to go to the beach house, I'll tell him there under the stars," she paused, remembering the shooting star and the wish she made when she saw it. "I got my wish," she mused happily.

"You should tell him before he thinks he has to tell you," Bliss said, wisely giving advice. She'd said many times that she wished she would have understood all the ins and outs of pregnancy better when she first discovered her plight as well as how they would affect the father. Yet she'd been left with few options when Broc refused to answer her messages.

Chelsea mulled over her words. "I suppose you're right, but if you think he already knows, what difference would it make."

"A lot," Bliss said. "He wants you to tell him everything you know. Honesty is important. It would not have mattered if you didn't know now."

"It's a manly thing," Hope laughed.

"They believe they should know everything," Lacie added with knowledge suddenly beyond her years.

Chelsea fell back for a moment, adjusting her shawl. Suddenly, she was yanked off her feet, a hand covering her mouth. The sunshine faded as a cloudy haze covered her eyes.

She was aware but she wasn't able to move or react. Rough hands stuffed her inside a moving vehicle. Minutes passed and she didn't know anything more while she seemed to float in a dream world. Where was Victor and what happened to her sisters and Hope?

Her head pounded and the groan she heard was coming from her. When she tried to open her eyes, they seemed stuck closed. She groaned again, rolling over, pulling her knees close to her body.

Trying to calm herself, she lay as still as possible, thinking. Her senses seemed to return at a maddening pace. Even as she began to feel her arms and legs, she realized every part of her body ached.

From somewhere, she heard music playing and laughter. The scent of cigar smoke filtered through the door as well as strong perfume. For several minutes she kept her eyes closed, thinking about what happened while remembering almost nothing.

So little came to mind, the rough calloused hands that grabbed her from behind before shoving her into another man then the vehicle. The smell of something at her nose then the darkness. Minutes more rushed by before she slowly opened her eyes. With each passing second, she was growing stronger.

A clock chimed once telling her nothing about the time she'd spent here. A chill swept through her. She rubbed her arms, trying to minimize the goose bumps, realizing now she was not dressed the same as before. What seemed to be a skimpy gown covered her.

Panicked, she ran her hands down her body. Suddenly, she sat up, groaning as her head thundered with pain. With eyes wide open she gazed at herself, nausea rolling in her belly.

The flimsy white gown veiling her, showed her off as if she had no clothes on at all. Heat rose to her cheeks while she wondered why anyone would do this to her. With trembling legs, she pushed herself off the bed. Struggling to walk to a full-length mirror, she stared unbelieving at herself.

"No." She was shaking her head, tears filling her throat as she tried to back away from the horrible vision in front of her. Unable to remain standing, she sunk to the ground, curling into a tight ball. Trying for the ability to stand again, she failed. Inhaling huge gulps of air, she remained on the floor, moisture filling her throat and eyes.

"Miss?" The door to her room slowly creaked open and a woman poked her head inside. "You're awake? That's good but you shouldn't be on the floor. You need your rest."

"Where am I?" Through a fog she stared at the young woman who entered the room.

"At a brothel." The woman said her voice calm as if she tried to reassure. "You must do everything they say and all will be fine. No harm will come to you if you do that. I will take care of you until someone..."

Unable to help herself, she interrupted. "What brothel? Why?" Questions pummeled through her head. She found herself shaking again, her body quivering in fear of her life. The sultan bought a woman at a brothel. Was this how she was dressed when Arie purchased her? How she felt? She would never forgive Arie, and next time she saw him she would tell him exactly what she thought about all of this.

"Men will come to bid on you and examine you by sight only. They will look at you but they are forbidden to touch, yet no one will stop them if that's what they choose. You must let them do whatever pleases them or it will not bode well for you." The woman tidied the bed where Chelsea had been placed before she turned to look at her.

"Who dressed me in this?" Escaping this room was at the forefront of her mind. If she had any say about what was going to happen to her, she wouldn't be here for anyone to scrutinize or touch her...or bid on her. She wasn't for sale.

Never would be.

"I did and I'm sorry for that but I knew you were not used to anything like this, so I insisted. The others can be callous and unfeeling. I want you to understand, I treated you with care and respect."

"Why would anyone be used to anything like this?" None of what the woman was saying made sense to her. "This is disgusting, abhorrent..."

"Women are bought and sold here on a regular basis. Most of the time they are beautiful just like you. Men use them for whatever they want." The woman shrugged her shoulders slightly. "It is just the way of the world. Men do with unprotected women as they please."

"Not my world. That's sickening. Why are you here?" Curiosity at her fate and this young woman's was paramount.

"I was sold too, but I'm lucky because I'm not beautiful. My scar..." She touched her face with a fingertip.

"I'm sorry," Chelsea whispered.

"Don't be. Instead of being a whore, I'm a trusted servant. Over time I've been given more duties, better duties. I don't have to clean the rooms after they've been used any longer and many times I'm asked to wait on the madam. It's the best life I could have possibly had and I've no regrets."

"You prepare women for sale to evil and immoral men and that's the best life?" Chelsea couldn't keep the hatred from her words and Arie was one of those immoral men. No wonder Cam detested him so. "You should refuse."

Her small laugh surprised Chelsea, but the woman went on to say. "That is true and it's my job to keep you sedated now so you won't do anything rash that might harm you or make things worse. There will be one man every half hour to an hour and they will have ten minutes with you. They can do anything but touch as I said, though they will do what they want. I will stay with you throughout so you won't be too frightened."

"Sedated?"

"Yes, the drugs are in the water I bring you. I must make sure you drink the entire glass as soon as one man leaves and before the next one comes to see you. The medication will help you live through the nightmare that is about to be visited on you."

"And if I refuse?" She didn't intend to drink the water or let anyone look at her or touch her. She would find a way from the room.

"There is a man outside this door who will make sure you drink everything. You really have no choice in this matter. They can tell if you are not drugged. As I said, I will help you through this ordeal, but once you are bought, I can no longer give assistance."

It seemed to Chelsea the woman had an answer for everything. Well, of course she would. "Will you help me escape?" she blurted. Asking even when she knew what the answer would be.

"I cannot." The woman bowed her head, hands clasped in front of her. "Even though I would like to do just that, I would never jeopardize my future. I do not want to be a slave and that's what would happen to me if I helped you. There is no other recourse for you than to accept your fate as I have mine."

"Of course you can. If you help, I will give you a job in my home. You can be my maid." She didn't know where that job offer came from. A maid she could not trust was not something she should bargain for. She also wondered how Jana would react to sharing her job.

The woman looked up for a moment, clearly appearing to consider Chelsea's proposal and shaking her head once again, she said, "I cannot. What if we were caught? The risk for me is too great."

"That won't happen. There are people even as we speak who are looking for me. This is illegal in Scotland, the selling of women. I'm a viscountess. They won't get away with it even if we don't try to leave." She was very nearly pleading, but during the time she found she was slowly regaining her strength, the drugs wearing off.

Still the woman was shaking her head and wringing her hands, terrified of defying the people who had owned her for so long. "There is no way out of here, no way to get out of this room without being caught."

Chelsea looked to the window, believing otherwise.

"We are on the third floor for that very reason. You are not the first to have ideas of escape nor will you be the last."

"What is your name?"

"Bernadette."

"Bernadette, we will go out the window one way or the other."

~ * ~

The madam paced, distraught, wringing her hands. She was never told Arie had a vested interest in the young woman upstairs being prepared for the private showing and auction later this year. Bloody eyes, no one told her. The sultan would seek revenge against any person who did him wrong, but she could find no way out of these circumstances that had been set in motion hours ago.

The showing would go on for several months. Letters had been sent to patrons who would be interested and were in the process of being delivered even while she strove to find a way out of this predicament she inadvertently found herself in. Two men had arrived already. She coughed, knowing they were here only because they wanted to ogle the woman, perhaps touch when they weren't supposed to touch.

In order to look one must pledge a huge sum of money and prove themselves as capable of paying that as well as any further expenses that would be accrued. In any case, the sale of this woman would bring her a fortune. Money she would never be able to use because Arie would exact his vengeance.

If she went through with this, she would not live to spend any of the wealth she meant to acquire.

Back to Arie, though, and the revenge he would seek against her. She would most likely end up in a brothel somewhere or a harem and even if she lived, she would never be able to see the fortune from this sale.

"Madam, the woman has been prepared. She is ready for the first viewing."

"And has she been sedated properly? She must not panic when things happen that will be beyond her control or experiences." She pressed her fingers to her temples. The headache she'd been experiencing seeming to grow more painful over the hours that Chelsea MacEwen Viscountess of Rosehill had been imprisoned on the third-floor room.

"Very well, what are you doing with lord MacEwan? Her would be rescuer," the madam asked.

"He is ensconced in a second-floor room. At the moment he is still unconscious. I will keep him that way until it is too late for him to help her." She should have expected the lady's husband to look for her.

"Fine, see that he stays incapable of protecting his wife. You need to escort the first man upstairs then make sure Bernadette has more water to give her charge when he is finished. Try to keep each showing thirty minutes apart. Perhaps only these two men will arrive tonight and there will be some respite for the lady." And a chance for Arie to set a rescue in motion, the lady's as well as her husband's.

This was not going to end well for her. The sinking feeling in her belly was growing worse while she held her hands tightly together to restrain the shaking. This scenario seemed to take on a life of its own, and she didn't know what she could do about it. She certainly didn't intend to end up in a harem somewhere in the Ottoman Empire.

She watched as the first man was escorted to the showing of this woman who shouldn't be here at all. This woman, whose very presence here was going to turn her well-ordered life up-side down if she didn't think of a way out quickly.

She inhaled long and deep, seeking a solution to this, knowing all the while she would have to contact Arie about all of the details. He should know everything, if she had any chance of keeping her life as it was here in Glasgow.

The lady's husband should be set lose to find a way to bid on her. Perhaps he could rescue her if his room was left unlocked. She had to find a way out of this before the situation escalated, as she was sure it would.

There were days though, days where anything could happen. Arie would have a plan and she had pretty much assured him Chelsea would not actually be sold.

Chapter Eight

Bernadette had been right about the facts here. If she refused the water she would be held down and forced to swallow the contents of the glass. Now she stood in the middle of the room, swaying slightly as she watched the man who had been let in. The room swirled slowly around her as did the floor. For a moment she closed her eyes, hoping to steady herself, but when she opened them, she stared into hollow, uncaring eyes.

This man was older, thin yet intimidating by his stance. The sneer on his face sent her skin crawling as if vermin raced up her arm. She swallowed, defiantly lifting her chin, determined to see this through without showing fear. A feat she was finding impossible.

Sweat broke out on her forehead, moisture sliding down her cheeks. He reached out as if to touch her, but slowly drew his hand back, the leer on his face growing. She swayed slightly, unable to remain upright. It gave him the opportunity to touch her, to pick her up and carry her to the bed. She hit his shoulders, but the act served only to make him laugh.

"Alas this will be my only opportunity with you," he said. "Suppose I should make the most of my time. Don't have the funds to bid along with the men who will come after me."

He sat beside her, his hand resting near her body, his eyes darkening as his brows drew together. When he looked to her protector, the man nodded, seeming to give consent to something. Slowly his mouth descended toward her, touching her lips, tracing the line of her mouth with his tongue while one hand cupped her veiled breast.

She moaned in despair and pain, giving him the opportunity to taste her. Trying to cry out against the invasion, she was unable to form words. She wanted to yell no, but nothing happened. He held her head with his hands, even as she tried to jerk away from him.

"You're very beautiful, lass. Sadly, as I said before, I don't have the funds to keep up with the bidding. But you were worth the huge fee just to see you, taste your essence, feel your breast beneath my hand. Ah, too bad I cannot sample you more thoroughly. "He rose then, striding away from her and out the door.

When the door closed behind the two men, Bernadette was at her side, her eyes seeming to beg for something. "Sit up, lass. You must walk off the drug before I give you more. Otherwise you will not be able to rise from the bed and if that happens, the guard will not deny any of the men anything. You must be awake and able to stand or it will go badly for you. This will continue all night, as long as there are men paying to see you."

"No, no more. Just let me go out the window." Chelsea closed her eyes, terrified of what the men would do to her as the evening progressed. If this man had not been a contender what would the others do? The men who might buy her? The ones who had the funds?

Bernadette moved to the window, looking down. "No, lass. It's too far. You would surely fall to your death. Besides if I allow you to escape, I will be punished."

"It's not too far." Chelsea stood beside her, pulling her bottom lip into her mouth. "It's one floor to another roof. We can tie the sheets together. I have to do this. Look, there is a tree over there." She could not survive more of these encounters, another man then another, staring at her, finding an excuse to touch and explore places she would deny if she could. She supposed as more money was involved, the men at the showing would be given more liberties.

"You have to be strong and patient," Bernadette said as if trying to reassure her that her life had not changed irrevocably. "Everything will all work out. Someone nice will purchase you and give you a home. They won't mistreat you," Bernadette added as if she tried to reassure herself.

"Not for me, not unless I risk everything. Nothing will work out. I can't. I won't stay here and let someone else decide my fate. I won't go with a man who wants to buy me." The drugs were fading from her system, and she found she could not stop the horrible shaking that encased her body.

"In your condition, you'll not survive if you go out that window. You cannot even stand straight," Bernadette said forcefully. "Would you rather die than endure a man's touch?"

"Death would be better than what is yet to come, the groping hands, the lecherous grins." Chelsea shuddered, still in a daze and not entirely free of the effects of the drug. With difficulty but with determination, she pulled both sheets from the bed, smoothing the quilt covering over the mattress.

"It's time for another drink. You must be ready for the next man." Bernadette picked up the new glass of water that had been placed on a table near the door when the first man left. She handed it to Chelsea, "Drink. You will feel no pain."

Chelsea poured it out the open window, feeling in control for the first time. "There." She brushed her hands together. "I want to be able to decide my fate for myself."

"No," Bernadette cried, rushing to the window as if she could retrieve the water. "This will all be so much worse if...they will be able to tell and they will give you even more drugs. That was so reckless of you. Everything is measured correctly to keep you just the way the madam wants you."

"I'll pretend." Chelsea was determined now, a plan set in motion and she would save herself. Going out the window drugged was not an option. A clear head was needed for what she planned. She tried to channel the feelings the drug concocted while she tied the two sheets together, waiting for the next man to enter.

"If you leave, I'll be punished if I don't say anything, if I help you. You can't do this to me," Bernadette was nearly sobbing.

"Then you'll have to come with me. It's really your only option. I don't want you to be punished or demoted from this position you seem to covet." Chelsea couldn't help the sarcasm and grimaced at the change of expression on Bernadette's face.

"It's time. I hear them on the steps. Hide the sheets quickly or this will all be over before it has begun. You have no idea what they will do to you, if they think you are trying to escape."

Chelsea slipped the sheets under the bed before sitting and waiting to see who walked into the room. She sat watching the door open and the second man enter.

"Why isn't she standing in the middle of the room as promised? I want to see all of her, every curve, everything." His voice hoarse and throaty echoed in the tiny room. "She needs to stand now. I want to see what I plan on bidding for. Exactly what I'll be getting myself into. A man needs to know and see."

"She," Bernadette licked her lips "she couldn't walk so I let her sit on the bed. Can you help me?"

"Too much of the drug?" the guard queried, laughing, seemingly unconcerned for her well-being. "She isn't very big. I'll fix that next time."

Chelsea closed her eyes when the man slipped his hands beneath her arms, lifting her, his fingers brushing against her breasts. She pretended she couldn't walk, dragging her feet and moaning. "No... not again. Please..."

"Let her drink half when this man is finished with her," the guard said, backing away from her. "Need her to be able to stand at least for a few seconds. Don't want the madam to hear any complaints."

Chelsea tried to let her mind drift to a more pleasant place, tried to think of Cam when the man walked around her, trailing a finger along the low cut bodice of the dress she wore. His shadowed face told her nothing about what he was feeling.

She shuddered when his thumb and finger pinched the tip of one breast, her knees very nearly buckling. Gulping in a breath of air and with Bernadette's help. she steadied herself.

"You like that." His eyebrows drew together. He was shorter and broader than the last man. His dark beard sported strands of white hair. "Be assured that if you don't like my attentions now then you will learn."

She couldn't help herself, she was shaking her head, stepping backward, trying to deny him. "Ah, but you will." Holding the back of her head with one hand, he molded his mouth across hers, forcing her lips apart so he found entrance with his tongue. His other hand slid down her leg, lifting the fabric of the gown so his hand touched her intimately.

Trying to push away, fighting his advances, she could not move him. He continued a path up her ribcage, while his tongue nearly gaged her. When he drew away, gazing at her, "No!" She pushed wildly on his shoulders.

"You're a spirited woman. I will have fun bringing you to my will. You will know when to say yes. No will not be a word I allow you to use."

"Never."

His grin sent a chill through her, pounding into her head. "Oh, but you will or you will be punished."

The showing continued much like the first time then the room was empty again except for her and Bernadette. Once again Chelsea poured what was left of the drink out the window with another moan from Bernadette following.

The next breath she inhaled was special. She felt slightly better, her head a bit clearer than before and her thoughts cohesive for the first time this evening. Looking out the window with a strong purpose, she knew she would succeed in her quest. The question was the role Bernadette would play and how many more men would come this evening. She'd been told they would go on all night as long as there were men.

"Is the lady ready?" The knock and the door opening seemed to happen far too soon, but Bernadette quickly managed to get her positioned in the center of the room.

"Yes." Bernadette stepped back, holding her hands in front of her and staring at the floor.

"This is the last man," the guard said as he held the door open. "I see we've found the right amount for the little lady. She looks perfect, just a tiny bit glassy eyed and not quite able to stand with a bit of swaying. Perfect. The man will be pleased."

"I believe we have," Bernadette agreed.

Chelsea wavered, closing her eyes while she licked her lips, a bout of nausea rushing through her. Enduring one more man seemed impossible, but she had to survive this so she could leave. If this man was truly the last person to come tonight, then she would have hours before anyone would notice that she was no longer on the premises.

The session went the same as the others. When they were alone, Chelsea let out a long sigh, closing her eyes for a few precious seconds, trying to shake thoughts of those men from her head as well as the drugs, which she still felt. She looked up, "It's time and you're coming with me. I'm not going to leave you here."

Bernadette seemed to freeze in place before she finally nodded her head, accepting what they were about to do.

"You go first," Chelsea said, hoping Bernadette would do as she asked, afraid if she left the room before Bernadette, she wouldn't have the courage to follow.

"What if I fall?" Bernadette's voice quivered in fear.

"You won't. Just hang on to the end and I'll try to let you down slowly." Climbing down by herself would be easier, but Chelsea realized that wasn't going to happen now that Bernadette joined her.

Bernadette stood in front of the window looking down, her body visibly shaking. For a second, she looked to Chelsea, imploring her.

"I'm going to tie the sheet around your waist." Chelsea smiled at her, trying to give her more confidence. "There."

"I can't." Bernadette stepped away.

"Then I'm going by myself. We don't have enough time for you to hesitate or for me to try to convince you. I want to be out of this awful place before the sun rises and everyone is looking for me. If you don't have the courage, tell me now. Remember though, you'll be punished if you stay." Chelsea had grown impatient as well as annoyed. She'd never realized she had so little use for a woman who was terrified of her shadow or all shadows for that matter.

Of course, she didn't know if that was true or fair having no idea what Bernadette's life had been like. What she did know was that Cam would most likely faint if he knew what she planned then when he discovered this course, he would lecture on the all the dangers. He would expect her to wait for him to come to her rescue. That wasn't going to happen before the sun rose, and she didn't plan on being ogled by more men, waiting for Cam to put in an appearance.

"Well?" Hands on her hips, Chelsea tapped her foot, anticipating. "What's it going to be? Stay or Go?"

Bernadette peered over the window again, her face fading in color. Then with a long gulp of air. "I can do this. I know I can."

"Good, climb out the window. I've wrapped this around the bedpost and I can let it down slowly. I'll stop when your feet hit the rooftop. Do you understand?" Chelsea asked, praying the girl would come through and find the courage.

Bernadette nodded while she placed one leg over the windowsill, holding on to it with both hands, the sheet rigid. It seemed to Chelsea she couldn't bring herself to remove her hands from the ledge.

"Now, Bernadette. Let go and trust me."

Seconds turned into what seemed like hours before Bernadette finally let go, trusting her to keep her safe. Using the leverage from the bedpost, Chelsea slowly lowered the woman. When the sheet lost all tension, Chelsea peered over the sill, smiling.

"Wait for me," she whispered, even knowing Bernadette wouldn't know what to do going forward without her.

Using the knots she tied strategically in the sheets, she climbed down. Landing, she dusted her hands before looking for the next step.

Pointing to the tree at the adjacent corner. "That's where we're headed. Do you think you can use that tree to get to the ground, crawl across the big limb overhanging the roof then the trunk?" Chelsea didn't expect enthusiasm, just hoped for compliance. Changing the direction of her thoughts and not waiting for an answer, "Stay close to the house and follow me."

Chelsea decided not to look back. Bernadette made her choice and if she didn't want her life to end up in shambles, she would stay close to her side. She reached a window peering inside before passing two people who were asleep inside.

Looking back to Bernadette, she motioned for her to get down. Crawling on all fours, her heart pounding, she passed beneath the window then waited for Bernadette.

Once the first window was behind them, she stood up, sweat beading on her forehead. She tried to steady herself, her nerves and her shaking legs making the feat nearly impossible. Two more windows to go, she smiled at Bernadette.

Circumstances would improve for Bernadette if she could find an empty room. They could try to leave through more conventional means. Walking down the servant staircase might prove easier for the woman who had now placed her life in Chelsea's hands instead of climbing down the tree.

The last window, Chelsea tensed, sensing something was different here. Peering inside, she nearly cried out.

The side of the house gave her the steadying she needed. She looked again, letting her breath rush out slowly. "Cam," she whispered softly, her heart in her throat. "What did they do to you?"

Bernadette seemed to notice her distress. "What is it?"

"Cam is in there. He's unconscious." Surprisingly, she opened the window. Just as she had not expected her window to open, this one slid open. She supposed no one besides her ever tried to leave in this unconventional manner.

"You can't go inside. They'll catch you. Maybe they already know you've left and they put him there to catch us."

She was shaking her head, disbelieving Bernadette's words. "Plans have changed, at least for the moment. You can go on by yourself or stay with me. Suit yourself."

"I'll stay with you. Nothing could get any worse and I don't know what I would do, if you weren't telling me."

Inside Chelsea knelt by Cam. "What happened to you?" She smoothed his hair, wishing for him to wake up. He would make this right, solve everything. Perhaps he couldn't. He must have tried and lost the battle with the madam's men.

"Cam, wake up." She touched his face, traced the line of his jaw. When she felt the steady pulse at his neck, she sighed with relief.

"He won't wake up that way," Bernadette said before pouring a pitcher of water on his head.

Cam sputtered, struggling to sit up, his arms swinging wildly. Then it seemed he noticed her. Despite his inability to help her, his eyes darkened, narrowing with seeming displeasure. "What the bloody hell are you doing?" His words were slow and measured, reeking of disapproval.

Chelsea had not been prepared for this scenario. Instead she thought he'd be grateful but now that she was standing in front of her husband she retorted, "Saving you."

He swiped his hands across his face and chest getting rid of the excess water. "How do you plan on doing that? I don't need saving. You, on the other hand..."

"I'm saving myself also. You can either go with me and Bernadette of course, or you can stay here and see what happens in the morning."

He seemed to appreciate what she said even though he had a look of skepticism clearly drawn on his face. "How?"

A single word but very clear to Chelsea, "Haven't decided yet. Either out the window and down the tree or perhaps the servant staircase, Bernadette says it's close."

"I see."

"Well, what do you think? The stairs or the tree? We must decide quickly. If another man shows up..." She thought better of telling Cam the rest. He shouldn't know what she'd been put through, at least not yet and maybe not even later.

"When was the last time you shimmied up or down a tree. Wouldn't want you to fall and hurt yourself," Cam asked as if he still wanted to play the part of knight in shining armor rescuing the damsel in distress.

"When was your last time?" she queried, a smug feeling rushing forward, even while she understood the urgency of the situation. Arguing in this upstairs room would be a waste of valuable time. "Last year for me."

"You have me beat. Didn't know you were a lady who liked to climb trees," he muttered through clenched teeth. "In any case, perhaps we should navigate the staircase. We shouldn't see anyone who has a vested interest in either of us."

"My sentiments exactly. It's after midnight so chances of running into someone are slim. Seems we do agree on something every now and then." Chelsea turned. "Bernadette, will you take a look out the door?"

The ghostly shade covering Bernadette's face gave Chelsea more reason to fear for her. This was not something she was prepared to do. "Yes, ma'am," she said, her voice whisper soft, seemingly used to taking commands.

Chelsea's heart went out to her, but what Bernadette didn't know was that after tonight, her life would be infinitely easier. Bernadette moved so slowly, Chelsea wasn't sure if the sun would rise before she opened the door.

Finally, "It's clear. Everyone should be sleeping." She stepped back. "I think we should go now."

Cam, wrapped her in his arms, "Thank you," he whispered. "Now stay close and if I tell you to run, don't ask questions."

She nodded quickly, understanding Cam was back in control. When he took her hand in his, she felt her life had finally reached some kind of normalcy even though they were still in the brothel. Now that she found Cam, she was more than willing to let him lead the way, rescue her. Knowing how to handle the unexpected was not something she felt confident with.

The rush down the staircase and out the back door was met with no resistance. The house did seem to be asleep but when they stepped outside, the sun was beginning to rise. Somewhere nearby a rooster crowed and a dog barked.

"We made it," Bernadette whispered.

"Not until we're in my townhouse," Cam said, his hard body alert and seemingly ready to take on any foe. "How far do you think you can walk?"

She wasn't sure how to answer. She wore no shoes and the gown... her back stiffened, "As far as necessary."

He looked at her then and for the first time seemed to realize she was very nearly naked. Quickly, he slipped from his jacket then wrapped it around her shoulders. "What the bloody hell did they do to you?"

She licked her parched lips in an attempt to answer, embarrassment suddenly heating her face and understanding she was still under the effects of the drug. The last thing she needed to do was waste time regaling him with the facts of her night.

Seeming to read her thoughts. "Never mind, you can tell me later." He swept her into his arms, "You wouldn't make it one block barefoot. Are you coming Bernadette?"

$$\sim * \sim$$

Arie spoke quickly to Victor, the words curt and to the point. He was disappointed in himself and the fact he failed to protect Chelsea and her husband. When he discovered the ruse hatched by Fletcher and Leod, his anger nearly overwhelmed him. He had thought the first lesson he taught Leod would have been sufficient. Yet, with a few calming breaths, he realized this should have immediately been done to both men when he discovered the fact they sold Chelsea to the brothel.

With Victor at his side, he set the strategies in motion. The two men would not escape his vengeance today, and they would pay dearly for the rest of their lives, just as they intended Chelsea to pay for the rest of her life.

"Your proposals will be carried out exactly as you have described them to me. Do you want me to see the men all the way to their destination?" Victor asked, the grin on his face told Arie Victor would delight in the job but Arie needed him here. Perhaps not, maybe he should oversee the endeavor then he could report back in detail.

"I changed my mind, go ahead even though the captain of my ship has the authority to do business in my name. Just make sure the men are secured then return home. His presence is all that is necessary and I trust him, nearly as much as I trust you. His loyalty has been proven multiple times. You are needed here, by my side." Arie strode to the sideboard and poured himself and Victor a whiskey.

"I'm sure those two will enjoy their new lodgings," Victor said, admitting then, "Almost like to go with them so I can watch how they react to what's in store for them. Would enjoy the sight and how they'll endure what they've put two women through over the year. Almost too good to be true."

"As would I, but we've more pressing business here," Arie sipped his drink, thinking of what was about to happen and enjoying the thoughts more each time his mind imagined the different scenes enfolding.

"What could be more pressing than seeing these two meet their just end?" Victor laughed. "I wonder how they will like making love to a man or by a man?"

Arie let out a long breath of air, "Very little and as much as I would like to see their faces when they realize they'll be sold to the highest bidder and the fact they'll endure the voyage in chains naked. I cannot waste precious time. Suppose I'll have to rely on my imagination." Arie would have joined Victor in his laughter, but he had other more serious business to attend to this morning.

"You will see to Chelsea?" Victor asked. "Is there anything you'd like me to do for you?"

"Soon enough but the madam has spent a great deal of money on this endeavor. I would see her compensated despite her lack of judgment. Perhaps you can have the captain of my ship purchase a young woman to take Chelsea's place. He could find a dark-haired virgin with unique features who would see an improvement in her status in the brothel here in Scotland. I don't want any more auctions. The lady will have to agree, but if she is moved from a harem to a place where she has some say in her life, I doubt if there will be any objections."

"I will pass on the word to the captain." Victor bowed, grinning before he turned to leave.

Auctions and abductions of young women was not acceptable any longer, although he had no delusions. He was still having trouble coming to terms with this notion. Alison was still in his possession, and he couldn't find a way to give her up. He would work on himself. As long as there were men on this earth, women as well as children would be bought and sold. Arie spent the next hour getting papers in order and deciding on the right way to approach the madam. He bought the brothel earlier this morning. Now he had to bring the news to the madam and release Chelsea before she had to endure anything more.

In any case the lady would stay in charge. He didn't want anything to do with the day-to-day routine of the whorehouse. But as to the larger dealings and decisions, he would dictate everything.

He thought of Ali, needing to see her, check on her well-being. Several days had passed since he was able to visit with her. Her mother would also be on that ship bound for the Middle East. As to her role in her new home, Arie wasn't sure. He would have to speak with Ali before making a final decision. In any case there was time. His ship wasn't leaving until this evening, and he planned on seeing her right after.

Today, he dressed in traditional European garb. He didn't want to stand out. Walking from his apartment, he settled a hat on his head. Twirling his cane, he set out to right the wrongs done by Leod and Fletcher.

~ * ~

Victor strode the gangplank to Arie's ship with directions for the captain dictated by Arie. As he walked by the two men, Leod and Fletcher, he grinned. At the moment they were bound to the main mast as the sailors passing by directed vulgar comments their way, mostly directed to their tiny man parts.

Taking a step back, Victor gave his thorough contemplation to the men for a few seconds before turning his attention to the captain.

"These two men are to be sold to the highest bidder. Preferably a man who keeps men in his harem. Arie would like the funds as soon as possible. So, your return trip is to be quick. He doesn't care about the nature of the men bidding just that there will be no escape for Leod or Fletcher. Arie wants to make sure these two spend the rest of their lives in servitude as well as humiliation."

"That will not be a problem. Arie sent me the names of several men who will be interested in purchasing these two for their personal carnal delights. What about the woman?"

Victor rubbed his chin, "Arie was uncertain about Alison's mother but after speaking with her, he has decided to be lenient. Alison doesn't want her mother hurt or to pay too dearly for the abuse. She also had been given few choices in her life. When she consented to the sale of her daughter, Ali didn't believe she knew what would happen to her."

"Sold as a servant then, to someone who is generous and doesn't beat their help," the captain said.

"I believe that is what Arie would want."

A loud roar echoed across the bow of the ship as various men were examining the prisoners as if they were women. He chuckled. Leod was visibly aroused by the attention. Victor would have something to report back to Arie who he was sure would appreciate the similarities.

Before leaving the ship, Victor stopped in front of the men. He allowed his gaze to roam the length of them, up then down. "Interesting that you are both aroused," Victor said. "You two enjoy men. Best you get used to this. There will be more when you are sold." For a moment Victor looked away then, "You should have understood Arie's threat the first time."

Fletcher spat at him but missed.

Victor roared with laughter. "I see you do not learn fast. Perhaps

Leod will be quicker to come to heel. The less time it takes to adjust to your new environment the less pain you will have to endure."

"I will kill them," Leod said. "Both Arie and Cam."

"You will never get that chance."

Chapter Nine

Cam pushed open the door to the observatory before setting Chelsea on one of the chairs. Her face seemed to have taken on the hue of a ghost, and her body shook with the chill of the night or the withdrawal from whatever drug they gave her. Fear for her resonated through his body, surging within a powerful force driving him.

"What is this building? Never seen anything like it," Bernadette asked, clearly baffled by the structure situated on top of a hill in a sparsely populated part of town only a few blocks from the brothel. Stepping inside, she seemed to look at everything with awe and curiosity.

"It's a place I use to look at the sky." He was concerned about Chelsea's feet as well as her physical state. At first, she seemed almost normal but as the sun continued to rise and the long walk progressed, she began to slur her words, clinging to him as he carried her the distance. Her head hung limp now, resting on the side of the chair.

"The drugs they gave her," Bernadette said, seeming concerned. For a moment she looked away and when she turned back, "They must still be affecting her. She tried to throw them away, but they forced more on her."

"What happened to her tonight? Why drug her?" Cam was beside himself with worry, fear for her so real it nearly brought him to his knees. He poured from a pitcher of water, soaking his handkerchief, touching her forehead, which was burning with fever.

"She should probably tell you herself. Let me do that," Bernadette reached out for the cloth.

"No, I'll take care of my wife. Seems you've done quite enough already." Cam knew his words would sting but until he discovered all the truths revolving around this evening and why the madam saw fit to drug his wife, he wasn't about to trust this woman. She had been a part of what happened to Chelsea even though Cam understood the woman could have done nothing to stop whatever events took place.

Gently, he cleaned Chels' feet. With the blood washed off, he saw the small scratches and a couple deep cuts. She wouldn't walk for a while, at least not without pain.

"I thought the drugs they used faded or I wouldn't have let her climb out that window. She could have fallen. I'm sorry—so sorry. You have to believe me. I didn't want any part of the auction, but it's my job. If I had refused, I would have been punished and she would have been given someone who didn't care." Bernadette's hands were gripped tightly in front of her while tears slipped from her eyes and down her face.

Cam looked up, displeasure coursing through him. Everything Bernadette said about falling to her death could have come true. The woman should have stopped Chels from climbing out the window.

He wanted to shake sense into his wife yet there was no way he could think to do it without hurting her and making her fragile condition worse. She thought she had the wits and strength of a man. She did not. She should have waited for him to rescue her.

This was not well done of her.

"Cam?" It seemed Chelsea struggled to sit. Pushing hair from her eyes, "Where?"

"I'm here, and yes we're away from the brothel, just as you intended. Needed to stop and rest. Don't think Bernadette could have made it all the way to my townhouse. I saw no carriages for hire on our route or I would have purchased a ride." He touched her face with his hand. "You are safe and in the observatory. Before you ask, Bernadette is fine too."

"What happened to me?" She pushed to a sitting position then fell back, her strength seeming to evaporate. "I don't remember..." she paused, looking at him as if he could answer.

"You're still drugged," Cam said. "You thought you were fine. Now, we'll take a few minutes to rest then we'll go to my other townhouse. I've a carriage there we can use and we can always go inside if need be. Even though mother will most likely wonder what has happened to you."

"Do you think they're looking for us?" Chels said, her voice a whisper thin, a thready sound in the tiny confines of the room. "I don't want to go back there and Bernadette..." She closed her eyes, seemingly exhausted by the few words. "Bernadette will be punished. I won't stand for that. She helped me endure something so horrible..."

Waving his hand in the air, he didn't have time for anyone except Chelsea, "Bernadette is no concern of yours. She is with us only because it seems you wanted her." His voice was curt and he knew it. Didn't care though. Bernadette could fend for herself.

Finding a blanket on one side of the room, he wrapped the thin fabric around her shoulders. Dear Lord, but she was cold to his touch, her breathing slow and too shallow while sweat beaded on her forehead. His heart in his throat, "Bloody hell."

He understood all too well she would never make it to his townhouse even if he carried her. Turning to Bernadette, "Will you watch her? Make sure she stays warm?"

With huge terror filled eyes the woman slowly nodded. "Of course, but..." It seemed to Cam she couldn't meet his gaze and might mean to argue with him. "Where are you going? You're not planning on leaving us."

"To bring a carriage. Neither of you can make it to my residence. I'm going by myself."

"You don't mean to leave us here? Alone?" Her voice shuttered as her body seemed to waver where she stood. "You can't sir. What if they come for us? What if..."

"I've no choice and neither do you. I'll lock the door behind me. The sun is about to rise. No one will intrude, but don't open that door to anyone except me." He bent close to Chelsea, whispering in her ear, so terrified for her. "Don't leave me or be afraid. I'll be right back."

She opened her eyes for a moment then smiling, her hand rested on his chest. "Why would I do that? Open the door?"

"You wouldn't. Bernadette is going to stay here with you. I'll be back before you know it." Quickly he kissed her on the forehead.

Running through the streets, his mind raced over all the scenarios of last evening. The girls' night out together and their walk back home. It had all seemed so boring and safe. Nothing untoward should have happened. He would have never thought anyone would attack them, take

Chelsea to the brothel to be sold in auction.

When Arie showed up with the information and the fact there was nothing he could do that evening, his mind exploded with rage then worry for her. Chelsea would not be compliant. She would fight. He knew he had to act before she did something stupid.

He ran past street vendors setting up for the day, past homeless people as well as men returning from a night of entertainment. With two blocks to go, he slowed his pace, inhaled, filling his lungs with much needed air.

Time seemed to pass in slow motion then a black and white cat dashed across his path while a few squirrels darted up the big oak trees in the neighborhood. Somewhere down the street a rooster crowed and birds began to sing. Still, he ran, pacing himself.

On the horizon a wealth of colors painted the sky. He prayed Chels would be fine as well as their child, telling himself he would never let her from his sight again. Would never allow her to spend an evening without him unless she was inside his house. Bloody eyes, but he'd keep her under lock and key.

He'd heard about auctions and what happened but this one was different. He didn't know how but only people of wealth were allowed to see her. Arie didn't tell him much and he supposed the lack of facts was meant to keep him from barging into the house and demanding her release.

That was what he did though and look at what it got him. He was unable to free Chelsea. He had to smile. When he did wake up, she was standing over him. In a sense she rescued herself and him. In her condition and dressed as she was, she would have never made it a block let alone manage an escape. At least he had been there to lend her the aide she needed.

Reaching his townhouse, he strode to the building behind. The young man he hired to feed and take care of his horses was shoveling manure.

"I need my carriage, the larger one and my driver. Bring it around to the front of the house as soon as you've got the horses hitched then...no, you can drive. Don't have time for anything else."

He left for the main house, intending to find another blanket and hoping at the same time his mother was still asleep. An explanation would take too much time. Entering through the back door, he stopped abruptly, the worst possible scenario enfolding in front of him.

"Mother."

"Colin, oh my goodness. What are you doing here at this hour? You don't usually rise this early." She leaned forward. "Do you? Did I invite you and forget all about it?"

He waved his hand in the air, impatient to be on his way. "I'm usually up at the crack of dawn. Now, I'm here and no I don't have time for a cup of tea. Just wanted to find a blanket."

"Well, I'm sure there is an extra one somewhere. Do sit though for a few minutes. I haven't seen you in several days. We can catch up. Oh, and how is your lovely wife? Doing fine I hope." She poured him a cup of tea despite what he said. "Just when are you going to have a reception."

"Just fine," he murmured, heading out the kitchen door then taking the steps two at a time to the upstairs bedroom.

"I'm sure there is one, a blanket, by the porch swing," his mother called out. "Really, you could give your mother a few minutes of your time."

"Thank you. I'll look there." In his haste he knocked over a vase, hearing it crash to the floor behind him as he retraced his steps to the first floor. "I'll pay for that as soon as I get a chance."

"Colin..."

"Sorry mother. Just don't have the time to talk." In the kitchen, he grabbed a loaf of bread. She would be hungry once the drugs vanished from her body and thirsty as well. He didn't want to grab a bottle of wine though. There was nothing to do, he hoped for the best. This meager faire would have to suffice for the short drive to his home.

"What are you doing?" She stood, hands on her ample hips, watching him race around as if crazy.

"Don't worry about anything, mother." Before he passed her, heading out the front door and to the carriage, he gave her a quick kiss on the cheek. "On second thought, send someone, anyone, your maid if you don't have anyone else, for a doctor. At my place, I'd be grateful."

"You need to explain yourself." She stood in the doorway watching him.

"Not now, don't have the time. I'll tell you everything later." He smiled at her, looking over his shoulder. By the time he saw her again, she would have forgotten what transpired here.

He could pray.

At times his mother would wrestle with an idea never letting it go. News of a grandchild soon might help her disregard this bizarre morning. He wished he could forget and he wondered what revenge Arie would exact on the perpetrators of this crime. Leaving them naked in the city center would not be good enough for those two men.

Inside the carriage, loaf of bread and a blanket on his lap, he closed his eyes, trying to relax but his neck and shoulders were so stiff he knew they would ache for days. This was the first time he realized his head pounded, blood seemed to throb against his temples.

Inhaling sharply, he put the throbbing to the back of his mind. He could not give into the pain while Chelsea still needed him. For the few minutes that were left of the trip, he closed his eyes again, steadying himself and concentrating on his wife.

She would be fine. He could tell himself a million times but it wouldn't make it true.

When the carriage rolled to a sudden stop, he jumped from the vehicle. Striding to the observatory door, he prayed he would find Chelsea awake and alert.

"Bernadette, open the door. It's me, Cam." He heard the lock turn.

"Chelsea?" He pushed open the door.

"She is sleeping," Bernadette told him, her voice soft. "Did you bring the carriage?"

Kneeling beside his wife, he stroked her cheek, hoping she would open her eyes. His finger at her pulse, he was pleased to find the beat steady and strong. Perhaps she was just sleeping off the drugs. In the interim, some color had returned to her cheeks.

"Chelsea...can you hear me?" He studied her intensely, watching the even rise and fall of her breasts. She would be fine in time. "Chelsea, I'm back and the carriage is sitting right outside. We'll be home in a few minutes."

A soft moan followed then her eyes opened. "Cam..." Her hand touched his cheek then fell to her lap.

"How do you feel?" He almost laughed at the expression on her face. "That good?"

"No, nothing good. My head aches and my stomach is rolling." She ran her hands up then down her arms, shivering. "Cold."

He wrapped the blanket he brought from the carriage around her shoulders. "Tell me where it hurts?"

She tried to straighten but groaned, falling back on the chair. "My head mostly but the world isn't spinning like it was before you left and last night when..." she stopped, shuddering, her eyes closing.

"You don't want to know," Bernadette told him, touching him on the shoulder. "It will only make you angry and we need to take care of her. The anger as well as the revenge can come later."

He already guessed what happened and his guesses couldn't be worse than the truth. At least he prayed they couldn't but Bernadette was right, the information could certainly wait for a more appropriate time.

"I'm going to carry you to the carriage. Mother has sent for a doctor to check you out when we get home."

"Don't want a doctor, just you," she murmured then when he tried to pick her up, "I can walk."

"Of course you can," he agreed with her, moving back to give her the space she needed to stand.

She pushed on the arms of the chair but after a second or two, she fell back with a groan. "Guess I was wrong but thank you."

"For what?"

"Letting me try. You knew all along I wasn't going to be able to stand up and you let me prove myself wrong."

He had no answer for her statement. Scooping her in his arms, he carried her to the waiting vehicle. Once Chelsea was inside, he helped Bernadette into the carriage then tapped on the roof.

With Chelsea sitting beside him, the trip to his home seemed to take less time than he expected. When they entered the house, the physician had already arrived.

"I'm taking her upstairs. She seems better now."

The doctor as well as Bernadette followed him to his chamber. Placing her on the bed, he stepped back, swallowing his fear.

He took his time with the examination and it seemed to Cam that as time passed, she grew stronger.

"Do you know what it was they gave her?" the doctor asked.

"I believe it was an opiate," Bernadette said. "Over the course of the night, she must have swallowed quite a lot. They gave her some every half hour or so. We tried to toss as much as we could. She managed a few times, but her guard was adamant and seemed to think he had to watch her drink before he was satisfied."

Cam felt his gut tighten, his fists clenching at his sides. He had failed Chelsea. It was as simple as that one fact. As her husband, he was supposed to protect his wife.

He failed.

"Make sure she gets plenty of rest and give her water to flush it out of her system." With that said, he took his leave.

"What would you like me to do, sir? She told me I could be her maid. That is why I came with milady. But I see she already has one, a maid."

"No other reason?" he asked, sarcasm filling his voice. "You didn't have some ulterior motive for following her?"

"Of course there was more than one reason. I knew I would be better off and not at the whim of the madam. She convinced me this would make things nicer for me. My life would be better." Once again she was wringing her hands. "I can't go back and I've no where to go if you put me on the streets."

"He won't," Chelsea said from her bed, trying to smile. "Now, I would like something to eat. Perhaps Cook has breakfast ready. Could you go see? I'd like to speak with my husband for a few minutes."

Cam watched Bernadette leave before turning to his wife. "What can I do for you? Anything you need or want?"

She was shaking her head, tears slipping down her cheeks. "Don't ask me about last night. It's not something I want to remember or recount to you or anyone else. I don't want you to know what happened in that room."

He picked up her hands in his, tracing circles on her wrists. "For me, it's not debatable, I have to know. If you won't tell me, I'll ask Bernadette or Arie. He will tell me everything."

"All I'm willing to say is that it was a nightmare. I'm fine... Can't you please leave it at that?" she paused inhaling a gulp of air, clearly distraught. "Don't go to Bernadette."

He wanted to know if she was violated. Yet the next thought entering his head was why. Knowledge of something so despicable would not change his feeling for her. He needed her just to breathe. Anything that happened to her would not change the course of their future and the things he wanted with Chelsea by his side.

"I need..." He stopped himself reconsidering the situation and reversed his thoughts asking once again, "What do you need?"

"For you to trust in me." Yet she seemed to hesitate as if thinking about what she needed to say. "I don't want someone else to speculate or for Bernadette to try to explain. No one was supposed to touch."

"But they did touch. I won't judge." He encouraged, hoping the answer was no. Men were men and he saw her now with the clothing she wore when she was presented to the bidders. He understood lust and her appearance, her beauty, would create that lust in any man gazing at her.

"They weren't supposed to." Her body shuddered as she gulped a breath of air, looking into his eyes. "I don't know... I don't think. Bernadette would know. She was there throughout. There is nothing to do about what happened now. Men are never punished."

"You want her to tell me what you went through? How you felt? I don't want you to go through this alone. Supporting you is what is important to me. Nothing else. I'm sure talking about what happened will help." He realized the truth of those words. "I do believe it would be best for you to talk about last night even if it hurts. If you won't talk to me then Bernadette, or your sisters."

"There is so little I remember. I thought I would recall everything, but it now seems to be such a haze in my mind."

"Perhaps that is for the best," he told her, wondering about this world, buying and selling women. This was Arie's world, not his. But here they were. In order to discover what happened, a conversation with Arie seemed imperative at this point.

"I don't know how I convinced Bernadette to climb out that window and now, when I think about it, I don't know how I did it without falling. I just knew I had to get away, couldn't wait one minute in hopes you would find me." She smiled at him for the first time since bringing her into the bedroom.

"You have a way with words," he laughed then. "You can convince me of almost anything, even when I know it is wrong or bad for you."

"I remember feeling better. I thought I had not," she paused. "That I wasn't drugged. Believed I tossed everything out the window."

"It was the drugs playing with your mind. I've seen people who are addicted to opiates. Sometimes they seem lucid and other times they've no control of themselves."

"No sense, doesn't make any sense at all."

"We don't need to talk." He sat on the bed, drawing her close, reveling in the feel of her against him. She was safe and back in their home. That was all that mattered at the moment, her safety and that of their unborn child.

"I've breakfast." Bernadette entered with a tray in her hands, a smile on her face when she saw them. "More than enough for the both of you. Hope the two of you are feeling hungry."

"Thank you. Make sure you get something to eat. I'll take care of you as soon as Chelsea is resting," Cam said. "You need a room."

She set the food on the table by the bed before leaving.

"Bernadette will be fine. I'm sure Cook will feed her. Probably more than she wants to eat."

Chelsea laughed softly. "There is enough here for..."

"Six people?"

"True. Really Cam, all I want is a bite or two then I need to sleep. Do you want to sleep with me?"

"Let's eat then I'll put you to bed and see to Bernadette. When all of that is done, I'll join you platonically for a few hours then I need to find Arie and have a much needed discussion with him."

"Arie, did he play a part in any of this?"

"No, found out about it when the madam sent a message asking for help. She was smart enough to understand if she didn't buy you..." he didn't know how much to tell her. "He might not have been able to do anything to save you."

"Who then?"

He paused wondering how much he dared tell her. "Leod and Fletcher. Fletcher knows Alison. She was her mother's lover."

"Arie's Alison?"

~ * ~

"I'll lie down beside you as soon as I return. Sleep, it's what you need. I'll be back before you wake up." He kissed her on the forehead before he left the room.

"You can't know that," she whispered to his back.

Chelsea watched Cam leave the room and the door quietly shut behind him. Just like her, he needed rest. The bruise on the side of his head gave credence to the blow he must have taken in her defense. She closed her eyes, inhaling long and deep while she tried desperately to remember every moment.

"Bernadette?" she asked as the door creaked d open and the woman she met last night peeked through the opening. "I'm glad you are here."

"I ordered a bath for you. Thought you might like one before you go to sleep. Do you need any more food?"

"Thank you," she said, watching as Bernadette set another tray down and gave orders for the bath. "And thank you too for not sharing with my husband. I don't know how much and if ever I will tell him. He'll be so angry. I'm afraid of what he'll do."

"It is your business and I'm not proud of the part I played, but I hope it is all in the past. Are you going to eat any of this food? You should have something before you go to sleep." Bernadette deftly changed the subject.

"A little, leave it. For the time being..." She paused, watching the servants bringing in the water and wondering about her time in the whorehouse. Cam, she was sure, had been there to rescue her. The madam clearly didn't think of him as a risk, or perhaps his capture was just for show.

"Do you want me to stay?" Bernadette asked while she poured a glass of wine for Chelsea. A few seconds later the wine sat on a chair beside the tub.

"No, but check on me in a little bit. I'm still not feeling that well. I..." she paused again, grimacing, "I seem to have some cramps."

Bernadette's face paled, "No, milady, no. Are you with child? The madam I'm sure didn't know. She gave me no instructions."

"I believe so. It's too soon to know for sure." Chelsea settled her hands on her belly, wondering and thinking about the life that might be growing inside her. "I..." She didn't know where to begin or what to think.

Bernadette straightened her shoulders. "Take your bath and ring for me as soon as you are finished. If I don't hear from you, I'll check. If the cramps grow stronger, let me know right away. Promise."

She nodded, wondering at the new urgency in Bernadette's voice. "I promise but I don't really think it is a concern."

"Good, then I'll leave. Call for me if anything changes."

Chelsea stood, hesitantly walking to the bathing room, grimacing with each step. The water looked divine. She slipped the gauzy dress over her head, kicking it aside with her foot. She meant to tell Bernadette to burn the gown, never wanting to see it or remember it again.

For a few seconds the water stung when it touched her feet. She had no shoes. She recalled that but not the cuts she now saw.

Hot water surrounding her, she rested her head on the rim of the tub, closing her eyes. She didn't have to force her mind to remember the men. Their despicable touches upon her body. They appeared to her in order of their appearance in her room. The way they smelled, their eyes and how they made her feel as if they owned her.

She shuddered.

What she couldn't remember was the escape. Bernadette told her they climbed out the window and they were going to shimmy down a tree. But that didn't happen. Cam found her or did they find Cam?

Everything was such a huge fog in her mind.

They were in the observatory and she didn't remember how they got there. Then Cam disappeared and it seemed the silence echoed through her. Bernadette stayed with her.

She fell asleep but Bernadette sang. She was singing to her and her voice was beautiful. Visions of the men floated through her mind. When she tried to wake up and push them away, they laughed.

That was everything she could and couldn't recall. A cramp gripped her belly and she cried out, surprised by the sudden force of it. She sat up splashing water out of the tub. The pain vanished though just as quickly as it had burst upon her. If she didn't remember the agony, she would have thought it part of her dream.

But it wasn't. The cramps were real and frightening.

Picking up the wine Bernadette left, she sipped. What else could she remember? The ride to his townhouse and the way Cam gently carried her upstairs. She wanted to know if he'd be angry with her if he learned what the men had done, sure that she recalled most of it.

He would not think it her fault, would he? She had too many unanswered questions and no one to help her with the answers. If he learned of that night, would he have the marriage annulled?

Quickly, she brushed tears from her eyes. Cam didn't love her but he'd told her he wanted her, needed her even, couldn't live without her. He left her as soon as possible, telling her he needed to speak with people, Arie maybe or the madam? She couldn't remember. Her mind had been foggy, still was a little bit.

Finished with the bath she stepped out then wrapped a large bath sheet around herself. Bernadette left a platter of food as well as the bottle of wine. She was hungry trying to remember the last time she ate. Dinner the night before came to mind, the sister's night out. A piece of something here and there.

She picked at the food, nothing seeming to taste good to her. The wine on the other hand was nice. It tasted sweet and appeared to satisfy her small craving. Wandering around the room, she found that Bernadette had set out a nightgown, not one of the revealing negligees Cam bought her but one of her old gowns that covered her thoroughly from head to toe. A protective covering, just what she needed.

Chelsea slipped the gown over her head, realizing she liked the security it gave her. Bernadette seemed to understand. Her new maid had experience in these things. Cam might very well be disappointed when he returned and joined her in bed. Since they'd been wed, they slept naked every night. Heat rose to her cheeks at the memories.

She didn't want to sleep naked tonight.

She plopped down on the bed, closing her eyes for a moment and yawning while she ran her hands along her legs. Sleep... she inhaled a deep breath of air. Setting the glass on the nightstand and swinging her feet onto the bed, she curled up, a pillow nestled tightly against her.

"Miss Chelsea?" Bernadette stood beside the bed. "You fine now? No more cramps?"

"I think so. Just tired," she whispered, wishing she could stop thinking about the past and fall asleep.

"You had some wine? That will help you sleep. Maybe you should finish the glass and have something else to eat. It will all make you feel better when you wake up."

"I suppose so." She was nodding her head in agreement and pushing herself to a sitting position.

Bernadette held out the glass of wine until she accepted it. "A berry tart would be nice. Sweet and it will put something in your stomach. I'm sure I should hear it growling."

"I really don't feel well. At times I'm hungry and the next second I think I might lose the contents of my stomach." She sipped a few times, enjoying the wine. When she tried to set the glass on the table, Bernadette held out her hand to stop her.

"Drink all of it. You will sleep and the memories will fade with time. Before you know it, you and your husband will be playing with your baby and all will be forgotten." She stood, tapping her foot impatiently, seeming to wait for Chelsea to do her bidding.

She downed the entire glass. "There."

"Let me help you pull back the covers." Bernadette wasn't waiting for permission. The covers were pushed aside and ready for Chelsea to slip beneath.

"I appreciate what you've done here. I'll make sure Cam does too. He blames you, doesn't he?" Chelsea asked, vaguely recalling a few things Cam said to Bernadette. "He wasn't very nice to you."

"It's normal. I didn't buy or sell you but my part in this was to show you off in the most provocative manner possible. I did that and must accept responsibility."

"You had no choice."

"There is a choice in everything. I did what was best for me, not you. Of course your husband is angry with me. You must tell him one thing though."

"What is that," she asked her curiosity peaked.

"That you were not forced or violated. He needs to know that one thing, nothing else. It is the truth, not a lie. No one forced you. Remember to tell him."

"What would have happened to you if you refused to let the men see me?" Chelsea asked, wondering what kind of choices Bernadette really had.

Bernadette shrugged, lifting her shoulders slightly. "My choices don't make a bit of difference. I'm not beautiful so..."

"So?" Chelsea prompted. "What were they?"

"I would have serviced the men who could not pay the exorbitant prices to have the more beautiful ladies or I would have been sold as a slave. Madam had little use for anyone who could not bring her money or perform a much needed service. I survived at other people's expense."

"I would not want to be a slave either. I would have made the same choices as you." Chelsea settled into the bed again.

Bernadette pulled the covers over her. "I'm sure you'll sleep better now that you drank the wine."

Chelsea closed her eyes, thinking of Cam. The warmth of his body next to hers always comforted and gave her feelings of security and safety. His big body surrounded her, his hand cupping her breast. She sighed, wishing this wasn't a dream and he really was lying beside her.

Sweet, soft, gentle kisses floated across the back of her neck then her ear. "Chelsea, how are you feeling?"

She didn't want to open her eyes, effectively ending her dream. She snuggled into the warmth offered her, sighing softly. His quiet laughter warmed her heart and still, easygoing, moist, slow yet exciting, provocative kisses trailed across her shoulder.

Contact changed from soft and gentle to nipping and intoxicating. Unable to help herself, she turned in his arms.

Opening her eyes, "Cam, you came back." She touched his face with her hand, trying to memorize the textures as well as the angles and planes. "I wasn't sure when you left."

"Of course, did you think I might leave you?" he asked, seemingly confused as well as a bit irritated.

She looked at the ceiling then back to him, shaking her head as she watched the expressions flit across his handsome face. "I wasn't sure. What..." she couldn't speak the words, didn't want to think or verbalize what took place in that third story room. As Bernadette told her, she should tell him the worst scenario didn't happen. She would when the right time presented itself.

"Hush, you don't have to say anything else. I'm your husband and I'll always stay with you. Never leave. You can't get rid of me."

"Do you mean it?" She traced his jawline. *I love you.*

"Never more sure of anything. Are you rested?" he asked, his voice still filled with concern.

"I don't know. I'm just trying to wake up. Maybe. I still don't want to get out of bed." She wanted to stay here for as long as possible.

"Good, because we've got a lot of things to talk about. More wine?"

He sat up then, pouring them each a glass of wine and handing her one before walking to the fire and adding more wood.

"How long have I been asleep?" She pushed hair from her face so it lay behind her back.

"A few hours. Dinner is waiting downstairs if you feel up to dressing or we can have someone bring it to the room."

When she pushed away from the mattress to lean against the headboard, her nightgown slipped from her shoulders, barring one breast. Quickly she looked at Cam to see him grinning then lifting his broad shoulders.

"Couldn't help myself. I undid all the buttons. You're so beautiful."

She adjusted the gown, trying then to fasten the buttons with one hand. "Where did you go? Did you tell me? If you did, I'm sorry but I don't remember. Doesn't seem I remember much of anything right now."

He set his glass on the stand before brushing her hands away, laughing softly. "Let me help you with those although I'd rather unfasten all of them. I understand you need time to heal, come to terms with the events of last night."

"Cam, I really don't..." she couldn't finish. She'd never denied him before and hated herself now.

"Before we get into that, how do you feel? Bernadette told me you had some cramping." He sat down on the bed beside her, leaning against the headboard and crossing his long legs.

He was so much in command and even though he appeared relaxed and carefree, an undercurrent of raw energy seemed to possess his body.

"I feel," she paused a moment, "better than before but not as well as I should." She wasn't sure how much she should tell him about the cramps and for that matter didn't know what they meant if anything. Hours had passed since her last cramp. Perhaps it was nothing. She should, however, tell him she was pregnant.

"Time and rest will bring you back to your normal self."

"Things are still a little bit hazy." It appeared he was asking questions but not completely paying attention to her answers.

"And I've been sick to my stomach." Except for the wine, which seemed to make her stomach stop rolling, she'd been nauseas most of the day.

"Did you want to dress for dinner?" he asked again.

Perhaps his lack of attentiveness was a good thing. She could avoid answering in depth. "No, the world is clearer now but food isn't appealing to my stomach yet. Do you think the opiates would cause that?"

"That and all the other side effects you've endured. You will be stronger soon and able to eat again, perhaps later tonight. I promise. You just need to be patient."

"You know how patient I am," she laughed softly.

"What do you remember from last night?" The question was pointed, demanding an answer.

She didn't want to answer him so she closed her eyes, remaining silent until she thought she might explode.

"Chelsea..."

She smushed her lips together. He placed a fingertip on her chin, lifting until she would stare into his eyes if she had the courage to open hers. Nervous energy possessed her sending tingling sensations up her arms. "What?" She finally opened her eyes.

"You have memories. What are they? I would only try to help." His gentle slow encouragement sent a feeling of hope to her. "Nothing that happened is your fault."

Resisting, she turned away. "I don't want to talk about what they did...to me...ever. Even though Bernadette says..."

"Bernadette says...?"

"Nothing." She shifted nervously beneath the covers.

"I really do believe talking would help ease the pain and erase the memories. If you don't want to talk to me or Bernadette, then perhaps your grams or Bliss. They would listen."

"More wine, please?" She held out her glass, trying to smile yet she was sure he saw through her ploy.

"Whatever you like." He did as she asked. "You cannot avoid the issue forever. Obviously, you talked to Bernadette and she gave you advice."

Tears suddenly flowed unbidden and she brushed them away. Everything she wanted to avoid just happened. "Bernadette knows everything. I don't need to recount the events to her."

"I'd like to ask her."

"No!" Her hand shook so violently wine sloshed from her glass. "No, you can't." She tried to stay calm, breathing slowly in then out. "Please don't. I don't think I could live with that."

"If you're going to worry about what I might do, don't." Cam was running his hands through his hair, clearly distraught. She would give almost anything to make him feel better.

"Cam." She swallowed hard, placing her hand on his arm, understanding why Bernadette wanted to tell him she wasn't forced, but... "I'm..." she looked down, "embarrassed, mortified. I didn't want any of it and prayed every second it would all go away."

When she looked at him, his brows were drawn together in a deep frown and his eyes blazed with emotion she didn't understand.

"What are you really afraid of, Chelsea?"

Once again she looked away, her heart pounding inside her chest. She couldn't form the words or force them from her mouth.

Finally, "Nothing. Nothing. I'm not afraid."

He took her glass from her, pouring her more wine. A few seconds later. "These grapes are very good as well as the tomatoes and cucumbers. Perhaps you would try a piece of cheese or slice of bread. Are you still nauseous?"

With the glass of wine in her possession, he handed her a piece of cheese on top of the bread he mentioned.

She bit into the appetizer, chewing even though her stomach churned. "Why are you changing the subject?"

"Just doing what my wife wants. If she doesn't want to tell me about last night, she doesn't have to but she needs to understand that one way or another, I'll discover the truth." His charming smile stretched across his face, giving her reason to question his intentions. "I'd rather my wife told me though."

Then, "I want you to make love to me." She needed reassurance he still wanted her even after what was done last night in the brothel.

"If I do then you'll tell me everything I want to know?"

"No."

"I see. I would like nothing more than to give and receive pleasure right now, but you aren't ready for that, your mind or your body."

She bristled at his words. "How would you know?"

"Hmmm..." He sipped his wine, studying her closely. "First, your eyes. They don't have that sparkle I'm used to seeing."

For a moment she was taken aback. She wanted to look at her eyes and wondered what he saw. "My eyes? No sparkle? How on earth..."

"You are not as alert as usual either. I wonder at that. There is a vagueness about the way you look at me as well as the way you are talking. Perhaps the drugs still linger in your body."

"Just my eyes?"

"Your face is pale then at times flushed. And your breathing in very slow, not at all normal."

"Cam?" Her voice shook. He was terrifying her now.

"What aren't you telling me?" His query sent her into a tailspin.

"Just last night," she said.

It was his turn to shake his head, his debonair smile changing to an expression of serious concern. "No, there is something else you aren't telling me. Again, I'd prefer my wife would say the words."

She knew he would continue the questioning with a determined purpose she didn't have the will to resist then turning her back on him. "I don't know what you mean."

"Neither do I but that doesn't change the fact that you aren't telling me something."

Chelsea was looking for some way to dissuade him, to change the subject or both. "It's nothing. Really." She was plucking at the fabric. Her nerves were stretched to the breaking point, and her only wish was for him to go away and leave her alone.

The pause seemed to last forever while all she could do was hear the beat of her heart and her labored breathing as well as the tick of the clock. It seemed her heart assumed the same beat.

"I saw Arie this afternoon."

Once again silence seemed to encompass everything she was as well as all her thoughts. "What did he have to say?" If anyone would know what happened to her during the auctions, Arie would.

"Everything."

"Everything?" she asked, her heart in her throat. Perhaps it would have been better if she told Cam. After all, he gave her the chances. She truly didn't want to lie to him but the words were so terribly hard to form.

"Should we start where you might feel more comfortable?" His question held a wealth of meaning.

"Where would that be? I don't feel comfortable talking about any of this. There is so much we've shared but still, there is so much I'm awkward with, mortified to be exact. You seem to take everything in stride, can speak of the most intimate details between us and I..." She moistened her lips hesitating, "I'm still embarrassed with sexual things."

"Leod and Fletcher." He picked up her hand holding it in his, tracing lazy gentle circles on the underside.

"Were they responsible for what happened to me?" She had no idea who kidnapped her, bringing her to the whorehouse.

"They were responsible."

"And Arie knows?" She knew he had more resources than any man alive. Arie lived in the world where women were bought and sold into harems to be subservient to men. His world was different from hers, yet she'd fallen into his and almost paid the ultimate price.

"Arie seems to be in complete control of this. In any case, neither Leod nor Fletcher will be seen in Glasgow ever again. They are gone and you need never fear them again."

An agonizing cramp stole through her. Clutching her belly, she cried out, a loud piercing cry doubling over in pain. She'd never felt anything so horrible before. The cramps and the pain seemed to go on and on.

~ * ~

Arie whistled as he strode up the steps to the now infamous whorehouse. Gossip spread quickly through the city of Glasgow. Men flocked to the house to hear more about what transpired and how the beautiful woman escaped the evil madam's clutches.

Arie had to shake his head at Chelsea's antics. She couldn't wait for a man to rescue her. She had to do it herself. Hers was a horrible price to pay though. She could have killed herself in the process. Cam needed to teach her patience.

"Madam." He hugged the woman who seemed to scowl at him. She was shaking, afraid of him as well she should be. He held the power of life or death over her.

"Arie, to what do I owe this visit?"

"You mean why am I here? I'm sure you know by now that your young woman who was to be sold to the highest bidder had different ideas. You should have released her to me when I came for her and you would have avoided all this scandal."

"I don't know what you mean," she persisted, her hands clasped tightly in front of her.

"We need to speak some place private. Perhaps your living quarters would be appropriate, and I would like the best brandy you have in the house." He smiled at her. "Then I want the truth from you." He turned, "Victor."

The two men followed the lady into a room near the front of the home. Arie sat down, tapping his cane on the floor while he waited for the glass of brandy. True, he was impatient. This woman defied him and if her answers were not what he wanted to hear, the truth, he would uproot her from this position of leisure.

"I couldn't speak candidly in the main room. There are men who are waiting to see the lady who was advertised. It will not bode well for me when they discover there is no lady. I hope you have a plan in place."

"I'm sure you will survive and thrive as well as long as you do my bidding." He waved his hand in the air. "None of this matters though. You must understand I will not tolerate any more auctions."

"You won't tolerate?" Her hands fisted at her sides, she was clearly angry with him and as yet had no idea how much control he possessed in this situation.

He leaned back in his chair, his long legs stretched out in front of him. She needed to learn a valuable lesson and quickly. "You don't understand the crux of the matter."

"And what would that be?" She downed her brandy then poured another one, her hands shaking.

He leaned forward, grinning, "I own this place and you as well. You will always do as I command."

She paled and sat down abruptly. "You're my boss."

"I am, but I'm not going to poke my head into the day to day running of this house as long as everything goes as planned. I trust you know what will happen if you overstep my boundaries. There will be no more auctions, among other things. A woman has the right to refuse employment. No sex slaves."

She crossed her arms in front of her. "That's fine with me. I've not had anything but trouble with them including the one where you bought Alison. Can I assume you've let her go?"

He nodded briefly, acknowledging her statement and unwilling to answer her questions. He would never allow Ali to leave him. "But I benefited immensely."

"Beside telling me you're my new boss, why are you here?" she asked, siting up straighter, seemingly preparing herself for his orders. "I know you have another agenda."

Again, he smiled, watching the madam pale again. "I wanted to tell you what happens to people who cross me or my friends. You should understand the consequences of crossing me."

"Leod and Fletcher." There was a long pause, "And me."

"Nothing untoward will happen towards you as long as you behave yourself." For Arie this was a moment of complete satisfaction.

"So, are you going to tell me their fate? Are they naked in the city center again? Seems as if Leod should have remembered the first time. I know I would." She sat down with another glass of brandy in hand. "You don't have to worry about me as long as you make all your rules clear I will follow them to the letter."

"They were delivered naked onto one of my ships bound for the Middle East."

The knock surprised both of them, "Madam? Lord MacEwen says it is urgent business. Shall I let him in?"

Not giving the madam a chance to answer, "Yes, he will enjoy this story as much as I do." Then he turned to the madam. "Please take note of what happens to people who disturb me."

When Cam entered the room, Arie stood, "Brandy?" he asked.

Cam looked from one person to the other, seeming to take stock of the situation, "Yes."

Arie nodded to the madam who delivered a drink to Cam.

"I was just telling the madam a little story. Thought you might like to hear this tale also."

"Whatever you think best." Cam sat, drink in hand watching and Arie knew, listening carefully. It seemed Cam's jealousy and anger towards him had vanished.

"I was just telling the madam that the boys, Leod and Fletcher, were delivered to one of my ships today, naked. They will stay that way for the duration of the trip and most likely for the rest of their lives."

Cam sat forward on his chair, "And after the trip. I'm hoping they will never set foot in Glasgow again. What do you have planned that will keep them waylaid and harmless?"

"If they find a way to escape their owners, they'll be broken men. Even if they could find the means to make their way back to Glasgow, they would prove to be no problem."

"They'll be slaves then?" Cam asked, seeming eager to hear more.

"Sex slaves to men." Arie smiled then turning to the madam. "You understand the power I have over people as well as their lives. At the moment you have a life filled with luxuries. That can change in an instant."

"I will heed your advice," she said, her face a sheet of white.

"Good, I'm glad you understand."

She didn't answer and Arie was sure he recognized the moisture in her eyes as compliance. "Completely."

He stood then, extending a hand to Cam to proceed in front of him. "How is your wife?"

"She will survive. At the moment she is still suffering from the effects of the opiates she was given. I'm sure that will pass but there is something she is not telling me. You wouldn't happen to have some idea what that could be. What happened to her in that third story room."

"True. She was taken against her will, but she wasn't raped. Forced to be touched as well as fondled in ways that would make you want to kill the men, she was not violated."

"I don't want to ask, yet perhaps she would confide in you."

"You humble me, but no, Chelsea might tell me but she would never forgive me if I forced her to say the words and the resentment would go soul deep. You must solve this tiny problem yourself."

"Tiny problem?"

"In the scope of things, yes."

Chapter Ten

"No!" Chelsea cried out, curling into a tiny ball. "No, no, no..." the last word Cam could barely hear. She moaned in agony, her eyes closed.

Cam rushed to her side, his hand resting on her hip. "What is it?" He didn't know what to do for his wife or what was happening to her. He rang for Bernadette, wishing she had told him whatever it was she hid. She'd told him it was nothing. Perhaps it was.

Most likely not.

"Where do you hurt?" His words were intense, vibrating through his body, needing to find a way to help her through this. "I can't do anything for you if you don't tell me what is happening to you."

She was moaning in pain, her eyes closed and shaking her head. "My..." she clutched her belly while she gulped for air. "I don't know what's wrong. Help me..."

Bernadette stepped through the door. "Sir?"

Before he had time enough to answer, Bernadette was by her side, her hand on Chelsea's forehead.

"You need to help my wife. What is wrong with her?" Sweat beaded on his forehead his nerves seemingly ripped apart. Bernadette seemed far too calm in this situation.

"I can only guess."

"What then?" He needed answers not guesses. His patience thinning as seconds ticked by.

"You need to leave the room, Sir. She doesn't need a hysterical male watching her. She needs peace and calm. Time to let nature takes its natural course," Bernadette spoke to him as if he wasn't capable of understanding.

Frustration and anger filled his soul. "No, I'm not leaving. I'm not an idiot nor am I incapable of understanding." What the bloody hell did she mean by nature taking its natural course.

"She doesn't need you right now." Bernadette persisted while pulling the covers over her tiny form. "This is private and not part of a man's world. Go downstairs and wait."

What the bloody hell did that mean? "I'm staying here."

Bernadette held onto his arm turning him, pushing him from the room. "As I just told you, she needs peace and calm. I'll call you when it is done. There is nothing you can do here except get in the way."

His body shook with fear for his wife. "When what is done? Just explain yourself and I can decide if I should leave or stay. I'm not letting you, a woman I don't know, dictate to me."

"I understand why you don't trust me and I don't blame you. But you are not needed here."

She was still so frustratingly calm he wanted to shake her. "I can take you back to the brothel." He didn't like himself much for threatening and he knew Chelsea would chastise him for it, but nevertheless, he meant every word.

"I believe she is losing the child." Stiffening, Bernadette spoke with a quietness about her Cam didn't understand when his world as he knew it seemed to be falling apart. "You can't be in this room," she repeated, this time more forcefully. "Threaten me all you want, but I'm not changing my mind. This is no place for a man. You will only get in the way. All you can do now is comfort her when this is over."

Cam ran his fingers through his hair. "Bloody hell." But he didn't want to leave. While he was thinking, Bernadette pushed him out the door and closed it tightly behind him as he heard the lock click into place.

In a fog, he wandered down the steps. Worry over Chelsea eating at him. He needed to be with her yet he sensed Bernadette might be right. Chelsea might not want him there. They had been intimate but they'd never shared private times like a woman's monthly. They'd never had the need. Nothing to do about the situation now except heed Bernadette's wishes or push his way back into his bedroom and in the process breaking the lock.

Wandering down the stairs, he walked aimlessly from one room to another. Silence seemed to echo in his ears as he tried to understand the scope of all the things Chelsea had been through in less than twenty-four hours. She was strong and resilient she would survive this.

She was losing their child. The impact of the realization hit him in the gut. Even though he told himself they would have another one, they were sure to have a second chance, he couldn't hold back the tears sliding down his cheeks. Gut wrenching sobs shook his body. This was his fault. He failed to protect her and rather than rushing inside the brothel, he should have waited as Arie bid.

Perhaps she would not have been drugged and traumatized if he'd bowed to superior knowledge.

Cam looked to the ceiling, needing to go back inside his room. Loss of control was not something he could accept willingly. Determined, he started up the steps, his hand resting on the railing, a breath away from forcing his way inside to be close to Chelsea.

"You should stay here. I made sure Nial came with me so he could keep you company. The two of you can share tales over glasses of brandy or whatever men talk about while we take care of your wife. Flynt and Hope are also on their way." Grams strode up the steps, her back stiff, leaving him behind to wonder at his submissiveness in the face of this controversy. Wondering, too, when exactly Hope and Chelsea's grandmother had been summoned. Bernadette must have had some inkling this would happen.

Cam watched as the older man set his hand on Cam's shoulder. "Shall we have a drink and wait?"

"I need—" Cam began but he was cut off.

"You need to let the women folk take care of whatever they need to take care of. This isn't about your needs but your wife's," he spoke softly, his eyes filled with tender concern. "You should think of Chelsea, not yourself, no matter how difficult that will be for you. Hope has more knowledge about women things, births and everything else than anyone. She will make sure Chelsea survives and will be able to bear you more children if that is what the two of you will want."

He'd read so much about childbirth, talked to physicians at the university when he first thought she might carry his child. He wasn't sure he trusted anyone with her life.

"Was it the opiates?" he asked not expecting an answer.

"Most likely," Arie strode into the house with Cam's mother. "Any drug can have a negative effect on an unborn child. It is early and it might not have been the drugs at all. Many babies are lost in the first few months, but no one really knows why."

"I might have only born one child but I had numerous experiences. All of our travels were not in countries where one could call a doctor at a moment's notice. I've helped more than one woman in childbirth as well as a few with miscarriages. When they were healthy in the beginning, they nearly all survived," Carmine spoke only to her son seeming to dismiss the others as well as their fears.

"I don't..."

"You don't trust anyone but yourself. In that, you are just like your father but you must begin to believe in the women in your life. We're intelligent and strong. We can endure more than most men. Now, I must go upstairs and see what I can do for your wife even if it's only to give solace at the loss."

He had just been most thoroughly put in his place by an almost nonexistent mother. Still, he needed to argue, give his opinion on something that set him back a few thoughts, "We all know men are stronger and smarter than women."

His mother's smile caught him by surprise. The expression was one of indulgence not acceptance. "Someday, son, you will realize women are far stronger, faster as well as smarter than nearly all men. We will endure and survive when men are..." She waved her hand in the air before pausing for a moment to think. "You men do what you do second best and I'll go upstairs."

"What just happened here?" Cam asked, sitting on the step to the upstairs rooms and where he wanted to be with his wife. He understood all he thought about were his needs, but he equated them with Chelsea's needs also. His mother just implied that wasn't true, setting him back a few strides and seemingly putting him in a place he was not accustomed to.

"A sandstorm called Carmine just swept through," Arie laughed. "But in so many ways your mother is right. If we men had to give birth, most likely the species would disappear from the earth. We cannot handle pain and are absolute babies when we are sick."

"Women are not stronger or smarter," Cam mumbled, clearly

distraught by his mother's ranting's and unwilling to believe her as well. "Men protect and keep the household running smoothly because they are more intelligent and stronger. That fact can't be disputed."

"Of course women are stronger and while I'm not willing to admit they are smarter, they truly have more common sense." Arie laughed before pouring himself a drink and finding an empty chair. "Women are definitely a superior species. They have to endure more than a mere man could ever imagine. That's why I love to be around women. They always seem to put me in my place quite handily."

"Then why..." Cam stopped short and thought for a few seconds, because women understand only they can birth a child. It must take a tremendous amount of strength and fortitude to carry a child for nine months then endure the agony of childbirth. He'd never really thought about it before or even that there was pain involved. Men were just content to have their heirs and rarely if ever thought beyond that.

"They have the patience and understanding that if they didn't let us have our way in so many things, the most important events in our lives would never happen," Arie continued to provoke ideas.

"Babies?" Cam wasn't sure if babies were more important than other things, but he was beginning to think he didn't want to put Chelsea through another pregnancy.

"Yes, and they allow us to puff out our chest and prance around like the peacocks we are while they do all of the hard work. In so many respects, women are stronger and smarter than men, not too sure about the faster part though," Arie mused thoughtfully. "Perhaps in some things. Maybe quicker is the better terminology."

"Because they don't think with their cock." Flynt stepped through the door and into his living room unannounced. "Couldn't help overhearing your conversation. Grams always insisted that was true and in so many ways she is right. We fail miserably at times because all we have on our minds is sex."

"That's why you are the bad boys," Arie said. "You must truly learn to think as well as react along different lines."

"You're just as bad as the rest of us if not more. I don't..." Cam began but stopped himself. While he wanted to put himself above that little piece of information, he realized that was what he'd done with Chelsea even though he'd tried to avoid doing just that.

"Of course you do and so does Flynt, but I've managed to enlighten him of that fact and he does a much better job now days," Hope said before she strode up the staircase leaving the men behind.

"Hope has educated me on the ways of women as well as men. She is a wealth of information." Then he turned to Arie. "Thank you for being the catalyst who brought Hope to me. I couldn't live without her. She has become the backbone of my household as well as my life. I never thought..." he paused before clearing his throat. "Nothing."

He seemed to gloss over his pause not wondering what it was he was about to say. "You are so welcome. At least one of us has seen reason. Hope has always had that way about her as did her mother. I do believe that is why father fell so deeply in love with her he made her his only woman."

Cam was beside himself, learning this. Hope was and always would be an enigma to him. She was unlike any woman he'd ever known. Her time growing up in a harem would do that to her.

"We need to wait until the women tell us the time is right," Flynt said, sitting down before he stretched out his legs. "Relax. We might have all night."

"Not possible," Cam muttered as his gaze wandered to the second floor. He couldn't sit still, didn't want to in any case. Meandering through the house for a second time that night, he finally stepped outside. The summer air was still warm with the scent of roses filling his senses. He inhaled deeply, wishing Chelsea was by his side, sharing the evening with him.

The day was changing to night. An array of colors swept across the horizon and one planet sat just above the treetops. He could take solace in the stars, but it was too light to see any yet.

Flynt joined him, standing beside him, his hands clasped behind his back. "She's going to be fine, you know. With Hope and Bernadette, Grams too, she is in good hands. Hope knows what she's doing where it comes to women things."

"I don't know anything of the sort. This has been my fault, all of it." He strode down the walkway, looking at the garden for the first time in so very long. The staff had kept it up quite well, he supposed. In the small gazebo, he sat down his head in his hands, holding his breath for a few seconds, trying to keep debilitating tears from his eyes.

The light in the upstairs master chamber shone brightly, almost as if something cheery was happening in the room. It wasn't.

He knew different.

He was losing his first born.

Shadows of women passed back and forth across the window. He tried to make out who they were but with no success. All he knew was that none of them was Chelsea.

"You should probably go inside now. I'd wager you'll be summoned soon," Flynt told him as he too watched the window.

"How would you know that?" Cam asked skeptically, looking his friend up then down.

Flynt lifted his shoulders in a shrug, "Just a hunch. Besides if it was me sitting down here moping, I'd want to be as close as possible when the women folk told me I could see my wife."

Cam inhaled a deep breath of air, running his hands through his hair at the same time. The frustration gnawed at him, and he wondered if he would have the patience to stay away if Chelsea was in labor. "What am I going to say to her? I've no idea how to console her or ease her grief."

"Do you mourn the loss too?" Flynt asked, putting him on the spot. "I see by the tears in your eyes you do."

"Wasn't even positive she was pregnant before tonight. I'd guessed though. Was waiting for Chels to tell me. When she was in pain, I didn't even think of the fact she was losing our child," he inhaled long and deep, trying to think of the words. "The notion is all too new."

"But you had a pretty good guess. You understand the repercussions of what you do in bed," Flynt challenged, watching him as if he waited for an admission of truth or guilt, he wasn't too sure.

Cam nodded, confirming. "Still don't know what to tell her."

"Neither would I but perhaps you should hold her until she wants to talk. There isn't a lot you can say that will take the pain away. Even though she wasn't far enough along to even tell for sure she carried a child or announce it to her family, a human life died today. Your child didn't survive long enough to see the light of day."

"I suppose we can have more," Cam said, wondering if there was truth to that. "He prayed there was.

"Probably should allow Chelsea to mourn the loss of this child before you make plans to replace the lost babe."

Flynt was right on that count as well as the others. His advice seemed to be sound. Besides, making love to her might not be the best for Chelsea. He supposed she would know when the time was right for that.

A figure exiting the backdoor caught his attention. "Cam..." there was a slight hesitation. "You out here?"

He stood, striding toward his home. "I'm here. How is Chels?"

Chelsea's grams stood silent and still seeming to wait for his approach. "You can see her now. She lost the child as we all suspected. Since the pregnancy was at it's very beginning, there should be no complications. Hope will tell you more about what you can and can't do and when."

"How is she?" His thoughts were only for his wife. He quickened his pace, not waiting for a reply.

Grams fell in beside him, "Sad but otherwise fine. She needs your comfort more than anything. All the ladies except Hope are downstairs now. I will stay the night but I'm sending everyone else home so the two of you can be together uninterrupted. Flynt might stay also because Hope will be here through the night in case she needs a woman's touch."

He stopped then and taking Catherine's hands in his, "Thank you and thank the others for me."

Racing into the house and two-stepping the stairs, he stopped at the bedroom door. Breathing raggedly a few times, he stepped inside, nodding to Hope.

"I will be downstairs for the time being then in the guest bedroom if Chelsea needs anything you can't help her with. Bernadette will also remain close by." Hope backed from the room. "Bernadette will need a place to sleep. Would you like me to find somewhere?"

"Thank you and yes. There are several unoccupied rooms upstairs. She can pick whichever she would like," he said again, this time to Hope.

When he finally looked at Chelsea, her eyes were red, he supposed from crying and she appeared exhausted by the ordeal. Her strength had been tested for over twenty-four hours now. Perhaps she was stronger than he ever thought possible.

"Can I get you anything?" He sat on the bed, placing her hand in his. "Anything at all."

She broke into sobs as he drew her into his arms. Her tears soaked his shirt while he stroked her back. He remembered Flynt's advice. *Just hold her until she wants to talk.*

Seconds turned to minutes and he had no idea how many passed before she pushed slightly away from him. "I'm sorry." Her words were a thin whisper in the fading light.

He pushed wayward strands of hair behind her ears, smiling gently. "I am too, but we can not change the past. We can only do our best to make the future better." He tried to be pragmatic but once again he didn't know what was the right thing to say.

"The baby, I lost him or her. I shouldn't have gone out that night without you." She gulped air, tears streaming down her cheeks. "Should have stayed home with you. Been a better wife."

"Hush, stop with those thoughts. We had no way of knowing. This is not your fault but the fault of the men who wanted revenge on me, not you. Some of the blame was mine for not realizing sooner the gravity of the situation with Leod." She couldn't possibly understand how he goaded Leod, taunted him with his lack of manly prowess. At first, he believed what he told the man was good advice, nothing more but it was now evident Leod didn't see things in the same light.

Her cheek rested against his chest now and the gut wrenching sobs had died down. "I thought..." Her tiny fingers gripped his shirt and he was assailed by her fragility yet she, as Arie had pointed out, was strong, deep inside where it counted; she was strong, much stronger than he could ever be.

"Yes." He lifted her chin, hoping to read something in her eyes. "What is it that you're thinking? Tell me anything or everything you want."

"I don't know." She looked up, caressing his jawline with a soft fingertip. The touch was bittersweet yet tender. So fragile yet...

"I want to be here for you, but I don't know what that entails." He lay down beside her now, pulling her into his arms. She was everything he wasn't.

"If you're hungry, Catherine and Hope made sure there was food and wine. You should help yourself," she told him, once again looking after his needs rather than her own.

"Don't think I'll ever be hungry again," he murmured, tightening his hold, intending to never let her go.

"Me neither." She rolled over in his arms. He looked into her tear-swollen eyes. "Hope said we have to wait to make love. That we should postpone trying for another child."

Cam had second thoughts about children now. He needed Chelsea beside him forever and he was beginning to understand the dangers of childbirth. He'd been cocky and arrogant before but now, now he would make sure nothing happened to her. "We'll take precautions when Hope says sex is alright. We don't have to have children."

"But you..."

Sure that he understood what she hesitated saying, "I don't need sex or an heir. I like it, adore making love to you, but I don't want to risk another pregnancy and perhaps the loss of the one bloody good thing that has come into my life. You."

"You don't want children? I thought you would be happy that I carried your child? Was I so wrong? Wrong about everything?" Her voice wavered on the last words as more tears slid down her face.

He brushed the fresh tears from her cheeks, knowing he botched that up. "It's not that I wouldn't love children. I don't want to risk losing you."

She closed her eyes and he thought she might have fallen asleep, she was so very quiet and still. Then, "When we make love again, I don't want you to take precautions. Hope has already volunteered to be my midwife when we have another child. Grams is also a midwife. Nothing will happen to me."

He almost laughed at her words. Even as tired and sad as she was now, she took control. She wasn't going to allow him to be a martyr. He was a man doomed. "We can talk about this later," he murmured. "When you are stronger and I'm not in fear for your life."

"Now." She rose above him, her hands pressing on his chest while her hair fell in beautiful disarray around her shoulders. He picked up a strand, reveling in the silken feel as he held it between two fingers. "We'll talk about this now or I won't be able to sleep. You do want me to sleep?"

He realized how very light she was, such a small woman to possess such power and strength. He could almost hear her saying she was stronger and smarter and faster than he was so of course they would do as she said.

"You have an urgent need to speak of having more children now? This instant?" He wanted to wait until they both had a good night's sleep and perhaps a meal inside their bellies before a confrontation that was sure to go bad for him. For a man always in control this was a new feeling for him. They would share their thoughts, something they never did before they wed.

They would share, even though he understood all too well he would succumb to her wishes. He would do whatever it was she wanted. He would give her the stars and the moon if she would ask. For now, he would treat her as if she just had a miscarriage. He could listen but make no commitments.

"I do." She let herself down on his chest. "Children are important to me. I've always thought I would have them. I won't give up on that part of my life."

"Having children is a serious decision." He began thinking of the words he wanted to say. "In any case the decision need not be made today. We've a few weeks at least before we can be intimate."

"What you're thinking will weigh on me for those weeks. I want to have another child as soon as possible. I've already decided."

He chuckled softly. "And I, the husband, have no say in this matter."

"You need an heir."

"We could adopt a child. There are too many orphans running in the streets of Glasgow. I'm sure one would like a home such as ours."

"Sex." She toyed with his chest hairs and he couldn't help the tiny groan of desire that rumbled up from his chest.

"Don't need it." He lied.

"I'm not going to allow you to exhaust your base needs with a whore or a mistress."

"My base needs. I only want you. There are ways to keep my seed from taking root."

"Your seed will take root. I want a child, perhaps even five or six." She shocked him, leaving him speechless.

~ * ~

Chelsea spent the day lazily planning Cam's seduction in her mind. At the beach house for the last three weeks, she meant to finally show her husband she was fit and ready to be intimate with him once more. She wanted children and his fear for her wasn't going to stand in the way of her happiness of their happiness. To Chelsea it seemed irrational to stand in terror of childbirth. She equated it to being afraid to walk across the street.

She wouldn't allow him to wallow in his fear for her life.

Both Jana and Bernadette had accompanied them to the beach house. Together, and while Cam was fishing, they decorated the roof and the protected shelter where they would sleep. She wanted to set up the telescope but didn't trust herself with the expensive equipment.

She thought this was the perfect atmosphere to seduce the man she loved. And she truly didn't believe for one second he would think to use this protection he talked about and she also didn't believe he had the willpower to lose his seed outside of her body instead of inside. If he did succeed in having his way tonight, there would be other times.

Hope and Bernadette both taught her countless ways to seduce a man so he had no rational thoughts left in his head. Hope's experiences came from listening to the women in the harem and Bernadette's the women in the brothel.

But this time was special and she decided she'd just be herself and let the physical intimacies proceed naturally. Lies between them would not bring her the joy she wanted. He would resent her as well as the baby if he were forced to be part of something he didn't agree with.

Seduction was different and he'd used the ploy on her many times. She was sure he'd be a willing participant.

Now she stood at the railing overlooking the ocean, watching the sun dip behind the water, the breeze blowing her hair. She remembered the night they were married and her first view of the ocean from the balcony. It was dark then, clouds covering the sky. Now the sight was brilliant but she almost wished for a thunderstorm like the one that happened on the night of their marriage. The energy was inescapable, vibrant and all-consuming that night. Waves pounded against the rocks, sending spray high into the air. Seagulls swooped then caught air currents, soaring on the wind.

She wore a thin negligee that both Hope and Bernadette assured her showed off every curve as well as nearly every intimate part of her. They told her Cam wouldn't be able to resist. Running her hands down her sides, she felt a moment of insecurity. Since the miscarriage she lost weight but was slowly gaining it back. He'd told her she was too thin then quickly corrected himself saying she was beautiful just the way she was, but she understood he worried about her health not her appearance.

Chelsea smiled thinking about the man she cared so deeply for. Telling him she loved him was on the tip of her tongue, had been since their wedding night. Tonight, if all went well, she would say the words and pray he could return the sentiment.

And if he didn't?

She would be disappointed but considering everything about their marriage, she was lucky to have him whether he loved her or not. Life would be infinitely perfect, if he did love her though. Children would be a part of their world. She would find some way to convince him of that.

"Chelsea?"

She turned from the spectacular view to one that caught her breath and sent her pulse pounding hard and fast. Cam was infinitely more beautiful than the view. He had bathed and now he stood in front of her, his dark hair damp and disheveled. His naked chest broad, narrowing to slim hips, sent her body thrumming with heated desire. Reckless passion swept within. Her hand on her chest she wondered if she'd ever be able to breathe again.

It seemed like an eternity since he loved her, since she knew pleasure from his hands.

His vivid green eyes were dark with the raw passion, smoldering now with the uncontrolled desire she'd come to recognize when they were intimate but she hadn't seen the expression for some time. "Cam? You're back early. I wasn't expecting you for..."

"It seems I couldn't stay away." Long quick strides brought him to a position in front of her. "I like what you're wearing." He pulled her into his arms for a long deep kiss that left her nearly swooning.

When he let her go, "I'm glad. I like what' you're not wearing." She looked down, suddenly feeling shy, thoughts of her planned seduction flying from her brain. When he wasn't with her, she had felt emboldened, but now she wondered at his thoughts and how he would feel about making love tonight.

"You mean to seduce me this evening?" he asked, lifting her chin until their gazes met. He was smiling at her, chuckling as if he was thinking of something amusing.

"Always." She moistened her lips, hoping he appreciated her efforts. "Do you like this?" As she turned then motioned to the scene behind them, "The flowers and the pillows. There is food and wine. I thought about Guinness and oysters but," she paused, "truly I didn't want to eat them."

"It's beautiful but not as beautiful as you. You've done a lot of work." He pointed to the sheltered sleeping area as he placed her hand in his and walked toward the structure. "Where did you find the flowers?"

"Hope brought them from Glasgow. She and Flynt are staying in a guest room downstairs tonight. Jana and Bernadette promised to make sure we have everything we need then they too will retire for the evening."

"Was there a question about your health? Is that why Hope is here?" He sat down pulling her into his arms and onto his lap, smoothing his hand gently down her back. "I thought when I saw you..."

"I'm healthy and you're right about what you saw." She placed her hands on either side of his face, pulling him closer. His hands settled around her waist, working their way higher. "I want to kiss you again."

He grinned at her and she wondered at the look on his face. "Then you should do that. In these three weeks have you forgotten how?"

"No, but I thought you would..." She hesitated then let out a ragged little breath.

"Thought," he prompted.

He was laughing and shaking his head. "You wanted to seduce me so I plan on letting you do just that. Kiss me now, my sweet treasure, *moer stilis*."

A wave of confusion passed through her. Sucking her bottom lip beneath her teeth, she waited as if that would provoke him to do something besides stare at her.

Then after it seemed an eternity, "I'm not sure..." She shivered as she thought about all the wonderful things that would come along with any intimacy.

"Kiss me, Chels, just put your mouth on mine and tease my lips apart with yours and your sweet little tongue. You'll figure it out. I've got other plans while you're kissing me."

His grin left her breathless and gasping for tiny wisps of air. His fingers brushed across her veiled nipples. It seemed he didn't mean to wait until she figured out how she wanted to kiss him. Tiny sounds of pleasures escaped her while he cupped her breasts in his hands, rolling the hard buds with his fingers.

"You have to come closer. I can't reach you." Her words were whispered as his big hands slid down her ribcage to rest on her hips and pull her against his hard arousal. She shuddered, trembling with the pleasure he gave her with his hands.

"Do I have to do everything?" he asked with a petulant voice but he did move his head close enough for her to reach him.

She tentatively touched his lips with her tongue, drew a path across the closure, heard the tiny groan escape his chest. Seduction was easier when he was in charge, yet his hands still roamed her body, touching and exploring until she gasped for air.

His lips drew apart, his breath whispering so close to her, an intimacy she'd lost and missed for the last few weeks so amazing now that he wanted her again. An odd breathless feeling snaked through her and it seemed to Chelsea he could hold back no longer.

Yet he did.

Drawing away from her, he brushed hair from her face, tracing her chin with a calloused fingertip. "Would you like some wine and food? Perhaps look at a few stars before this reaches its proper conclusion."

She gulped trying to fill her lungs barely able to breathe those few seconds. This seduction turned on her and it seemed he meant to stop it before she could barely kiss him "What?"

"Wine or food?"

"Wine?" her voice a thin wail. "You don't want to...you don't want me." She wasn't at all sure of herself and now he put doubt in her mind when she'd been so positive about the outcome.

"I want my wife to have something to eat and enjoy the evening as well. If we succumb to the bed now," he paused. "There will be no stargazing or food. The seduction will be infinitely more pleasurable if we take this slow and easy. I want to enjoy every facet of the night."

"I thought I did something wrong."

"Everything you do is perfect." He watched her with heavy lidded eyes before he kissed her then another long deep kiss that seemed to go on for minutes and more minutes, leaving her speechless and left her dragging her lungs for air.

Her fingernails raked across his shoulders and down his chest over his tiny nipples. She gave into all that he did.

When he ended the kiss, he touched her lips. "Did you know how beautiful your lips are when they are moist and kiss-swollen?" Then he rose, leaving her on the sofa by herself. With the wine poured and two plates of food, he handed her the glass and one of the plates.

"I'm not hungry for food." She ran her tongue across her lips. "Just you, only you. Can't food wait until we are...?"

"Ach, lass, you are hungry for me then? I like that but we must have sustenance first." He chuckled softly, seeming to thoroughly enjoy himself. "Something to eat, the stars then loving. You must have patience. After that we can spend the entire night loving each other. Whatever you want."

"Don't know why I need patience, seems overrated to me." She understood now she lost control of the evening and realized she never had been in control and would never be able to reclaim it. He dictated everything and now it seemed he meant to tease and torment. She had no idea to what purpose.

"You want to be intimate with me? You must put some food in your belly as well as some wine. We will enjoy the stars first then I will touch you in all the secret places I know you like. You can explore me as much as you want."

For some reason her mind once again strayed to the oysters and that meal they shared. She'd asked awkward questions that she now understood. Leslie and Donal laughed at her innocence, but it had not been at her expense. The scope of the teasing had been directed at Cam and what he was trying to do to her or perhaps prepare her for whatever might ensue.

"After we eat you will make love to me?" she asked wishing she didn't feel so awkward and shy. This felt like the first time.

"We will look at the stars first." He placed a bit of cheese in her mouth, running a fingertip across her lips. His gaze focused on her mouth as if he wanted to kiss her again. "Then perhaps some more wine."

Mindlessly, she was nodding her head in agreement even as he handed her more food. "I want to look at the stars, but it's not dark yet."

"No but it will be when you've finished eating everything on your plate as well as drinking all your wine." He cupped a breast in one hand, lazily sending shivers through her, while he teased the hard tip and made her groan with the pleasure he induced.

She knew then he had ulterior motives and he wasn't going to forget about protection or anything else he'd told her he would use to keep from having a child. Her heart danced a crazy spin of despair inside her chest. She had to make him mindless just as she was and unable to think to such a degree he would forget his plans.

"I can't eat all of this," she told him as she downed her wine and held her glass out for more.

"Then you will drink, no, we will drink the bottle. But you must have food. I insist."

He placed something else on her tongue. Dutifully she chewed and swallowed, but she wasn't entirely sure what it was she ate.

"I wanted to seduce you," she spoke softly, admitting the truth to him. "I believed..."

"So I would forget about protection." He handed her another glass of wine. "That's not going to happen and I'm never going to forget what you went through that night three weeks ago as well as the dangers of childbirth. Your pain is mine."

"Children though," she paused, sipping the wine he'd handed her and closing her eyes, trying to end the tears threatening to fall. "I've always wanted my own children."

"Are very important to you. I know that but your life is more important to me. Chels, I can't live without you and if having a child could take you from me, I would also die. I'm not going to let that happen."

She was beside herself with frustration now as well as despair. He wasn't listening, didn't understand, wasn't going to change his mind. She didn't know how to convince him, how to make him see things her way.

"I'm willing to take that chance." She needed to persuade him. He had to know how important children were to her, but she didn't know any other ways to tell him.

"I'm not. Come, let's take our wine and the plates of food and look at the stars and the ocean. The sun has dipped beneath the water and the skies will soon be dark enough to see the brilliance they have to offer."

He'd suddenly closed himself to her. She was at his mercy yet she could still hope he would not use that protection he spoke of. Perhaps when they did make love, he would forget. It didn't have to be tonight. There would be many times after this for him to forget.

She sat down on a chair while she watched him take the telescope from its sheltered home and set it up. He fiddled with different gadgets before he finally sat down beside her.

"I've made you unhappy." He pulled her to him for a quick hug. "That was never my intention."

"I'm not fragile and I don't want you to feel as if you have to protect me every moment of everyday. I'm strong and very capable of bearing children. I won't die." The argument had been made several times and there was just nothing else for her to say.

He kissed her again but it was chaste by his standards and left her wanting so much more. Wrapping an arm around her before pulling her closer, "You have no way of knowing that."

Her Cam had left her again. "And I could die crossing the street in Glasgow," she shot back, still trying to point out life was precarious at best. "Or I could fall off my horse and be trampled when I was out for a pleasant afternoon ride." Anger at his stubbornness now consumed her until she shook. She tried to tamp down the unwelcome tears threatening to erupt.

"Then I should keep you out of the Glasgow streets and off horses, shouldn't I?"

She hit him with a fist and elicited a tiny grunt from him. "Beast."

For the time being he ignored her as he finished with the telescope. "Do you remember anything about the stars?"

She decided to let him have his way with this issue for now. He would anyway. So, she would try another tact. "Let me see. The North Star, Polaris and Ursa Major and Minor. I remember. That night was one of the most special of my life." Then she shrugged, deciding to play with him, remembering all the directions and how one found each constellation. "I suppose they are all up in the sky somewhere. Don't you think?"

The expression he shot her sent her heart into a tailspin. His eyes narrowed, eyebrows drawing together while his lips thinned. She tried not to laugh but couldn't help herself. When he realized what she'd done, he slowly strode toward her.

"You will be sorry for that," he spoke just as slowly as he approached her. "I mean to exact my revenge. It wasn't well done of you to tease me so outrageously."

She tossed her hair back, "I don't think so." Yet suddenly she thought better of her words. The look in his eyes told her he wanted retaliation of some sort. Forgetting she couldn't out run him, she turned, racing to the gazebo, trying to put a barrier between them.

"Chels, don't run from me," he said, his voice a throaty whisper. "You are not faster a foot than me. You cannot escape."

She wanted to cry out, or what? But she didn't dare, her heart racing, her breaths coming in tiny spurts, she ran.

In a matter of a few seconds she put some distance between them only because he stood still watching her. She stood beside one of the poles holding up the structure. It was meager protection but it did provide a small barrier between them.

He closed the distance. The expression on his face was one of a hunter. She did feel as if she were his prey, but for some reason wanted him to catch her just as she had that first night so long ago. It reminded her of the night they shared their first kiss.

"Cam..." She remained behind the pole, keeping her distance and moving with him so the barrier remained in place. "I lied."

"Chels..."

He moved quickly, grabbing at her and was left with a handful of air as she sprinted away. "Bloody hell, Chels, all I wanted to do was look at stars. What has gotten into you?"

Chelsea watched him, unsure of the concentrated look on his face. His dark green eyes gleamed with purpose. When he looked straight at her, she understood deep down that she'd lose. She also knew she wanted to lose this tiny battle between them if she could someway win the war. She didn't even remember how it began. Then, perhaps it wasn't really losing at all if he caught her. Perhaps letting him would get her what she wanted more than almost anything. He was now thinking of something other than protecting her from himself. He wanted revenge for her teasing. This might well work in her favor.

He feinted left then in a flash dipped right and was on her in the next moment. She yelled, turned, but he swept her into his arms. She beat on his chest, protesting weakly his masculine advantage.

"I've got you," he said with great relish and kissed her hard. "I have got you, Chelsea, forever, for the rest of our lives together." He kissed her again, his tongue sweeping across her lips. "You will cease this chatter about having children. We will find a way without putting your life in danger in the process, and dammit, you will admit that I'm right."

She wasn't about to admit anything like that, but she did want that kiss, and another one after that and another until perhaps he would forget his threat of no children. She needed to be able to do that to him, make him think only of her and how it felt when he was deep inside her. She needed him to think with his cock not his head.

"Put me down, Cam. Put me on that bed and make love to me, hold me, give me those sensations I've come to love. I need to feel your hard body on top of me and your rod deep inside."

He groaned low in his throat as her arms went around his back and she felt the smoothness and the muscles as he moved against her. He fell on the bed with her atop him. His lips found hers and he deepened his kiss. His tongue lightly explored her mouth, not ravishing as he sometimes did but slowly and methodically as if he wanted to savor all of her.

She matched his fervor with her own, more than eager to feel him deep inside, to know that his seed would take root and they would have that baby. She would make no more comments about children but she would do her best to keep him inside when they made love.

He stroked down her back and cupped her bottom in his hands, lifting her against him, pressing her hard against his rod. Heat exploded inside her and she could only pray he felt the same unrequited desires.

He was so hard and she squirmed against him, her hands smoothing along his chest, before tangling in his hair, her mouth ravishing his. She needed so much more and he gave her everything she craved. Her frenzy for him seemed to consume her. She made small mewling sounds in the back of her throat.

"My God, Chelsea, it's been so long." Then it seemed he pulled away from her, distancing himself for a moment before his lips sucked a nipple into his mouth. He was holding her above him now, his hands around her waist as he kissed and laved each nipple over and over again.

"I want you too," she sighed softly, wishing he would quit teasing her.

He stopped then, "This evening is about a slow seduction, Chelsea. I want you to crave me more than anything else in this world. Tell me about the stars."

After changing the subject, he rose above her, moving from the bed to pour more wine. He had to walk to the telescope to retrieve the plates and the glasses they left there.

She knew her eyes were glazed over and at this moment she wanted to throw something at him but didn't dare. This seducing thing was going to be the death of her. Her overheated body yearned for him, and he left her without giving and receiving pleasure. This wasn't like her Cam, but she understood he was making a point.

He could control his lust and he would. They would never have children of their own. Sobs suddenly wracked her body. He had won the game they played and she felt as if she lost everything. But for her it was no game.

No, it was her life.

When he sat down beside her with the wine in hand, she wanted to toss it at him, nearly did. "You can take your bloody stars and send them all to hell!" With fisted hands she pummeled his chest, surprising him and sending the wine sloshing from the glasses.

He didn't seem to care what she did. "Why are you crying?" With gentle hands, he brushed tears from her face.

"Don't touch me." She turned from him, unwilling to continue the evening, which held such promise only a few hours ago. "I can't bear it when you seduce then leave me needing you."

"You're my wife. I'll touch you any damn time I want, but for now tell me why you're crying." He ran his hand up then down her back. "Is it because I stopped touching you? I can fix that."

She shrugged away from him, moving off the bed and to the railing overlooking the ocean. Over and over she told him what mattered to her and how she felt. He refused to listen or even try to meet her half way. When he stood beside her again, "Only if you change your mind."

"Change my mind?" he asked, sounding confused by the statement. Then, "Is that what the tears are about?" Now he almost sounded angry.

She turned to look at him, gazing into his eyes. He had, she realized, put their discussion about children in the deepest darkest recesses of his mind. Well, two could play at this game.

"I won't willingly make love to you until you've come around to my way of thinking." This was not going to be easy. He was a determined man and one who believed himself to be right in this instance but he would never force her.

"Which is?" Wrapping his arms around her, he pulled her against his chest as if there was nothing wrong.

"Don't play stupid. You bloody well know what it is." She pushed away from him, walking to another corner.

Beside her again, this time he didn't touch her. "Look at me, Chelsea."

She was shaking her head, beside herself and frustrated. "No, I won't, Cam. I won't do this your way. Not this time."

"I won't make excuses for how I feel and I'm not going to be the reason you die."

"No, of course you won't." Furious she brushed more tears from her face. "I mean it, you'll have to force me." She understood all he needed do was kiss her and she'd turn into a mindless, spineless pool at his feet.

"If I kissed you now, would you tell me no?"

His was a fair question. "Yes, at first, but...Cam, you would still be forcing me because I'm telling you now I don't want you to touch me. You need to honor that because I'm not willing as long as you refuse to at least try to have children."

"I'm your husband. I've every lawful right to have sex with you whether you say nay or yay. Blackmail does not suit you." His voice rose as it seemed he was becoming angry but she didn't care.

She waved one hand in the air, pursuing this conversation in hopes he might come around to her way of thinking. "All you say is true but it doesn't make it right. Would you be proud of yourself if you made love to me when I told you no? If you forced me because you know you can make me want you?"

He ran his hands through his hair, for a moment appearing defeated. "I'm terrified for your life? Thoughts of... God, Chels, if you died because I got you pregnant... I would never forgive myself."

"I've Hope and Bernadette at my side, and Grams. I won't die. Can we take this one child at a time?"

"One child at a time," he repeated sounding thoroughly defeated. "Very well."

Epilogue

He had given in to her that night at the beach house along with many more nights and days as well. Not because she threatened him with no sex but because of the tears. Giving her whatever she wanted or needed was the crux of the matter. In the end he could deny her nothing. She had never realized the power she held over him.

The moon and the stars, the entire universe as well would be hers if she asked and he was able to give them. He chuckled softly as his son, Houston they called him, crawled onto his lap. The baby was nine months old now, and Chelsea was already talking about another child.

He supposed she would get her way. She had won. The pregnancy as well as the childbirth had been uneventful. Indeed, she was barely sick the first few months.

Chelsea picked the little boy up, cradling him in her arms.

"Are you happy, Cam?" she asked. She exposed a breast, feeding her son.

"Perhaps you were right," Cam reluctantly admitted. "I'm very happy and I'm willing to try again if that's what you want."

"You know it is."

Lazily he leaned on one elbow, stretching his legs out. He enjoyed watching her with their son.

"He will be walking soon, another couple of months then we will have to make sure everything is set far enough away he can't get into trouble."

"Would you like a little girl now that you have a son?" She sipped the cup of tea he set beside her. "You laced it with whiskey."

"As always, Hope told me it helps relax a mother and makes breast feeding easier."

"I really do appreciate all the help we've had with the baby. Hope and Bernadette are wonderful. But I don't want another child right away."

"I'm surprised. Whatever you want," he told her, trying to be as agreeable as possible.

"We should enjoy our son and the time we have with him. They grow up so fast. Bliss' twins are running around terrorizing everyone."

"Then," he prompted, hoping for an answer.

"Let's just say we should wait another year or two. There is no hurry."

He took the baby from her hands before taking him upstairs and putting him in the crib. When he returned, he pulled her into his arms for a long drugging kiss.

When he finished. "You will have to use that protection you talked about. Good Lord, it seems an eternity since that night at the beach."

"I was terrified of the possibility of losing you, Chelsea."

"And I was going to tell you I loved you until you made me so angry I couldn't breathe."

"You love me?" he grinned, realizing then how deeply he loved her. "I love you too, Chels."

"I don't just love you, Cam. I'm crazy for you."

"Crazy for Cam. I like that and I do believe I'm crazy for you too."

Coming Soon
by
Christine Young
at
Rogue Phoenix Press

Falling for Flynt

September 1825

Flynt MacTavish dismounted, handing the reins to the stable hand. He'd just spent the last few hours bored to tears with the beautiful Melessand. When he asked her to go riding with him, he never believed the time spent would be gossiping about the latest fashion and just how beautiful she was.

He looked at the dark sky. Riding home this late had not been prudent, but he needed to expend some energy and weigh the pros and cons of the lovely Melessand while he considered spending the rest of his life with her. "Bloody hell, why did he suddenly decide he needed an heir. His sister Bliss with his best friend, Broc, had two boys and Chelsea, another sister and her husband, Cam, had a son. Two of the bad boys had met their demise. So why did he want to follow them? This courting thing was taking its toll on him.

A crisp breeze hit Flynt in the face when he strode outside the stable, a breath of fresh air, a much-needed one. Autumn was upon them. Leaves cluttered the ground, making swishing noises as he walked through them. A full moon appeared in the almost cloudless sky.

For a moment, he thought about Beatrice, his second choice for a wife and to be the mother of his heir. She didn't prove much more interesting than Melessand. At least she didn't spend hour upon hour expecting compliments but she had very little to say if anything. While he enjoyed silence at times, with Beatrice the silence was absolute and overpowering as well.

He sighed heavily, wondering why this had to be so complicated and uninspiring. Just a year ago he had no intentions of marrying anytime soon, enjoying his life at the fullest. Then his friends, the bad boys, started dropping like flies, to his sisters no less.

Ah, he thought about Hope. Hope came to him quite unexpectedly. The sister of one of his friends, one of the bad boys, she was fragile yet beautiful and unassuming. Her memory of her past life was nearly nonexistent. Much of what she seemed to know was instinct, not memory. Hope was unlike any woman he'd ever known. Her friendship was priceless and he'd do most anything to keep it, including staying away from her.

As he strode up the front porch steps, he noticed a light shining in the parlor. Hope must still be up. He would enjoy talking to her while having a nightcap as he wondered if she'd waited up for him. Conversation with Hope always proved delightful, sometimes so spontaneous, her words could leave him roaring with laughter or stealing his breath

"Hello," he said as he stepped into the parlor after leaving his jacket and hat by the front door. "You're up late."

She sat up, pushing a few strands of flyaway hair from her eyes. "Hello, I must have fallen asleep. And no, I didn't wait up for you. I was reading." She showed him the book.

Her clothes were wrinkled and out of place while her face was slightly flushed. He thought she'd never looked more perfect, beautiful. In the light of the candle he could see a spattering of freckles across her nose and cheeks. He was, he thought, bored with perfection. The Melessands of the world be damned.

"Didn't mean to wake you." He grinned, striding to the sideboard and pouring himself a brandy. He turned to speak to Hope, holding up a glass, "Would you like anything?"

She made an attempt to smooth her gown into place and rearrange her luscious red hair, pushing back the delightful tendrils that had come lose from the matronly chignon she wore. "Whatever you're having, I suppose."

"Did you wait up for me?" he finally asked, curious as he brought her a full glass before sitting down beside her. "I know you said you didn't, but I'm not sure I believe you."

"I guess I did. I've something to tell you. Talk about." She looked at the brandy, swirling it around.

"You've peaked my interest." He watched her closely, picking up her hand in his as he smoothed a thumb across her wrist. "What is it you want to tell me?"

"How was your outing today with Miss Melessand? I do hope it was an enjoyable adventure" She avoided his question, which peaked his curiosity even more.

"So, it's to be this way, is it?" He laughed, appreciating her antics even though she appeared to be serious. "Take your time. I'm not in a hurry tonight. In fact I'm wide awake and will relish some time spent in the company of an intelligent woman."

"Melessand is very beautiful, arguably the most beautiful woman in this part of Scotland." She smiled sweetly at him. "But I'm intelligent. Thank you. I suppose those are words that should make a woman pleased."

Truly he thought Hope to be more beautiful, not in the classic way of great beauties but inside and out. "To hear the lady tell it, she is the most beautiful in all of Scotland and England, perhaps the world."

"That lovely?" She sipped, grimacing slightly when with the heat of the liquor as she swallowed.

He roared with laughter. "Her face, yes. Nothing else that comes to mind, however."

"Are you going to marry her?" she asked bluntly.

Rubbing his chin he thought for a few seconds. "Not any time soon, if ever." No, he was never going to tie the knot with that woman. His life would be over as soon as he said the words, I do.

"You do need an heir," she reminded him. "I suppose you should think more seriously about that. Is Beatrice a better choice for you? She isn't as sweetly, sickening beautiful, but she is adequate. I suppose she would do in a pinch."

Do in a pinch that was hardly good enough. He didn't want a life mate that would work in a pinch. "Yes, but I've just begun to look." He scrubbed his hands through his hair, frustrated, irritated as well as thoroughly annoyed with this process. Instead of courting, he could spend his time in a more productive manner. Anything would be more productive. A lifetime with either of these two ladies, he realized, was not tenable.

"Neither Melessand or Beatrice will do for you?" She plucked at her skirts, not meeting his gaze. "I wonder why you're being so picky?"

He rose, agitated, pacing. "I don't have any other possibilities." Certainly not the sister of his best friend even though said friend seduced his sister and finally married her just before she gave birth to his twins.

"There are no other women who appeal to you?"

"Not in these parts," he said, understanding the lie even as he spoke the words.

When he turned his attention back to her, the look in Hope's eyes was sad. "That's too bad. Perhaps you should try your luck in Edinburgh. I've heard the women there are bonny lasses."

"Enough about me and my prospects. What about you? Do you have possibilities?" He was suddenly concerned some of this strange conversation with her revolved around her, realizing the last thing he wanted was for her to see someone.

"You don't have to limit yourself to those two women." She smiled, setting her finished brandy glass on an end table.

He shouldn't let her put this off much longer, but at the moment he was enjoying the conversation. "They are both twits." Needing something to do, he picked up her empty glass. "More?" He lifted an eyebrow studying her but didn't wait. He strode to the sidebar and the bottle of brandy.

She didn't answer, just nodded a wistful look now on her face. Then, "Please. I suppose another glass or two wouldn't hurt."

"Perhaps I will take a trip to Edinburgh for just that purpose. You could come with me. I've heard the earl of Sanford is planning a ball. There will be debutants there and gentleman as well searching for a woman to wed. Maybe one of those new young ladies will be more palatable to me." He handed her the refilled glass. "What do you think? Would you like to travel with me?"

She lifted her shoulders in a delicate move he appreciated. "You will do what you want, I believe. And no, the gossip would never end if I visited Edinburgh with you."

He laughed again. "You know me well. Yes, I do believe I should consider the ball in Edinburgh. Nothing better for me to do than to put myself at the scrutiny of young debutants searching for a husband. I've been bored these last few months and the trip might prove interesting. Would be more interesting with you as my guest though."

"When you put it that way," she spoke softly. "I wonder what a man like you must go through to find that perfect woman to fill his life and give him an heir. Seems a bit beastly to me."

"No more beastly than a woman searching for a husband of wealth who can give her baubles and gowns, as many as she wants." He rubbed his chin thoughtfully. "I would have to be careful with her pin money, wouldn't I? A woman who wanted nothing more than what I could give her would be worse than if I was a wastrel."

"Would you be heavy handed?" she asked. "Knowing you, if you loved her you would most likely give her anything she asked for."

"Within reason. But love..."he paused a moment in thought, "don't know what that is. I do believe it's a feeling, some emotion that would make a man weak and vulnerable."

"And your perfect manly self would never be weak," she said, watching him it seemed for a reaction to her statement.

No, he would never consider himself weak and neither would he fall in love. That was not for him. "I would have to keep the upper hand in a relationship. Love is not for me." Changing the subject, "We still haven't spoken about you. What was it you want to talk to me about?"

Her eyes closed as she waved a hand in front of her face. "I'm exhausted. Perhaps we could speak of it tomorrow."

"Too much brandy," he murmured huskily, even while he poured her more, unsure if the alcohol would loosen her tongue or put her to sleep.

She sat up straight, her back stiff, eyes flashing. "Then why do you keep giving me more?"

"Hmm... That's a good question. I don't know except I do enjoy you when you are more relaxed, not intoxicated, just sleepy-eyed and stress-free. Sometimes your back is just too stiff. You seem to hold everything inside yourself." He sat down next to her again. Her hand in his, he pressed gentle circles on her wrist, enjoying the way her eyes grew wide and seemed to shine with what he new to be desire.

What would it be like to experience her raw passion? She had learned so many ways in the harem she grew up in to please a man. At least that's what she'd told him. Perhaps it would be nice to experience those sweet things she knew but kept to herself.

She swallowed, looking away from him but not withdrawing her hand from his. "I'm going to move out."

The earth seemed to stop for an instant. "You're what?" He felt blindsided by her sudden statement. He'd never imagined when he walked into the parlor she would shock him this way. When she said she needed to talk, he'd thought it would be something frivolous like buying more rose bushes, which of course he would say yes to.

Moistening her lips then tucking the bottom one beneath her teeth, "I'm moving out," she repeated quickly as if she was trying to convince herself. "There is nothing here for me. I feel as if my life has no meaning and that it is passing me by. I, too, would like find someone I can share my life with."

"You can do that and still live here. Why?" he asked abruptly, his heart racing. He didn't want her to go anywhere. She was a constant in his home as well as his life. Bloody hell, but she was an intricate part of his life, a meaningful part.

She met his gaze now, seeming to make her point. "I just told you. Just as you want an heir, a family, a wife, I need to move on and find some of those things for myself. When you wed, I'll be in the way and underfoot. I don't want that for myself."

"I don't understand." She was a servant, a trusted one but a servant nonetheless. "Why would you be in the way?"

"I would feel out of place. That's all." She didn't meet his gaze as she smoothed her skirt.

"Blessed hell, I don't see why. You're a servant."

"Nothing more," she finished for him, a small tear sliding from her eye which she turned from him and quickly brushed it away with the back of her hand. "And not really a servant. I work for you only because I don't want to be in my brother's way or underfoot in his household."

Anger built inside him. "You know that's not true. You're more than someone who works for me. You're important to me."

"Do I? Whatever have you done or said to make me feel as if I was more than a servant to you?"

"I don't understand."

"Of course you don't. Needless to say, I don't believe you. If you ever took the time to listen, you would comprehend everything I'm telling you." Her back stiffened again. "I'm moving out."

"Where will you go? My ex-mistresses townhouse is available." He knew the moment he uttered the words, it was wrong of him. She would never accept a proposition of the nature he just offered.

"I will give you the benefit of the doubt. Not for a second do I believe you meant that the way it sounded. You would never ask me to be your mistress. I also don't think I have to tell you, I'll never become your mistress, just as I risked my life to leave the harem for a similar reason."

Trying to tamp down the rising anger, his fists clenched at his sides, "Where will you go then?" Yet he understood she had options. Her brother, Broc, would provide for her. His sister, Chelsea, would do the same if she asked. And Arie, the sultan who followed her to Glasgow, he would make sure she lived in comfort.

"My brother has offered me his ex's home. However unlike your offer, the good people of Glasgow won't believe me to be my brother's good horizontal." She seemed beside herself with emotions, anger rising with the force of each word.

She was cross now and perhaps annoyed as well. He read it in the lines around her eyes as well as the pursing of her lips. "My apologies." He bowed deeply. "Guess I don't want to see you leave. I enjoy your company too much. You are a breath of fresh air in this crazy world I've found myself in."

"Life goes on. It makes no difference in the scheme of things if we have good conversation or not. There is nothing here for me and like you, I'd like a family, husband and children."

A sudden wave of jealousy swamped him. He'd do anything in his power to stop that from happening, but that was all wrong too. He forced a calm to settle inside, something he truly didn't feel. "Do you have someone in mind? A suitor who would be appropriate for a husband."

She plucked at her skirts again. "I do but I haven't met him yet."

Her voice was so soft and small he needed to bend over to hear her. "Does this person have a name?"

Her face slightly flushed as she blinked and stared at him, "He does."

"And..." It seemed to Flynt she was forcing him to drag the information from her. She didn't want to give him any information he didn't ask directly for.

"Angus," she told him then with a bit more volume, "Angus Kinross. He works with Cam at the university."

"How did you meet him?" He tapped a finger on his chin. "You've barely been anywhere." He didn't like this idea, Hope being courted by a male. Well, the devil, who else would court her?

She shrugged, looking away from him, seemingly unwilling to meet his gaze. "As I said earlier, but you don't listen, I haven't yet."

And he knew once again his friends, the bad boys, were interfering in his life. He was happy though, she had still to meet this man who was taking her away from him. "How do you know you'll like him?"

She smiled then, "Cam says he's ever so nice and gentle as well. He called him a gentle giant."

"That must be nice," Flynt murmured, wishing he had a better hold on this conversation while he planned to pay Cam a visit tomorrow in order to find out exactly who this Angus Kinross was and what he did to deserve to court Hope. "Cam should keep to his own business," he blurted.

"Why would you say that?" Hope sounded defensive, her frown lines deepening with each of his questions. "Brock told him I was moving out and why. Seems you should keep to your business. This really doesn't concern you. You have no hold on me. I am, after all, your servant."

Yes, he should but he always thought Hope would be part of his life forever. His voice hoarse and heavy with unspoken emotions, "Want to see you safe and happy, that's all."

"That sounds better." She smoothed her skirts again, her fingers winding into the fabric negating the previous gesture.

He would give just about anything to know what she was really feeling, thinking, other than nervous. "When are you going to meet this guy? And how did you say Cam knows him?"

"You haven't been listening to anything I've said. "This guy is Angus and he's a mathematician at the university. Top of his field, he does these amazing calculations for Cam and his astronomy. You know, they chart the stars and the galaxies, things like that."

"What the devil do you mean?"

"I'm not sure. Cam said something about charting the distances to stars and other things. It's all somewhat over my head since I cannot even add a few numbers. Would like to learn though."

"A real paragon of virtue," Flynt said sarcastically, an intelligent man. He wondered if he was just smart or wise in the ways of the world. If they wed, would he know how to give her a woman's pleasure?

"You don't have to act that way." She stared at him, his lips actually.

"Back to my first question. When are you going to see this mathematician?" Flynt couldn't tamp down the jealousy. Didn't want to in any case.

"This weekend, don't know if I should tell you anything else." She yawned, slumping a bit in the chair. "I am tired. We should put off the rest of this discussion until tomorrow."

"There is more?" He sat down beside her again, wishing he dared kiss her. She was staring at his mouth and he had the distinct impression she wanted him to kiss her, no, was subconsciously begging him.

"He is taking me to a competition, caber tossing I believe was what Cam said. He's a contestant. It's a highland celebration."

Flynt was nodding his head, thinking of all the things to do. "I suppose he's the best too."

"That's what Cam told me. He almost always wins." She yawned again, seeming to suggest other things.

"Suppose he's wearing a kilt also." The thought sent another jealous bolt knifing through him

"That I wouldn't know, but I can only assume. What does one wear to toss a cabor?" She yawned again, closing her eyes. "Should probably go to bed, before I'm forced to sleep here on the sofa."

"I wouldn't allow that." Smiling, he watched her as she tried to stand, pushing from the couch only to find herself back in the same position as she was before.

"Can I help?" He extended a hand as an offering before he swept her into his arms and to her bedroom.

She nodded her approval, "Perhaps I drank too much."

"Perhaps you did," he agreed, wondering just how he was going to keep himself from kissing her or tossing her on her bed and making love to her and in the process ruining her for Angus Kinross. With Hope in his arms, Flynt carried her to her bedroom.

Sitting on Hope's bed and with her in his arms, he felt one with the world. This feeling inside him was right, so what was he going to do about it?

She sighed softly, opening her eyes now. One soft fingertip stroked his jawline. "Kiss me."

"Kiss you?" He chuckled, "You're smashed."

"No really, I want you to kiss me. Need to have something to compare." Her tongue darted out to moisten her lips, her gaze resting on his mouth.

She must not realize how provocative that simple gesture was. When he stepped into his parlor a few hours ago, he had no idea the evening would end this way. He wasn't going to turn down an invitation such as this one, even though she was half asleep and had clearly drunk too much.

"If you insist, I never turn down a lady," he whispered so close to her lips he was sure she would feel his breath.

"I do," she closed her eyes, waiting. "Insist."

"Open your eyes, sweet lassie." Then his lips found hers, touched, explored before his tongue delved inside. She was sweet and hot. Her softness intrigued him as well as her willingness to allow him inside her. Her tiny sounds of pleasure sent him over the edge. All he could think of was discovering more of her, all of her. That discovery would have to wait for another time. He liked his women willing but also of clear mind when he pleased them with his sexual expertise. He wondered if Angus could claim that thought.

Then it seemed she relaxed in his arms. She was asleep, soundly asleep. He laughed at himself as well as well as his thoughts of making love to her. Even with her strange and erotic upbringing, she was by far too innocent for the likes of him.

What to do now.

She wouldn't sleep well, not if she went to bed wearing her clothes as well as her corset. He could undress her, perhaps without looking at her. No, don't get too far ahead of yourself, old chap. No way in hell could he do that when presented with such a golden opportunity.

With Hope totally uncooperative, Flynt managed to remove her dress and corset, leaving her with only her chemise to cover her. He looked at her then, her soft feminine curves. Groaning, he pushed more carnal thoughts from his head.

He couldn't help himself. He continued looking, dreaming about her as well. She was slim, her breasts perfect, seeming to invite him to taste. Nope. Walk away before you do something you'll forever regret. Pulling the covers over her, she woke.

"Flynt?" The question in her voice stopped him as she sat up, her covering slipping to her waist.

"Yes," he sat beside her, wishing he had permission to touch and explore, to curl up beside her.

"Stay with me tonight." Her hands rested against his chest, imploring him to heed her request.

"You wouldn't like it when you woke up," he argued to no avail. "There would be regrets and recriminations on your part.

"I don't like to be alone. And you're here with me now." She closed her eyes for a second. "Please don't go away. I've been so lonely. Sometimes I wanted to cry."

"You won't like it in the morning," he told her again, knowing he was too close to accepting her proposition.

"I don't care." Her voice was soft, her breathing shallow. He could see the pulse point at her neck, which was beating rapidly.

Blessed hell, but she wanted him. It wouldn't hurt he told himself. Her invitation was not the one he would have preferred right now. Nonetheless, how could he refuse. "Very well."

He strode to the other side of the bed, unbuttoning his shirt and sitting on the bed to remove his boots. Prudence told him he should leave his buckskins on despite his preference to sleep naked.

She watched him, staring at him as he settled in next to her. Pulling a quilt from the end of the bed over him, he wrapped her in his arms. "Go to sleep now. I'm here and I won't leave until morning."

This was heaven and he was a saint for his gentlemanly behavior. In the morning he could give himself a pat on the back. In the morning, she would be shocked to find him in her bed He could effectively get rid of Angus by regaling him about her and their escapades.

He was a cad, yet...

The raging thought held too many beautiful possibilities

~ * ~

"Bloody eyes," Hope murmured as she opened blurry eyes to discover a pounding head and a man's arms enfolding her. The sweet kisses, she paused in thought. It had to be Flynt but why was he in her bed? The feel of his mouth against the back of her neck then down her backbone sent a myriad of shivers down her spine as it did every where else.

She wore next to nothing, she realized as she ran her hands along his strong arms. Turning in his embrace and discovering him naked, sleeping with her didn't seem prudent. This was exactly what she'd been trying to avoid for years. Why her mother helped her escape the harem and the fate that waited for her if she stayed. What to do now?

With his lips he caressed her ear, tickling the lobe before gently biting. Her body heated, reacted as she unconsciously pushed against him in response. She wanted more. And yet...

"No." She pushed away, sitting up her sheet held tightly to her breasts. "Flynt, stop. What are you doing in bed with me?"

When she finally turned and looked at him, he grinned at her, a charming very Flynt grin. "Why?" he asked, his voice husky with what she could only assume was desire. "After last night and what we did together, I would think you'd be more than willing to do those wonderful things again. You are wonderful, you know. Besides, you invited me into your bed. Don't you remember?"

"I did not. What did we do last night?" Her breaths were rapid little pants, which she tried desperately to slow but to no avail. She clung to the sheet, her grip tight, not wanting to let the meager covering go. Her modesty had been important to her, but he must have seen all of her, touched and explored her. She groaned, thinking of all the possible consequences and the fact she was no longer a virgin.

"You don't remember? Well, you did have a bit too much to drink and while I'd never taken advantage of a woman in an inebriated state, you did beg me. I recall your sweet please clearly. So, I thought to myself. What to do? I couldn't very well let you down. After all you begged me to make love to you."

She wanted to cosh him over the head with something, but all she could find was her pillow. "I did nothing of the sort. I didn't beg for you. I wouldn't. I've never wanted such a thing for myself."

He smiled again, gazing at her lips for a second. "I'm sorry you don't remember. Perhaps we could try again tonight or right now for that matter. It is a disappointment to me when a woman doesn't remember the pleasure I gave to them."

"Stop it." Her hands on her face, she felt the rush of heat to her cheeks. Quickly, she reached for the sheet, which had fallen. "Don't say another word." She pointed at him, her hands shaking. "I think I would know if we did that. If you did that."

"Did what?" His grin widened.

"You know."

Now his grin seemed to reach nearly from ear to ear. The silence unnerved her more than his accusations.

"Go away." She pushed the sheet away from her then looked at herself and the view she presented to him. Her body had been his to see yet he still wore his buckskins and while his shirt was unfastened, it hung loosely from his shoulders. His chest was well muscled, his body so hard and fascinating, intriguing. Her fingers itched to caress, explore, and discover every hard inch of him.

"Cook sent coffee and pastries," he finally spoke. "Are you as hungry as I am?" he stared at her breasts as if he wished to devour them.

"Cook knows you spent the night? Stop looking at me like that." She swallowed hard, thinking, trying to defuse the gossip before the rumors found their way to Glasgow.

"Like how?"

"As if you want to devour me."

"Oh, can't help it. It's true." Changing the topic back to the cook. "All she knows is that I brought you breakfast. Told her you had a headache and she claims her coffee will cure everything that ails a person. She also sent a bit of laudanum if you wish it. I would advise against it though. Heard it could be addicting."

"My stomach is churning." She inhaled deeply, terrified of asking her next question. "I'm not a virgin anymore?"

"I wouldn't say that." His voice took on a different tone. One she couldn't define. When she looked at him, she couldn't stop the tears from flowing. This was not how she planned her life.

He sat beside her, pulling her into his arms, running his hands along her nearly naked back. "I'm sorry. That was not well done of me. I got caught up in the moment and wanted to tease you. We didn't do anything last night. Had I taken your virginity, there would be blood as well as my seed on you as well as the sheets. Forgive me for being so blunt but..."

She remembered the women in the harem after sex. What he said was true. She coshed him on the head with her pillow. "I'll never forgive you for that." She hit him again and again, until he roared with laughter, falling back onto the bed.

"Telling the truth? I give up. I surrender. Promise to lie to you just so you won't hit me."

"Don't you laugh at me." She hit him again then again, putting all her efforts behind each blow.

Grinning still, he tackled her, rolling on the bed with her, laughing, holding her hands over her head. She stared at his mouth, couldn't help herself.

He was resting on top of her, bracing himself with his forearms. "You shouldn't do that. It's foolhardy of you."

"What?" She felt his length against her, his sex hard against her belly. Somehow he'd spread her legs and he was lying between them. She gulped air.

"Stare at my mouth." His eyes blazed with raw passion and desire and a hunger she'd never seen blazing in his eyes before. Letting go of her hands, he traced her eyebrows, then along her jawline. "I'm hard pressed to resist you. You enthrall me, never bore me and you're definitely not a twit."

From what her mother had told her about men, he hungered for her. She couldn't help the sigh. "Your mouth, it's beautiful and soft, so different from the rest of you."

"You know your lips are asking me to kiss them."

Hearing his words sent a wave of desire rippling through her. "That's impossible." She tried to be strong. "My mouth wouldn't ask that."

He chuckled. "Little liar, nothing is impossible." With his teeth he gently tugged at her bottom lip, pulling the soft flesh into his mouth, running his tongue across it, soothing the tiny nip.

Her fingers beneath the fabric of his open shirt, she clung to him, reveling in the way he felt against her hands. She yearned for more than she should, more than she had any right to ask for. Tell him no. But she couldn't, in any case she didn't want to lose this magical moment with him. These few seconds might well be the last for her.

His breath whispered against hers, "Open for me sweet lassie. Open your mouth so I can reach inside."

Unable to resist the temptation he offered, she did as he bade, felt the pressure of his lips as they closed over hers, gasped as his tongue slid inside caressing hers. He explored and she reciprocated. Primal hunger filled her, touched her soul. She loved him. Loved him desperately yet he didn't reciprocate all he wanted was sex with her. She understood what drove him. Still she couldn't refuse.

His hands settled on her waist then rose, enticing, caressing over her slightly veiled body, the chemise she wore would never protect her from the raw desire he enticed. Heat raced through her, the inferno building with each mysterious stroke of his fingers. The fantasy he wove around her would vanish as soon as he left. Then her world would crash down around her and bring her shame.

His lips found hers again and again. She moaned, unable to stop herself. Running her hands down his torso, she basked in the feelings encompassing her. She should stop him now. *Stop.* Now before it was too late and she really did lose her virginity.

Her body arched against his as his lips found a nipple. "Flynt..."

"Sweet, sweet lassie, you taste so wonderful." He paused in his attentions to her, smoothing her hair away from her face, gazing down at her. "I should stop. You should tell me to go away."

"I can't," she sighed into his mouth as it once again closed over hers. And it was true. Sometime in the last minutes, she lost the will to turn him away. It seemed he didn't want to stop either. If this would be her undoing, she would have no regrets.

She held on to him, pulling him closer, never wanting to let him go. Against her belly she felt his hard arousal, pulsing against her. She arched, searching for something, for some fulfillment she didn't understand.

"Sweet lassie." His hands roamed the length of her leg. "I want to kiss you everywhere. It's just kisses," he whispered. "Kisses never hurt anything. Innocent kisses." Again his lips closed over a veiled nipple as he pulled it deep into his mouth.

She was mindless now, quivering, needing him and knowing his kisses were not innocent. "Flynt," she sighed again. "What you do to me..."

Suddenly he left her, pulled away by an unforeseeable force. "Get off my sister." She heard the words, tried to register them in her head. *Broc?*

Sounds of knuckles hitting flesh, grunts then a moment of silence while hard breathing followed. She sat up, once again holding the sheet against her, shocked to see her brother standing over Flynt, his hands fisted at his sides.

Siting on the floor, Flynt rubbed his chin, "Guess I deserved that." He was staring at her though, still smiling. "Suppose I should leave now."

"Not so fast." Broc stepped between him and the door, looking from Hope to Flynt. "What are your intentions? I'm not going to make the same mistakes you did."

"Ironic, don't you think," Flynt said. "You get to make love to my sister, leave town never caring to find out if your seed took root and now you want to hold me accountable for something I haven't done yet."

"Only because I got here before you could take what you wanted. Did you ask her for her hand? Did you commit to her in any way?" Broc gritted out, the lines in his face still pressed together in fury.

"I wasn't going to take what I wanted," he spoke, shrugging nonchalantly.

"Get out, both of you." The men turned to Hope. "Get out now and Flynt, don't come back until I'm gone. Broc you can wait for me downstairs. This has been the most horrendous night and morning. Both of you, you've mortified me." She couldn't stop the tears from filling her eyes.

"I promise you, Hope, I will come back. We've things to talk about, and I'm not going to leave them unsaid." Flynt grabbed his boots, heading out the door. Before the door closed, he stopped to look at her one more time.

"Go to the devil." She didn't want to see either man. Embarrassment heated her, rushed through her. Covering herself with the sheet, she hid from them, holding her breath until she heard the door close and both men's booted steps heading away from her room and down the stairs.

Trying to calm herself, her shaking nerves as well as come to terms with what she'd just allowed Flynt, she was shocked to hear the door open. A very soft feminine voice followed. "I've your bath water, Miss Hope. Master Flynt ordered it. May we come in?"

Still beneath the sheet, "Yes," her voice wavered as she still felt nearly spineless from the encounter with Flynt. None of this should have happened. She knew better. Thank her lucky stars Broc came by.

What did her brother want?

Well, she supposed she'd find out soon enough. She didn't understand men, didn't think she ever would. Now, she meant to take her time and make them stew downstairs for as long as possible, hoping they would have something better to do with their time and leave.

"Your bath is ready, Hope." The maid left the room. Once again Hope waited to hear the door close behind the woman.

Warily she sat up, still clutching the sheet against her. They were gone, thank god, but Broc would expect her to explain herself to him. Well, her brother could wait in hell. After all she was an adult woman and the only person she needed to explain herself to was her.

Now she began to understand Bliss' feelings a bit better. Bliss gave her brother all of herself and he'd run away, afraid to commit to her. Blessed hell, Bliss had twins just seconds after they were married. What kind of man did that to the woman he loved?

What possessed her to offer herself up as a virgin sacrifice to Flynt when she knew better, had counseled other women against doing just this sort of thing. She was smarter than that, but she suddenly realized this sex thing had nothing to do with intelligence.

Slipping into the hot water, she tried to rid her mind of the morning events. She found the feat impossible even while she closed her eyes. Shutting her eyes made it all worse. With her eyes closed, she imagined every heated caress, the evocative ways he stroked and kissed her, nothing innocent about his kisses and where he placed those kisses.

With a heavy sigh she sat up, washing all of her, retouching every place Flynt stroked. "I'm going to forget about Flynt, a man I can never have. Angus, a gentle giant, he sounded just right for her. She hoped his kisses would be as nice as Flynt's. If no, he would just have to do."

She supposed Broc was here to see how she was doing, maybe tell her a bit about Angus. She stiffened suddenly, water sloshing over the rim of the tub. What if Angus was here, right now, waiting downstairs with Broc to meet her? Good god, he wouldn't do that to her, would he?

Angus would know she had been with Flynt when Flynt walked through the parlor to leave. No, you silly ninny, Broc would never tell him and Flynt would never leave his home unless that was what he wanted.

But Flynt might tell everything. This had all started because Flynt didn't think Angus was the right man for her. He wouldn't say the words outright, but he might imply by subtle innuendos that he just came from her bed.

He wouldn't dare.

Of course he would.

Well she still meant to take her time getting ready to meet her fate. Whatever that was. Letting the water sluice from her as she stood, she reached for the bath towel that had been set out for her.

Let them stew.

An hour later, unable to find anything else to do, she walked down the steps to find her brother sitting with Angus, visiting and seeming to enjoy each other's company.

He was handsome, in a medieval sort of way. When the two stood, Angus, she assumed the man was Angus, towered over her brother by almost a head and her brother was a tall man. His shirt tightened around his shoulders when he reached forward to place her hand in his. He brought her hand to his lips, gently kissing the back. "Hope."

"Angus?"

Against her skin, his red beard was soft and when he smiled at her, his green eyes twinkling, the expression was tender. "I'm very pleased to meet you, Hope. May I call you Hope?"

Beside herself with worry, she didn't know how to react to this man who seemed so sincere. He would realize soon she didn't reciprocate that tenderness, "Of course." At least the first question was easy.

She sat down, smoothing her skirts wondering, "Why are the two of you here? It's a long ways to come without good reason. I doubt if it was just to meet me."

"It was," Broc smiled at her "Cam thought you should meet Angus before Saturday's outing, and I wanted to accompany you to your new home in Glasgow. Angus thought he would help out." Broc's voice was tight with emotions she was sure he didn't want to show.

"Flynt would have seen me to the house. Neither of you needed to come here." *And humiliate me.* The words were out before she could take them back. "Where is Flynt?"

"He left," Broc bit out, clearly still displeased with what he saw earlier.

"For town? For a ride? This is his home, why should he leave?" she asked, knowing she was ruffling her brother with each inquiry.

"Didn't ask and don't care," Broc said with a masculine shrug and an air of indifference. "Well then, perhaps we should be on our way. Is Angus coming with us also? I've packed a couple of valises. They are upstairs and they are really quite heavy. You should go get them."

Angus stood, shifting from one foot to the other, "Lass, do you still want to go with me tomorrow? You seem a bit restrained. And after Flynt left..."

"My apologies," she murmured, lowering her lashes for a second, then, "My brother showing up here today without a note or anything to let me know he intended to surprise me not only with himself but you has left me a bit on edge. I don't appreciate surprises such as this. It seems my morning has been filled with surprises."

"I would not have taken such liberties, rest assured if Broc and Cam had not made sure to tell me multiple times that my presence would not be an imposition. Were they wrong?"

She felt the flush of color rise to her face. "It's not an imposition. Truly, I was looking forward to getting to meet you, of learning about you more thoroughly and intimately but not with an audience." She shot her brother an angry glare.

"You are not going to be intimate with Angus," Broc said, his voice harsh.

She noticed a flush rise on the part of his face the beard didn't cover. "Why don't you get my bags?" she asked Broc. "Angus and I could use a few moments."

"Of course," Broc said, reluctantly rising from his seat, his glare furious.

"I can certainly help," Angus started to stand.

Broc looked at his sister then Angus. "No, Hope does have a point. The two of you should have an opportunity to speak without big brother hovering. Perhaps the two of you can find something in common to share."

She watched her brother's back as he strode upstairs. "Take your time," she called after him.

"You're a bonny lass," Angus told her when she returned her attention to him. "One I would like to get to know."

"Thank you. Cam tells me you are a mathematician. Goodness, it's all I can do to add and subtract a few numbers. I would love to have your skills."

"I could teach you," he offered, a grin beneath the beard.

She waved her hand smiling. "You would probably just confuse me. You see, my education was not in numbers and letters. I was taught other things." Other things, such as how to seduce a man and how not to be seduced by one. She had not learned the second lesson at all, Flynt being proof of that fact.

"What did you learn? History perhaps, maybe literature."

Pursuing another answer was not what she expected. She smiled then knowing she couldn't tell him the truth. Flynt, she could be honest with him, because he knew most of her history if not all.

"I don't want to shock you. I would have thought Cam would have told you that I grew up in a harem. My mother was captured and made a concubine of a wealthy Turkish sultan. My education has been unorthodox at best."

"'Tis nothing to be ashamed of. One cannot control their past and the life they were born into. It's what you do after the fact that counts."

Goodness, but he was just too nice. "So you don't care that I've learned a lot of things our society would scorn." He needed to know the truth before they invested too much time together and she wanted to know how much of her past he could accept.

"No, but you've piqued my curiosity." He smiled at her, siting down on the sofa beside her. "Tell me whatever you feel comfortable sharing."

"Perhaps another time, if there is another time. I take it you're not one of the bad boys." She started another line of questioning, eager to leave her past behind at least for the time being.

"Bad boy?" He lifted an eyebrow. "Don't know what you speak of.

I've spent my entire life trying to be good."

Of course he had. "Didn't think you were one, but you're not boring like most who I've met who are not."

"Was there a compliment in there somewhere?" He laughed outright and she liked the sound of it.

She couldn't help but shrug her shoulders flirtatiously. "I have a way of saying what is on my mind. I suppose a compliment did exist in the words. Tell me about your family and later I'll speak more of my life before I escaped and found my way here. You should know some things about me so you can make a decision."

His eyes grew wide as she thought they would yet his smile remained. "I'm guessing, compared to your story mine will inevitably bore the tears from your eyes."

"Try me. Do you have siblings? I've one, Broc, and he can be overbearing as you just witnessed."

"I've seven siblings, four sisters and three brothers. Guess one could say we grew up poor even though my parents made sure we wanted for nothing, at least until they passed away."

"In a sense, at least until I came to Scotland, I had more siblings than you. In the harem there was always someone to play with as there was always a new baby. We are all half brother's and sisters. My mother only had me. I was never quite sure why until I was older."

He watched her with what seemed like avid curiosity. "I always excelled in school, numbers more precisely. Being crofters, the likely hood of attending the university was nonexistent."

"How did you get so lucky, assuming that's what you wanted?" She was curious now, intrigued by this man who worked his way to a better life.

"More than anything. The man overseeing the crofters and the crops noticed my capabilities and brought me to the attention of the lord who owned the land. One good thing led to another and I found myself studying to become a mathematician. It was the best thing that ever happened to me, and now I'm hoping you will take that place."

She swallowed hard, deciding she had to give this man a chance and forget about Flynt who obviously wanted her for only one thing." You'll have to show me where you work."

"A tour would be in order. We can speak of a time after the

competition. Perhaps on Sunday after, the students wouldn't be there."

"What do they do at games besides the cabor toss?" She was interested in the highland games. "I've never been to anything like this. In some ways I'm a foreigner in the land I should have grown up in."

"Ah so many things, dancing, piping, the toss and the hammer throw. I do both of those."

"It's time," Broc let the bags fall to the floor with a crash.

Her hand flew to her chest, surprised by the jarring noise. "You don't need to be rude."

"You should have let me get the bags. They look heavy," Angus said, rising to give assistance.

A slight flush rose to her brother's cheeks. "Nothing I couldn't handle. Did the two of you get enough private time?"

"Not nearly enough for me, but we'll talk again on Saturday and we do have the ride into town to further discuss what we would like to do and perhaps the direction of our relationship." Angus picked up one of the bags before offering Hope an arm.

"I must tell you nothing happened upstairs with Flynt," Hope blurted as the stepped onto the porch.

~ * ~

Cam paced the parlor in his Glasgow town house, his heart thundering in his chest. He just set something in motion he wasn't proud of but would have to live with. He stopped his pacing to watch his wife.

Chelsea sat in a chair, studying him while shaking her head. She was knitting something, booties or a baby blanket. He could never be sure until she finished. He was always amazed, the yarn coupled with the needles ever turned into anything substantial or recognizable.

"Cam, please sit down and talk to me. You're making me nervous and you're about to wear a hole in the carpet," She set her work aside to listen to him, her gaze pointedly riveted on him.

He knew she wasn't going to let this go and perhaps it was for the best. "I set something in motion I now regret and it's too late to take it back. Even though I understood how Flynt felt about Hope, I did it anyway. Thought to put a spur on his behind, but I'm afraid it might have backfired."

He watched her inhale a deep breath of air, her breasts rising then falling as she exhaled. "Very well then, tell me what this is all about." She closed her eyes, sighing softly a sound that was very endearing to Cam. "What does Flynt feel where Hope is concerned? I didn't realize there was anything between them. If there is something there, they both have managed to hide their feelings very well."

Cam strode behind his wife, his hands on her shoulders before bending to whisper into her ear. "He is just as enamored of Hope as I am of you. He just won't admit to his feelings. I believe she reciprocates those emotions, but Hope on the other hand is hell bent not to be his mistress, which of course makes complete sense."

He felt the shiver his whisper created, thinking to take his wife to bed and forego this conversation, one that would inevitably result in an argument if he didn't do something to waylay it.

She turned then, pointing across the room. "Stop it. You brought this up so until we are finished, you need to sit in that chair. I need to understand more than just these abstract notions you have about the two of them."

"You do have a point, but your lovely ears, and neck, and well...your soft lips. I get side tracked way to easily. You have to do your part and stop enticing me." He wondered why he didn't bring up this problem with Hope and Flynt after he bedded his wife. Too late now though, he would have to do her bidding. He left her side, striding across the room and taking a seat. He grinned at her.

"Cam, what makes you think my brother is in love with Hope? He's courting two women at the moment."

"Ah, yes," Cam stood again but prudently retook his seat across the room. Uncharacteristically placing his hands in his lap, "Have you ever noticed the way he stares at her? He's smitten, I tell you."

"So you say. What about Melessand and Beatrice? Has he no feelings for either of them? He has certainly put enough time into courting them." She picked up her knitting and the needles seemed to fly.

He drew in a long deep breath, concerned now that Chelsea wouldn't understand or agree with him. "Melessand is a twit. There is no other way to describe the woman and Beatrice is a total bore. Lovely as she may be, she cannot keep her nose out of books. He could not possibly fall in love with either, and if he wed either one, he'd regret it the day after."

She paused in her knitting "Let me get this straight. Flynt is in love with Hope but doesn't know it and the two women he's courting, neither one is good enough for him. Am I right? And what is wrong with reading. Beatrice must be very intelligent."

"That's it in a nutshell." He knew when he mentioned the books, he would be in trouble with his wife, and he didn't know how to explain himself.

"So, moving on, what is it you did that you now have regrets about?" She smiled at him. "This tale could prove to be very interesting."

"I told Broc about a man I know, a professor at the university, a mathematician. He's single and I thought it would be fun for Hope to meet someone, have a choice, you understand and perhaps make Flynt a wee bit jealous."

"And you also thought this man's attentions where Hope is concerned would prompt Flynt to make a commitment of some sort. So you assumed Flynt would be jealous." She was staring at his mouth.

"Yes. Angus is a very nice man. And yes, I hoped Flynt would be jealous. You have an extraordinary way of reading my poor man's brain." He wanted to laugh at the emotions sweeping across Chelsea's beautiful face.

"So, he would be good for Hope if she liked him."

"If she liked him," Cam agreed.

"Yes."

"If you keep that up, I'll toss your skirts right here in the parlor." He rose, striding toward his wife.

"Not in the parlor and the middle of the day." She set the needles down again, then with a laugh she picked up her skirts and raced up the steps.

He roared with laughter, knowing he would catch her before the bedroom. Perhaps he would lift her skirts and make love to her in the hallway. The bed would do for a second round.

Other Books by Christine Young
Available at Rogue Phoenix Press

My Sweet Broc

He's a bad bad boy...

Broc Wallace is a fun-loving rake who never thought any beautiful woman could melt his heart. He lives life in the present enjoying the camaraderie of his friends and the pleasures of his mistress. When Bliss races into his life, he is ill prepared to deal with her secrets or give up the tenor of his life. When the truth is revealed, he finds himself unable to forgive and forget the betrayal.

...but she's sweet for him

Bliss MacTavish knows she's playing with fire when she refuses to tell this bad boy her name. He tempts her with sweet whispers of seduction knowing her innocent nature will be unable to refuse all he yearns to give her. Deciding to follow her heart, she finds the repercussions more than she bargains for when she gives herself to this bad boy.

Foolish for Piper

The pickpocket...

Piper has spent her life surviving the streets of St. Giles Parish in London, a den of iniquity and crime. Masquerading as a boy she escapes the whorehouses the young girls are sent to as they come of age. The day she encounters Brett MacLachlan begins the same as every other one. When she picks his pocket, she has no idea her life is going to change irreversibly.

...and the mark

Handsome aristocrat Brett MacLachlan has come to London for his amusement only to find his world turned upside down by a thief and her dog. From the moment he spots her, Brett knows there is something intrinsically wrong. In his arms, Piper discovers passion and joy. Yet secrets of her past haunt her, and a scar will tell the true tale as well as her identity.

Taylor's Destiny

She traveled to another time and place to change destiny...

Enjoying a day of sailing, Taylor Maxwell never expected after a suffering a concussion she would wake up in another century. A resilient independent woman in the twenty-first century, the blond beauty is ill prepared for life in the 1800s. Her first sight of the naval captain who rescues her makes her heart stop, giving her hope for her future.

His life is transformed by a woman who appears from nowhere...

Born to a life of ease, Reid Stewart defies the dictates of those born to aristocracy and chooses a life of adventure in the navy and as a spy for the crown. When he discovers a nearly naked woman on the bow of small sailing ship, his heart warms. His love for Taylor and his need to protect her from a man who pursues her might cost him his life as well as hers.

Caitlin's Duke

She played a fiddle in an Irish pub....

Caitlin O'Shea Is the most beautiful woman Roc Leighton has ever seen. With her blue violet eyes and long black hair she captivates him. In turn he mesmerizes Caitlin. Caught in the power of his gaze as he watches her, she is wise enough to know he desires her but will never give his heart to her. Caitlin has vowed to never be any man's mistress.

And fell in love with an English Lord...

Roc knows the first time he watches her play the fiddle and dance around the pub, she will be his next mistress. Despite her protest, he will find a way to convince her that her place is with him. While Caitlin's determination to keep her vows, fate takes a cruel turn and she is forced to seek refuge with Roc.

Catching Meara
Book One in the McKenna Clan Series

Meara Thorton was a feisty, world-class computer hacker—cornered by the FBI and shockingly given the chance to be their newly acquired technical analyst. Brilliant and intuitive, yet aching with the loss of everyone she has cared about, her restless heart led her to discover a love she fought and a world she didn't know could possibly exist.

Sweet Sexy Sadie
Book Two in the McKenna Clan Series

From the first time Sadie's eyes met those of Brody McKenna in the hot Sierra Madre Mountains, theirs was a potent attraction—not gentle, slow, and easy, but hot, hard, and all-consuming. The daughter of a dysfunctional family, Sadie had dreams no man could wrench from her with hot sex and an all-consuming passion. She'd challenge this alpha male with all the strength she possessed. But her red hair, fiery temperament, and indomitable spirit obsessed Brody...and he knew he had to find a way to show her he was more than he appeared and convince her to make a life with him.

Sweet Misbehavin'
Book Three in the McKenna Clan Series

Cast adrift after fleeing the home of Jokul, the ice demon, Atantsi, a firestarter, grew to womanhood as she moved through time to keep the demon from finding her. Though stubborn and courageous, she was ill prepared to use powers she had not been taught. Her first sight of the intoxicating Carr McKenna left her breathless, and her second encounter gave her hope for a future she never thought she had.

A playboy, a second son and a shifter, a man who thought his life would be carefree, Carr McKenna was shocked to discover the woman he'd paid as an escort is a firestarter who is running for her life. He is the leader of all the McKennas around the world and that he has multiple powers. His passion for Margo and the need to defend her might cost him his life as well as hers.

Sweet Talkin' Sugar
Book Four in the McKenna Clan Series

Lyonesse McKenna, was dreaming or was she? From the instant Lyn saw Deacon McClain across a black jack table in a crowed Las Vegas casino the unmistakable attraction sent Lyn's senses flying into overdrive. Her family of shapeshifters believed in soul mates. She'd always been skeptical yet she couldn't help but question the way her heart sped when he looked at her.

When Deacon appeared in Las Vegas he knew his first job was to save Lyn from a Sea Demon, but the next order of business was to convince her he would someday mean more to her than she'd ever expected. But her stubborn nature and unbendable spirit consumed Deacon...and he had to chase away all the demons real and imagined in order to win her heart.

Sweet Surrender
Book Five in the McKenna Clan Series

Ripped from her family at the top of Infinity Cliff, Kimi McKenna finds herself thrust somewhere into the future. Dark elements threaten to destroy the earth unless Kimi can work together with the white witch to stop the destruction. Confused by her mate's role in the conspiracy, she refuses to acknowledge the connection. But amidst raging fire and attacks on the people she is coming to hold dear, she allows Maska O'keefe into her heart.

Maska O'keefe has loved the beautiful shapeshifter for years. Unable to save her life years ago, he vows to watch over her as he is given a second chance to convince her that even though he is a witch and not a shifter, they are indeed soul mates. Kimi's divided loyalties between her family and the cause she is now a part of will determine their relationship. Only the part she plays as the messiah can bring this to a conclusion in the final battle.

Dakota's Bride
The first book in the Lakota/Pinkerton Series

When Emma St. John received her brother's letter imploring her to escape her stepfather's vengeful scheme and to trust Dakota Barringer with her life, she was willing to chance it. But the handsome, brooding riverboat owner Emma found in Natchez a danger of another kind. For Emma soon found herself surrendering to an unrelenting desire.

Raised by the Sioux when his parents were killed, Dakota had been betrayed once before by a white woman. He wasn't about to trust another, especially one claiming that her stepfather, a powerful U.S. senator, had framed her as a murderess. But he couldn't let Emma's intoxicating effect on him. Now Dakota would risk his very life to protect the innocent beauty who had seduced him with her tender love.

My Angel
The second book in the Lakota/Pinkerton Series

A BEAUTY IN BUCKSKINS
When her father decided to send her to a finishing school back East, Angela Chamberlain refused to be confined to stuffy drawing rooms. Instead, the daring spitfire who could shoot like a man and ride like the wind longed for a life of adventure and romance—and she knew exactly who could give it to her. Devil Blackmoor was a hired gun with a dangerous reputation. But Angela was willing to go to the ends of the earth to capture the handsome devil's heart.

A DEVIL IN DISGUISE
He'd come to America looking for excitement, but Devil Blackmoor got more than he bargained for when he encountered a beautiful rebel who answered his kisses with a wild innocence that touched his very soul. Yet standing between them were more obstacles than either ever dreamed. For Devil had strapped on a gun for the wrong man. And that made Angela his enemy. Now he'll have to choose between his duty and the woman he loves more than life.

The Locket
The third book in the Lakota/Pinkerton Series

The year is 1894. Seeking revenge for crimes against his family, Misha Petrovich follows a path that leads straight to Ariel Cameron's boarding house in Mist Harbor, Oregon. A family heirloom in Ariel's possession leads Misha to believe she is guilty. The locket has been handed down to the oldest girl in the Petrovich family for generations. Ariel is innocent of wrong doing, but her father is not. Misha is torn by his feelings for Ariel and his need for restitution against her father. Knowing that the relationship between them is fragile, Misha does everything in his power to protect Ariel's father. His efforts are to no avail when her father is shot. Ariel comes to realize Misha's steadfast courage and determination to protect her and her father despite what has happened to his family. Ariel's love and devotion heals Misha's heart.

The Talisman
The fourth book in the Lakota/Pinkerton Series

Running from a marriage that lasted one night, Dr. Moriah McKeown discovers the land she has settled on is coveted by determined and lawless men. Yet the proud young woman who once vowed never to abandon her home has second thoughts when her adopted children are threatened. Her only recourse is to enlist the aid of a dark, dangerous gun for hire.
Haunted by the past and a betrayal he will never forgive, Ian Civanovich uses his fast gun and his reckless courage to forget the faithlessness of a woman in his past. He will trust no female—nor will he rest until the threat hovering over Moriah McKeown is put to rest.

Forever His
The fifth book in the Lakota/Pinkerton Series

Struggling to come to terms with the part she played in Jacob St. John's death, Etta Barringer resigns from Pinkerton Agency and seeks peace and solace in a Rocky Mountain Cabin.
Jacob has vowed to discover the reason Etta has betrayed him, sold him out to his enemy and left him for dead.
Isolated in their cabin, they discover their love for each other and learn to trust. But the trust is shattered when Jacob learns she is married to his sworn enemy; the man who left him in the desert to die.

Allura's Secret
Twelve Dancing Princesses Book One

Allura McClellan is horrified by her father's decision to take out an ad in the Times awarding her to the man strong enough and smart enough to win her hand and uncover her secrets. She's an intelligent young woman who takes great delight in the freedom allotted to her by her father. She's well aware that marriage would effectively curtail the adventures she's shared with her sisters and cousins.

Hunter Gray is nothing like the other men who've arrived to vie for Allura's hand in marriage and everything that goes along with it. However, he is the first to refuse to concede defeat and pursue her despite her attempts to disguise her true appearance. It's her temperament that is of more concern to him than her looks. Hunter has worked all his life with the hope of someday owning his own land. Now that it looks like there's a very real possibility that everything he's ever wanted is within reach nothing is going to deter him – including Miss Allura's disagreeable disposition.

Amorica's Wager
Twelve Dancing Princesses Book Two

Amorica Hepburn was sent to London to find a husband. Finding a man was the last item on her agenda. With her two cousins, Amorica wagers she can dissuade her suitor before the others. Despite her efforts she discovers a chemistry that cannot be denied. Suddenly she is the arrogant man's wife, pledged to a marriage neither desire. But swept off to his ancestral home above the Dover cliffs and into his strong embrace, Amorica is soon possessed by a raging passion for the husband she had vowed to despise… Damian Andrews couldn't afford to trust the emerald-eyed spitfire who happened upon his secret. Amorica's hatred of all men of his kind only inflames the war that rages between them. Still, he can not control the intense desire his stubborn bride inspires, or make her surrender to his will until he has conquered the headstrong beauty on the battlefield of love…

Ravyn's Marriage of Inconvenience
Twelve Dancing Princesses Book Three

A REGAL BEAUTY

When the duchess decides to wed her to a wastrel and a fop, Ravyn Grahm takes matters into her own hands and declares her engagement to another man. Instead of fessing up and telling her great aunt what she has done, she goes through with the pretense. Aric Lakeland is the bastard son of an earl and has a dangerous reputation. But Ravyn is willing to do most anything to keep the duchess from discovering the lie.

A DEVIL-MAY-CARE SMUGGLER
He'd bought land in America, looking to put down roots and end his life of adventure, but Aric Lakeland got more than he bargained for when he encountered a beautiful heiress who made a promise she didn't want to keep. But the promise could not be undone and standing between them were more obstacles than either ever dreamed. Aric had made plans to spend the rest of his life in America and that was at odds with Ravyn's plan of living in England and running her father's estate. Now, he'll have to choose between his dreams and the woman he loves more than life.

Christel's Sunrise
Twelve Dancing Princesses Book Four

He Made Her An Offer...

Life has thrown Christel McClellan some experiences that could have devastated a less determined woman. Beautiful, self-assured and fiercely independent, she is trying to forget the loss of her stillborn child. But is the child alive?

She Couldn't Deny...

Life is carefree for Ryder MacLaren who loves to see what is on the other side of the sunrise. Laird of Clan MacLaren, he is wealthy, handsome and happily unencumbered...until stunning Christel McClellan enters his life. When he hears her story, he believes the child she thought dead has been sold to a wealthy buyer.

Storm's Passion
Twelve Dancing Princesses Book Five

SHE MADE A PROPOSAL...

Life strikes Storm Graham a shattering blow when she learns her father has bartered her to a man she detests. Storm is beautiful, self–assured and fiercely independent, and refuses to be a pawn in her father's schemes, yet she can find no way out of this bargain made in hell. Going on the offensive she asks the wealthiest man on the eastern coast of England to marry her, never believing she might fall in love.

HE TRIED TO REFUSE...

For Hadden Johnston life has provided everything he ever wanted, including a sanctuary for homeless children. He is wealthy, handsome and happily unencumbered...until stunning Storm Graham marches into his life and proposes a marriage of convenience. Yet this type of marriage to a woman who inflames his senses is far from acceptable. If he's going to be tied down, he will move heaven and earth to have this woman warming his bed.

Gotta Have Fayth
Twelve Dancing Princesses Book Six

A regal beauty with raven hair and piercing blue eyes, Fayth Graham is unwilling to parade herself in front of the wealthy Lords of England during the season. Seeking a means to dissuade any man wishing to wed her, she seeks a way to ruin herself for marriage. When she unexpectedly meets a man with sparkling gray eyes and an infectious grin, she decides this is the man who will keep her from agreeing to obey.

He returned from six months at sea, looking for a few nights of pleasure with a willing lass, but Jarret Kinsley got more than he bargained for when he met a beautiful debutant who responded to his kisses with a wild innocence that touched his heart. Yet the obstacles looming between them might rip them apart. Both had vowed never to marry, so when consequences of their dalliances got in the way, Jarret would have to choose between the life he's always desired and the woman he loves more than life.

Ella's Pleasure
Twelve Dancing Princesses Book Seven

A WHISPER OF PLEASURE

Ella Hepburn was an auburn haired debutant from the harsh Scottish coastline—a wild innocent to be seduced and tamed. A spirited beauty, she captivated Drake Montgomerie's jaded heart—while succumbing to the smoldering desire she felt for her unyielding suitor.

A WHISPER OF DANGER

In Drake Montgomerie's glittering world of money and privilege, young Ella discovered passion and desire could overcome everything she'd been taught to resist—entangling Drake, the heir apparent, in a lethal coil of aristocratic family intrigue. But grave peril would only nurse the sparks of a love that knew no limits and a magnificent ecstasy that would not be denied.

Eveleen's Seduction
Twelve Dancing Princesses Book Eight

A WHISPER OF SEDUCTION

A brutal attack on Eveleen Hepburn's cherished island off the Scottish coastline leaves her shattered and bewildered. Learning a man she once trusted can kill as easily as he can breathe even though the deed saves her life, creates questions that need answers. An innocent beauty, she enchants

Logan Maxwell's cynical heart—giving in to the raging passion she feels for her mysterious suitor.

A WHISPER OF INTRIGUE

In Logan's Maxwell's world of espionage and privilege, young Eveleen discovers truths about herself she never expected, and a need for passion and love can overcome all her fears if she learns to accept certain truths. She finds herself entangled in a lethal battle for land that was once owned by French nobility, taken from them during the revolution and sold to Maxwell. But grave peril would unleash the flames of love that simmers, creating a magical union that cannot be refuted.

Tavia's Deception
Twelve Dancing Princesses Book Nine

WHISPERS OF DECEPTION

When her father decides to send her to London for her season, Tavia Hepburn resolves to see the world instead. The raven haired beauty decides to disguise herself as a lad and find employment on a ship bound for Barcelona as a cabin boy. But she never bargains on finding passion and love to a red haired sea captain who rescues her from certain death.

WHISPERS OF MURDER

For James Macmurra, the world is black and white until he meets a young debutante, who turns his world upside down. He's unable to deny Tavia's intoxicating effect on him. In a match tense with obstacles, unwillingness to divulge secrets, and unforeseen peril, irresistible desire and passion grows into undeniable love. James would risk his life to shelter and protect the innocent debutante who seduces him with her sweet love.

Larena's Fascination
Twelve Dancing Princesses Book Ten

WHISPERS OF FASCINATION

Fiery, free spirited Larena Graham never wanted to marry a duke. She is thrilled to be in love with the fourth son of an aristocrat, Gavin Broon. But when it seems Gavin ignores her, she set her sights on politics and bettering human life. Unsuspecting intrigue and a plot against her, she continues her dangerous plans despite Gavin's wishes.

WHISPERS OF TRUST

Gavin has every intention of properly courting the beautiful Larena until he must leave the city in order to put his affairs in order. Returning to London, he finds the woman he means to make his own is embroiled in political protests that could lead to a prison ship. Larena must learn to trust the handsome Scotsman whose most pressing mission is to protect her and keep her from harm.

Tira's Education
Twelve Dancing Princesses Book Eleven

WHISPERS OF EDUCATION

Learning how to build ships is Tira Hepburn's only dream until she meets Jamie Lundin and her world is turned upside down. With her raven black hair and vivid green eyes, she tempts Jamie and pushes him to defy his vows. She never bargains on finding an irrevocable love and a passion to a man who cannot fulfill her dreams despite his burning desire for her.

WHISPERS OF A BARGAIN

Arrogant and self-assured Jamie is brought up short when Tira captures his heart. All his carefully made plans are put to the test when he decides to teach her the art of ship building if she will spend a week with him alone on his ship. He is unable to deny Tira's intoxicating effect on him. When Tira leaves him behind unwilling to live with him without the benefit of marriage, he races after her. Jamie will risk everything to shelter and protect the innocent debutante who seduces him with her sweet love.

Aidan's Love
Twelve Dancing Princesses Book Twelve
Whispers of Love

Aidan McLellan has loved since she first set eyes on him as a young girl. Spontaneous, wild and eager to grow up, Aidan haunts his waking thoughts day and night, insinuating herself into his life. With her fiery red hair and sparkling sapphire eyes, she seizes Blade's heart even while he tries to resist the innocent child until she becomes a woman.

Whispers of Courage

Blade has waited what seems a lifetime to claim the woman who captures his heart as a little girl. Claiming his inheritance before his younger brother takes what is rightfully his, Blade must convince Aidan of his sincerity after years of avoidance and wed her before his father dies so he can return home, securing his rightful place. Everything is put to the test when his life as well as Aidan's is threatened by the man who once called him brother.

Twelve Days to Love

When Archer Steele shows up at Calanthe Durand's failing plantation with an alligator over his shoulder, Cali thinks she's never seen a more handsome man. During the war she had to defend herself and her servants from both union and confederate soldiers. Independent and self-sufficient, she vows to never marry.

But Archer Steele has different ideas. The first time Archer sees Cali in town, he feels an instant attraction. He decides he will do everything and anything to convince the beautiful Miss Durand he is worthy of her love. During the weeks leading up to Christmas, he gives her twelve gifts in hopes she will fall in love with him. Yet they are faced with challenges they must overcome before Cali can commit to a marriage.

Door to Heaven

Jessica Lawrence is the stepdaughter of a woman born in the twentieth century transported back in time to the year 1868. An acclaimed suffragette, she raises Jessica to believe in the equality of women. Jess Law believes everything she was taught, and when the time is right she becomes a private investigator. Courageous and impetuous, Jess finds danger in her quest to save all women from white slavery. Her passionate mission results in a wedding to Roc Newman, a man she knows can steal her heart...

Roc can't trust the sapphire-eyed spitfire who invades his home in search of secret papers and knocks him flat with her karate moves. Jessica's refusal to obey his wishes serves to inflame the war between them. Still, he cannot control the intense desire his reluctant bride inspires, or make her surrender her independence, until he has conquered the headstrong beauty on the battlefield of love...

Rebel Heart

HER REBEL SPIRIT DEFIED HIS OUTSIDERS SOUL...SEP She was velvet and silk, eyes the color of a summer storm and amber hair. Victoria DeMontville, because of a promise and a codicil to her father's will, was forced to marry one man to protect her from another. She hated Cameron Savage with a fierce passion. But to hold on to her genetic research and find a cure for the deadly Signe virus, she must pretend to love the enemy at her door, come with weapons of fire to melt her icy heart...

HIS OUTSIDERS TOUCH IGNITED RAGING PASSIONS...SEP He wore

a mask, disguised as the Phantom, a true legend come to life. Even as war and debate over new genetic research engulfed them all, he would find his greatest adversary in the beauty who'd branded him an outsider and barbarian, the woman he was born to possess, his soul mate.

Safari Moon

Solo St. John, a wildlife photographer, is preparing for a trip to Alaska. Suddenly, Solo finds women of all sorts invading his privacy, his home and his office, all cooing nonsense words and blatantly throwing themselves at him. Solo doesn't know why, and he has no idea how to rid himself of the persistent women. He finally decides to beg a favor of his best buddy Nyssa Harrington.

In love with Solo for the past ten years and knowing he doesn't return her feelings Nyssa doesn't want to talk to Solo. She knows if she accepts his phone call, she will not be able to resist the temptation to hope again.

Straight to Heaven

Running from demons, Alexandra McMurdie stumbles into Forbidden Ground where up is down and elements of nature are contested. Though a strong independent woman in the twenty-first century' she is unprepared for life in the 1800s. Her first site of the formidable James Lawrence makes her heart skip a beat, giving her cause to reconsider her desperate need to find a way home.

Born with a silver spoon, James' life was torn apart during the War Between the States. Moving west he vows to put the life he once knew in the past. When he discovers a half-frozen woman near Gold Hill, his heart begins to thaw. His love for Alexandra and his need to keep her from a man who has pursued her through time might cost him his life as well as hers.

A Valentine's Anthology

The Lending Library-a fantasy by Christie L. Kraemer

Faeries try to fit into the human world when the forest where they make their home is destroyed by a mysterious enemy.

Chasing Rainbows-a contemporary romance by Genene Valleau

An eccentric aunt, an inventive uncle, a mother who wears poodle skirts, and a brother who wears pearls provide a hilarious backdrop for the courtship of a young woman who yearns for a "normal" family.

The Gift-an historical romance by Christine Young

A man and a woman on opposite sides of the Civil War get a second chance at love after one final battle returns soldiers to their war-torn homes to rebuild their lives.

A St. Patrick's Day Tale
by
Christine Young, C. L. Kraemer, Genene Valleau

Tumble through time…

…to Ireland in 1817, when tensions are high between Protestants and Catholics and fae people guide the fate of villagers. A lovely Catholic lass stumbles upon the weakly ritual fisticuffing between Irish lads. She falls into the lap of a handsome young Protestant. Family ties, grudges, and two conniving faeries threaten their budding love. But the faeries outsmart themselves when they hijack a time machine that has mysteriously appeared in their forest and are whisked to…

…Eugene, Oregon in the 20th century, amid a property feud between the local faeries and night elves. The conniving faeries from Olde Ireland try to stir up more mischief. However, a warrior gnome convinces the magic folk to control their own destiny, and forces the intruding faeries to take refuge in the time machine again, spinning their way toward…

…A modern day castle in western Oregon. An eccentric inventor is determined to reclaim his wayward time machine and save his beloved wife from her latest misadventure. If only they can travel safely past the black hole…

a May Day Anthology
by
Christine Young, C. L. Kraemer, Rosemary Indra, Genene Valleau

Highland Miracle — Christine Young

HURTLED THROUGH TIME, Sean Michael Sterling, landed in the midst of a May Day celebration he didn't understand, assuming the role of Laird Sterling.
ILLIGITAMATE CHILD OF NOBILITY, Reagan Douglas searches for a way out of her half brother's house.

Defying the Odds — C.L. Kraemer

The night elves on the hill aren't happy without their magic. They concoct a plan to punish those who were involved in the act that rendered them almost human. Meanwhile, Uther, the rogue night elf, has returned to woo the Librarian to be his eternal mate.

Love in Bloom — Rosemary Indra

When childhood friends reunite it takes two fairies and a matchmaking daughter to help them admit their true love for each other.

No More Poodle Skirts — Genie Gabriel

After drifting for years in the innocent age of the 1950s, a woman struggles to join today's world by finding a career and a new love, with some help from her zany family.

Once Upon a Christmas Moon
by
Christine Young, C. L. Kraemer, Genene Valleau

TWELVE DAYS TO LOVE

When Archer Steele shows up at Calanthe Durand's failing plantation with an alligator over his shoulder, Cali thinks she's never seen a more handsome man. During the war she had to defend herself and her servants from both union and confederate soldiers. Independent and self-sufficient, she vows to never marry. But Archer Steele has different ideas. The first time Archer sees Cali in town, he feels an instant attraction. He decides he will do everything and anything to convince the beautiful Miss Durand he is worthy of her love. During the weeks leading up to Christmas, he gives her twelve gifts in hopes she will fall in love with him.

BOOTS AND BLADES

An ancient evil from the old country has arrived in the high desert of Oregon. Gnome children are vanishing then re-appearing, showing various stages of traumatization. Tiamoon, warrior gnome, will put her skills to use alongside Killian, a handsome warrior, also in need of a cause.

CHRISTMAS PAWSIBILITIES

With their world destroyed and their space ship malfunctioning, the dogizens of Planet Canid have little choice but to crash land on Earth. They face tortuous experiments at the hands of the Geeks in Green...or they can trust an eccentric inventor and his zany family to deliver the Canine Queen's puppies and help them celebrate new lives.